IN SEARCH OF THE FALLEN DIVINA MARIA CALLAS

NORMAN BEAUPRÉ

In Search of the Fallen Divina Maria Callas

ISBN: 978-1-951901-12-7 [Paperback Edition]
978-1-951901-13-4 [eBook Edition]

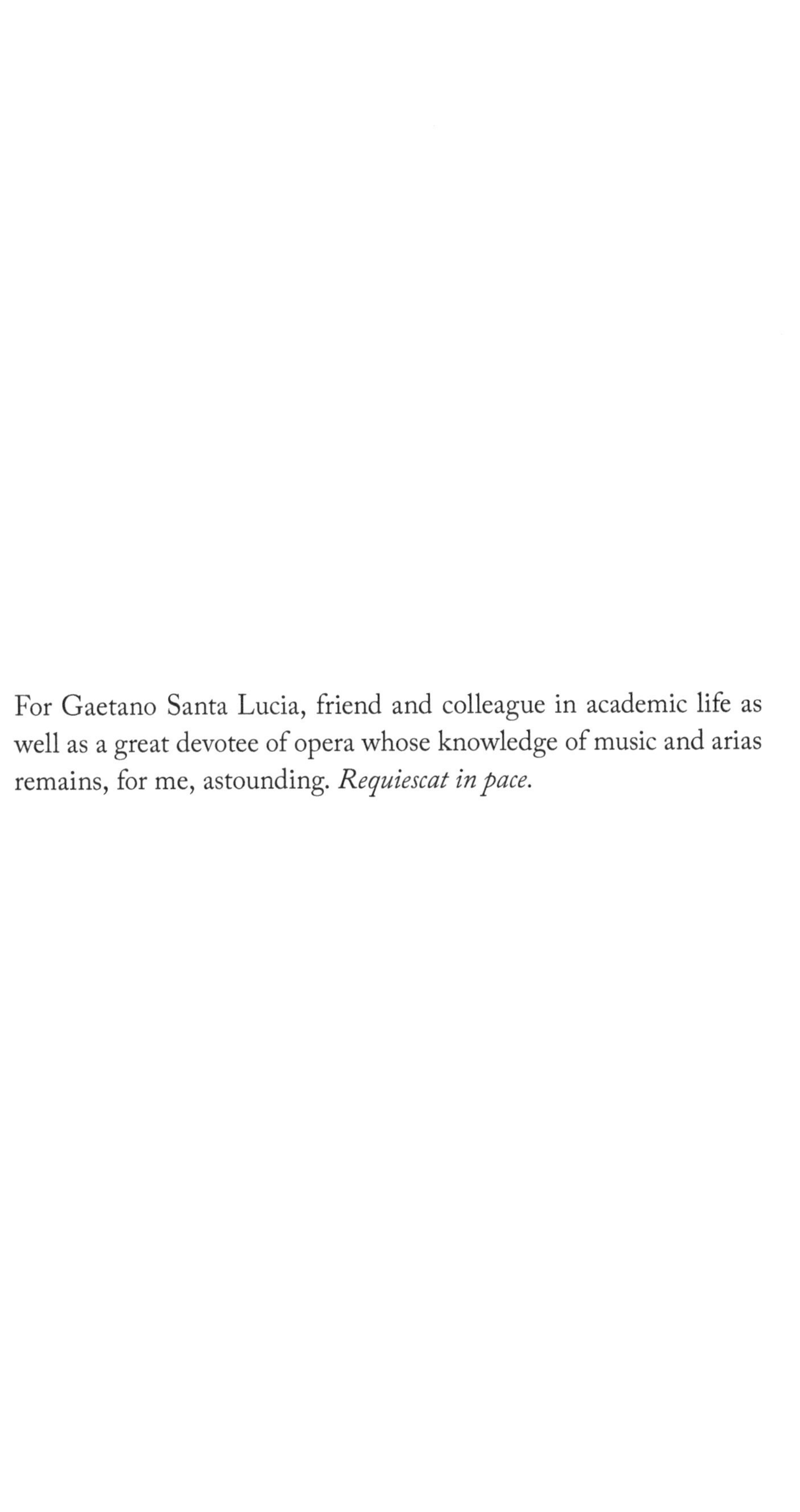

For Gaetano Santa Lucia, friend and colleague in academic life as well as a great devotee of opera whose knowledge of music and arias remains, for me, astounding. *Requiescat in pace.*

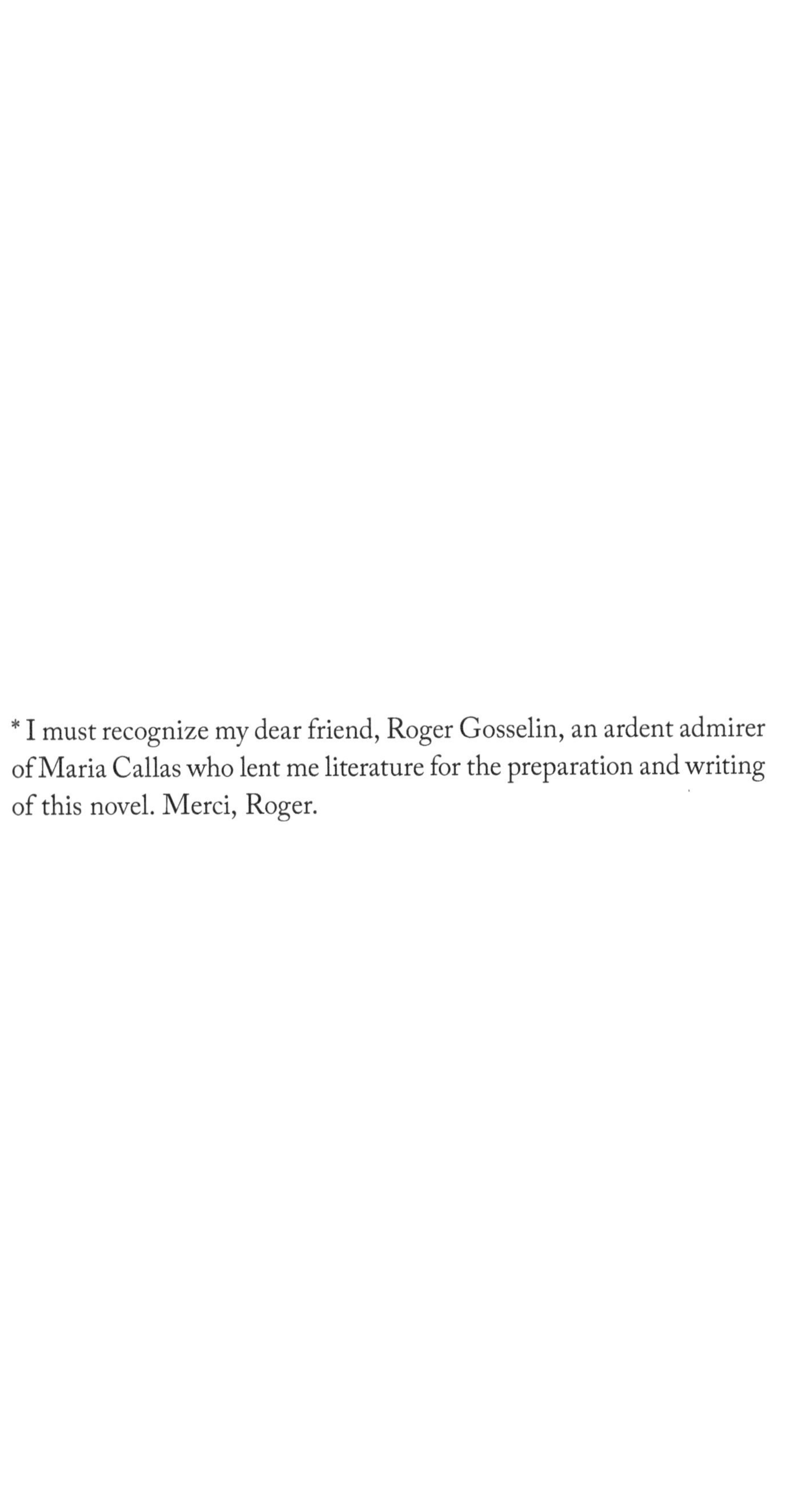

* I must recognize my dear friend, Roger Gosselin, an ardent admirer of Maria Callas who lent me literature for the preparation and writing of this novel. Merci, Roger.

Other works by the same author :

1. *L'Enclume et le couteau, the Life and Work of Adelard Coté, Folk Artist. NMDC,* Manchester, N.H. 1982. Reprint by Llumina Press, Coral Springs, FL 2007.
2. *Le Petit Mangeur de Fleurs,* Éd. JCL, Chicoutimi, Québec, 1999.
3. *Lumineau,* Éd. JCL, Chicoutimi, Québec, 2002.
4. *Marginal Enemies,* Llumina Press, Coral Springs, FL, 2004.
5. *Deux Femmes, Deux Rêves,* Llumina Press, Coral Springs, FL, 2005.
6. *La Souillonne, Monologue sur scène,* Llumina Press, Coral Springs, FL, 2006.
7. *Before All Dignity Is Lost,* Llumina Press, Coral Springs, FL, 2006.
8. *Trails Within, Meditations on the Walking Trails at the Ghost Ranch in Abiquiu, New Mexico,* Llumina Press, Coral Springs, FL, 2007.
9. *La Souillonne, deusse,* Llumina Press, Coral Springs, FL. 2008.
10. *The Boy with the Blue Cap---Van Gogh in Arles,* Llumina Press, Coral Springs, FL, 2009.
11. *Voix Francophones de chez nous, contes et histoires,* Llumina Press, Coral Springs, FL, 2009.
12. *La Souillonne, Dramatic Monologue,* tr. from French by the author, Llumina Press, Coral Springs, FL, 2009.
13. *The Man With the Easel of Horn---The Life and Works of Émile Friant,* Llumina Press, Coral Springs, FL, 2010.
14. *The Little Eater of Bleeding Hearts,* tr. from French by the author, Llumina Press, Coral Springs, FL, 2010.
15. *Simplicity in the Life of the Gospels, Spiritual Reflections,* Llumina Press, Coral Springs, 2011.
16. *Madame Athanase T. Brindamour, raconteuse, histoires et folies,* Llumina Press, Coral Springs, FL, 2012.

17. *Cajetan the Stargazer*, Llumina Press, Coral Springs, FL. 2012.
18. *L'Étranger Extraterrestre*, Llumina Press, Coral Springs, FL, 2013.
19. *Marie-Quat'e-Poches et Sarah Foshay*, Llumina Press, Coral Springs, FL, 2013.

Contents

1. Ena

My name is not important. Who I am, where I come from and what I do in life is of little consequence. I'm the narrator. This is the story of my friend, François, whom I have known for a very long time. I will tell it to you exactly as he told his story to me. You see François had an ambitious project in mind and eventually he overcame whatever obstacles he encountered and was able to reach his objectives. It was a very ambitious project and I'm delighted that he entrusted me with his story. First, I will let him speak and later I will take over this very interesting story of his. I must say that most of the story will be told by François himself. It gives the story a more personal *cachet,* as the French say. However, François wanted me narrate some parts in order to introduce some objectivity to the entire story.

My name is François Basil Spirounias and I was born in a very small town in upper Maine not far from the Atlantic coast where the winter months are harsh and bitterly cold, springtime, when it comes, tender and bursting with blossoms, summer erotically hot on some days and breezy with salty air on other days, while the fall can be the most glorious of days with spectacularly colorful leaves on the hills and mountainside. My friends call me Frankie, my mother calls me François and my father calls me, "Hey you" and sometimes "Hey, Greek face." He likes to tease me and make fun of me whenever he can. I never know if he implies scorn or admiration for my being half Greek. I take my ethnic Greek half from him; he was born in Greece and his parents emigrated to the U.S. when he was but a child. They came to New York under the guiding torch that the Statue of Liberty holds beckoning all immigrants to this country. "Give me your tired, your poor,/Your huddled masses yearning to breathe free/The wretched refuse of your teeming shore./Send these, the homeless, tempest-tost to me." Well, I don't know if they were part of the wretched refuse or even the homeless, but I'm sure they were tired and quite possibly poor. My father hardly ever talked to me and my mother about his and his parents' condition as immigrants, but I'm sure he grew up wanting to be part of the American dream, whatever that was for him and his family. All I know is that my father's family found a home with some relatives who had preceded them to New York. My mother told me one day that my father hated to talk about his family and his Greek relatives because he did not like them and they did not like him. Because he would not fit in, he told her. "What do you mean, 'not fit in'?" she asked him. He never replied to her many questions about growing up in New York and later on moving away to New Jersey and then to Massachusetts. Somehow and some way he managed to come to Maine and that's where he met my mother. Way up northern Maine where the dogs bay at the moon and the cows come home to be milked by some potato farmer. I never knew why my father did not like his own Greek culture or why he didn't like anything that was Greek. Why? Of course, he drank Ouzo. That's one thing he accepted as part of his ethnic self. My father was a handsome man, strong, vibrant, but painfully shy in some way and reclusive. He was no Zorba, vibrant, expressive and full of life. Not at all like this energetic and filled with the passion of living and love. He had dark shiny curly hair and a strong chin that jutted out like a promontory of flesh and bones. He had a ruddy complexion and strong hands. They were large hands with big thumbs and well-manicured nails. He did not work in the dirt nor did he labor in the mills or shoe shops where a man can get his fingers and nails full of dirty grease and oil. No, he worked for himself and by himself making furniture. They were fine pieces masterfully made of hard wood such as rock maple or white birch. He had learned his trade with a master finish carpenter and cabinetmaker somewhere in and around Boston. He had garnered a fine reputation for himself as a master furniture maker. He was good at making chairs and tables polished to a fine luster. People sought him out. We lived well and never lacked for anything for he was a good provider. The only thing I knew about him was that he had wanted to move away from big cities and live in the country where things were slow-paced and tranquil. He chose northern Maine as his place of refuge. His shyness and reclusive nature matched his lifestyle as a lone furniture-maker who did not like to be harassed with questions about his life. Once a year, he would go to the local Aimilianos Greek Club somehow affiliated with the main chapter in Lowell, Massachusetts to meet up with his close friend, Socrates Agnosistos. I suppose they chatted together and drank Ouzo. Talked about what, I don't know. Neither did my mother. That's all the socializing my father ever did. The whole thing stopped when Mister Agnosistos died.

I was born not too far from St Croix where Champlain established his Habitation but he returned to France because he realized that the winter months at his Habitation would be much too cold for himself and his men. He didn't want to freeze all winter long. That's the kind of weather we around here have to contend with. However, the weather changes with the seasons. That's all part of living in New England. Everything changes while remaining the same. I mean, the seasons change and people change, some die while others move away to find better means of living. The constant in all of this is that the real Maine character or attitude never deeply changes. Of course, you have the Yankee features, the Irish steadfastness, the French stubbornness and *joie de vivre* and so many other variations of life style that immigration with its flux and generational hand-me-down of customs and values have left their mark on the Mainer. I suppose that I'm a Mainer having lived my childhood days in Maine. As I said, my father was of Greek origin while my mother's family was Acadian French and came from New Brunswick. My mother told me that she had met my father in a restaurant where Greek food was offered and very much enjoyed by the clientele. The restaurant was owned by distant relatives of my uncle, Plato Throuvincios and had been in the family for four generations. My mother whose name was Valéda Louise Arcand, fell in love with my father, Basil Spirounias, the very first time she met him. Well, I don't really know if it was true love or the folly of love. She had been dazzled by him, his way of looking at her with his deep dark and piercing eyes and his bright sensuous smile much like Zorba the Greek in the film with Anthony Quinn playing the part of the lover of life and women. Such a performance, such dramatic tour de force. And the poor widow who grieved for her husband and so very much maligned by the villagers for not abiding strictly by the old traditions and not marrying the young suitor who eventually drowns himself. And how about Madame Hortense, the lonely French woman who craved for and needed love in her empty life. My mother and I loved the film *Zorba the Greek*. We would sit for hours at the local cinema watching this film while my father told us that Zorba was not really Greek and that he was a romanticized version of a Greek man whose dream project with the monks on top of the steep hill came to a total disaster. His life was a disaster, my father said. But we retorted that Zorba's life was an adventure in living and deeply and sensuously enjoying every moment of his existence on a lonely and barren corner of the world where love was embodied in a man who loved to dance. Dancing for Zorba was the linking of his soul to the stars and the expression of inner zest for life. My father would just walk away mumbling that all of this was rubbish on the dunghill of life. It seemed strange to me that mamma was more consciously appreciative of Greek life and the measure of all things Greek than my father was.

"You two live in a fantasy," he would tell us, "a goddamn fantasy of broken dreams."

"Who cares?" my mother would say, "as long as one has dreams to live on. Without dreams life is but a desert devoid of flowers and life-giving waters. *C'est du sable qui coule entre les mains,*" she would tell him and he would simply say,

"Yeah, yeah, yeah, sand running through the fingers, right."

I grew up appreciating the Greek culture while being immersed in the French cultural values and traditions of the Northeastern part of the United States that shared a culture nourished by the French language and traditions. People did not understand my zeal for the Greek culture especially when they knew that my father had very little respect for it except for the Ouzo. I suppose he had not been raised in it and his family had not shared that culture with him. He once told me that his grandmother had tried to teach him the language and bits and parts of the Greek traditions but her health was failing as well as her mind and she never got around to it. She died uttering repeatedly *"Oros Olympos, Oros Olympos, Mousai."* My cousin Pietros explained to me that grandmother was calling the muses on Mount Olympus for her own father had often referred to the sacred mountain and the habitation of the muses whose spirit and breath of inspiration called upon the great poets of Greek history. Grandmother Spirounias had studied at the University of Athens and was steeped in mythology, literature and music. Hard as she tried she could never inspire her son, my father, to commit himself to knowledge and the understanding and appreciation of Greek culture. She kept telling him that he had no *logos* and would wind up a pillar of stone, hard-headed like many Greek men. However, she did inspire me, François, at a very tender age to at least try to delve into my father's culture and know and accept that part of myself, the son, was Greek. I never repudiated my Greek culture while maintaining ties to my French heritage. As a matter of fact, I loved the Greek culture for what it could teach me and how it made me a lover of life in all of its capacities. In high school, I devoured books on Greek mythology and Greek literature and I owe much of what I learned to a teacher named Mister Kolophon who helped me in my pursuit of Greek culture. He had even planned to take me with him to visit Greece in my senior year. However, he left quite unexpectedly at the end of our junior year. I was utterly disappointed and even wanted to change high school. My mother insisted that I persevere in my studies where I was and think about a college where there would certainly be another Mister Kolophon. I stayed on to graduate and had already selected a college where Greek culture and history was being taught by superb teachers. It was all part of their humanities program and I went there feeling that I had finally arrived at the promised land of studies and cultural experiences. This college run by Franciscan friars who came down from Canada in the early part of the twentieth century had a study abroad program that offered a semester in Athens and the surrounding towns and villages. My mother was so very happy while my father said nothing more than,

"It's your choice, your traveling circus into a foreign land."

I did not attempt to explain to him why I was doing this and what it meant to me.

"Why Greece?" he asked.

"Because," I answered, letting the whole thing drop.

The college that I selected for my undergraduate studies was a small liberal arts institution and had very little as an endowment but enjoyed a very strong and faithful alumni association who believed in the future of the college. Although the student body as a whole was aware of the importance of jobs and skills, most students cared less about future jobs and more about getting an education. Some said that this was idealistic and not very practical in our world of business, investments and technology. The philosophy and objectives of the small college were immersed in the thought and ideals of a group of Franciscan monks and teachers who strongly believed in the educational worth of a liberal arts education founded on philosophy, theology, history, literature, fine arts, languages and the sciences. Math and economics were also part of the program but the emphasis was on thinking and being able to create and verbalize intelligently thoughts and ideas. My father insisted that I think over my choice of an education that did not include what he considered practical.

"What's the sense of cramming your head with nonsensical stuff," he said. "Good sense, practical sense does not come from books but through living and hard work. You were never one to be practical anyhow."

I earnestly tried to explain to him what my thoughts and feelings were on education as a formation of the mind and soul, and I just could not interest him in such a plan of getting an education. To him education meant jobs, money and a career that will guarantee the good life, he said. I asked him what the good life was and he said that if I did not know what a good life was then he was not about to explain it to me.

"I can tell you what the good life means to me," I told him, but he wasn't at all interested in my philosophy of life. So, we drifted further and further apart in thoughts and feelings. I was the shit that practical people refused to bear, he told me. I was the dreamer that stunted growth, real growth, he insisted. How could I end up anywhere with anything, he asked. A real man does not spend his life daydreaming and reading about culture, he insisted. A man is a man, is a man, and that's all.

"Are you a man?" I asked, and I could see that his face was as red as a hot iron. That's when I decided not to pursue the matter.

It was a good thing that I was away from home to study for I would have been in constant turmoil with my feelings while my father would have been in constant anger over my choices of living the way I wanted. The two of us were not on the same wavelength and I could not bring myself to try and understand him and his strong opinions on things especially on cultural views, his very own culture that I so highly respected and treasured. I took advantage of my four years in college to explore the many avenues of education, my education, as I saw it. I sought a holistic formation that would shape me into a human being well connected to the many facets of learning that would open up for me new avenues and different ways of seeing and appreciating things. Some of my friends asked about my goal in life, a goal that would lead to a career that would insure that I had a valid life, as they put it.

"What do you mean by valid?" I asked.

"Well, you know, a job, money, travel, political and social contacts and all that," they replied.

"Valid means other things for me."

"Other things?"

"Yes, other things such as dignity, self-worth, compassion for others, an open mind, a well-formed spirit and a literate capacity to absorb the rich and varied poetry of a world fashioned by poets who have nurtured the creative powers of the imagination and established world literature as a fountainhead of human development and achievement."

They all looked at me as if I was from another planet and did not realize that they had their feet firmly planted on this earth while mine floated above the clouds. I knew their way of seeing things and the thoughts behind their motives for insisting that I was wrong and so very impractical.

"Wake up, man," they said, "you're living in a dream world of your own. You're way above us. Your head is beyond the stars and into the nebulae of fantasy. Wake up, Frankie boy."

I was awake but they did not know that my awakening had begun a long time ago when my mother and I realized that a life without dreams is a life not worth living. In the meantime, I pursued my education and plunged into the books that allowed me to soar beyond the stars and the nebulae and into the world of philosophy, theology and especially literature. I also realized that my education would not be complete if I did not study music. Really study it in order to discover its ramifications as fine arts and the way music reaches the soul in order to make it sing or play on the chords of the soul's harp. I would have given anything to be able to play the violin or the piano but found out that I had no talent for these instruments of making ethereal sounds that pierce the heart and mind and go straight to the soul. So I resigned myself to singing and listening to music. My voice was not the best but it wasn't bad either. At least I had rhythm and a good ear for music. I had never before I listened to opera music much less gone to an opera. I was an opera ignoramus on his way to becoming an opera buff, but that would be several years away. Opera for me was full of loud and at times stringent sounds coupled with words that were foreign and not too well pronounced by the artist that was, I'm sure, renowned in the musical field. Paris, New York, Milan, Venice, Berlin and so many other large cosmopolitan cities where I had never been and would most probably never go due to a lack of music appreciation and, of course, money. I had no incentive and absolutely no one to bring me across the bridge of high culture. I remained in the marshes of social strata where I was born and most probably would remain for the rest of my innocent and ignorant life. That's what I constantly told myself. My mother did not agree with me but left me to my thoughts and low expectations in life although I know that she kept me in her prayers that someday I would discover my hidden talent for travel and cultural exploration and especially my love for books. They were my only solace and my only adventure in the realm of thoughts and desires. I read voraciously and admired those heroes and heroines who went beyond their capacities in life and flushed out their talent for travel and adventure. They never backed away from them. They never refused to acknowledge their skills and talents for reaching for the sun. The moon was not sufficient for them. No, they had to reach for the sun in spite of the inner warnings of their fatherly soul-Daedalus. The Icarean flight is engraved deep down in the soul of an adventurer so that it becomes a haunting and a passion that will never go away, never be erased. It must be attempted or else the adventurer will die, not a mortal death but a death in the soul. If the sun does not melt away the waxen wings of flight, it will certainly scorch the soul enough to be in constant pain. The pain of never-reached immortality and for the artist, this is very painful. The work of an artist forever doomed in the marshes of the forgotten, is a painful experience if not a disdainful one.

The great passion of my college years was reading Nikos Kazantzakis. I knew that he had written "Zorba the Greek" but that was all I knew about him until I started to delve into his life and his marvelously written work. He was an inspiration for me and I seriously thought of becoming a writer myself. However, I realized that I did not have the talent to be a writer. It takes that special calling to put things into words and have them resonate with power and passion. Nikos Kazantzakis was such a towering figure in my mind and in the mind of his readers and followers that I knew I could never measure up to him as a poet, a mythic artificer, a maker and forger of words much like Hephaestus, the legendary smithy of ancient Greece. When I was deep into Greek mythology spending nights and even days reading about the Greek deities and their skills, I learned that several epithets were attached to Hephaestus' name, one of which was *Klutotékhnēs*, the renowned artificer. He embodied, for me, the creative spirit that makes and forges magnificent artifices so that the human imagination can live and thrive in this glorious celebration of creativeness. I only wished then that the great Greek artificer had considered giving me the talent to be word-creative. However, I knew that my talent lay elsewhere, but where? And so I plunged into the writings of Nikos Kazantzakis. I read with ardent desire of grasping things his early works,

After college, I hunted weeks and months for a job, a meaningful one. I ended up with not-so-much of a meaningful job but an absurd one as my existential penchant saw it. I became a runner boy in a small firm that made so-called fancy women shoes and distributed them by courier, me. I ran here and there making my daily rounds of drop-offs. Some were small companies, some stores calling themselves boutiques, *une boutique nulle,* I called them, and some directly to homes where the ladies who purchased a pair of fancy shoes awaited their delivery with a quarter tip in their hand. I took the tip but I wanted to give it back so frustrated if not infuriated was I at my lot in post-college life. My father thought I was losing my time and my education and should have gone directly into a trade right out of high school without even considering higher education. Higher education meant higher costs and no job opportunities that made sense according to him.

"Don't buck the flow," he used to tell me, "you were born for the swamps and you'll remain there even though you fight it and refuse to consider your plight in life. That's part of the Greek tragedy, I'll have you know, pride, unfulfilled pride, unabated pride, foolish pride, tragic pride, the hubris of the tragic hero, that's what it is. You see, I know what Greek tragedy is all about and I did not have to study it in college. I lived it, my boy, I experienced it."

"How?"

"Someday I'll tell you but not now."

"Why not?"

"Because you're not ready for it. You're still wet behind the ears, practically if not totally inexperienced. You are tragic in a sense because you do not aspire for the really important things in life, true life. To me you're tragic because you aspire for the things beyond your reach and like Icarus your wings are melting."

My mother would tell him to stop that thoughtless chiding and that I was not tragic by any means but destined to live a life of magical and adventurous journeys. My father would just walk out of the house when she started to say things like that. He had a very low tolerance for people who could not understand Greek tragedy and Greek feelings the way he viewed it.

"You're French and not at all Greek," he would tell her, "you're not Helen of Troy, you're not Medea, and you're absolutely not Melina Mercouri or Irene Papas."

"Who do you think you are, my husband, Homer the poet or Jason with the sacred fleece, Anthony Quinn, the Zorba, or the billionaire Aristotle Onassis? You see I know some Greek names of famous people."

"Aristotle Onassis is a bastard Greek, a good-for-nothing womanizer. He's a manipulator and a scumbag, as far as I'm concerned."

"You say that about a co-citizen of your country?"

"Yes. He's no true Greek. Besides, my good wife, Anthony Quinn is not Greek but Mexican. Don't you know that?"

She looked at me and all I could do was shrug my shoulders and whisper,

"It's true, mom."

"As for Onassis, he's but a fat ass who soaks himself now and then in Greek country and sails in his fancy billionaire yacht."

"Shame on you, Basil, shame on you, talking like that."

"Shame on him for what he did to Maria Callas, shame, Greek shame."

It was the first time I had heard the name of Maria Callas. What had my father meant by Greek shame? I needed to look into it.

2. Dyo

I went away to college with a sense of freedom and release from the tensions of father and son's distraught feelings. I grew to resent my father's constant grudge against my own feelings that I nurtured in my heart and even in my guts so deep were these feelings of self-confidence and, at times, self-denial. I denied myself the comfort of being close to my father because I could not approach him the way I would have wanted to physically and emotionally, and I might even add culturally if not spiritually. Was he really my father? He might have been my biological father but I did not harbor any sentiment about his being my real father. His sperm had fertilized my mother's egg in her womb but that was about all I felt about the father-son relationship. I did not want to feel that way about my father but I could not help myself. Where was the closeness and intimacy that belong to such a relationship? I asked myself. Did he resent my being his son? I wondered. Did he wish that I had been born of another sex or of another personality than the one I had? Why were we in constant opposition to one another? At least, that's the way if felt to me. I kept pushing back my true sentiments about him and trying constantly to understand this man who was my father, but try as I may, I could not come to terms with the fact that he was indeed my father. Why could we not be like the ancient Greeks who had such a close relationship with one another especially between father and son? I loved Greek mythology and it was one of my best courses in college. I spent endless hours reading with my nose buried in supplemental texts above and beyond the required readings assigned by Dr. Felamon. He was such an accomplished master of Greek mythology for he knew everything there was to know about Greek myths and he delivered his lectures with great enthusiasm and vibrancy that most of us in the classroom just fell under his spell. He taught me how to love the myths as stories that exemplified the behavior of human beings and their heroic gestures as well as their quirks. These mythical characters were heroic and at the same time they displayed weaknesses that made them humanly real, for me anyways. I realized that the relationship between father and son in Greek mythology was not always harmonious but, at least, it was genuine and in many ways intimate. However, there were some who nurtured harmonious relationships and displayed a real sense of parental and filial love. Take Daedalus and Icarus, for example, Aegeus and Theseus, Odysseus and Telemachus, Priam and Hector and Peleus and Achilles just to name the most significant father/son relationships. On the other hand there's the relationship between King Laius and his son Oedipus. I call it a very strange and strained relationship much like my dad and I. Strained beyond compare. Laius is so afraid that the prophecy of his son killing him will come to fruition that he sentences him to complete exile and abandonment to the wild beasts. That's a pathetic move on the part of a father. Figuratively, that's what my father did to me. As for Aegeus and Theseus, the father is long separated from his son, Theseus, who is finally recognized by his father only when he is handed a cup of poison by the infamous and malicious Medea and the father, in a surprising recognition scene, knocks the cup from the son's hand. But the most salient scene of this father/son relationship occurs when the father, Aegeus, thinking that his son was killed by the Minotaur, jumps in the sea and is drowned thinking his son is lost forever. I doubt that my father would ever do that for me. As for Daedalus and Icarus, well that's a very well-known story. We all know that Daedalus wanted desperately to get away from Crete so he fabricated wings to fly over land and sea. He did the same thing for his son, Icarus.

However, much to the dismay of his father, the son disregarded his father's instructions and flew too close to the sun that melted the wax on his wings. He fell to his death into the sea. We are told that his father cried bitterly over his son's death and lamented his own arts. I remember so very well that Professor Felamon had reminded us of James Joyce's hero, Stephen Daedalus, in his novel, *Portrait of the Artist as a Young Man* in which the artist wants desperately to fly over the nets of his own ethnicity. Mythic heroes do live on and fashion the lives of literary characters by their authors. And I must not forget Priam and Hector as well as Peleus and Achilles for the two sets of father/son relationships do intertwine. When Hector is killed in battle by Achilles, the Greek warrior treats the body of Hector with disrespect and refuses to give it back. It was emphasized in one of our classes that refusing to give a Greek proper burial is tantamount to sacrilege. We knew that by the reading of the tragedy, *Antigone* . So the gods intervene and Priam, Hector's father, is brought to the enemy's camp and there he pleads with Achilles for the return of his son's body. He invokes the memory of Achilles's own father, Peleus. He tells Achilles that he has endured what no other man had endured before and he put his lips on the hand of the man who killed his son. Achilles is deeply moved and thus relents. I wonder if my father would do that for me, I mean, go that far to rescue me from disgrace and dishonor. To some degree, all of them suffer from tensions created by the elements of fate and destiny. I learned that fate could be defined as man's vulnerability to the whims of the gods while destiny could be defined as the design of the stars that controls man's ultimate unfolding as a human being. I still struggle with both of these but I think I'm beginning to understand them as related to me, François Basil Spirounias, and my being as a thinking man. The Greeks put so much emphasis on philosophy as well as poetry that plumbed the inner meaning of living and dying. I will never be able to attain the full depth of the thinking and even the feeling as a Greek does. At least, the ancient or mythological Greek as far as I'm concerned. The contemporary Greek man has lost most of the essence of this way of being. He has lost the true spirit of the *logos* also. A contemporary Greek like my father, exiled so to speak from his homeland, does not appreciate his culture or his being Greek. Not in my book, at least. Why am I being so harsh on my father? I don't really know except that I fault him for not living out his culture and heritage. For not understanding what makes a true Greek function as a man. Zorba does and so do the poets who write about what it means to be Greek. I may be totally wrong, but that‘s the way I feel and think about all of this. Maybe, my heart has overtaken my brain or the other way round. I do not know.

I don't know why I even bother to try and fathom the Greek essence and especially what makes my father tick, as they say. I guess, I'll never know. My mother does not know either and she lives with it always trying to console herself and reconcile herself to the mystery of not living one's culture. It seems a bit strange to me why she places so much emphasis on her husband's culture. Not that she underestimates her own, but it seems to me that she wishes that I, the son, take on the burden of the father‘s cultural abandonment. She certainly knows that I am half Greek and half French since I have both cultures flowing in my veins, but more and more do I think that she wants me to compensate for the mistakes and faulty sins of my father. To her, cultural abandonment is not only a mistake but a sin against the Creator who blessed all of his creatures with the gift of cultural identity. For her, to believe in the Holy Trinity is to believe in the Triune God that includes God the Father and Creator. That is why she puts so much of herself in the admiration of the Greek icons especially the one they call The Holy Trinity by Andrei Rublev. My mother kept urging my father to go and see these icons that she loved so much but he would not even step into a church that had them in resplendent and glorious colors as painted by experts in the art of the Greek icon. I went to see them and as many times as I saw t hem I could not tear myself away from this artistic wonder. What a beautiful rendition of faith and cultural belief. What is art for one is but a picture or a scribbling for another, I suppose. That was the case for my father. Don't talk about art with my father. That was a lot of bullshit, a made-up word to cover all kinds of drawings and paintings to be sold at the highest price and fool those who fell for art, he would say. Art is the gilding of the lily and the lie is in the beholder's eye, he liked to say. My mother and I would simply leave him alone in his thinking and ways of seeing or, I should say, not truly seeing things. Damn, he was stubborn! He had no appreciation of art in whatever form or shape. He was not Greek. That's what I told my mother who insisted that Basil her husband, my father, was indeed Greek since he had been born in Greece.

"He may be Greek by birth and homeland," I told her, "but he's not truly Greek in his rejection of his cultural heritage. That comes from the heart, no, the soul of a man. The Zorba soul," I insisted.

She knew what I meant but wished her husband, my father, had it in his soul to proclaim it loud and clear. On that point, he was mute and dispirited. He had been castrated by the gods who refused to shower him with the greatest of gifts a god could bestow on a man, his true identity. Would my father and husband of my mother find it someday? I've always wondered. My father was a lost soul and a lost poet as it is seen by the Greeks. They had the gift of looking deep into the soul of anyone especially another Greek and perceive the flaw, the tragic flaw of a tragic man like my father. Was Basil Spirounias, my father, lost in the miasma of the nebulae and planets and especially the creative will of the Aristotelian First Cause that set the trajectory of stars and of men in the immense firmament of living and dying? Who knows?

What I learned in college was both useful and formative in my spirit and my thinking. I learned how to manage things and how to perceive the practical sides of being alive. However, what I appreciated the most was how to conceive of principles and set them to creative means of interpreting my life as a human being. I learned how to ask questions since asking questions is a sign of intelligence one of my professors told us in his class of philosophy and science. He had told us that a true scientist was a thinking being, one who could ask pertinent questions and try to resolve problems even though the answer was not always there. Pertinent questions do not always have answers, he told us just like problems do not always have resolutions. The key, he said, was to ask the right question and to look at a particular problem with a keen eye and an inquisitive mind. My father would have been astounded what the professor had told his students since my father believed only in practical answers to practical questions and problems. No turning round and round in circles, he would say. Come to the point, he insisted, and give me the right answer, that's all, he would say. But there is no single answer to any given pertinent question, a question that has any depth to it, I would respond. Stop giving me that philosophical bullshit that you learned in college, he would say. All that money wasted on philosophical bullshit! What a waste! He would say exasperatingly. How could I give any answer to someone who always ended on a note of bullshit, I do not know. College may be bullshit for some but for me it was taking the bull by the horns and running with it in the right direction, the direction of the stars and not the marshes of the earth.

I needed to get away, as far away as I could and yet I felt within me the attraction of being home. I knew I could come home whenever I needed to or wanted to, but in order to miss home I had to get away from it. My father's constant presence, I would not miss. As for my mother's, well she was starting to get on my nerves with her constant prodding and pushing that I get closer to my father in some way. I got tired of having someone, even and especially my mother, telling me what to do. After all, I had grown up and could very well make my own decisions. So what if I made mistakes, everyone made mistakes, but the worst mistake is to think you cannot make mistakes. I learned that quickly. The more you make mistakes, the more you realize that the mind and heart cannot always lead you in the unmistaken path of what is called life. I soon realized that one does learn by his own mistakes and rash judgments. Most of the time what is truly needed is an open sense of creativity. Wide open to all kinds of creative outlets. I mean taking chances. Yes, taking chances even though it means making mistakes. After all, a mistake is a learned opportunity. College showed me how to be creative although I was told that I was already creative before I even attended college. However, having the skills and the talent to be creative does not mean that one is creatively constructive. I mean, one cannot be creative if one does not already know about words, art, culture, history, geography, philosophy and theology, science in a way that Einstein defined science or in the way some of my favorite scientists like, Newton, Lavoisier, Leo Szilard defined it. They were all linked to the humanities in some fashion and respected its values as permanent and steadfast values that guided them to the absolute truths. I learned that a true scientist is a person of ideas, a being who believes in the great movement of creation and believes in himself or herself as a creator. Some questioned this but these scientists were ever constant in their declaration of the true scientist. I also learned that it's not a matter of mathematics, physics, chemistry, calculus and other scientific disciplines. It's a matter of using these as tools and not as an end in themselves. And, you must learn how to ask questions, not about petty things such as what's the color of the moon or what makes the sky blue or the reason for a light or heavy snowfall. No, ask what makes us think and aspire for the stars. Learn how to ask questions like Socrates did. He always said that he knew nothing and had to learn by asking a plenitude of questions that eventually ended up with pertinent answers that were formulated by the one who responded to the question. That's because Socrates knew how to ask questions and extract the answers by making people think rationally and cogently. You see, they had the answers in themselves but needed to uncover them. And in the process they learned how to create with words and ideas. One does not create in the void, you see, that's for the Great Creator, but for us human beings we need to use what we already have but fail to recognize it in a creative way. One philosopher that I greatly admired was Henri Bergson for his views on creativity and for his stimulating élan vital concept. Bergson gave me the impetus to understand that I was capable of being creative without trying to tie everything to the intellect. We have all the germinating seeds inside us and we need to uncover them and let them grow if we are to be truly creative. It took time to fully grasp these thoughts and the teachings of great scientists, philosophers and creative literary artists, but I came round to it and eventually I made these thoughts my own. Once I leaned to meld the humanities with the scientific truths I owned them and I could now use them at will in my process of creativity. I had learned to ask questions and questions are not the possession of any specific discipline.

Another scientist I learned to emulate and appreciate was Carl Sagan the contemporary astrophysicist and cosmologist who firmly believed in extraterrestrial intelligence and popularized the notion of science and cosmology so that people started to listen to a scientist who really had something to say about the universe. It was in college that I started to delve into the notion of scientific philosophy or philosophical science as I called it. Our professors called it the philosophy of science and some gave courses on it. The best course I took in college was given as a team-teaching effort by a professor of science matched with a professor of philosophy. I learned not to compartmentalize knowledge but to approach it with a holistic view and understanding. Teachers and students do not own academic disciplines. Students are too prone to attain GPA's that favor their majors and often avoid challenges in other disciplines that enhance their knowledge and skills of asking pertinent questions. Students are not to blame. Teachers, counselors and administrators are because they are so prone to redirect students to areas of study that enhance majors in which they have invested critical resources in their pursuit of reaching numbers and quota goals.

When I graduated from college I felt compelled to spread my wings and fly higher than a kite as high as the sun would not fail me and ruin my waxen wings of discovery and adventure. I had felt secure at the college where my most adventurous ambitions had been to wander in the countryside seeking peace and tranquility and not looking for lustful adventures. Not that I wasn't like other young men full of vinegar and sexual desires, but I did not want to become addicted to such desires and irrational motivation. People used to say that I was caught up in my Greekness and was thoroughly platonic in my quest for intimacy and love. I did have friends, men and women, but they remained friends and did not become lovers.

Was I impervious to sexual love? Did I not crave for human intimacy? Was I not like others who seek an adventurous life full of hunger and cravings for the body and its inimitable lustful seeking? I was human after all, but my cravings were for the mind and heart and especially the soul. Yes, I had a soul, a spirit that craved for eternal truths and never ending debates with my two selves, body and soul. Would my body have it over my soul? I used to ask myself in a never-ending debate full of heart-wrenching doubts and ever increasing frustrations. Would I ever be at peace with myself? Would I? I found some measure of peace in music. Music became my passion. I had attained a point in my life whereby I entered what I called the sublime measure of total and complete ecstasy of sounds and music with the poetry of words all combined with the power of musical instruments played masterfully by creative magicians of sounds so pleasing to the ears and the inner soul. But, what rendered me so attentive to the music was the colorful and mystical sounds of the voice attuned to the music so that the music that was attained by voice and instruments became, for me, a kind of mystical reverie where I found myself to be totally intrigued and lulled by music so that the enrichment of it was so intently created in my heart and soul that I yearned to become oblivious to everything else in my life. It was as if there had been a transformation deep within me that I had neither sensed nor anticipated. It was a gift, a gift offering from heaven, a heavenly grace, I told myself. How else would I receive this gift, the gift of music? When I told my father about this he looked at me and said in his obsequious voice,

"That's bullshit! Wake up son, wake up and smell the coffee. Come down from the clouds and be a man not a robot or a monster of an angel with waxen wings."

My mother used to tell him,

"Stop harassing the boy, Basil, he's not a monster."

"He's not a boy, mother, he's a man or, at least, he's supposed to be a man. I sure hope he hasn't turned out to be a fag."

My mother turned as white as a sheet and hollered at my father,

"Don't call him that. He's a bright and beautiful boy...man...our son. Please do not use language like that in my home. Yes, my home, Basil, my home. Not yours, but mine. I've earned it, it's mine. You never made it a home for François and me. Not with your spite and your damn acid-spitting mouth, always spewing dirt and vulgarities. You are not Greek, Basil, you are not Greek."

"And you think you are, my French *tartine*?"

I told them to stop it and to please be more civilized.

"The Greeks were civilized and taught us to be civilized," I said.

"Yeah," answered my father, "as civilized as the barbarians of Greek playwrights and poets such as Homer who only lived to produce garbage. Garbage, I say. I can't relate to them or their works. It stinks to high heaven, I tell you. It's all imaginary stuff not fit for decent and rational people. His so-called epics and the plays of high-fallutin so-called thinkers and writers such as Sophocles and that guy, Aeschylus, are nothing but trash. Trash, I tell you, junk. A son killing his father and then marrying his own mother because it's a curse on the family? High society killing each other off and then they call it tragic? All of this was rammed down my throat when I was young and they called it culture, Greek culture and literature. Curses, tragic flaw, destiny, gods that run after the wives of others and fight among each other, and that one there who kills her own children to get vengeance, that's all crazy stuff, I tell you. My ancestors were nuts for telling such ridiculous stories. Bah! I say Bah!"

"Stop it, Basil, stop it. You're now infringing on the civilized rights of your own people and I'll have none of that."

My father left in a huff and slammed the door so hard that everyone on our street must have heard the clamor and wondered what was happening. I left home for good that same year.

I had no job, hardly any money except for what my mother had given me out of her pitiful savings that I had, at first, refused, but then accepted telling her that someday I would give the money back to her. She hated to see me leave like that, for she knew that I would live precariously without any guarantee of finding a place to live and sleep. I told her that I had the names of a few college friends and that I would take their invitation seriously and with gratitude to stay with them for a few nights until such time I would find my own shelter and be able to afford a decent place to live once I had a job. I was truly taking a chance that my luck would turn out to be favorable. All I had in my small used leather suitcase was my college degree, a few shirts, underwear and some other items that I had thrown together thinking that I would probably need like toothpaste, soap, and razor. I really didn't need much to survive. All I wanted was to get away so that I could think in peace and start mapping my life by myself. In the short run it would work but I wondered if in the long run it would turn out to be what I wanted or even needed. I was taking a chance and I knew it. Life is one big fat chance, I told myself. Destiny is a fat chance also. I just simply could not wait until my destiny had been carved out for me for I knew that it did not work out that way. If we all knew what was going to happen to us early in life we might not be courageous enough to dare and seek adventure and the hope that one day things would be just fine. There are detours in life and the road is often rocky and not always straight. We must live with paths that lead us nowhere and, at times, somewhere. It's a chance that we must take. What I knew and what I thought was true was that I had talent and creativity at my disposal and all I had to do was to nurture them and rely on my powers of intelligent questioning. I could sling hash, I could deliver newspapers, I could do handyman jobs, and I could learn to survive somewhere and somehow. And, I could always rely on the knowledge that I had learned the lessons of the humanities come what may. Nobody could take that away from me. These lessons might not give me a job right away but I could learn skills and I could reason and I could think and I could do whatever as long as I held on to my courage of believing in myself. Thank God for my music, I kept repeating over and over. For music is the sublime balm of the soul that soothes tensions and releases it from the stressful urges of life from having to cope with them with a sense of urgency. Besides the pop music that I liked, I had learned to appreciate "deep" music as I called it, classical, operatic, symphonic, and all that was called longhaired by some. Every day, it seemed, I learned something new about music and the performers. How I wished I had had the time and talent to learn how to play an instrument like the piano and the violin, my favorites. My mother wanted me to but I refused to commit myself to any task that would take up much of my time and effort. How foolish the reasoning of a recalcitrant youngster. I so much appreciated and felt jealous of those who did play the piano or the violin. How did they learn such disciplines of mind, body and soul, I wondered. It had to be very hard to learn the intricacies of music as applied to any instrument and with what patience and perseverance undeniably earned. I first learned to appreciate the "deep" music by forcing myself to go to a concert. It was a concert during my senior year in college when a friend of mine, Charlie Vargas, invited me, no, bribed me with flattery and a promise of a bottle of wine, to go with him to hear the music of Beethoven as played by master musicians under the auspices of the fine arts club. I told him that I did not want to but then changed my mind thinking that a good bottle of fine wine would be just the right thing after a couple of hours listening to music that I did not much care about. The muses must have been working overtime trying to convince me that my humanities courses would not be complete without the ravishment of music for I ceded to their prodding inspiration.

The concert was fabulous, more entertaining and bewitching than I would have ever thought. Long hair music had not been my favorite distraction or entertainment. I was not brought up with it and therefore I mistrusted it for what, I considered it to be a waste of my time. I did not understand it, I did not and could not get into it as so many people did, and I rebelled against the sounds that I overheard now and then. I told myself that I could never stand still listening to such noise that infuriated my ears. Besides, I just could not get into it and my mind had not been open to such music for it really bothered me to believe that people spent long hours listening to such sounds. Mozart, Beethoven, Bach and Liszt were composers' names that I had heard but not taken the time to really get to know them and their music. One cannot appreciate what one does not know and refuses to know. I was stubborn and I knew it. I had inherited a streak of my father's stubbornness when it came to cultural opportunities. The more you sink into stubbornness the more you get to be entrenched into it and therefore, you can only see and appreciate what the stubborn mind and heart allow you to see and appreciate. It becomes a *cul-de-sac* more or less. No exit, no open door. Yet, I was not one to be stubborn in anything, but I saw myself becoming a stubborn ass in spite of my reluctance to be one as far as music was concerned. And, as far as opera was concerned, forget it, that was a no man's land for me, as much as I looked at it and tried to listen to it. There is nothing worse than music obfuscated by words that one does not understand to turn you into an opera anti-buff. I used to tell my friends who listened to opera on Saturday afternoons that they were just wasting their time and could in no way lure me by any means to even pay the slightest attention to it. I would listen to LUX PRESENTS HOLLYWOOD, the radio theater, and throw myself into the movie stories with an ardor that belied my self-proclaimed objectivity to entertainment, but I would not, absolutely not, listen to the Metropolitan Opera radio broadcasts sponsored by Texaco and introduced by the announcer, Milton Cross, both staples of this live broadcast. One Saturday afternoon when I was sharing a beer with some of my friends, they surreptitiously turned on the radio to have me listen to the opera of the day which was **Carmen** with Risë Stevens. I stubbornly refused to even hear of it and tried to dash out of the apartment. Charlie convinced me to, at the very least, sit down and listen for a few minutes to the opera for, as he said, my stubbornness would probably melt away if I stood still for five minutes and listened to what he called exquisite music. I told him that opera was not exquisite. It was a lot of screeching noise interfering with the music itself. I told him I had tried to listen to it before but had been totally disillusioned by opera.

"But did you really listen to it?" he said.

"What do you mean?"

"I mean give it a chance to sink in your mind and heart?"

"How could I with all the conflicting noise I was being given right and left? That wasn't singing. It was loud babble."

"But you have to learn how to listen to opera, you must learn to adapt your mind, heart and ears to the whole of it. First you have to befriend the story, and learn how to appreciate the libretto and then how to absorb the music as it lends itself to the entire performance. It's a whole learning process for one is not born with it and only the very few have a penchant for opera."

"I'm not one of those."

"I know Frankie. Your dispositions are elsewhere but you could learn to appreciate opera if you could only get rid of your stubbornness."

"I'm not stubborn, Charlie, I may be in certain things but I'm not totally stubborn."

"Then learn to get rid of it when it comes to music and opera. It's well worth it, my friend."

And so, I let go of it for a little while when I tried to pay attention to my first opera, **Carmen**. It seemed better when I could hear the words and understand them since the opera was in French. I also learned that it was composed by Bizet and he was deemed to be one of the greats in opera, at least in the opinion of some. I really liked the overture since it was so vibrant and catchy, as Charlie said, especially the "Toreador" music. I managed to listen to the opera for half an hour but then I declined to further my listening capabilities and turned to Charlie and offered my excuses. He simply waived me off. I have to admit that the music of **Carmen** that I had heard became stuck in my head and I could hear it over and over again like a haunting melody that one cannot escape. And that was my introduction to opera. It would take me several years to completely enjoy opera. I did suffer through some of them but in the process I learned to be more patient and less stubborn and let the entire genre sink into the very fibers of my listening capabilities. I remember listening to parts of **Rigoletto** where the hunch-backed court jester becomes outraged over his daughter Gilda's love affair with the Duke of Mantua resulting in the fruition of a curse put on the Duke and Gilda and ending in Gilda's death as she sings, "*La maledizione.*" And of course, I fell in love with the song "*La donna è mobile.*" I was told the morning after the very first performance of **Rigoletto,** everybody out in the streets was singing this song. I understand why since it's a very catchy melody.

Gradually, I started to listen to more operas on the radio, Gounod's **Faust** and Massenet's **Manon.** I found **Faust** to be highly dramatic to a point of extreme romanticism what with the evil spirits and the angels, and the devil himself signing a pact with a human being in order to get his immortal soul. And the ending with Marguerite in prison ready to die for having killed her own flesh and blood. But the final scene, so religiously romantic, is her apotheosis and redemption---*Anges purs, anges radieux*----and she is *Sauvée!* I had a hard time swallowing that romantic pablum, I have to say, even though I'm a romantic at heart. As for **Manon** I found Massenet's music lyrical and heartwarming probably because I was getting used to opera and I was finally getting into it, I suppose. I like the Saint Sulpice scene where Manon lures her lover away from the seminary and she asks for God's forgiveness in *Pardonnez-moi, Dieu de toute puissance.* What a touching and sentimental scene, probably a bit too sentimental for some. Then I discovered Puccini, the great Puccini. What an artist of distinction, I thought. By then I was freely discussing operas with Charlie and he could not believe how far I had come in appreciating this genre of music and how much I had learned on my own. One scene that I preferred over all the other scenes and their music, is from **Tosca** when Cavaradossi hears the matins bells echoing in the valley and he launches inspiringly into the aria, *E lucevan le stelle.* I could feel it stirring in my soul. Not to forget either Tosca's aria, *Vissi d'arte, so* well known by so many people even those who are not opera buffs. I thought that Puccini had truly mastered his craft with this opera and was without a doubt, as far as I'm concerned, a great composer and musician. So many people love his work and rely on his operas to bring them the satisfaction of music that stirs the soul as I felt about his operas.

After a while, I realized that what I had learned and had absorbed about opera was not much, not much more than what most people knew and treasured. I had to dig deeper and discover the wealth of operatic music and librettos. How about Mozart, Bellini, Rossini,

Donizetti, Cherubini, and other master composers? Was I willing to devote time and energy to opera? I wondered. Charlie thought that I was going overboard with opera, but he encouraged me to delve deeper and deeper into it and more profoundly in my mind and my soul until such time I would evolve into a true opera lover. However, I could not do that simply on listening since opera was meant to be heard and seen. It had to be live on stage with great performers, artists that captured the essence of any given opera. Artists who could convey their art and the art of the composer to an audience some of whom had become true connoisseurs of opera. These sophisticated people, sophisticated not by their status in life but sophisticated by their talent and courage of learning what had to be learned in order to truly understand and appreciate music with words and action. Opera was after all, a dramatic art. I knew that and I realized that if I ever came to know fully opera as a dramatic art form, I would have to find an operatic performer who truly brought drama to her or his art. It took me a long time to do so but I did find her in Maria Callas. But, that's for later on in my story and my development into opera.

3. Tria

When I did return home for a brief visit, I just could not completely avoid my parents nor cut them off entirely from my life, I told them about my musical development or better said, my music appreciation, and detailed for them my growth into opera. My mother did not fully understand my love for it or why I was spending so much time listening to music that was beyond her capabilities to grasp. As for my father, well, he went blank, no response, no arguments, no sign that he approved of my journey into opera. My mother asked him why he did not respond and he just said that it wasn't worth it since it was, as he said, another waste of time and effort on my part. That was all. He then left the room quietly and a bit despondently. I was not disappointed nor was I expecting much more from him. There had never been very much communication between my father and I. Why would I expect some now? My mother told me to be patient with him and that someday he would open up to me.

"Ma," I said," he's so closed up like a clam, that I wonder if he will ever open up his shell to me."

"He will, just give him a chance."

"I don't know, ma, I really don't know."

It was simply the kind of father and son relationship that one encounters in literature or in everyday life where neither father nor son fit nicely in one another's communication skills and receptivity like a piece of puzzle that snaps right into place as soon as the hand places it there. Of course, there are good father and son relationships but so many are not so good, even bad ones as far I can see it. One very good father and son relationship comes to us in Homer's epic story of the *Odyssey* between Odysseus and his son Telemachus. Oddly enough the relationship develops at a distance for Odysseus has been away from home for some twenty years. Absence creates a caring and dutiful relationship here. As a matter of fact, a good portion of the *Odyssey* is lent to the quest of Telemachus for his father. In contemporary literature we have the father and son relationship that develops into full bloom with some of the best known literary characters. There are also bad relationships between fathers and sons in literature and the one I like is the "Letter to Father" by Franz Kafka that tears the father apart for his evil ways. Then there's "My Two Wars" by Moritz Thomsen in which he talks about his two catastrophes, World War II and his father. Tolstoy's "The Death of Ivan Ilych" addresses the problem of getting old and dying and reminiscing about one's life and accomplishments to a point where one asks himself, what have I done with my life as a man, a father, a husband and as one who did everything right. Then, of course, there's Willy Loman in "Death of a Salesman" who tries so very hard to bond with his two sons and be understood by them. I've always loved their story ever since I first read it in high school. Poor Willy Loman who loses everything, his job, his career as a salesman and even his self-esteem. I tried to compare it with the relationship between me and my father. It was easy to see that there was hardly any relationship between him and me. Whatever there was when I was very young seemed to have either vanished with the years or never had been there in the first place. I believe that he had made the initial act of engendering and then had left my mother to take care of whatever relations necessary for the upbringing of a child. I don't know if there was any kind of a relationship between my father and his father, or between any in the generations before him. What a sad and lonely existence it must have been. No male intimacy, no male relationship worth anything. That wasn't Greek nor was it French.

It was nothing. Am I the product of a void male relationship? I must have been affected in some ways with the Oedipus complex, I suppose. But enough of that. I must go beyond male intimacy and father bonding to reach and maintain my sanity. Try as I may, I can never go there. I can never reach my dad. I can never go beyond my reach for some form of closeness with my father. I know that and I accept it. However, it's not easy.

I have got to stop living in a dream, a dream that one day I will be free to do whatever I want, free to go wherever I want and free to do anything I want. But then I ask myself what is freedom. Freedom from want, freedom from that gnawing feeling of nastiness that twists my soul and makes it uncomfortable when all I want is comfort and ease. What is nasty anyway, I ask myself. Am I the forger of my own ennui? Yes, the age old ennui that's the malady of the soul. I've come across that in literature and so many times in my young life that I cannot fully comprehend it. My father would call this a feeling of longing for something impossible to get and not worth seeking for it. A waste of time and effort. Is that it? A wasted soul and a wasted soul journey? I do not know any more if I'm coming or going. Going where? The more I read and the more I try to deepen my knowledge of self and others, the more I am confused. *Approfondir mes connaissances, c'est dégonfler la science de me connaître à fond* [to deepen my knowledge is to deflate the science of knowing myself], my philosophy teacher would say. He was a philosophy teacher but not a philosopher, he would say. To deepen is oftentimes to burst the balloon of knowing oneself, to put it in a nutshell. He's the one who used to tell his students that philosophers are blind persons who search for dark matters in a dark room never encountering anything concrete and worthwhile. Then why do you teach philosophy? we would ask. To make people like you try to understand that the pursuit of ideas is a meaningless if not worthless endeavor, he would say. Yet, he was a brilliant educator and a man of letters. He had read practically all that is to be known in the realm of philosophy. Was he like Faustus perhaps, sick and tired of knowledge and yearning for that transcendental knowledge that breaks open the kernel of the mind and soul to let in the final and wherewithal human knowledge that touches upon divine *sapientiae*? Was I getting to be that blind man searching in a dark room for some dark knowledge of some kind? Like a lifeless being in search of himself and his identity as a human being? What did it mean to be a human being? I kept asking myself. The mind is a very precious thing and the thinking soul or the *logos* is an irretrievable part of our existence once we have denied it. However, we are not transcendence only. We are what we are body and soul, feelings and thoughts. How can I thrive in an oblique world of ideas where Plato's cave binds us together as ignoramuses while on the outside lies the blinding light of the sun-truth? Plato's sense and theory of idealism is for the Platonists and the not-so-wary of veritable human existence. Am I a Platonist, an existentialist, a realist, or an abstractionist whose feet are in the mire of abstractions and irrationality? Am I in touch with reality? Who am I? No! No! No! I told myself. I do not want that. I don't want to dwell in the confines of my mind. I want to return to my full humanity as a person, not some kind of philosophical robot. So, I stopped thinking, thinking in philosophical modes and terms and I started drinking in music like a drunken man who cannot stop himself from taking a drink no matter what the consequences are. Getting inebriated on music is a marvelous way of dealing with ennui. After all, the soul needs harmony and delight. It needs that kind of energy in order to revitalize itself and become less lethargic and definitely more in stride with living and not wasting away in some dark corner of the mind where ideas deteriorate and become lifeless. I wanted spontaneity, joy, freedom of the mind from preordained thoughts, freedom to let go, and freedom to be myself. I needed a conduit, a channel where I could exercise my passion, if I had one, and enjoy the expression of self in a world that so often denies true self-expression. But where would I find that? And so I found it in music. Music the wonderful and marvelous conduit of the soul that has finally been exorcised of all ennui.

4. Tessera

Music, music, music! I did not want the music of the natives or the music of the fleeting times. I wanted the music of the ages that lasts on and on. I wanted real music. The music that clenches one's soul and hangs on to it like a dog that holds on desperately to his bone. I wanted to sink my teeth into it, chew it and taste its full flavor like one who savors the delight of a ripened fruit. I wanted to make it a sensual experience while enjoying its mystique as an art form. I wanted to suck fully of its milk like a young child sucks on his mother's breasts. Music regales and broadens your delights as a human being, I thought. What other art form can do that? Of course, there's literature, but literature has its own richness and delight. Painting? Well, painting, drawing, sculpture and other forms of the plastic arts, render the soul pliant to forms, colors and visions of things or beings conceived by the artist who either mimics nature or surpasses it to find new ways of seeing things. Music has its very own cachet and once it's unlocked, the whole embodiment of its richness pours out like a river or a stream ready to assuage you and mellow you or spin you out into the galaxies of stars and wonderment. *Le mystère de l'envoûtement de la musique,*"[the mystery of the spell of music] as my teacher, Monsieur Tisserand, used to say. He used to tell us, his students in fine arts, that his name meant "weaver" and that indeed he was a weaver of dreams and musicality. *Pauvre Monsieur Tisserand*, he liked to say that dreams are composed by the imagination in a musical trance since music is part and parcel of our human being. Even babies at birth respond to music, he said. Their very first lullaby is "*le bercement des eaux de la mère,*" he liked to say, the rocking movement of the mother's amniotic fluid. Quite a character was he this Monsieur Tisserand.

Yes, I was on a journey. It was a journey of the soul searching for its essence. What I mean by essence is that the soul has a core or a basic truthfulness that cannot be wiped out. It cannot exist without its essence since it would then deny its very existence. I know, I'm getting a bit too philosophical here but I'm trying to define what the soul truly is and I can't find the right words. It's very hard to define something that's transcendental, immutable, spiritual and non-material. Do we really have living in all of us human beings an element that is beyond matter? Yes, because we are fused with the spark of life itself. Some say that the God-spark or the touch of the divine in all of us. We could not live without it. We were all created with it and by it, Creator blessed and infused by the spark of the great Maker, or as the Greeks would say, the *poien.* You see the *poien* is the factor of creation or image-maker that resolves all questions of creativity. To the Greeks *poien* meant creation by the mind and soul, a creation that expresses the essence of soul-creativity. Some would use the word imagination, but imagination is a bypass used to mean not real, like you're imagining things. The Greeks had several words that translated the power of thought and the process of thinking like *logos* for independent thought and *nous* for the capacity or principle of the cosmic mind or soul responsible for the rational order of the cosmos. Whatever word is used or whatever power of creativity is employed to define what is transcendentally creative in all of us, doesn't matter, as long as we believe in its power to sustain life and its essential meaning of being alive and creative.

However, words and definitions quite often escape us. They're slippery like earthworms and eels. They tend to confuse us thought-makers and thought-graspers. We tend to grasp at straws as some would say. One thing that Mr. Kolophon taught me was to use simple words and simple definitions to express your thoughts, he said. What is thought clearly and precisely can only be said clearly and precisely, he said. No twisting things, no convoluting things and no going around things. Just plain and clear. Thoughts and ideas need clarity, he insisted. But, ever since I got a taste of philosophy, theology and other –ologies, I tend to use words that render definitions somewhat obscure as they become slippery and hard to communicate. They're slippery and fall oftentimes on deaf ears. It's like a star-catcher trying to catch a shooting star with a butterfly net. What is clear to me and precise as an idea is not always clear and precise to another. I know that. How do I communicate my ideas and definitions to another especially when we are not on the same wavelength? Well, I found out that it can work if you use a catalyst. Like what? you may ask. Like music. Music for me renders things more concrete since it's linked directly to the senses, especially that of hearing. I am told that certain people feel music and touch music. Some may even taste music. Can you imagine? I can. It takes a catalyst to turn the power of thought and ideas into reality. Mine was music. It still is. It's easier to understand what I'm trying to get at when I use the catalyst. Music for me became my catch word, my *passe-partout*, my creative gate through which I could pass unharmed from the scathing moments of each given day. No day is perfect and no day has every moment as bright as a star. There are clouds and crevices, dark spots and gloom-filled interstices. Music is not a panacea for all ills and reversals but it sure has the magic of setting things right. For me anyways. What if but for a moment we all lost the sense of hearing and the world became deaf and dumb? No sound, no music, no sense of the mysteriousness sound. Just blank and soundless. What a loss that would be. I knew a woman, Ruth, who told me one day that she would prefer to lose her sight than lose her hearing for she adored music, and as much as she loved reading from a book, she knew that she could somehow recapture the sense of reading through Braille or having someone read to her. But to completely lose the gift of hearing and listening music? No, that would have been tragic for her. Not to be able to ingest music like a being ingests food or nourishment that, to her, would have been disastrous and downright reprehensible. You may not like music or even stand it but you could not live without the soothing, joyous, even the lugubrious sounds of music in all of its modes and nuances. Some say that music elevates the soul but I say music is the soul in mystifying vibrations and resonating vibes. True music, real music, ageless music, everlasting music. Music crafted by musicians who have talent and know their craft, either as a composer, a musician or an singing artist. Now, you may ask me what is true music and I would have to tell you that you will have to discover that by yourself. I cannot and will not tell you something that only you can get to really know. I'm still learning.

Well, music came into my life as a sorceress who entices you by her seductive glances and slow movements of her limbs that bind you to her and her everlasting caresses of alluring love and sensuality. The limbs of a music sorceress are her heart wrenching movements of compelling sounds and passionate stirrings of the heart. Just like a *pieuvre,* an octopus, that encircles you and sucks you in with its many tentacles. I became enthralled and under the spell of her enchantment, the enchantment of music. Music drilled into me by sheer delight and sudden discovery of lyrics and sweet sounds. How could I resist such delight? How could my soul remain submissive to the aridity of the desert devoid of beauty and the lush verdant growth. The cool roaring rush of the waters of a waterfall emit sounds that captivate not only your hearing like a sudden burst of music but also your perception of sensual things that resonate deep into your soul. Some are left without any feelings in such a case. They're like stone, motionless and flat. But, I am always fascinated by waterfalls and all that's gloriously rendered by the sight and sound of water whatever it may be, ocean, rivers or lakes, and even quiet ponds with water lilies that call to mind Monet's evocative paintings, or even gurgling streams that can be heard from afar in lonely woods. I love the sounds of water and I love the sounds of music when they are rendered with sublime craft and passion. *La musique calme l'âme et rend éternel son pouvoir de rejoindre les doux chants des anges dans le ciel,"*[music calms the soul and renders eternal its power to rejoin the sweet chants of the angels in the heavens], our music teacher, Monsieur Paradis, who loved to swoon poetically over music, used to say, and we would all fall into a deep mocking swoon. Ahhhhhh. He would just smile and seemed pleasantly gratified. I just thought that he was off the tree limb into some mode of stupidity. But he was right, of course. Music could reach the angels in heaven. However, music is not magic nor is it devoid of all manners of hard work. It's crafted by it and it takes hours and hours of practice and deep perseverance. It also takes talent, the gift of the gods. Some have it and some have more than others and I will learn later that Maria Callas had the most of it, more than anyone ever had who sang opera with such élan and passion. Nothing is truly worthwhile if not done with passion, especially music and writing.

5. Pente

So, how do I translate my catalyst into verbal tones, tones that mean something to me and to you out there? I mean how do I speak to you so that you can fully grasp the meaning of what I am saying in writing? Writing is so easy when one knows what he is trying to say. I don't like he/she nor do I like "they" when I want to use the singular pronoun. It's too complicated when attempting to follow the rules of grammar and at the same time trying to be politically correct. Society oftentimes complicates things when it comes to gender equality. Now, I'm getting further and further away from explaining my catalyst. The Greeks did not have such a hard time doing it. They used poetry to explain things of the mind and of the soul. *Logos* and *nous* served them well. The Greeks knew precisely what was meant by these two concepts and they applied them with deliberate preciseness. Although they used them in philosophical debates and writings, they often preferred the creativity of the poem. They produced theater, wrote epic poetry and expressed themselves clearly and precisely enough to last a lifetime, more than a lifetime because their literature and philosophy have transcended time. That's why we have it today and we are able to study their ways of looking at things and their ways of gathering information and turning it into definitions that make sense to us. They had and used catalysts. Yes, they did and they did it in a masterful and precisely clear way. The Greeks used myth as one of their splendid catalysts. Myth has the power to elicit a human response. It is the essence of *poien,* I might say. There's that word again. I like it because it exemplifies the very power of creativity and, it's time to say it, the imagination at work. Imagination is not necessarily untruth and the non-real. No, imagination is truth in the making. Not the hard scientific truth as many people like it but truth as the mind and soul can conceive it. Anyhow, that's the way I see things. Am I not right? *N'ai-je pas raison*?

I may just fall apart here and now since my mind is wandering and it's not exactly in tune with my thoughts and my words at this very moment. It appears that I'm in the process of writing without knowing what to write about. It's like a hiatus, a pause, an empty space in time and thought. However, nothing is completely void and empty. I know that. The wheels are spinning and the thoughts and ideas are evolving. They have to merge concretely and coherently with words in order to fashion speech out loud or mute. Is speech ever mute? you might ask. I don't know. Speech is speech and it's voiced, isn't it? Otherwise it remains thought unvoiced. It doesn't really matter does it? What I'm doing here is to replicate the passage of writing. Yes, passage. From the mind and soul through the path of speech and then voiced out loud in order to communicate with others who listen with their ears wide open to the sounds of my voice. That's why communication is important and it must be clear and precise communication. Human communication needs coherence and preciseness. What I'm really trying to do here is to reveal to you listeners and readers the workings of writing in the process of distilling itself and rendering itself communicable. If it's plain writing like biography, history, technology, science or whatever is straight communication of the source to those who read it, then it's fairly easy. But, if it's creativity at work, if the creative process is sought and the imagination lends itself to the processes of creativity, then it's not so easy. Much effort has to be put into it so that the ideas and the words coalesce with the story that's being told. Human beings are essentially storytellers. Myths are the essential forms of storytelling and the Greeks knew that and showed us the way. Not that the reporting of facts and figures, the telling or retelling of historical facts and the statements of formulas and scientific thoughts and findings are not difficult to produce. They're part of a different process of telling things through thought and words. Now I'm really straying from my writing and telling you about what the real story is about. After all, I am writing a story. Well, what is it? you might ask. Stop beating about the bush, as the old saying goes. I am, I am. Right now. I was just collecting my thoughts, I'll have you know.

Where was I? I was attempting to define creativity and the expression of it in writing. Here I go again. Empty and meaningless words. They're not really meaningless but here in context they do not make any sense to the reader or listener. So, stop it. I will. Telling the story, we agree, is the essence of the novel and since this is a novel, as such, well I must tell the story. Here I go. No, here I continue after a long hiatus. But it wasn't a meaningless one since I was trying to resolve things, as you know. But, don't fall into the trap again, you might add. I agree. Let's get out of the mire of words upon words and without too much meaning. But, I might add, they were NOT without sense and meaning. Yeah, yeah, yeah.

Where was I? I was at the juncture of telling you about my catalyst and my reason for writing this story. As I said, my catalyst was and is music. Delicious, soul warming, exquisite, entertaining, and breathtaking music that sparks the intelligence into forming ideas about what is being created in the mind by sounds and what elevates the soul to a higher plateau of capturing sweet and harmonious sounds as perceived by the ears fully opened to the sounds of music.

Music. How does one define it? I mean how does one render justice to music if not by composing music, listening appreciatively to it or absorbing it through flesh and soul? I do not really know how to define music except to say that not everything in life can be defined. Yes, there are definitions and many attempts at defining music have been made, but personally I cannot define music. I can only appreciate it and falling in love with it the more I listen to it and absorb it into my inner being which is my soul. I resist saying my mind because one cannot truly and effectively define and appreciate music strictly by intelligence. Sure, some people do it very well and they define music in elaborate terms. For sure music teachers, at least some of them, do it professionally and they do it well, but do they define music in its very core. I don't know. Music is an art and art is not defined by words and thoughts. It must be expressed. I like the description or definition that one of my artist friends proposed to me: "Fine arts must be engendered by the fingers and pass through the mind to finally end up in the gut." That's really what art means to her and to me. I understand the process. Art and music must be produced and felt with the guts. That's probably where the soul lies but I understand what people call the "gut feeling." Well, gut creativity is certainly one way of defining music. When I am listening to music, brilliant and soul- soaring music, I can feel it in my entrails, my gut to be blunt about it. Enough of this and let me get to the core of my story

My story continues when I remember my very first experience of being in love. I met this girl in Boston when I was studying music at the Berklee School of Music. I was not matriculating there but rather I was auditing some courses, officially and unofficially. Her name was Ange-Aimée. She originally came from the Quebec Province then moved to Maine and later on moved to Massachusetts with relatives to study music. She had a lovely voice, one that could enchant the angels as her mother said. Her mother was nice and her father was also nice but extremely shy. He hardly talked. Ange-Aimée used to tell me that her mother was the opposite that if you did not tell her mother to stop talking, she would go on indefinitely without much interruption. Rose-Éva was her name and she told me once that she had to talk for two since her husband hardly ever spoke, and she laughed. Rose-Éva was a charming lady and a beautiful woman with a beautiful and lush complexion but she was a possessive woman who liked to manage her children's lives and practically restrain them from being who they really were. She choked them, strangled them so-to-speak into being mama's possession what with her words of intense correction and her psychological beating with coerced feelings. She left them no breathing space, no room to become men and women. She had four children, two girls and two boys.

Ange-Aimée was the youngest and probably the most rebellious of the four. The two boys got married very young just to get out of the house and find peace in their lives, Ange-Aimée told me. As for the sister, her name was Amanda, she remained glued to her mother's apron strings. As she grew older, she took on the habit of folding up into her shell just like a turtle. She was polite, courteous and gentle but so very squeamish and afraid of almost everything especially bugs and animals such as snakes and spiders. She hardly went out except with her parents. Amanda never spoke much and that's why her mother took it upon herself to speak for her. I think she did not speak much because her mother had taken over her life. Amanda was not free to express herself because she was held captive in her mother's restraining hold. I told myself, what a life to live like a caged animal, psychologically and emotionally dependent on the woman who had given life to her. Ange-Aimée tried to explain things to me one day, but she couldn't. She knew all too well that she was defending her mother while trying to liberate her sister from the terrifying hold of parent-possession. Why do parents do that? I wondered. Some like my own father drive their children away while others hold on to them like God-given possessions. They think they own them and do not want to lose them to maturity, so they cling to them with raw determination. Even animals do not do that. They let their young grow up and they teach them to be on their own. Well, Ange-Aimée would not let her mother own her to a point of crushing her spirit. Her spirit was music and music needs freedom of the heart and soul and free expression. What surprised me the most was the fact that the mother, Rose-Éva, truly thought that her children were free to choose, free to express themselves fully and free to do whatever came to their minds. However, freedom coerced by strained emotions with the free spirit chained to what is perceived as duty to family and not to oneself is freedom unclaimed. Ange-Aimée knew that and that is why she moved to Boston. Yes, it was to find her soul in music but it was also to loosen the chains that the mother had fashioned since childhood. Ange-Aimée was going to once and for all break those chains. Not that she did not like her mother, she loved her, but love is never a choke-hold. That's when I realized that my mother truly loved me for love blossoms in free space and develops into the flower of give and take. Love is an exchange, a giving of oneself in exchange of getting back what has been given but better for the given has been transformed into a wondrous gift, the gift of self to others who need love. Selfless love is true love since it does not grab anything to turn the other into a thing-being but transforms the giver and the receiver into joint receptacles of caring and giving of oneself. It's so hard to define love; it needs to be expressed and shared in order to experience its power of transformation. I believe that Ange-Aimée and my mother knew that and understood it quite well to a point that they did it resolutely and naturally. As for my father, I'm still trying to fathom him. I know he loves me but in a rather strange way that I cannot fully grasp and understand. Father and son love can be strange and elusive, I think. If I ever become a father I will try to the best of my ability to give love freely and to receive it freely, open and transparent.

6. EXSI

Ange-Aimée loved me and I loved her. It was as simple as that. How did I know that she loved me? Well, I knew it because of what she expressed and how she expressed it. It was not carnal love but rather the love that attracts two people to one another as friends and companions. You could say that it was platonic but at the same time it was sensuously real. Love needs to be expressed fully and clearly, not hidden under some bushel of lies and tortuous ambiguities. She expressed what she learned about music as well as the great talent for music that she had. Music does reveal what one really is deep inside. When one is lonely or sad, melancholic or tenebrous like a cold cavern, or even when one is bursting with joy and filled with the wonder of the stars, then music can transform these feelings or moments into lustrous expressions of self-abandonment to being who you are deep inside and vibrantly outside. I learned in my Transcultural Health and Being course with Dr. Banachevko that if you're not well inside you're not going to be well outside. He used to quote Carl Hammerschlag to us taken from his book, "The Dancing Healers". There were many notable quotes that really enlighten me as to the holistic approach to health care. Although I did not intend to major in this field of studies the whole notion of holistic health was fascinating and made me think about all of life's endeavors being thought out holistically, even music. One quote that I really liked dealt with mental health. It's quite simple but captivating. I cannot remember it word for word but paraphrasing it comes out as having your head, mouth, and heart in a straight alignment. Mental health happens when what you say is what you truly believe in your heart. When the mouth is on the same pathway as your heart, then you are mentally straight. But how do you know if your mouth and your heart are on the same pathway? One knows. How do I know? Through music, yes, through the catalyst of music. That's how I know. The more the music resonates in my heart and soul, the more I know that I am mentally sane and soulfully healthy. I know that music is not magic but it is magical in the sense that it has the power to stir in me the magic of thoughtful and emotional well-being. I should not say magical but mystical. When I tried to explain all of that to Ange-Aimée she understood. What a delightful feeling of accomplishment when you're on the same wavelength or the same pathway as the person you know well enough to share your mysteries. Not that I have mysteries inside me but they're something like mysteries that I cannot always explain. I believe that love helps to make someone believe what you say. I certainly would not try that on my father, but perhaps someday I'll do it with my mother. Who knows?

Ange-Aimée and I used to go to classes with enthusiasm and pride in our hearts of being able to absorb music and everything that surrounded music such as the instruments, the lyrics of songs, the melodies, the strains of different bars of music, the full notes, the half notes, the sharp, the modulations of tones and even the loud banging sounds of the snare drum. Moreover, the sweet, vibrant and melodious sounds of a violin to me was sheer delight to my inner self and especially to my gut where the physical reality of feelings resides for me. I still did not know which instrument I preferred, the violin or the piano. I never did. And the brass, the loud, the riveting and sassy sounds of the brass instruments always made me shimmer inside just like when I'm listening to Ravel's "Bolero" or Gershwin's **Porgy and Bess**. Of course, "Bolero" is not just brass but an entire harmony of sounds rising above all in crescendos until the heartbeats slow down to almost a halt after having pounded in your chest so fast and so wildly tumultuous. And so I keep asking myself what is there that music can and cannot do. I know that it can do so many things. It can soothe, it can stir up emotions, it can rev up your power to feel and it can simply be there for you to enjoy. As for Gershwin, well he knocks the socks off of you as they say. His many talents inspire you to dream on and to be creative with the talents that you have. And to think that he died of a brain tumor when he was still at the height of his musical career. Cruel fate, cruel death. Tragic, in my book. I can just imagine what music he would have composed later on in his life. I'm sure that he and Ravel are making wild music together in the other world. His **Porgy and Bess** that he named folk opera, is truly outstanding in lyrics, music and the rendition of sassy, brassy, soul-defying sounds that pierce your armor of know-it-all-don't-need-to-know-more. There's true grit under the spell of Gershwin's melodies and Catfish Row becomes the cauldron of broken dreams and unblemished hopes for a future that will overcome hardships and desperation. Gershwin's **Porgy and Bess** has melodic richness and rhythmic punch much like Ravel's "Bolero, I think. I remember one evening I tried to listen carefully and attentively to **Porgy and Bess** while "Bolero" was playing in the background. I deliberately put on "Bolero" just to get a comparison and contrast with the folk opera. I thought that it made a marvelously rich complement to Gershwin's musical composition. I was not distracted from the opera at all, but soaked in both compositions in tandem and with great gusto. "Bolero" kept egging me on and pounding my thirst for crescendos while the folk opera brought me to heights of nerve-wrenching thrills. The two complemented one another quite well, at least that was my thoughts on it. I may be wrong but music does complement whatever is going on in your listening or simply hearing. I wonder if anyone has ever thought of doing what I did on stage. I wonder.

Ange-Aimée and I truly relished our days at the Berklee School of Music in the heart of Boston. It was a well-known and well-respected school with a curriculum and a faculty that truly knew music and knew it in their bones and in their gut. Just like I wanted it and liked it. It suited my longings and my tastes. I did not go there to learn an instrument but to learn music and how to learn it and interpret it the way musicians know and love it. Of course, Ange-Aimée knew how to play the piano and the violin so she had already the very notion of music in her hands and in her heart. She tried to teach me the piano but I was not the clay that she wanted and needed as a potter. She could not fashion me into a musician. However, she had the patience to teach me how to love music and develop an appreciation of the art of music. She used to tell me that music was an art and that any art must be learned with the soul for to really gain knowledge of the art of music one must have the passion for it. Just like writing, I may add. Without passion, writing goes flat and meaningless. It evaporates into thin air just like broken dreams and soap bubbles. Some play at writing just as some play at learning and practicing music but that's all, they're players, game players simply for entertainment, mostly self-entertainment. Ange-Aimée tried ever so hard to insist that learning and appreciating music is very hard work. You must practice and practice and practice not only with an instrument but with all of the skills at your disposition be it voice, composition, film, stage performance, listening, or even simply closing your eyes to fully experience the sounds of music enter into your soul. You must be ravished by music and you must treat it like a mistress who enchants and seduces you, she said. She was right, of course, since she echoed very well the instructions and convictions of the teachers. The teachers loved her and encouraged her to expand her horizons.

I had chosen Berklee but I did not want another bachelor's degree. I already had one in the liberal arts. Besides, I had very little money and I was living very simply and could certainly not afford the high cost of full tuition. I audited one or two courses and with others, I sneaked in without the professor saying much of anything. At least he did not throw me out of class. I had made it my craft of bypassing formal registration without taking anything away from the school, I thought. Ange-Aimée was just starting out a freshman and she was talented especially in music. Both of us often spent the better part of an evening into early morning when the day breaks discussing the Music Curriculum at Berklee as well as their liberal arts curriculum. She told me that she would prefer to stick particularly to the core of music courses since it was hinged on music and that she tolerated the liberal arts only because it seemed important to her education. However, the philosophy of Berklee towards the liberal arts had convinced her that it was not only important but vital to her full development as an artist. I told her that Berklee was right on target as far as an education was concerned. Ange-Aimée was ten years younger than me and she could be easily swayed by my claims although she could never be fooled. She had a bright mind and she was a resourceful person always asking questions that sometimes baffled me. I was fascinated by her ability to grasp things that so many others do not quite get immediately. She was smart. She was my sounding board and my life when it came to music. Then came Katerina Woyzovniek into my life.

7. EPTA

Katerina Woyzovniek was a stunning blond with deep dark blue eyes and lips that could enthrall anyone who favored the shape and color of sultry lips. She was a knock-out. She started hanging around me without my first noticing it until one day Ange-Aimée asked me "Who is that girl?" I told her that I had not noticed her before and did not really care who she was or where she came from, until....Until I started really noticing her and looking at her more intently. She was dazzling, like a movie star or a first-class model. At first, she stayed aloof and kept her distance, and she did not speak to me. She just stood there, motionless and attractive in her imperious stance. I told myself, she must be from some royalty somewhere for she did not look American, I mean like the run-of-the-mill American girl. She was always dressed very well and displayed a charm that models do. It looked to me that she came from money, I mean, her family must have a lot of money and she was wallowing in riches. That's how I measured her. I refused to pay too much attention to her until...Until, one day she stepped forward and started to speak to me. She spoke in a low, sultry voice and with an accent that sounded to me as being Eastern European. She did not say much except to ask me what my name was and I told her François Basil Spirounias.

"Oh, you're Greek," she said.

"No, I'm half Greek. My father is Greek. My mother is French-Acadian."

"What a marvelous coalition, Greek and French."

"Yes, I think so."

"Are you from the states?"

"I live here but I'm originally from Eastern Europe. My parents still live there but they travel a lot."

"Are you Hungarian or some other Eastern European nationality?"

"Well, I'm a mixture of ethnic sources, part Russian on my mother's side, part Hungarian on my father's side and part gypsy on my grandmother's side."

"On your grandmother's side?"

"Yes, on my paternal grandmother's side of the family. Her mother was the daughter of a gypsy king.

"That's interesting."

"Yes. As for my maternal grandmother, she is a cousin four-times removed of the Empress Alexandra Feodorovna, so she told me. And, you know that Alexandra was Queen Victoria's granddaughter. So, I'm very proud of that side of the family. You see, I have royal blood."

"Sure, a very small if not tiny drop perhaps."

"Don't make fun of my royal heritage."

"I'm not. It's just that I don't see the importance of it all."

"Well, it's important to me."

"What about the other side?"

"Well, that's my father's heritage and that is tinged with gypsy blood."

"Don't you like gypsy blood?"

"Yes and no. I don't really know."

"You don't know?"

"Stop harping on it, François."

"I'm not harping on it, I simply want to know why you don't like it as much your mother's side."

"I have preferences, that's all."

"What don't you like about the gypsy part?"

"If I tell you I don't want you to repeat it to no one. Do you understand?"

"Yes, of course."

"Well, my grandmother brought me to Saintes-Maries-de-la Mer in southern France when they were having their big festival celebrating Sara-la-Kâli, the black saint. They were all so boisterous and low class revelers that I was turned off the minute I set eyes on them. Gypsies are noisy people, loud-mouths and frivolous people and they're robbers and cheats on top of it all. I just do not like that side of my family, that's all. I always thought they were sleazy and worthless clans of people. Now don't question me about it anymore."

"Who told you they were robbers and cheats? Aren't you making up stories about gypsies and stereotyping them like so many people do? You're a racist, Katerina."

"Don't call me that. Don't you call me that. You have no right to call me a racist."

"But...."

She cut me short.

"François let's not get into an argument about something that's not so very important and really does not concern you. What if I started saying things about your Greek side of the family that you did not like?"

"There are some things about my father that I don't like and I'm not at all afraid to open up the subject. I'm not prejudiced on his account."

"Neither am I. So, let's be done with this matter, François. Let's talk about something more pleasant, shall we not?"

I realized that I would not be able to delve into her little peeves and dislikes and most probably her discrimination of some people with which she did not want to associate. She left in a hurry and as quickly as she entered my life, as quickly she disappeared. I did not see her for days, even months. Until the beginning of the following spring when all was in bloom and the air was filled with gentle perfume and mild weather in New England. I had not seen Ange-Aimée either. My life had become void of women closeness. We did not even get together to discuss music. She was busy with her courses and I felt despondent not seeing her or having her close to me. I missed her music and her constant awareness of music and joy that filled her soul. I would have clung to any small vestige of closeness whatever the source at that point. Not that Ange-Aimée had abandoned me, but she was caught up with her music and her classmates who cautioned her about me and Katerina. Yes, it seems that almost everyone knew about Katerina and her ways with people, her wiles and her proud attempt at being who she was not, they said. Ange-Aimée did not care about such things and she did not mind at all that I see or frequent Katerina. All that mattered to her was her music. One thing for sure, she would not let me get in the way of her music. I knew that.

So, one April afternoon, who do I meet but Katerina wearing a lovely lemon yellow chiffon dress and carrying a matching parasol walking across the yard behind maple grove. She rushed over to me and started telling me that the reason she was carrying a parasol was that the sun was very bright and that it might blemish her complexion, a lovely and delicate alabaster complexion that she wanted to keep that way. I did not ask her why I had not seen her for such a long time for that would have been cause for alarm, perhaps, and most certainly cause for negative reactions to my questioning her about the situation. Katerina did not like being questioned about her behavior or about her tendency to obviate things she did not like. I was a bit despondent and slightly lonesome that day, so I welcomed her presence and especially her perfume that wafted all around me like an alluring scent seducing the butterflies in a butterfly bush. I felt as if I was in the presence of the most of feminine allures and wiles. She knew that I wanted her with me and that she had neglected me for some time and she didn't seem to care one bit. Obviously she needed someone to remind her that she was alluring and desirable. I was the one. Why didn't I simply walk away? I thought of it but I could not restrain myself from doing so. I stood there as if frozen and numb. Where was my brain then? I asked myself. Certainly not thinking but rather drooling over feminine wiles and allures. I felt stupid and at the same time relieved that I had Katerina with me and she was paying some attention to me and my need to be lifted out of despondency. I also knew that she knew that I was despondent there and then. I must have shown it in my face and in my way of walking as if my movements were aimless. We sat down and started to talk. Just small talk at first but then things got somewhat exciting. She asked me to go to New York with her to enjoy the sights and sounds of the great city. I told her I could not afford to do that because I was now on the edge of poverty. I was scrimping on everything, food, clothes, transportation and even necessities like toothpaste and soap.

"Where do you live?" she asked me.

I was ashamed to tell her that I was living in a slum area of Boston and had contemplated welfare.

"You can't do that."

"But I have very little choice knowing that things will get worse."

"Yes, you do. Stick with me."

"I'm not going to crash in on your lifestyle and become a beggar. I'd rather be a tramp for that matter."

"Don't be self-deprecating with me, François. I know you better."

"I can't help it, Katerina."

"Yes, you can. All you have to do is to rely on me."

"And what am I expected to give in return?"

"Just yourself, just yourself."

"But I don't want to owe you nothing. I'm independent that way."

"You will not owe me anything. I already own you."

"What do you mean by that?"

"I mean that I have you in my net just like a flighty butterfly and I mean to enjoy my butterfly."

"I'm not a butterfly that can be caught easily. You're toying with me and you're trying to exploit my penniless situation. I'll have you know that I'm without money but I'm not poor enough to be exploited."

"Poor child. I'm not exploiting you, I'm simply helping you to come out of your dire situation. No money, no circus, my friend."

"No money, no play with the circus mistress."

"Now, come on, François, I'm not that bad, aren't I?"

"No, but you're the coy temptress of the Nile.

"You mean like Cleopatra?"

"Choose your temptress."

"I'll have you know that I'm not a temptress but if I were I would certainly not put my claws into you."

"Why not?"

"Because, just because."

I didn't want to pursue the subject and I certainly did not want to prolong the conversation that was turning a bit ridiculous. However, I did need shelter and a friend to be with so I was willing to give it a try fully knowing that I was left with very few choices in my life at the very moment. I just could not go back home to Maine with my mother and father. My father would have jumped on me and laughed his head off. He would tell me bluntly that I was a failure and that I was wasting my life with more school, music, and just tramping around the big city. What was my liberal arts education doing for me now? How well was it serving me or was it?

"Come on," he would say, "be practical and get a real job. Earn some honest money."

I know all that he would tell me. Nothing had changed with him. Nothing ever will. My mother would be more conciliatory and try to understand my predicament, but her hands were tied when it came to money and helping me find a job. I know that she would prefer for me to be more self-reliant and more productive in a society that treats people like me with mistrust and doubts. Had I hit the bottom of the barrel? So, I decided to take Katerina's offer and go to New York with her. After all, she was footing the bill, she told me. I wasn't proud. I wasn't ashamed to accept help from a lovely woman who apparently was loaded with money. My penchant for the *petits luxes* acquiesced easily enough through gratuities did not in any way affect my masculine pride. I had become a sugar-mommy's man, I suppose. I didn't mind. I was going to the big city. I had Ange-Aimée completely out of my mind. It did not mean that I was leaving music behind. No way, I told myself. This was a hiatus, that's all. Broadway, here I come.

We stayed at the Waldorf-Astoria, the luxury hotel where the wealthy stay. I would have never dreamt that someday I would stay at the Waldorf-Astoria. Never in my wildest dreams. Man, talk about luxury. Everything glitters and there's always someone ready to wait on you hovering behind silently ever knowing what to do and how to do it. I was overwhelmed with wonderment at such gratuitous service. After a while I started to feel as if I were out of my element, a poor beggar in the den of luxury. A half-Greek playing the part of a god, that's what I felt like.

I met Katerina's parents and began to see why she was what she was, a spoiled and coddled child of the plentiful class. Her father seemed like a kind and gentle man ever soothing the frustrated whims of his daughter. He was proud but not haughty, stern but not belligerent, and most of all he indulged his wife and his daughter. He seemed to have nothing else to do. His East European polish shined through his deliberate want to appear somewhat Americanized or at least fashioned in some way with American ways and demeanor. I realized that he did not want to lose his true identity as a citizen of the old world in order to adapt to the new. It would have been stupid and a lack of self-assertion, but he played the game well and his daughter seemed content that he did.

As for his wife, Katerina's mother, she was something else. Strikingly beautiful with deep blue eyes, velvety blond hair without a single strand of hair out of place in an elaborate hairdo that must have taken hours to fashion, and she knew all too well that she had been graced by the gods with beauty, intelligence and self-confidence. I could not keep my eyes off her. I could recognize the Russian strain in her demeanor, bold, haughty and unreserved in her way of asserting herself. She was class in my book but, at the same time, I believe she was shallow and pretentious. She noticed my endless glances at her and she seemed to appreciate my focused attention on her all the while seemingly flirting with the maître'D. She occasionally looked at me askance but she did not in any way rivet her eyes on me. I suppose that I did not matter in her world. I was but a fly on the wall of higher society and she could easily swat me down. I did not care. I had Katerina with me and she was my key that was to unlock the pleasures of a well-deserved and well-appreciated jaunt in New York City.

Katerina and I slept in a spacious room with all the accoutrements of luxury, gold faucets, polished marble tops, crystal lamps, soft and luxuriously heavy white towels in the bathroom and a bed that could sleep a half dozen people. The sheets were silk, the blankets of the finest merino wool. I wasn't accustomed to all that luxury and Katerina noticed my hesitancy to adapt to this kind of *grand luxe.* I began to feel like Odysseus on Calypso's island lured and tempted by the constant wiles and *gâteries du jour* by a nymph-like woman who sought to subdue and overpower her prey. I felt ravished by the moment and the luxury of the softness of the bed and Katerina's soft, delicious skin. I ran my fingers over every part of her body tasting all the while the fragrant and lush odor of it like a fox licking his fur and enjoying the delight of softness. I kissed and licked tenderly certain spots that I had caressed and now wanting more, I pressed my lips on her breasts and gingerly sucked the nipples that made her moan and swoon gutturally. I explored with my tongue and touch of my fingers every inch of that beautiful, soft, delicately pink and ivory flesh. It sent me into a kind of sexual delirium that can provoke savory yet acutely bewildering sensations to all of the senses. Katerina helped me along guiding my fingers to the most sensitive parts of her responsive body. She was certainly more mature than me in the pleasures of sex and the female body. Although younger than me in age, she was more mature in sexual responses. She recognized my inability to discover pleasurable experiences of the flesh while being taunted by my lack of experiential knowledge of the female openness to sexual pleasures. I was deliriously infatuated with her body, her breasts, her pelvic area, her slim waist and the way she gyrated when I touched her. It seemed that all of my senses became attuned to hers and we both formed a unison of fleshly desires being satisfied at any given moment. I could not prevent myself from moaning and groaning so vicarious were my responses to her pleasures acquired and avariciously received. There was no controlling my hunger and my pain of wanting more every moment I sought for more and desperately caught myself wanting more and more but could not satisfy my hunger that devoured me. Where was all of this leading to? I asked myself without wanting to interfere with the pleasures of the moment. Suddenly, I felt tense, surprised and bewildered by the intense thrust of pleasure and craving were building up in my loins. I could not seem to be able to control them so intense were they. All I could do is give it to them and let the flow of pleasurable intensity gush out of my hard and throbbing penis. Suddenly and without my wanting to, there was a burst of wet, gooey white fluid spurting out much like an explosion that cannot be stopped. My entire body at that very moment writhed in intense sexual delight as I was lying there close to Katerina's flushed body. She let out a loud cry and jumped up as if hit by some kind of offensive spray or something.

"Oh, my God, Oh my God," she shouted.

"What?"

"You dirty, filthy pig. You've infected my clean body with your awful sperm and look at me, I'm all covered with it. Auggh! I can't stand this. Get off me! I can't stand you either. Get the hell out!"

"I didn't mean to do it. It just came out, Katerina."

"Don't Katerina me, you filthy pig of a man. You're not a man, you're a child, a boy playing at sex. No real man would have done this. Not like this at all."

"It's not my fault if you excited me to a point of no return. I just could not help it. Don't you know how it is with a man who is brought practically to a point of sexual delirium and his involuntary ejaculation simply happens. It happens, Katerina. It's not being filthy at all. It's all part of making love even though such things happen without wanting to. I, I…."

"Oh, stop it. You're but a child, a worthless runt of a child in heat who cannot control his body."

"Don't call me that. Don't you ever call me that."

She started to whimper as she got out of bed and all I could hear in my mixed up mind was the echo of my father's words about not being a man. I just stood there ashamed and haunted by my inability to react in a manly manner to this sexual debacle. I stood there full of slime not being even able to cleanse myself of it and its shame. What a mess! All I could hear was the flow of water in the shower. Katerina was cleansing her violated body as she would say if she could at that moment. I knew what she was thinking. I knew her thoughts and her way of spitting out her bile. All I wanted to do at that moment was to jump in the shower myself and feel the hot water wash away my soiled body. I had not even enjoyed intercourse. All I had was the premature ejaculation of an aroused body wanting to fulfill the cravings of the flesh yet unsatisfied.

When Katerina stepped out of the shower wrapped in a large towel and sponging her wet hair with another one, she looked at me with a kind of disdain that goes right through you like a dagger ready for the kill. Her eyes were like brazen coals staring at me with contempt.

"Get out of here," she screamed so loud that I was afraid she would wake up the entire floor.

"I can't get out like that. Where would I go?"

"I don't care. Get out of my sight!"

"But Katerina, have pity on me. Don't I count for something in your life?"

"No, goddamn it, no!"

"No?"

"No. An absolute no. Go to hell for all I care, damn you. You're not a man, you're a spurting French frog."

"But, Katerina…"

"Don't call me Katerina. I'm no longer Katerina to you. I'll have you know I'm a lady with some royal blood in my veins. You are not worthy of me anymore. You're a vile animal of some kind. Not a man."

"But…."

"Go, François. Get the hell out of my life."

I did not know how to react to her anger and her harsh words.

However, she did allow me to get a shower and sleep the rest of the night on the divan in the other room. Early the next morning not wanting to offend her any more than I had already, I dressed very discretely and slipped out of the room not wanting to waken her and arouse once more her unwanted and unmerited anger. I went to the vast lobby and sat half hidden in a large stuffed chair where I dozed off now and then.

Around six-thirty when things started to come alive again in the *hôtel de luxe*, the touch of a hand on my right shoulder roused me. I looked up and there stood Katerina's father. He was impeccably dressed and had a faint smile on his face. He told me that Katerina had gone to see him and told him about last night while not revealing all of the details. All he knew was that she no longer wanted to see me again nor be with me in New York. He then handed me an envelope and told me that there was cash in it for me to stay a while longer and to get myself a modest hotel and perhaps enjoy a Broadway play before my departure. There was enough money to take a bus back to Boston, he said. His look was felicitous and warm and I felt as if I had been refreshed with a clean and tender smile. He then wished me good luck and told me that he had no bitter feelings towards me and that he simply wanted to smooth things over between me and his daughter and that I was not to try and contact her by any means. I reassured him that what had been between Katerina and me had been obliterated for good and that although I had had fond feelings for her I could never bring myself to even hold her hand nor even engage her in a conversation. He told me that he understood and that he and his wife had spoiled Katerina and that he, more than his wife, had learned to live with it. I shook his hand and I remained there in the lobby while he turned around and left. I couldn't imagine a nicer man than Monsieur Woyzovniek. He will ever be in my memory as a man of strength and integrity who had a beautiful but daring daughter filled with weakness and pretense.

I got myself a room at the Empire Hotel where students usually went to spend the night at a modest price. I found the hotel to be clean and the staff polite. I had very few articles with me and one change of clothes. They must have thought at the hotel that I was traveling very light or that I was somewhat poor in belongings. The truth was that I was both. I didn't care since I knew that I would be able to explore New York and its cultural dimensions as well as its entertainment venues on Broadway thanks to a gracious man who understood youth and its tender weaknesses.

I first explored the Broadway plays for that season of 1966. There was **The Appletree** that did not tempt me, **I do, I do** and **Sweet Charity** as well as **Mame**. I was drawn to the musical **Mame**. It was about an eccentric bohemian self-proclaimed *grande dame* in a selective society mad about itself and at a time between the Great Depression and the Second World War. Mame Dennis' famous motto, I read, was "Life is a banquet and most poor sons of bitches are starving to death." Wow! that really impressed me. That must be some wild musical, I told myself. It starred Angela Lansbury and Beatrice Arthur. That was enough to lure me to the scene of fun and musical romp, I thought. That's the play I was going to see. I couldn't. I could not get a ticket since it was sold out. Everybody, it seems, was talking about the musical **Mame** but not everyone could get tickets to go see it. So, I looked for another musical that might interest me and I found one at the Broadhurst Theater called **Cabaret**. It sounded very good and the man at the desk at the Empire Hotel told me that was the upcoming show stopper. I took his word for it and went to find this theater and its offering of **Cabaret**. I found out that it was about a brassy if not brazen singer named Sally Bowes played by Jill Haworth who sings in a bizarre Berlin cabaret in Nazi Germany and that the emcee played by Joel Grey was weirdly fantastic. That was enough to get me to buy a matinee ticket right then and there. I went to a matinee because I wanted to save money on the deal possibly enough to get me to the opera. That way I would be able to enjoy two venues of music during my short stay in New York. I must say that I truly enjoyed **Cabaret** and I have fond memories of the musical. It had a lot of *entrain* as we say in French, a lot of oomph and ah's. The setting was, as someone put it, a place of decadent celebration and I agreed with and enjoyed this proclamation of lost souls in the darkness of night in a seedy nightclub, and I especially liked the songs oftentimes belted out by the singers such as the "Willkommen" song at the beginning of the show. Such lecherous and devilish tones of welcome it was. Then there was "Don't Tell Mama" by the flirtatious Sally followed by the "Two Ladies" song as sung by the Emcee and two female companions commenting on the living conditions of Sally and her special friend. Later on in the second act, Sally belts out her anthem of sorts, "Life is a cabaret old chum" and rouses the audience to agree with her, at least, I did. I easily detected through the musical references oftentimes daringly provocative in Nazi society, a society that wavered between death and survival especially with the holocaust in the back of everyone's mind and heart sitting there in the audience. I was left with a feeling of impending doom and soul destruction at a time in history that demonstrated the bared weaknesses of man and his occasional triumph through a woman willing to mock the decadence and inhumanity of a Hitler and many like him who preceded him and followed later him. Will the decadence and destruction ever stop? I kept asking myself. To think that some people do not even believe that the holocaust ever took place. I also kept thinking of the Acadian expulsion of 1755 as related to me by my mother whose ancestors went through the hell of deportation and what she called in French "*l'effritement des siens par une armée britannique dite civilisée.*"[the crumbling away of your beloved ones by a British army said to be civilized]. Yes, it was truly the awful crumbling away of a group of people through the avaricious actions of the so-called civilized aggressors who sought to ravish the much desired Acadian land. I went back to the hotel with much thinking whirling in my mind and in my heart. I had practically forgotten Katerina and her antics of pleasure and inflicting pain on a poor and practically innocent young man who only wanted some sexual pleasure in his young life and got nothing but pain. Oh, well....

8. OKTW

Opera. Opera. That was all that I kept thinking about while in my room experiencing the loneliness of being alone in a strange place and at the same time anticipating some pleasure from music. Had I forgotten about my catalyst that drew me away from the pangs of self-torment and the difficult indictment of a father who could not understand my wanting to give myself to music instead of common labor. I did not need a job and I did not need a lot of money in my life. I managed and I scraped through an existence that was satisfying to me. Of course, it was not the lifestyle nor the dreams of many of my friends who had gone through college and anticipated the American dream to be fulfilled in their lifetime. I did not. What was the American dream anyway? Buying your own home, cashing in on the stock market, or getting a brand new car that cost a lot of money and maybe put you into debt for long period of time? And then there would be competition among the different ladders of society wanting and demanding more and more goods and rewards for work done in a competitive work place. How much is enough? I wondered. Was I being too platonically idealistic about my life in our American society? I didn't want to upset the apple cart but I did want to shy away from the American dream if it was going to tie me down to a dream filled with illusions and disappointments. I was told that I wasn't American enough and that I should get my act together if I was going to be part of the American dream. But,

I don't want the American dream or any part of it, I told those who said such things to me. They all thought I was crazy and that I was not living in the reality of things. Grow up, they said and that echoed my father's command. I was growing up and I wanted to grow up my way. That simply exacerbated the issue for them. I was swimming against the current of reality and sanity, they said. I didn't care for I wanted to get on the merry-go-round of life as I saw it not the way it was being foisted on me by society. Look what happened in Nazi Germany and how it eventually crumbled away into oblivion and into the sad pages of history for there are happy and sad pages of history, so many sad ones, if not tragic ones, and life is not always a cabaret.

Well, enough of my philosophizing and let's get back to opera. That's a much more pleasant subject in my book. It's because I kept seeing my life as a journey towards some worthwhile goal and I had not fully grasped it yet. Where was I going and when would I reach it was the big question in my life in November of 1968. As far as opera at the Met, well, I had to give up my dream of attending any opera there for the Metropolitan Opera House had been closed in the spring of 1966 after a lavish farewell performance and was to be demolished the following year. However, to my great surprise and delight I was told that a new Met had been built at Lincoln Center and that the new building opened in September of 1968 two months before my arrival in New York City and that the world premiere of Samuel Barber's "Anthony and Cleopatra" had been held. Although I was so very close to the Lincoln Center site since the Empire Hotel was not too removed from there, I had not noticed the new Met. I was so dazzled by New York and its tall buildings with its long avenues that I was totally ignorant of the happenings in and around the great city. What were my choices now? I checked my pockets for the money left after my two days in the city and discovered that I had barely enough money to pay my hotel bill and my bus fare to Boston not counting my meals for another day. I knew I could skimp on food and even skip a meal or two and that would probably afford me sufficient funds for an opera ticket. However, how much were opera tickets and would I be able to get a ticket, possibly a matinee? Besides what was playing at the Met? I asked myself. I wasn't going to miss my chance to see an opera at the Met. After all, I was in New York and what were my chances of coming back here in the near future. I had nothing to lose and only an opera to gain.

I started talking to the only person I got to know in New York, the desk clerk at the hotel whose name was Alexander Crutipustu and went with the name of Courtiss that was changed by his grandfather to better adapt to the American flow of things, he said. He lived with his parents in lower Manhattan and was educated in Connecticut at a private school. He was delaying college for he did not know where to go and what to study. He thought of the fine arts or some discipline that would satisfy his hunger for art and music. He wasn't sure. That's when I started having a discussion with him about the liberal arts and the possibility of expanding his horizons without crimping his soul and his desire to open up to his full potential whatever that would be. He was in no hurry, he told me. He did not want an education simply to get a job and probably hate it for the rest of his life. His parents did not worry about his delaying college studies but they did insist that he go out into the world, travel and try to discover what made him truly enjoy life without any strings attached or promises made to them. His parents were well off, he told me, and they could afford to provide him with sufficient funds to go on his journey of discovery without starving or being homeless. I envied him. However, he did want to work for a while and earn his own money. So, he got this job at the hotel and he got to meet many people who, in some fashion, enriched his life. He did not ask for much, simply the face to face encounters and the conversations that ensued. He had been to the opera with his uncle, an unmarried retired restaurateur who had made a considerable sum of money from the ground up building a clientele that was composed of some of the elite of New York and Hollywood. He got to know many a performer in the arts and some of them became his friends. He especially was fond of the opera star whom he had met after a performance at the old Met. Her name, Rosa Ponselle. The uncle's name was Konstantine Kapalodous, He had come to the states with his parents on a ship from Greece. Yes, he was Greek and proud of it. The desk clerk's mother was Konstantine's sister. Alexander told me that the big buzz in the city was the debut of a new artist named Pavarotti. He was heralded as a perfect fit for the role of Alfredo in **La Bohème**, and his voice supposedly was golden and could reach the high tenor notes without great difficulty. But wait until the opera critics get a hold of him, then we'll know if he is the success that people say he's going to be, said Alexander. The critics play a big role in the making or breaking of opera singers, he said.

"But why do critics play such an important role? They're just reporters of some kind aren't they?"

"Yes and no, François. It's because they influence so many people especially important people in the field and particularly because they have become the masters of marketing want to or not. People follow their opinions and they have faith in their evaluation of the singers and their performances as well as the delivery of music in general both by the singer and the orchestra including the conductor in whose hands the baton directs the movements of music and the voice rendition of those who sing. So you see the critics are important factors in the delivery of opera."

"But, Alexander, either an opera is good and even great or it is not. It doesn't depend on some critic sitting in the balcony listening and watching an opera and taking mental notes in order to write his critical evaluation."

"I see that you do not fully understand the art and business of the evaluation of the performing arts particularly opera, my friend. Most admired critics are well versed in the matter of their craft, be it drama on stage, a musical, a comedy or an opera. They have studied the designs, contents and the art of mastering a performance and they are thus able to render their evaluation or judgment as they see it with the perspective of an able connoisseur."

"I respect that and I am able to accept their evaluations and criticism but are they not, at times, wrong in their judgment?"

"Could be but they seldom are. And, that's why the patrons trust their word."

"I see."

"You see but you do not see. Like Oedipus you think you see but you are blinded by your own limited experiences and shortcomings. Pluck out your eyes of un-sight and see."

"Pluck out my eyes?"

"Yes, gouge them out of their sockets and see with your inner eye if you have one."

"What do you mean by that? I don't understand."

"No, of course not. You only understand with your limited perceptions and not through your full understanding of how things truly operate."

"You're being hard on me, Alexander. You don't know if I understand things or not. How can you?"

"Because I have gotten to know you even in a very short time and your perceptions of things especially in the performing arts need honing and polishing."

"How do I do that?"

"By experience and by education."

"I know I don't have much experience in the performing arts but I do have sufficient education to ponder things and evaluate them, enough to know what I like and what I do not like."

"That's just it. Your evaluation of the performing arts is based on your personal likes and dislikes and not entirely on sound educated judgment."

"Now see here Alexander, I may not be the most educated man on the performing arts and their excellence or lack of, but I'm not stupid nor am I entirely ignorant of these matters."

"I did not say you were, François and I am not condemning you, not in the least bit. I'm simply saying that you have a lot to learn about the world of music, the world of performers and the craft of putting together theatrical productions on stage. And, of course, the art and craft of being a truly knowledgeable and able critic."

"I know, I know. Please don't crush me with your own knowledge of the performing arts. I know very little and I realize you know much more than I do. Please forgive me my stupid ignorance in the art of performance and its criticism by experts. All I know is critics can be hard and terribly non-compassionate when it comes to the theater and opera."

"François, François it's not a matter of compassion but of objective quality and the evaluation or criticism of a particular play or opera based on the rendition of excellence by a given performer."

"I see, I see. I guess I have a lot to learn about the whole thing. How come you know so much about it?"

"Well, you see my father is an opera critic and he has discussed so very often with me not only his craft but his views on things in the theater but he has tried so very hard to make me see the nuances of quality versus the lack of it in a performer or a performance. He told me that it has to be one's passion in order to really probe the quality of any given thing such as opera and that takes courage and perspicacity. So that's where I got it and I'm still getting it from him. Furthermore, my father rubbed shoulders with critics such as Clive Barnes the dance and theater critic for the New York Times, Howard Taubman and Martin Bernheimer until he moved to Los Angeles last year. My father was known for his sound judgment and tact. He loved everybody even those who disagreed with him about opera. He once apologized to a performer for having passed judgment much too quickly on his performance. I'm not at liberty to name the performer nor the opera.

"So, your father is a well-known personality in and around New York."

"Yes, you might say that. I truly respect him and admire him for his years at the New York Times."

"You and your father are close then."

"Yes, very close."

"You're a lucky man and a very fortunate son, Alexander."

"I know."

That evening, I was getting hungry enough to eat whatever came my way and was cheap enough to allow me to still have money in my pocket. I looked around the neighborhood and discovered a small eating place called "Popeye and Olive" where they served sandwiches and soups. I looked at the menu posted outside on the large window and told myself I could afford a sandwich and a cup of soup. I went inside and was greeted warmly by a man and a portly woman with large brown eyes and a delightful smile. I sat down at a small table and asked if they were Popeye and Olive just to keep things happy although I did not want to make fun of them. I said it as a joke. They replied that the eatery was really named after them and that their names were Popeye and Olive after the comic strips. The man had been called Popeye most of his life by his buddies and the woman had adopted the girlfriend's name of Olive even though her real name was Ruth Anne and was called Baby Ruth by her mother and father. It all sounded so comically compatible with fun and games to me. It made me laugh and I needed a good laugh. I also needed some food. I ate a chicken salad sandwich with a cup of vegetable soup, the best soup I had ever had, even better than my mother's soups. Of course, I would never tell her that. I went back to the hotel and slept soundly that night.

In the morning, I was met with a beautiful November rising sun since I got up early enough to see the sun rise in the east through the tall buildings as if I was squinting at the crevices of mortar and stone rising heavenward in the cold air. My stomach was growling and I rushed to wash and shave and put on some clothes. I would grab a cup of coffee and possibly a donut if I could afford one. I was feeling the pressure of meager finances and that disturbed me to no end. As I stepped out of the elevator I met Alexander who was talking to an elderly gentleman in the lobby. He spotted me and waived his right hand beckoning me to him and the elderly man with him. I did not want to intrude in their conversation so I waived back to say that I was going out. He continued to beckon me and even walked in my direction to wish me good morning and to introduce the man to me.

"François I want you to meet my uncle, Konstantine Kapalodous. He's well-known in Manhattan and around for fine food and fine taste in clothing as well as opera."

I drew close to them and extended my hand in warm greeting.

"I'm glad to meet you young man. My nephew was telling me

about your first visit to our city and your nascent love for the opera. You do not know too much about this art of the angels as I call it?"

"No, sir."

"Well, may I teach you what I know about it then?"

"I don't think my uncle and yourself have enough time to learn everything he knows about opera."

"Come, come, Alexander. I can at least teach him the essentials of opera."

"Even that could be lengthy, uncle."

"Don't embarrass me Alexander by telling this young man that I'm full of wind."

"That's not what I meant, uncle. It's just that you know so much that you would have a hard time limiting yourself to the essentials."

"Let me be the judge of that, my nephew."

"Oh, yes, Mister Kapalodous. I really want to learn about opera especially from a master connoisseur like you."

"You flatter me, Basil. That's your name isn't it?"

"It's my middle name. My full name is François Basil Spirounias."

"So you are Greek?"

"Half Greek, sir. My mother is Acadian French. We're from northern Maine."

"And your father?"

"Pure Greek. His family came from Greece."

"It doesn't matter if you're half Greek or not. In my book you're Greek."

"Thank you. That's a delight to my ears and my heart."

"Were you brought up Greek? Didn't your father teach you everything he knew about his culture?"

"No. My father does not respect nor does he nurture his ethnic identity. He's become totally Americanized."

"That's too bad. But, you my son, you're not like your father. Do you love being at least half Greek?"

"Of course. I only wish my father had instructed me in his parents' ways, the old Mediterranean ways of living. However, my mother and

I have strong feelings for what is Greek. We especially love Zorba that great *bon vivant*."

"Yes, Zorba the Greek. But he's not the only one to exemplify the Greek culture."

"I know. There's the famous author Nikos Kazantzakis."

"Oh, you've read his works, have you?"

"Not all of them but several while I was in college."

"He's a great writer indeed. One that writers could emulate and learn from his style and ideas."

Alexander jumped in the conversation by saying,

"Listen you two, I can't wait here with you all day. I have things to do."

"It's alright, my nephew, Basil and I will continue our conversation elsewhere."

"Have a great day and I wish both of you enjoyment and good conversation," and Alexander left.

"Listen, Basil, are you planning on having lunch somewhere in the vicinity?"

"I haven't even had breakfast yet."

"Good, then we can have brunch at a nice Greek restaurant not too far from here."

"I don't know if Alexander told you about my financial ennui."

"You financial ennui?"

"Yes, I'm a poor soul who has very little money. I'm ashamed to admit it but I felt I had to tell you."

"Oh, don't worry about money. I have plenty of it and I want to share it with you, if you don't mind."

"Mind? Of course not."

"Then let's go eat somewhere."

Mister Kapalodous hailed a cab and off we went through the streets of New York to a destination I knew not where. We stopped in the middle of a small street off the main thoroughfare and we got out of the cab. I looked around me and there were several small restaurants that gave clients the choice of cuisine. My companion took me to a small restaurant next to a tiny Greek bakery and I could smell the rising dough and the flaky pasties. We went inside the restaurant and Mister Kapalodous was immediately greeted by this tall man with black curled hair as lustrous as the night. He sat us at a table and offered us something to drink. I took a small glass of Ouzo while my companion ordered some kind of drink fit for the gods, he told me.

"It's true nectar, Basil, veritable libation for the gods."

I drank my Ouzo while he sipped very carefully his drink.

"Now, let's talk about opera. What do you want to know?"

"Right now, I would like to go to one if that's all possible. I've never been to an opera at the Met."

"Well, let me tell you about the new Met at Lincoln Center. It's brand new. It opened its doors just last September. You should see the magnificent Chagall ceiling paintings. They're exquisite and the right fit for our Met the *grande dame* of opera in New York. The old Met was world famous and well known by the opera aficionados. It opened with a production of **Faust** in 1883. It was located at 1411 Broadway occupying the entire block between West 39th Street and West 40th Street. It was in the Garment District of Midtown Manhattan. It was nicknamed "The Yellow Brick Brewery" for its industrial looking exterior. Unfortunately it was gutted by fire in 1892 but was rebuilt and the interior was extensively redesigned. The golden auditorium with its sunburst chandelier and curved proscenium dates from this time."

The waiter came to our table and asked us if we were ready to order,

"In a little while," answered my elderly companion.

"Now where were we? Yes, did you know that the names of six famous composers were inscribed on the proscenium? Well, very few patrons know these names. They are Gluck, Mozart, Beethoven, Wagner, Gounod and Verdi."

"Mister Kapalodous, you know all these things, why you're like a walking encyclopedia of the Met."

"I know enough about my *grande dame* to fill a book. Now, let me see. Oh, yes, the curtains. The Met's first signature gold damask stage curtains were installed in 1906, completing the look that the old Metropolitan Opera House maintained until its closing."

"I remember seeing it in a magazine once. It was simply splendid and luxurious."

"Yes, I must admit that the old Met was sheer delight as a building and as an entertainment center of the *beau monde*. They had seats in the golden horseshoe for which they paid dearly, I'm sure."

"How about the poor people like me?"

"They had seats for anyone who chose to come and pay the price. They even had standing room places at the back of the opera house. Many a student stood there enthralled at watching an opera. I did it myself."

"You did?"

"Why yes. I wasn't always a person of means. It took years to do that. But, I always loved opera and did not deprive myself of it even it meant standing there watching intently **La Bohème, Carmen** or Gounod's **Faust**. Of course, I saw more than French operas, I saw **The Marriage of Figaro, Tosca** and many more."

"You were extremely fortunate to be living in New York then."

"Yes, as I am now. You can say that opera enriched my life. Yes, it did. I lived on the lyrics of opera, the music, its lavish sets and costumes, and, of course, the performances by the artists themselves. What marvelous voices enchanted the old Met. But, I must not linger too long on the old for I need to tell you about the new, the Metropolitan a t Lincoln Center."

At that point the waiter returned expecting our order for it was past one o'clock already. Mister Kapalodous excused himself and ordered a dish for me and for himself although I did not recognize the Greek names he ordered. After he had finally finished his drink that he had very slowly nursed, he looked at me in the eye and started to explain what he had ordered for us. There was on the menu, he explained, the fish of the day *Oreta* with lemon Greek potatoes with a beet salad, then there was moussaka with *pastichio* and *Spanakopita*, lamb shank with orzo and several other dishes. For us, he told me with a succulent glint in his eyes, we are to have the splendid *Avgolemono*, the Greek lemon chicken soup, followed by *Kolokitho Keftedes,* zucchini fritters fried to perfection, he insisted, then *Aginares Me Koukia*, artichokes and fava beans, followed by Pork Kebabs with cucumber-mint yogurt sauce with dessert to follow.

After ordering our meal, an elderly gentleman came over to our table and said to my companion, "*Pos Eisai*?" and Mister Kapalodous replied "*Yme kalA, efkharistO*." Then the gentleman turned to me and said the same thing in Greek to which I answered politely, "I'm fine, thank you." After a brief conversation between what seemed to be two friends, the gentleman returned to his table. Then Mister Kapalodous explained to me who the gentleman was. He was a retired tenor from the old Met and had sung there for twenty years. "He has a very fine and polished voice but he never had a lead role in an opera. He sung in the chorus with many other tenors of his vocal capacity and loved it. After all, the chorus is very important in an opera that requires one and it takes much training and constant practice."

"Did you ever sing in an opera, Mister Kapalodous?"

"No. I did not have the voice or the talent for it, Basil."

"But you are talented in some manner, I'm sure."

"My talents lie in good food and good service to my clientele when I was in the business of owning a restaurant. I used to own this restaurant but I had to sell it to the present owner, Spiro Bastonides, a fine man and a very good cook."

"How long were you in the restaurant business?"

"Thirty-nine years after I had worked for others in the trade. I loved every minute of it. I made many friends some of whom were patrons of the opera and even performers at the Met. My entire life was imbued with opera, Basil, my entire life."

"That's quite an artistic adventure."

"Yes, an adventure that gave me much pleasure and filled my heart and soul with memorable music. Music is the balm of my soul and soothes whatever ennui there may be in one's life."

"What is your favorite opera, Mister Kapalodous?"

"Oh, I have many but my very favorite is Puccini's **La Bohème** that I'm going to see tomorrow. Besides, it's the debut of a new and much talked about Italian tenor, Luciano Pavarotti."

"You are so very fortunate. I hear that it's virtually impossible to get tickets. Besides, I could never afford to buy one."

"Not only virtually impossible but really impossible for it's a sell-out. People are crying over the fact that tickets were not even available to some patrons who were caught unawares. Luckily, I'm a patron of longstanding and I was able to get two tickets for the matinee. Good seats too. You see, Pavarotti's debut is a matinee. But, I don't mind, I'm free anytime."

"Oh, how I wish I could attend such a performance. Poor people like me are so very often left out of gala performances. Besides, I'm due to leave tomorrow since I cannot afford to stay any longer at the hotel."

"Oh, it's not a gala but it's certainly a very big thing for the opera crowd as well as the Met. And, don't worry about your hotel bill, I've already taken care of it."

"I can't let you do that."

"It's already done, Basil."

"Thank you ever so much. I'm tongue-tied when I think about your generosity with me, a stranger. But, believe me I'm no beggar. I'm just not fortunate enough to have money right now and I don't want to ask my parents for some. I'm sure you understand."

"You're not a stranger to me, you are a guest and Greeks like me must welcome their guests lest they be the gods visiting them, remember?"

"Yes, I do. I certainly do. But why extend my stay in New York?"

"Listen, my boy, I have two tickets but can only use one since my invited friend, Ouros, cannot make it. He's sick in bed with a fever, so why not come with me?"

"I thank you ever so much but I'm not prepared for it. I don't have the proper clothes."

"We'll get you some. You can borrow Alexander's grey suit."

"Really?"

"Of course, why not? Things will work out well. You cannot

miss a performance like this one just on account of clothes. No, impossible."

"I feel so privileged to have met you and obtained not only your favor but your overwhelming generosity. I cannot thank you enough, kind sir. I'm practically in shame of having to rely so much on your financial generosity and especially you friendship."

"All if ask of you is that you enjoy yourself with this particular performance of a tremendous opera. Enjoy!"

"I'm going to say something that I never said to my father, '*SagapO*.'"

"I love you too, Basil. In the short time I've known you, I feel as though you are my son."

"If not your son at least your godchild. You have become like a godfather to me and you how important godfathers are in our culture."

So it was that I got to wear Alexander's grey suit, his white tailored shirt with French cuffs and his onyx cufflinks and a deep wine-colored silk tie. I hurried to give a good shine to my scuffed black shoes and there I was ready to meet my newly found godfather, Mister Kapalodous. Alexander came to greet his uncle and then offered me his black cashmere overcoat since it was quite cool if not cold outside this November day. Off we went like two gentlemen of the afternoon walking side by side, one a true amateur of opera and the other one but a half-Greek uninitiated opera lover. I didn't care who I was at that very moment or what people might say about me. I was François Basil Spirounias the young man on a journey of music that soothes the soul. We were off to the opera!

9. Ennea

The five tall oblong windows with the arches at the top allured me like lighted magnets for I could see the interior from the plaza and I knew I was at the Met at Lincoln Center. I could easily see the interior with its two murals created for the space by Marc Chagall, the exuberantly talented artist of folk themes that I had studied in college. My debut into opera at the Met that afternoon led me to feel like a male Cinderella stepping out of his coach onto the *parvis* where the fountain sprayed its glittering waters up towards the sky. Everything appeared like magic to me. Was I dreaming or was it real? I kept telling myself. I could not believe that such a serendipitous event was happening to me, little François Basil Spirounias from upper Maine. There was no doubt about it, it was serendipity that maneuvered things for me so that I might enjoy not only the delights of an opera but the fortunate debut of a tenor long anticipated, I am sure. This was better than sexual exploits with Katerina who had discarded me like a broken and undesired doll.

I kept walking with my head in the clouds although there were no clouds in the sky. I was living the metaphor while experiencing the glee of anticipation. I was at the Met! I couldn't help myself thinking of my father and wondering what he would say if he saw me now, but the thought soon vanished into nothingness, the nothingness of vain disappointment and the mist of despair. I had Mister Kapalodous at my side and for now that's all that mattered.

As we stepped into the lobby I saw people milling around, others rushing to find their seat, while still others engaged in conversation and not caring whether they were on time or not. These were the real patrons, the ones whose faces reflected the nonchalance of habitual opera goers. There was this one woman, an elderly well-corseted lady with a bosom well-defined in a cream-colored taffeta dress and whose makeup had surely been applied in many layers so as to give her the look of a mannequin. Her hair stood up like a tiered hornet's nest while, at her side, stood a younger man dressed all in black and sporting a brush mustache on pouting lips that looked like ripe crushed strawberries. The word elegant did not come to mind, rather it was another description that popped into it, the words being circus freaks, but I did not want to malign these two opera goers. After all, they were there to enjoy the moment and at the same time exploit their self-styled mock élégance du jour. I'm sure the lady once had style and elegance but they had faded away with the years and she had undoubtedly refused to accept the ravages of time and was living in a past that had once been favorable to her fresh stylish appearance. All that came to mind at that moment were the words, *Mais c'est une vieille prune démodée et artificielle,* as my mother would say, an outmoded and artificial old prune. My mother had a way with words especially in her Acadian dialect. "What did you say, Basil?" "Nothing, really nothing," as Mister Kapalodous tugged the sleeve of my right arm and told me to focus on the Chagall paintings. All I could think of was Katerina withering away in her old age resembling this faded *dame de l'opéra*. I shivered inside of me.

I stood there glancing upward at the many crystal chandeliers mesmerized by their starburst effect and their expansive glow. Mister Kapadolous kept directing my attention on the Chagall paintings as he explained to me their concepts. One was entitled, "The Triumph of Music" and the other "The Sources of Music." I thought they were magnificent embellishments for the eye to absorb. My companion remarked that such works of art are priceless and cannot be duplicated for they are one of a kind especially designed for the Met. Imagine my being right there contemplating two art treasures right at my fingertips. All of my senses reveled in them and I found my delight in the pleasure they were giving me for not only could I gaze at them but I could taste them, smell them and hear them and although I could not touch them with my fingers, I could touch them with the fingers of my soul. The chimes rang and it was time for the seating.

My companion and I followed the patrons and others into the fan-shaped auditorium decorated in gold and white. My head kept turning around to absorb all that I saw as meticulously as I could, but I was soon distracted by this huge pompous-looking man who growled and shifted awkwardly his feet before trying to sit down. He had a very hard time in doing so for his body resisted the exact space provided. "Harrr--oumph," he muttered out loud as he hailed one of the ushers. He demanded that they provide him with a seat that could accommodate his barrel torso. The usher looked embarrassed and took the man aside. They both left the auditorium and we did not see the huge man again. He was so huge that in measuring him with my eye, he must have weighed four hundred pounds or even more. My Lord! I wondered where they had placed him. Perhaps next to some very thin timorous patron or a student who did not complain about the poor corpulent man who kept growling all the time. Mister Kapalodous kept looking at me and smiled with his benevolent and amused smile. I simply put the huge man out of my mind and concentrated on the gold damask curtain awaiting the start of the opera. Suddenly the chandeliers in the auditorium were lifted up to the ceiling and the lights were dimmed. I was ready and eager to begin my journey into opera and Puccini's **La Bohème**.

I already knew the story behind the opera since I had done a project in one of my music courses based on Puccini's masterpiece. However, I was not familiar with either the score or the orchestration. Besides, the lyrics were in Italian and my mind juggled with them even though there was a certain familiarity that my French back ground and linguistic ability provided. I told myself to simply listen with my heart and my gut and shut off any desire to grasp every note and every word uttered by the singers. Soak it in, I told myself and let the strains of music fill your ears and your nascent receptivity to opera will do the rest. I created within me an ambience of silence that was conducive not only to the relaxation of every fiber in my body but especially to the harmony of soul and music in anticipation of the performance to which I was to witness in the hush of this vast auditorium as the curtain rose and the bohemian garret emerged.

I did not dare interrupt the train of thought that my companion was sure to have while his eyes and mind were fixed on the stage in front of us. I was sure too that the rapturous music was filtering into his heart and soul and that he would not have wanted any sudden interruption to the flow of music, lyrics and feelings that were being engaged as the conductor swayed the orchestra with his body movements while I watched him with amazement. I could only see the top of his torso and his arms and hands in sometimes smooth and other times vigorous motions that were meant to lead his instrumentalists. I did not want to concentrate too long on the conductor for I would miss the true performance on stage and that was the very core of the opera. All I knew was the performances of the singers that I saw and heard were much attuned to the music coming out of the orchestra pit. I also was somewhat nervous about Mister Pavarotti's debut since I had heard that he was an excellent tenor and that he would deliver a masterful vocal rendition of Puccini's arias. I sat there rigid in my body and taut inside awaiting this tenor's entrance onto the scene. I could not move for fear of distracting my opera companion or even letting on that I could hardly understand the lyrics being sung. However, I was able to follow the story and enjoy the music that Puccini had crafted so very well for his opera. I fell into a kind of a trance just sitting there motionless and letting the music carry me away while looking at the singers on stage performing their craft as performers and singers who had, no doubt, spent hours in rehearsals honing their talents and perfecting their delivery. I found myself in another world, a world of the down and out bohemians of Paris and particularly the much frequented section called Le Quartier Latin where the young artists and want-to-be artists find shelter and friends. This one is a world of poor young friends who struggle with everyday life and try to find comfort in each other and desperately want to make it in the world given them by fate and at times tragic destiny. Sitting there, I could sense their probing minds and haunted hearts for they were, if not at their wits ends, they appeared to be at the edge of mercy and want. I was hoping in my heart that they would not fall into desperation and hopelessness. I could feel that Puccini also felt it in his heart as a musician and composer. He rendered every cadence, every note, every beat with precise and tender emotion, I thought. So, I sat there next to my companion enjoying the unfolding of the opera in my head and in my heart as Puccini would have wanted me to, as part of an audience, capturing the full delight of his masterpiece.

The opera opens with an orchestral bang and I'm brought out of my stupor with my eyes on the stage. I read in my libretto that it's Christmas Eve and both Rodolfo and his friend, Marcelllo, are cold and hungry as they are looking for ways to get a little heat for the garret. Rodolfo decides to burn his manuscript but the flames are soon extinguished and there is no warmth in the small bare room. All that comes to mind is the word *dénudé* for my French serves me well. Enter Colline, the philosopher and Schaunard, the musician. I'm trying to concentrate on all three and the fast-paced music as if it's intertwined with the fast pace of a dialogue. Then, when Mimi comes onto the scene and the lovely music and singing of Rodolfo's "Che gelida manina" I can feel the growing strains of the romantic rhythms and we soon realize that it's love at first sight between the two. Pavarotti's rendition is clear and strong as well as tender. His voice has perfect pitch and draws me to him as a tenor who is well on his way to become an impassioned tenor. I can tell and I can feel it. I look at Mister Kapalodous and he looks back at me. We are sharing the moment without uttering a single word.

In Act II, we have the scene at the Café Momus where the friends gather for food and gaiety, after all it is Paris. It is there we encounter the sophisticated and richly dressed Musetta. Then we have her song known to so many as Musetta's waltz when she sings to her former lover, Marcello, whose eyes dare not leave those of his Musetta once his beloved. I sense that Colette Boky, the Musetta of the matinee is well qualified for her role. But I'm especially enthralled by the music and the voice of Mirella Freni as Mimi. Her voice is lusciously clear and resonates like a bell. I tell myself that the part suits her very well and she sings like a nightingale. That's what people say about a singer who sings so well that she imitates the lovely bird that sings so beautifully. Now I know why so many people are fully captivated by Puccini's music and style. I understand that Puccini's music in **La Bohème** is the music of the people for they go out of the theater humming and singing and will carry these melodies with them for days. I know I will. With the sounds of the children accompanying the military band we leave Act II and flow into Act III. Oh, there's been some misunderstandings and quarrels between Mimi and Rodolfo and we hear that from Mimi herself as she tells Marcello about it and the music seems to indicate that there is trouble in the small world of Mimi and Rodolfo. Mimi is dreadfully sick and Marcello says so with his "Mimi è tanto malata!"Mimi on her part says with sad and fateful feelings, "È finita!" It's over with. However, I'm glad when the two lovers are reunited and reconcile for Mimi tells Rodolfo that "We have the sun" with the strains of music to reveal her joy and reconciliation all the while Musetta and Marcello quarrel and proves to me that Puccini likes to work in tension and strain into his drama and music.

I'm just sitting there and glancing at the joy and contentment in Mister Kapalodous' face. He's really enjoying the opera and Luciano Pavarotti's debut. In the final act, we find Rodolfo and Marcello back in the garret as they sing the tender duet "O Mimi, will you not return?" I sense that there's a deep longing in both singers as they interpret Puccini's music especially on the part of Rodolfo. Puccini has the great talent of making us feel what the singers project their feelings and their talent as singers on stage. We have become part of the drama and music, we the partakers of the opera. There's a little bit of humor thrown in when Schaumard and Colline have a mock duel with andirons. I think it's to lighten the mood before Mimi arrives on the arms of Musetta terribly and desperately ill. Musetta has just found Mimi in the streets haggard and sick and asks her friend to bring her to Rodolfo. It's Musetta who tells of Mimi's words, "Voglio morir con lui," I want to die with him, a tender if not a pathetic scene. I mean with genuine pathos as in the Greek *pathētikos* that my teacher of Greek taught me. Mimi on her part repeats the melody and words heard before and it really touches one's heart, "'Che gelida manina'" There's that refrain again, that leitmotif, Mimi's song. I just seem to melt inside of myself when I I hear the softness of voices melded in with the softness of the muff offered to Mimi to warm her hands. We want Mimi, I want Mimi, to live but she dies as Musetta begs for her friend's life in prayer. Rodolfo can only cry out with tears Mimi's name, and I sit there transfixed and filled with regret for the two lovers. Two young lovers. Such a romantic opera, I tell myself and I can sense that it is what people at this opera feel as they exit out of the new and so lovely New York Opera. I just sit there motionless and Mister Kapalodous looks at me without saying one word until he rises and tells me that we are now going to the Russian Tea Room for a late afternoon meal anticipating the reviews. I look at him and I can tell that he doesn't want to talk right now for he is definitely regurgitating the opera in his soul of soul. He has been witness to and a participant to a very fine meal, and Greeks enjoy the superb quality of a fine meal. I now feel very much Greek.

The reviews, the reviews, everyone in New York is looking forward to them especially the producers, the performers and the audience, of course. Some do not care much for reviews for they seem to not represent entirely the views of the many, but they are an important factor in entertainment, I am told. Reviews are the gauges for success or lack of since they measure the possibility of success and money, the much sought receipts of the day, the week, the month and, if fortunate enough for the year and even years. And, I am told it's important for the international success of any opera.

Mister Kapalodous did not mention the reviews while we headed for the Russian Tea Room but he alerted me to the fine food served there. It happened to be one of his favorites. He told me that it was opened in 1927 by former members of the Russian Imperial Ballet as a gathering place for Russian expatriates. That it also became famous for those in the entertainment industry. It had been closed and reopened several times, said my companion who had followed the various stages of change in the Tea Room. As we entered through the front door I was mesmerized by the red ambience and the richly decorated room known as the Russian Tea Room for many years. We were seated and the waiter placed the menu in front of us. Mister Kapalodous told the waiter that we did not need a menu and that he had already decided what we were going to have. That is, he decided and I simply followed his lead and recommendation. He knew the place and its offerings and had a keen knowledge of what goes well after the opera, he told me. The Tea Room offered a Pre/Post Theater menu. He ordered for the first course, the Traditional Tea Room Red Borscht, an item that had to be indulged in, said my companion. Then for the main course, he ordered the *Kulebiaka*. It's salmon with slow cooked onions, mushrooms and vegetables wrapped in pastry, a traditional main course, he told me. "We'll order dessert later," he told the waiter. I did not say a word for I did not want to interrupt the finesse and knowledge of food of my dear companion. While waiting for our food, Mister Kapalodous began to talk about the opera **La Bohème** that we had just attended at that fabulous new opera house.

"I trust you fully enjoyed the performances of the singers," he said to me.

"Oh, yes, I certainly did. I enjoyed every part of the opera and I loved the singers and, of course, I was glad to be in attendance at Mister Pavarotti's debut. He's a very good tenor, don't you think so?"

"Yes, I certainly think so. Of course, it's his first time here in New York and it will take time for New Yorkers as well as for others to appreciate his voice. I do hope the papers give him good reviews."

"Do they, in general, give good reviews?"

"No, not in general. Quite often they give very bad reviews of certain entertainers like opera stars and legitimate theater performers. Only very seldom do they give rave reviews. It has to be a perfect performance by a perfectly well-trained singer who has mastered his or her voice to the music composed by a master musician and composer."

"Would you give this afternoon's performance a rave review?"

"No, not a rave review but a very good one. I like Puccini and his music. I don't know if you noticed but Puccini uses something called "thematic reminiscence" a favorite compositional technique of many Italian operatic composers wherein a melody or a melodic fragment recurs at appropriate moments in the opera. **Tosca** has its Scarpia chords, for example and **Madame Butterfly** has its suicide motif. As for **La Bohème** well, the themes attached to the bohemians and to Mimi are quite evident."

"Yes, I heard that and recognized the composer's efforts to remind us of the drama and its constant tensions."

"I see that you are quite observant and very discerning when it comes to opera. Keep it up."

"I enjoy it and I plan to continue enjoying this type of entertainment."

"Opera is not only entertainment but it is a gift of the gods to us humans who try to decipher the melodies of the stars."

"Well said, master."

"Puccini's manipulation of orchestral colors and techniques is unparalleled in Italian opera, I would say. Consider the change of mood from Mimi's aria in Act I to the duet "O soave fanciulla" where the orchestra completely envelopes the loving couple in a wash of romanticism."

"That's fascinating, sir, and I thank you for sharing this with me. I am not well educated in opera, as you must know. I must tell you that I felt the opera to be quite romantic and a bit overly so at times, but I refrained from judging it on the basis of romanticism and its heart filled inclination of sentimental values."

"Well, each and every one of us must take the time to learn. It has taken me several years to perfect my understanding of opera and its music and I'm still learning with every performance and every opportunity I have to listen to the great music of the stars be they the composers or the singers who interpret the music and its libretto. As for the sense of romanticism in Puccini's operas one must say that it does exists and is, at times, a bit too much. However, I do believe

Puccini masters his skills as a composer and is very much aware of the romantic s trains of his music. One knows also, that operas tend to be in the vein of exaggeration and overly amplified sentiments and expressions of anger, violence and illusions. That's the drama of the opera."

'I will ever be in debt to you for offering me the opportunity of attending this opera this afternoon. **La Bohème** is a supreme example of great music and of great art."

"You know, **La Bohème** is such a popular opera and such a vibrant tool for operatic singers that it has become one that is much talked about and remains one that is over-analyzed in the standard repertory. There isn't much more to be said about Puccini's masterpiece that has not been said before. Great works can tolerate analysis and commentaries, and, of course, reviews. Masterpieces in music, in the fine arts and in literature uplift us as human beings and we owe a great debt to the creative geniuses of the world."

"Amen."

We finished our salmon and sent our compliments to the chef. After a while, Mister Kapalodous ordered dessert and I was assuredly looking forward to it especially since it was free fare for me who was poor and regretfully so. It was the Chocolate Pyramid for me, a mousse with raspberry filling. Mister Kapalodous ordered for himself the Tiramisu. We both enjoyed the dessert anticipating the reviews that would come out in the morning with the sun. I could hardly wait.

While waiting for the reviews, for Mister told me that we could not go to bed before the reviews came out, we went to a small bar off Broadway and had a few drinks as we talked and talked about music and so many other things that interested both myself and my companion. The bar stayed opened until daybreak and catered to those who loved to linger after a show or an opera just to not be cut off quickly and completely from a performance and it's "*la joie de s'amuser.*" We waited and we chatted until the sun's rays began to filter through the blinds in the bar. I was getting a bit drowsy and perhaps would have enjoyed my sleep but I did not want to do contrary to the real amateurs of opera who waited and waited for the reviews. Mister ordered another drink and I told him that I could not take another one because I would fall dead asleep on the counter. He smiled and shook his head as if to acquiesce my youthful limitations.

Finally the reviews arrived. A young lad pushed open the door to the bar and offered its patrons copies of the morning papers. Mister Kapalodous rushed to get copies of two papers, The New York Daily News, The New York Times. The cultural headlines of the Daily News read in bold print, "MET GAINED A VIBRANT NEW 'BOHÈME' HERO.

"Look at this, Basil. Watt raves about Pavarotti and his performance. It's a good sign. He goes on to say that 'It was a pleasant surprise to find Luciano Pavarotti, a tenor seemingly born to the role, making his Met debut in Saturday afternoon's **La Bohème.'** Isn't that just wonderful, Basil?"

"Yes it is."

"Then Watt goes on to say that 'Not only is he the owner of a bright, ringing tenor in perfect tune, he is also an exuberant performer who gave buoyancy to the proceedings that few Rodolfos are capable of.' Isn't that marvelous, Basil?"

"Yes sir."

"Then Watt, the Douglas Watt of the New York Daily News states that 'With luck, his personality should brighten many a gloomy Met corner.' Well what do you know? It's a splendid review, don't you think, Basil?"

"Of course."

"'It as a winning **Bohème** all around,' he says and I agree with him."

"I'm so glad that he enjoyed the opera and its performers and especially Mister Pavarotti. I like Mister Luciano Pavarotti. He's going to go far in the world of the opera, I'm sure of that."

"Now, let's see what Mister Peter G. Davis has to say about yesterday's matinee of **La Bohème**. He's usually more severe in his criticism than Douglas Watt. It's not a long review but it merits my reading it in its entirety, you don't mind, do you?"

"Of course not."

"Well here is what he writes, 'The Metropolitan has to make the star system work for its **La Bohème**---the production is so faceless that only first –class operatic personalities in the leading roles can stir up any excitement onstage at all.' Now that's rudely frank of him. He can be so damn abrasive at times. He continues, 'Two performers managed to cut through the over-all bored routine of yesterday afternoon's presentation. One of them was Mirella Freni, and her Mimi is as fresh and lovely to the eye and ear as ever. She was romanced on this occasion by Luciano Pavarotti, who made his debut with the company in the role of Rodolfo.' Well, Mister Davis has kind words for Mister Pavarotti."

"I can see that. Good for him."

"Now he continues. 'Mr. Pavarotti triumphed principally through the natural beauty of his voice---a bright, open instrument with a nice metallic ping up top that warms into an even, burnished luster in midrange. Any tenor who can toss off high C's with such abandon, successfully negotiate delicate diminuendo effects and attack Puccinian phrases so fervently is going to win over any **La Bohème** audience, and Mr. Pavarotti had them eating out of his hand.' My God, "eating out of his hand" that's high praise for a debut performer/ tenor. Then he goes on to say, 'As far as acting tenors go, Mr. Pavarotti is not the worst, but his generally stiff and unconvincing sage presence did leave something to be desired.' There you have it, Mr. Peter G. Davis's review of the opera. I must confess that I agree with his assessment of Mister Pavarotti's stiff posture and stage presence. He's going to have to learn how to act and present himself fluidly on stage, I'm afraid. That takes time and effort and I take it he's still young in his craft."

"I am so very glad that the reviews are favorable to Mister Pavarotti."

"And those two are the main ones, the ones that readers swallow as whole. Well, the matinee was well spent, don't you think, Basil?"

"Very much so Mr. Kapalodous. I enjoyed the opera, the singers,

Mister Pavarotti and, of course, the splendid meal at the Russian Tea Room. It was a perfect day in perfect company."

"It was my delight, Basil, my delight indeed to have such a companion to the opera and the post opera meal in such a fine restaurant."

"Well, now I must be off and get some sleep if I can. I'm so filled with the excitement of the opera, the meal and the reviews that I don't know if I can fall asleep or not. I feel all jittery inside and my composure is unsteady. Oh, I'm so terribly sorry that I have to leave all of this tomorrow, but I must go. I must find myself and my voyage to somewhere."

"Your pilgrimage."

"Yes, my pilgrimage into the world out there. But first, I must go and see my mother."

"Don't forget you father, the Greek presence in your life."

"Yes, my father, the Greek, the thorn in my side."

"Basil, don't say that. He's your father and your generator who gave you life."

"My mother gave me life; my father gave the tiny sperm that fertilized the egg."

"Much more than that, Basil, he gave you your national identity as a Greek. That's very important in my book, I'll have you know."

"I know, I know, but it's not always easy for me to acknowledge that. My father is a tough nut to crack."

"Nut tough nuts give very sweet meats to those who persevere with delicate kindness."

We parted in the very early hours of the morning following a most delightful operatic adventure in the great city of New York. I regretted leaving Mister Kapalodous but I had to move on. Would I ever see him again?

10. Deka

I slept some fourteen hours the day following my operatic adventure in New York City. I call it an adventure because it was an adventure for me, an adventure into the world of opera, reviews, good eating and much pleasure. I had forgotten all about Kristina and my misadventures with her and I was well on my way of discovering my journey into the future. I had very little clues as to my findings but I was willing to search and find whatever would come my way be it the decree of fate or my own determination to reach out and make my own fate once I discovered the path. Where would I go and how do I start, was the question that I asked myself. I knew that I had to think about it seriously so I decided to seek meditation in a monastery where prayer and meditation were constant values and practices. There was a little Greek Orthodox Church, Saint Theotakos in the Boston area where I sometimes went when assailed by doubts and loneliness. I had not gone to church for months and had stayed away from church and religion because I had not felt the need for it. There were many Catholic and Protestant churches around but I seemed to be attracted to the Greek Church if not by faith at least by ethnic identity. It was like returning to my roots. Although I had wanted to stay away from them and my father, I felt the need to do so now. I don't really know why, but the need was there haunting me and it would not let me go. I felt the attraction like a magnet drawing the metal of my being. I knew I had a soul but

I did not know how to manage it nor accept it as my guiding light. Was it my heart that was telling me to placate my soul or was it my entire being calling out for mercy and love. I knew that I had a soul because music had touched it so very deep and long. And, I realized its presence in the very depth of me when I attended the opera **La Bohème** for the performance had invigorated not only my heart, my mind, and my senses, but especially my soul. That's what the opera did for me. It gave buoyancy to my soul and made me connect not only with myself but with a transcendence that I had not known before nor appreciated. Opera elevated my soul to a height unbeknownst to me. Was that transcendence, God or was it the movements of the stars and planets? However, I felt that there had to be more than that and that someone or something had caused the stars and planets to exist and that someone had to be transcendence itself. Was it the "unmoved mover" or the "uncaused cause" that Aristotle talks about? I knew very little of God and my knowledge was limited for I had not taken any theology courses in college nor did I mean to explore that aspect of my existence, that is, my creation by an "unmoved mover." If God existed, he had to be an all-loving being because I had read somewhere that's what he was all about. Probably in Saint John's writings that my mother used to read aloud to me when I was very young. But, then I strayed from such readings and preferred comic books and tales of adventure like "Treasure Island". All I know is If God is love then he must be merciful to his creatures for that would be in his nature to dispense mercy to us the lowly ones who struggle here on earth, on this very planet, where redemption was performed ages ago through a savior born of a virgin and who preached love and mercy as part of the New Covenant and through the simplicity of his gospels. That I knew since my mother had tried to instill in me those truths, as she called them. She tried so very hard to do that but I wandered and I strayed. My father, of course, did not help the matter for he was an unbeliever and practiced no religion. He didn't even practice the fundamental knowledge of his own identity. My father was an angry man and I never knew why. Was he angry with God? With his own father? With his fellow Greeks? With himself? I never could understand him and long ago I stopped trying to. As for God's love and mercy, I knew nothing of them and I refused for a long time to even admit of these transcendental qualities of a Creator God. I accepted the existence of such a God and I was I faithful to him and his act of kindness in creating me for I believed that my being was the result of transcendental kindness and mercy that I did not merit nor, at times, accepted. Besides, it was a free gift. Free to take or free to leave. So, as you can see, I was living in constant turmoil deep within my soul and I had to try, come what may, to resolve this issue. That was the beginning of my journey and most probably the start of my pilgrimage, my search for spiritual life and the comfort of finding it wherever it would lead me. That's why I thought of a long meditative journey in a Greek monastery where I would attempt to meld both transcendence and ethnic identity and try to get resolution to my problem of faith, trust and cultural belonging. But, first, I knew that I had to go back home and have a long talk with my mother. I felt that I had not seen her nor talked to her for months and that she most probably worried about me, her son François Basil. "*Ma pauvre petite maman,*" I kept repeating to myself. Poor mom.

After several months of deliberations, I went home and found my mother busy at making jams and jellies with the fruits of her little garden. Here she was in her kitchen her hands blotched with blueberry stains mixed with raspberry splotches. Her old apron, the one she kept for such chores, was also stained beyond the initial cotton fabric that she had taken to make herself a large apron. It was as if she was wearing tie dyed cloth around her body. She was singing an old familiar song, the one that the Acadian people sang when they had a "*veillée*": "*Ah les fraises et les framboises, du bon vin j'en ai bu...*" I just stood there behind her back listening to her and watching her pour the blueberry jam into a pot. When I joined in singing her song, she turned around totally surprised at seeing me there in her kitchen. "*François, qu'est-ce que tu fais ici*? What brings you here after such a long absence?" I looked at her and smiled and went over and gave her a big hug and kiss.

"I'm here to see you and to talk to you. I haven't been a good boy, you know for I've been bad in not touching base with you. Yes, it's been a very long time but I've been traveling and had a good time at discovering things and meeting people."

"Tell me all about it. Oh, it's so good having you here with me, with us, I should say. Your father will be so glad to see you."

"Where is he?"

"In the cellar. He keeps busy down there and hardly ever comes out except to go to bed at night. Curious behavior on his part, but I can't get him to change. You know your father, when he has something in his head there's nothing I can say or do to make him change what he has inside of him that haunts him night and day."

"He's haunted by something?"

"Yes, by his own illusions and disillusionment."

"Like what?"

"Like his fear of the sun and his preference for darkness. I've tried and tried to make him come up from his cellar, "*sa cave*" but he won't budge. *"C'est une tête-de-pioche, ton père.* He's hard-headed"

"Yes, I know he's stubborn but I never realized that he was so caught up his illusions."

"If I try to talk to him about it, he just shoves me off. I even have to bring his food downstairs to him. He won't come up, I tell you. He won't even talk to his friends who stopped coming by since he would not see them or even talk to them. Can you believe that?

"No."

"I want to go down the cellar and try to get him to come up and see you but I know he won't do it. It's stupid this affair of the cellar."

"Never mind, I'll go down there myself later, but first let's talk."

So it is that we talked for an hour and a half about things and especially about my venture into the big cities. The both of us sat on the back porch in the coolness of the day while enjoying the warmth and brightness of the sun. It was good being back home with mom and her bright smile of content. We talked about the neighbors that I knew so well, about Madame Molleur who passed away at ninety-eight, of Monsieur Latourelle who was now in a nursing home, of the young Mademoiselle Morin who had gotten a scholarship to go and study in the Canadian provinces out west somewhere. My mother did not know exactly where, but it did not matter. When it came time to tell my mother about my experiences at school and in New York, she sat there enthralled and hung onto my every word as if they were manna from the desert or honey from the bee.

I told my mother about Berklee and Ange-Aimée and how good a friend she had been to me. She asked me what I learned at Berklee and I told her that I was pursuing music for my own enrichment and pleasure. Then I slipped into the story of Katerina and her family and my stay in New York City. She asked me how I could afford all of that traveling and staying in hotels and the food and all that. You know how mothers are. I reassured her that I worked at odd jobs and that certain people had been very generous with me.

"But you can't live like that all the time. You can't depend on people for survival, François. That's sponging."

"No, 'ma. It's not sponging. It's accepting the good heartedness of people who offer you their kindness and empathy."

"But, why didn't you ask us for help?"

"Because."

"Because?"

"Yes, because I did not want to depend on you for my daily living."

"But, we're here to do just that, *mon fils.*"

"No, you're here because you are here and you need to take care of yourselves without having me bothering you with all of my cares and woes."

"What is a mother for anyways?"

"For love and mercy, mom."

I told her about my brief episode with Katerina without giving her all of the details. I told her that my brief encounter with her and her family was my opening to New York City. I mentioned the play **Cabaret** and how much I had enjoyed that musical. Then I told her about my encounter with Mister Kapalodous and his extensive generosity toward me. That he had taken me to the Metropolitan Opera, a new home for the operas, and that we had seen and heard the opera **La Bohème** with a new tenor called Luciano Pavarotti in his debut at the Met. She asked me how I found his voice and his performance for she was so interested in singers and their voices. She told me that she knew of the composer Puccini and his sweet music, sweet to the heart and soul, she said, and I concurred with her. I then told her of the Russian Tea Room and the exquisite food we had there.

"What did you have?"

"We had the salmon with onion and vegetables. It was delicious."

"And what did you have for dessert?"

"I had chocolate mousse with a raspberry filing and Mister Kapalodous had the tiramisu."

Oh, that's lovely that tiramisu. I only had it once in Quebec City."

The conversation ended on a happy note and I was content that I had shared my wandering experiences with her and she was content simply listening to me and learning about things she herself had never personally experienced.

"Now, François Basil, you must send that generous person, Mister Kapalodous, a long letter of appreciation and not just a thank you note. I wouldn't want him to think that you were not brought up well and responsive to someone's generosity. I brought you up to be a good boy and a thankful person."

"I know, 'ma."

I then told my mother that I had to see my father before I left and that I would not do it on the spot and that I had to wait until the following day to do that. I did not feel strong enough in my heart to be able to confront my father until I had rested and thought about it. My mother told me that it was alright and that I could see my father before he went to bed.

"Won't he come up from the cellar before then?"

"No. I have to bring his supper to him downstairs. I told you, he won't even come up for his meals. It's downright frustrating for me to live like that."

"What if I bring him his supper when it's ready?"

"That's a good idea. He's going to be so surprised. I'm sure he doesn't expect to see you. I can try to shout to him from upstairs if you want me to."

"No, let it be a surprise."

I couldn't imagine my father and mother living like that, one in the cellar, yes, *dans la cave* and one upstairs doing her laundry, her cooking and her *ménage.* One in the darkness of a cellar and one in the sunlight of the days spent in the routine of being busy and hiding her thoughts and her feelings the best she could. But, that's what my father and my mother always did wasn't it? They lived worlds apart. My father always sought the dark side of life it seemed. That was not at all Greek in my estimation. But, that was his character and his disposition, not Greek, not able to identify with his ethnic identity and not able to live with it. What made him do that, I wondered. But, I had been wondering about that all of my life. My father was my father and that was all. Nothing would ever change him. If only I could put sunshine in his life. If only I could ever bring him out of that cave that he himself had manufactured with his illusions and his deadly ways of coping with his faults as a human being. My father was dead inside. That was it wasn't it? *Mort comme un être figé et vide de vie qui attrape la mort par indifférence et devient enseveli comme une momie.* Dead as a doornail, dead and stiff and empty of life who catches death by his indifference and thus becomes wrapped up in the shroud of a mummy. That's what I thought of him. It wasn't nice but true. I could no longer hide the fact that I was estranged from my father and nothing would ever change that. God help him; God help me.

When suppertime came around I took my father's supper and slowly went down the stairs leading to the cellar. There was hardly any light there only the eerie glow of a single light bulb. I could see my father's shadow from across the wide open spaces that had been cleared by him. I softly walked over to him and gently place the tray of food next to him without saying a word. Not a single word. He turned around and I could see the surprise in his eyes. They were eyes without fire, without much response and dull like the bulb hanging overhead. My father never did have fire in the soul as far as I know, but he did have fire in his eyes much like Zorba. But, he had now lost even that. I felt pity for him.

"Hello, dad, it's me François Basil, your son."

"I no longer have a son. He's been gone too long. I have you but I don't really know you."

"But of course you know me. I'm your son. Half of me is Greek and I get that from you. Don't you know?"

"Half of you is Acadian and that's all. The rest of you is mongrel like a mongrel dog on the loose."

"Please don't ignore me and who I am."

"Who are you, François Basil?"

"I'm the son you never did seem to accept nor appreciate. I'm the son of the man who rejected him from birth, it seems."

"It's not true. I never rejected you."

"But why did you not ever acknowledge me as a son and as a human being?"

"Because you grew up to be unlike all of my expectations. You were never the man I wanted you to be."

"What did you expect of me? A superman, a man of lustful desires and lustful enthusiasm for sports and games? Did you expect me to measure up to your very own expectations of a son? Was that it?"

"At least a man who was strong and intelligent in the ways of a real Greek man."

"Who is that man? Who is the real Greek man? A person of valor, strength, courage, adventure, zealous endeavors and mighty deeds?"

"Yes, and much more."

"Like what exactly?"

"Like an Odysseus or a royal Priam. I must say however that Odysseus was at times a mandy-pandy."

"A mandy-pandy?"

"Yes, what I call a man who falls for the wiles of a Calypso or the sirens. He does not have the strength of courage to prevent himself from falling for such tricks."

"But Odysseus is a human being not a god. He is capable of human weaknesses like me, like you."

"But he's supposed to represent the qualities of a real man."

"What is exactly a real man, father?"

"A real man is a real is a real man and I need not define him for you. You know what I mean."

"No, I don't know what you mean. "Well if you don't know then I cannot define him for you, you who are supposed to be educated and intelligent."

"Education doesn't give you everything in life. One must earn education through experience and self-determination. School teaches one how and where to find it but you have to keep growing and searching."

"There you go again philosophizing."

"Call it what you want but I know what I believe in and I have learned to exploit it in order to keep growing in wisdom and strength of character. That's what the ancient Greeks sought in all of their searching for truth, *sapientiae* through *logos*.

"I know what *logos* means and you don't have to teach me about the power of independent thought. I know what it means."

"Then use it and don't feign ignorance."

"I'm an ignorant man."

"No you're not. You are a very intelligent man but you don't know how to use it properly."

"And you're going to show me how?"

"No, I can't."

"What do you mean you can't?"

"I can't because I don't know how to reach you."

"Reach me?"

"Yes, reach your heart and soul."

"Try."

"I've tried time and time again but I never succeeded .You are the carapace of a man."

"You mean I'm not real?"

"You are real but your reality exists in your mind and not in your heart and soul."

"So that's your assessment of me, your father."

"That's the best I can."

I had to stop since I did not know how to end this give and take that was leading us nowhere, like a ping pong ball being tapped across the net in an endless motion by two men who could not score.

"I'm leaving you to your supper now and I may see you before I leave."

"When are you leaving?"

"Soon, very soon."

"Oh……"

"Do you want me to stay longer?"

"No, not particularly."

"Then you want me to leave."

"No."

"But what exactly do you want?"

"I want you to stay with your mother. I'm afraid I'm no good any more to do any act of kindness with your mother."

"But you could try, at least."

"I have but it's not me anymore, it's not me."

"I don't understand."

"You see I have changed and I didn't want to change but I've changed. I'm a changed man not that I wanted it that way but I've changed….for the worse."

"Then change back to the man you were, not perfect but at least a man not an animal, a mouse living in the dark every day never seeking the sun."

"My eyes can't see the sun anymore. I can't face it anymore. The light blinds me."

"I'm afraid that it's more than sunlight that blinds you, father."

"I know, I know."

"Then do something about it."

"I can't."

With that short-ended conversation I rushed upstairs to be in the light of the day and forget that I had a father who rummaged through things in the darkness of a cellar. Where and how would all of that end? I wondered.

I left my parents' village, on my own, and told my mother that I had to get away and that I was contemplating on going to a monastery.

"Are you going to stay there and become a priest?"

"I'm going to stay there a while but not to become a priest."

"Please don't forget us, your father and me. Please, please stay in touch."

"I will, ma, I will." And I muttered to myself, "First I have to get in touch with myself. I must come to grips with what makes me be so nervous and edgy at times, so much so that I feel as if I'm going to fall apart and fritter away."

As I left mother slipped a small envelope in my side pocket. I told her that I did not need her money and to keep it for she would have need of it. She told me, "It's just pin money, François, just pin money that's all." Later on when I opened the envelope there was $250 in it mainly in twenty and ten dollar bills that she had folded quite evenly. I meant to send it back to her but I was in need of money and I thought that I would hurt her if I sent it back. I kept it.

11. Enteka

Two weeks later I found myself miserable and lonely in a small room in a cheap hotel in New Hampshire where I had lodged in order to come to grips with my *ennui*. That was certainly the old malady of the soul as we see it in world literature. I had written a thesis on the subject in my senior year in college. I had taken the prose writings of the French poet Lamartine and had analyzed the theme of *ennui* in his short novels such as his "Raphaël."In my thesis I found that I was able to glean enough material to be able to give the theme a good analysis of this sickness of the soul sometimes called melancholia. Even the Greeks mention in their writings that something like melancholia existed in some people especially in some creative and sensitive souls. Hippocrates and subsequent traditions associated melancholia with black bile, one of the four humours. Melancholia has been around for centuries and no one had a cure for it. It happened in the lives of saints and sinners, of the poor and the rich, but never, it seems, in the lives of common people, those who were too busy earning a living and not preoccupied with meaningless problems that seem to intrude in the lives of those who preoccupy themselves with ideas and dreams or the illusions of the soul. Disillusionment oftentimes linked to melancholy brings a wave of nausea to the soul and makes it vomit darkness and hopelessness. I certainly did not want to fall into that. I wanted to remain sane and free of nausea that causes one to feel tied to restlessness and obscure feelings. Albrecht Dürer's allegorical engraving entitled *Melencolia I* is well-known and is often interpreted as portraying melancholia as the state of waiting for inspiration to strike, and I can relate to that. I also read that the most extended treatment of melancholia comes from Robert Burton whose *Anatomy of Melancholy* treats the subject from both a literary and medical perspective. All I can say is that melancholia has been very well explored and written about.

I found in Lamartine's novels an *ennui* that stemmed from nostalgia and the lack of intimate relationships with others. The most intimate one is that of Lamartine and his mother whom he adored. She loved him to a point of extreme care and catered to his every whim. In other words, she spoiled him. He learned from her how to soften the blow of melancholy with religious practices and prayers often translated into poetry. It became the balm of soothing measures that reduced his anxiety and lack of vigor. I found his work, especially his three novels written towards the end of his life, to be filled with religious sentimentality and pathos that are often metamorphosed into a theatrical affectation. Much like other writers of his time, those who fall into the category of the Romantics, Lamartine wrote of and was afflicted with what was called the *mal du pays* and the *mal du siècle*. It's no more no less than romantic narcissism. However, I wrote my thesis knowing full well that Lamartine's novels were far from being masterpieces of literature but I found that important literary themes such as melancholy can be found in second rate works of literature. That was the case for me for choosing these novels. All I know is that after writing this thesis and having spent so much time doing research and writing about *ennui,* I was filled with a certain sense of melancholy myself and could not wait to get the work done and get completely away from such a malady that affected the soul. Even today as I reflect back on it, I do not want to fall into the vast and dark cavern of melancholy since I want to pursue light and adventure. So, I wanted to move on and not linger on my listlessness. What makes a person so listless and bored with life? I was bored because I did not have a Mister Kapalodous to be my companion and lead the way to the next adventure in my life. I certainly did not find it in my father in his eternal cellar.

That summer I met Jeffrey. Jeffrey was a round-faced, ever-smiling, energetic man with a shock of blond hair that was striking and blue eyes that glinted the light like a boy's marble. He was affable beyond compare and I liked him the moment I met him. As soon as I set eyes on him I knew we would become friends. I was drawn to him and I could not help myself from staring at him and looking into his eyes. He did not refrain from looking at me but asked me why I was staring at him for so long. I told him that I was drawn to beauty like a magnet and that I could not help myself. He blushed and told me that he did not think he was beautiful. Beauty belonged to women and to works of art, he told me. I replied that beauty belonged everywhere and to everyone, especially to people, men and women alike. Was it my fault if I found beauty in places and in people that I found likeable and filled with the esthetic qualities of a work of art? I know, I know, beauty is in the eye of the beholder, but beauty must first stimulate the beholder and seize him like one seizes a ripe plum or a golden pear ready to be bitten into. For me it's a sensual if not, at times, a sexual experience, beauty is. Oh, I could go on and on about beauty but I don't want to bore all of you to death.

Jeffrey and I realized that we had one great affinity and that was opera and music. Jeffrey was twelve years older than me and he had seen and heard many an opera. He's the one who told me about a friend of his, Wesley Boynton, and his Arundel Opera Theater in southern Maine. Although a small theater, it had fine acoustics and terrific performances by professionals who had not yet reached stardom or who were satisfied with simply being in opera on stage no matter where. He had seen the performances of **Carmen, Tosca** and **The Marriage of Figaro** and considered them of high quality.

"It's too bad that Wesley had to shut down his theater in the 1960's but he left a tremendous heritage of music, opera singers and good stage performances for a select public in a part of the world that would not have had the opportunity to enjoy opera had it not been for Wesley Boynton."

"You really think he was a superb musician and opera lover don't you?"

"Yes, I do. I don't know where he is right now but I do believe that he will find his niche somewhere and give people some opportunity to enjoy music and opera."

Jeffery and I lived together in my small apartment and we shared everything although we lived on a shoestring. He did not have a full-time job and neither did I but we managed. We often lunched on hamburgers and a coke. Sometimes when things got a little rough financially we ate beans in a can. We managed. I still had money left over from my mother's gift to me but I was saving some in case. Yes, in case because one never knows when one will need money in an emergency. Jeffrey was never demanding and seldom sad about our living condition. He did feel a bit under the weather when things got really difficult and we had to scrounge to find enough food to satisfy our hunger of the day, but we managed and we grew to take life as it came from day to day. We had fun and we enjoyed each other's company. We tried to give ourselves some measure of hope and cheer by planning an event in our lives that would bring joy and contentment like the time we agreed to save money to be able to go to Boston and go to an opera there put on by the Boston Opera Group under the leadership of Sarah Caldwell. Jeffrey told me all about her and her company and how she managed to put on opera productions. The Group even had a touring arm called the Opera New England.

Jeffrey got to know Sarah Caldwell and her brilliant mind as a masterful director and competent conductor when he volunteered for one of her productions, the opera **Marriage of Figaro** at the old Donnelly Theater. He told me that he was her runner boy of sorts and she entrusted him with all kinds of errands and she was pleased with his dutiful work. They kept in touch and she sent him programs and other correspondence from time to time. He also told me that she had invited him to any given performance and that she would have tickets for him. We decided that we would go down to Boston by bus and stay overnight at a cheap hotel that he knew and attend the performance of the Alban Berg's opera **Lulu**. Of course, I knew nothing of Alban Berg and his opera but I relied on Jeffrey to fill me in with the details. He was another Mister Kapalodous in my adventures with opera. I was so lucky to meet people like that for they filled my life with music and knowledge about opera.

We took the seven o'clock morning bus to Boston and while we were sitting there watching the early summer scenery go by, Jeffrey began to give me information about the opera we were about to see and its author. Alban Berg was an Austrian artist composer who was gained renown and praise for his first opera **Wozzeck**. He then started work on **Lulu**. However, Jeffrey told me that the opera was not completed due to the sudden death of its composer. Berg died of a poisonous sting and was not able to finish the opera as he had planned. For years, the opera was performed incomplete with the third act missing. Berg's widow tried desperately to have a friend named Arnold Schoenberg to complete the orchestration but after looking at the task he declined. There was even a silent film made of the opera **Lulu** but the original film is lost and only four stills remain. Jeffrey told me that the opera is not very often produced but once in a while you have a Sarah Caldwell who likes to produce operas not often presented to the public. She loved challenges and she put her heart and soul into them. I was so eager to meet her and see the opera. She would be one of my shining lights of my opera adventures, I told myself.

Jeffrey then proceeded to tell me about the story of Lulu as well as the opera itself since he had read as much as he could about them. Jeffrey was a well-informed man about what he loved, music and opera. He had a keen mind and a creative spirit. Too bad he did not get the opportunity to manifest the theatrical skills he possessed and that rich talent he had for music and performances. He would have made a great producer of musicals and operas, I thought. However, he was not interested in pursuing the job of producer, he told me. Sadly, I believe that he really wanted it but did not know how to enter the profession and therefore did not seek it out. Funny how some people have so much talent but do not know how to exploit it. They need a mentor, a guide of some kind. I knew my limitations and was satisfied with being a constant learner and never the maker or creative genius behind a production and certainly not opera. That was part and parcel of my journey in life, to learn and to be able to absorb what people in the know could give me be it history, literature, culture, music or opera. I was so glad that I had a liberal arts education on which I could build the rest of my learning experiences in life. As one of my professors had told me, the liberal arts are the windows or doors to one's solid education and I open them for you with my teaching and inspiration. I believed him and I always will.

Jeffrey took out his notes he had taken on **Lulu** for he had kept them and referred to them in time of need, he said. They were copious notes. Lulu's story is a complicated one, he added, for Alban Berg had quite an imagination and he had put it to work in his opera. There are all kinds of characters in it and several turns of events while the heroine, Lulu, is caught up in various love affairs and three weddings. It's a circus, a drama, an adventure and a strange cast of characters with performers taking more than on part under the directives of the composer. Jeffrey tried to explain to me the somewhat weird circumstances of the story and that there was a whole cast of characters: a painter, a doctor, an African Prince, a lesbian countess, an athlete, a schoolboy, a marquis, and even Jack the Ripper.

"Jack the Ripper?" I said totally surprised.

"Yes, Jack the Ripper who kills the heroine, Lulu."

"That's quite a cast of strange characters."

"It is but wait until you hear the story."

Jeffrey then proceeded to tell me the story referring now and then to his notes. In Act I Lulu is seen as a model for the Painter, no name given, who is painting her portrait. A certain Doctor Schön sits there. He's a newspaper editor. His son, Alwa, a musician, arrives on the scene and excuses himself for he has to go for a rehearsal. Both father and son depart. Lulu is left alone with the painter who makes strong and deliberate passes at her. She succumbs but in the meantime Lulu's husband arrives, breaks down the door and sees them together. Suddenly he dies of a heart attack. The painter leaves to fetch a doctor while Lulu remains with the corpse and reflects on the fact that she is now rich.

"Wow! That's quite a beginning for a story. Weird, Jeffrey."

"Wait there is more, much more."

Jeffrey then continued the story with the second scene in Act I. Lulu has married the Painter and is seen in their apartment. Dr. Schön is there with the Athlete and the Schoolboy and a heated discussion ensues. And the Painter interrupts the argument. Lulu leaves in a huff. Then Dr. Schön reveals his love affair with Lulu and various sordid details of her life. The painter is shocked that Lulu has hidden so much from him. Dr. Schön tells the husband that he should confront his wife with this matter. The Painter locks himself in the bathroom and horrible groans are heard. Alwa arrives to tell the doctor that revolution has broken out. Then the two of them break down the bathroom door only to find that the Painter has cut his throat. The in the next scene, Lulu is now a successful dancer and we see her in her dressing room with Alwa. The latter is contemplating writing an opera on Lulu's life but decides against it since, he says, the scenes are too gruesome. An alarm is heard and we are told that Lulu has fainted on the stage. In fact, she refuses to continue the performance because Dr. Schön and his fiancée are in the audience. Dr. Schön tries to convince Lulu to continue her performance but she tells him that she's running away with the Prince to Africa. Dr. Schön realizes that he cannot live without Lulu and decides to break off his engagement. Lulu than then leaves to continue the show.

"And that's the end of the first act."

"Weird, really a weird set of circumstances for an opera, Jeffrey."

"Wait until you hear about the second act."

Jeffrey sorted his notes and continued the story. In Act II we find Lulu in her home. She is now married to Dr. Schön who is filled with jealousy over her many admirers. One of them is the lesbian, Countess Geschwitz who visits her to invite her to a ball. Dr. Schön disapproves. Lulu and her husband leave for a stroll .Now comes the game of hide and seek. The Countess returns and hides. The Dr.

Schön also returns, alone, and hides in a different place. The two other admirers, Athlete and the Schoolboy, enter and begin to talk to Lulu when she returns. But when Alwa is announced they all hide.

"They all hide? What kind of a game is this?"

"It is a game, a game of chances and endless *virevoltes*. Let me continue the story."

Jeffrey then picked up where he had left off. Then Dr. Schön reveals himself and pushes Alwa from the room. He then starts an argument with Lulu ending with his offering Lulu a revolver and commands her to kill herself. When the Schoolboy jumps out from under the table Lulu is distracted and shoots Schön. The police arrive to arrest her. Then there is an interlude which consists of a silent film. In it we see Lulu's arrest, trial, conviction and imprisonment. Then she deliberately contracts cholera and is transferred to a hospital. The Countess visits her and they exchange clothing so that Lulu can escape.

Then we have Scene two with several characters in and out of Lulu's life. The scene ends with Alwa being seduced by Lulu and they go away to Paris.

In Act III Scene One we have Lulu in a luxurious apartment in Paris where there is a grand party going on. Everyone talks about money and their investments. There is blackmail on the part of the Marquis and the Athlete. They both want to embarrass Lulu and even turn her over to the police since she is still wanted for murder. She arranges her escape and flees. In Scene Two, Lulu is in London and Lulu is still on the run. She now works as a prostitute. The Countess arrives with a portrait of Lulu. When Lulu arrives with a client, Negro, he fights with Alwa and kills him. The Countess returns and contemplates suicide but she is interrupted by Lulu who arrives with another client. The Countess decides to return to Germany and become a lawyer fighting for women's rights but she is interrupted by Lulu's death screams offstage. The client is Jack the Ripper who emerges from a backroom and stabs the Countess and leaves. The Countess declares her eternal love for Lulu and dies.

"There you have it, François."

"What a weird story and an even weirder turning of events, so fast and so unreasonable. Berg made an opera out of that?"

"Yes, he did. Sarah Caldwell produced **Lulu** because she loves a challenge and is inclined to produce difficult and strange works. She's made that way."

"Well, I'm going with you to see this opera but I would never have gone by myself I'll have you know."

"Bear with me my friend."

We arrived in Boston, got off the bus and went straight to our hotel. We changed clothes and after a bite to eat, we went directly to the Schubert Theater. Sarah Caldwell had left tickets for us at the box office. We had good seats and I told myself that I was going to try and enjoy this opera no matter what. A portly woman to say the least came in and bowed. She was elegantly dressed and Jeffrey whispered to me that was Sarah Caldwell. Then the curtain went up.

I must say that I struggled to follow the opera, its story and its fast moving *déroulement*. However, I did enjoy the music though it was something I had not heard before. Jeffrey kept looking at me during the performance and I simply smiled my contentment at him not wanting to offend him with my inner discontent. Not that I hated the opera but I found it so strange, so irreconcilable with my sense of what an opera should be. Not after having seen and heard **La Bohème** in New York. Oh well, things are not always to one's liking and operas can be different in genres and style, I suppose.

I waited in the lobby for Jeffrey while he went to meet Sarah Caldwell for he told me that she had invited us for *un souper parisien* in a nearby restaurant after the performance. Jeffrey returned saying that we were to go ahead and that Madame Caldwell would follow us to the restaurant. He told me that Sarah Caldwell was known as the wonder woman of music and opera and that she was recognized internationally for her great talent. He asked me if I liked Sarah Caldwell. I told him that she was fat and energetic with the face of a bulldog. However, she was a very good conductor as far as I could see and certainly a good impresario. Jeffrey concurred with me but instructed me mot to tell her in her face that she looked like a bulldog. We laughed.

We had a nice fashionable *souper* and Sarah Caldwell was genuinely pleasant with the both of us. I could see why Jeffrey liked her and wanted to work with her. As we were having our coffee, Sarah Caldwell turned to me and asked,

"Did you like the opera **Lulu** young man?"

"Yes, it was nice."

"Nice means that you did not really enjoy it."

"Well I did enjoy it but to be frank I thought that it was weird."

"Weird, well weird is good for it stirs up the pot so-to-speak, don't you think?"

"I suppose so. Madame Caldwell what are some of your choices for your operas coming up?"

"Well, there's Arnold Schoenberg's **Moses and Arom**, Sergei Prokofiev's **War and Peace**, Hector Berlioz' **Les Troyens**, and **Benvenuto Cellini**, Luigi Nono's **Intolleranza**, Roger Sessions' **Montezuma**, and Peter Maxwell Davies's **Taverner** just to name a few."

"Wow! that's quite a list of challenges."

"I love challenges, my dear, I love to be challenged and come up with something different if not strange. Strange is only in the people's minds. Weird is but a qualifier for someone who is uninitiated."

"Like me."

"I suppose so."

"Did you ever think of sticking with the classics? You know what t I mean."

"Yes, I know what you mean and I have produced some of them. One of my first was **La Bohème**.

"I saw that one in New York recently."

"That was the one with Pavarotti's debut."

"Yes, and he was superb in it."

"That's what I heard. I would have loved to be there."

"I'm new to opera and I want to learn more about it. I know I have a lot to learn."

"Well, it's a good start. Too bad that Jeffrey brought you to see **Lulu** instead of a more standard fare but **Lulu** was a very good introduction to differences in opera and of course to Alban Berg."

"I'm glad that Jeffrey took me to Boston to meet you and to see one of your productions. I am told that you enjoy a great reputation as conductor and producer."

"It's not always easy for a woman to succeed in this business. There aren't too many of us. There are, of course, opera singers, the divas and those who are not established yet but some day there will be more and more women who will have climbed the ladder of operatic success as producers and stage managers, I'm sure."

"You have made it and you're definitely a pioneer."

"You can say that."

Jeffrey chimed in and said,

"Madame has great courage and a big talent to uncover talent and masterful compositions. Why haven't you written an opera of your own yet, Sarah?"

"Because I'm too busy producing them and conducting them as well as going after talent who can sing. Then there's the rehearsals and the many hours spent preparing for the stage. Not now. I'm satisfied with what I'm doing, Jeffrey."

We want to see more of your extraordinary talent, that's all."

"By the way, Jeffrey, when can you come back and work with me?"

"I'd love to but I wasn't invited to do so."

"You don't need an invitation, my dear. All you have to do is show up."

"Great, I'm here."

The following day, early morning, I took the bus back home alone. Jeffrey had decided to remain in Boston with Sarah Caldwell's troupe, and I was so happy for him. That's what he liked above all and that's what he would be doing, spending his time with the wonder woman of opera and filling his soul with wonderment.

I arrived home to my cheap hotel lonely and somewhat depressed. However, I did not want to fall into that pit of *ennui* again although I had avoided it at first but I knew what lay ahead of me if I let myself go and fall into melancholy, that sickness of the soul. I had to do something about it and I did. I decided to go to a monastery for a long and soul-filled retreat where I would be able to recapture the strength of my spiritual life and the vigor of my soul. What else could I really do? Stay like that and die. The death of a soul? NO!

12. Dwdeka

I was on my way to a small town in western Pennsylvania where I would find the Monastery of The Transfiguration run by Greek Orthodox monks who had been there for sixty years. They accepted people like me, searchers of the soul, they called them, and I responded to their call when I read about the monastery in a brochure that I found in the local supermarket. I did not have too much money left, just enough to take the bus to Pennsylvania and a bit left over to give my donation to the monastery as they requested. I knew that I would not see Jeffrey for a very long time and probably never, so I had to make a move to stay alive and remain vigorous. That's about the time I started thinking that my search would become my pilgrimage. It would take a leap of faith to do so and I was ready to thrust my soul towards the heavens and rely on God's mercy. What else did I have at my disposal?

It was a long trip and I slept the better part of the way since I was tired for a lack of sleep and a lack of good solid food. I was nervous, jittery and downright blue. I didn't know why I had the blues but I had them. I was probably on the edge of *ennui.* I hated that and I wanted to get away as far as I could from it. I had to be active in some way and my soul needed reinvigoration and I knew that. How would I get that was the only way I knew how and that was meditation and peaceful prayer. Not prayer with formulas but prayer associated with meditation and restful contemplation. The monks would show me how. At least I was hoping they would. They were in the business of contemplation themselves and they had been formed to lead others to contemplation. While thinking about monastic life and contemplation, I wondered what was troubling me. Was it my lack of self-identity, my lack of being sure of myself linked to my lack of confidence, or simply because I felt lost and listless? They were all part of my sense of emptiness and my sense of being void in the face of reality. How can one feel void and empty? Well, I was and I did not like it. Music seemed to assuage this emptiness but music can only do so much in one's life. Music needs a contributing factor and that's human responsiveness and I wasn't in the mood to respond as people who deal with music and wallow in it to the full extent. Sure I had the capacity to be creative but I was not being it and I was not in the act of creativity. I was simply on the edge of creativity and perhaps passive to its calling. I had to change things in my life and not allow it to take over my will and passion, if I had the passion to live and flourish as a human being. All these things troubled me and had me worrying about my state of affairs. Who was I? Where was I going? Who would teach me the right direction in my pursuit of good and unburdened living? Who indeed? What was wrong with me that I could not answer these questions by myself? After all, I had an education and a certain level of intelligence and curiosity as well as an active imagination. But, that was not enough. Not enough to feel secure and responsive to my calling in life. What was my calling by the way? I asked myself over and over again. My vocation as priests, nuns and religious people are wont to say. I could not go home, not now anyways, for I needed a place of comfort and not of turmoil. I needed self-assurance and not self-indulgence and narcissistic inclinations and satisfaction. My father was locked in his dark cellar by free will, at least that what I thought, although I wondered if he still exercised free will or was it a kind of spell cast over him. It's so strange how one's control over oneself and over things can be so easily lost. As for my mother, well, she was in her own little world of housekeeping and trying to find meaning in her own life by being a servant to her husband and mother to a son who was a wandering child. Mother never did take care of herself and her needs in life. She was the ever French-Acadian woman who had been formed early on by the dictates of Jansenism. It was a harsh view of life forever under the heel of fate and religious fervor. She needed to be liberated but who would teach her how? Yes, I needed to liberate myself from the past and forge ahead to wherever my search would take me. All I had right now was the compass of my soul and I needed to response to it in whatever shape of fashion.

When I reached the monastery evening was setting and I was reinvigorated by the thought that I had taken action and was on my way to rejuvenation as far as my heart and soul were concerned. In the bright and golden glow of the evening sun I could see the buildings of the monastery and I rejoiced that I had found a haven. I felt liberated and free to seek what I had been seeking, peace and tranquility. The monastery appeared to be the place where such spiritual comforts could be found. I would take advantage of its offerings and make them my own. That was my resolve even before I encountered any of the monks. My first encounter was the monk at the reception desk who was a tall man of assurance and boldness, I thought by his demeanor. He was welcoming and mild in his disposition. He was the right man for the position he held. He gave me one of those smiles that instantly brightens your day as he welcomed me and asked me my name and my interests in the monastery. I gave him the information he asked for and added that I wasn't sure what I was seeking here in the monastery but I was sure that I would find it once someone of knowledge and introspection allowed me to find it. He smiled and gave me the key to my room. I asked him about money and the fees and he told me that would be discussed later on. I only had a few dollars and some change on me. I was glad that money did not seem to be the primary care in this institution.

As I walked the passageways of the monastery I could hear chanting and I asked my guide what was that about since I was so happy to hear music again. He told me that it was vespers, part of the daily office that was sung every day at various times of the day. That was truly my welcoming sign into the monastery and I felt secure and happy inside. Signs like that are not serendipitous but they happen in time and space designated by the powers to be and here it was God's powers at work, I thought. I was already becoming part of the monastic life and I relaxed in mind, body and spirit. Oh, what joy, I thought, to be in the house of the Lord and be welcomed by him who welcomes strangers and wanderers. Monastic life was going to be stupendous. I was going to be part of a life designated as contemplative and mercifully tranquil. Part of me was already in tune with the harmony of the self and transcendence and that was why I was here in a monastery to seek that transcendence be it called God, the Almighty, the Creator Blessed or any other name. Names did not matter right now only the result of the power of transcendence. I was glad that I was beginning to lose my despondency and possible *ennui.* I never wanted to revisit that again.

The room that was given to me was very small and bare except for a small bed, one chair and some kind of a desk and next to this was a lavabo where the ablutions took place in the morning, I was told by my guide. He called the room a cell and that's what all of the monks had, he said. He left and a few moments later another monk brought me a tray with food on it. It consisted of bread, milk and some honey. I was told that the doorkeeper/receptionist had perceived in my face hunger and strain from the long trip and that I would enjoy some food to allay my immediate hunger for the next meal would only come at breakfast time early morning. I took the tray and could hardly wait to put that meager meal into my mouth and stomach. I was truly hungry. I knew that I would have to learn how to fast as part of the discipline of the monastery but right now I was hungry and did not want to think of fasting. That would come later. The sun set and my cell became dark and I looked for the light switch but found none. Instead there was a large candle in a candle holder next to my bed. I found a match and lit the candle. It gave a delicate and soft glow so that I was able to undress and slip into bed. I fell asleep as soon as my head hit the pillow.

The following morning, very early when it was still dark, I heard a soft knock on my door. I got up and opened the door to find out that there was a monk with a cowl holding a lighted candle in his right hand. He introduced himself as Brother Anthony, a delegate of the Abbot, he said, and he was to be my guide and companion for now until someone else, a monk priest, would be assigned to me. He told me that he was inviting me to attend Matins or *Orthros* in the Eastern Churches, the sunrise office, in the chapel and to please follow him. I dressed quickly and followed him to the chapel where all of the monks had congregated. This was the beginning of a new day and I was to follow the daily routine of monastic life starting now. All I could see were the black cowls of the monks, heads lowered in piety and humility, awaiting the first psalms to be sung. Then I heard it, the intonation of the initial psalm followed by the responsorial psalm all in harmony, raised voices in the silence of the sunrise. My guide gave me a book to follow the stream of prayers sung in solemn harmony. I did not have a hard time following them even though many of the psalms were sung in Latin and at times Greek. After the office my guide told me that the canonical hour itself was called Prime, the first hour at 6:00 a.m. The next one would be at 9:00 a.m. and it was called Terce. Mass was then said and we all received the Eucharist. It was a very devout ceremony celebrating the passion of our Lord Jesus Christ. After mass breakfast was served in the small cafeteria. We had hot coffee, a piece of dry bread, some jam and a fruit. All was served and eaten in silence. Then the guide brought me back to my room where I washed and shaved. I changed clothes but that's the only change of clothes I had with me. The guide told me that I could wear the monk's habit if I wanted to without the cowl and that would make me feel and be more monastic, he said. I agreed with him and that very evening I had a monk's habit laid out on my bed.

I did not follow every office hour of the day because my guide wanted to instruct me further about the daily monastic life and my role in the community. I told him that I was glad to be accepted as one of them and that I would follow every step that was prescribed to me. I was here to follow and learn and not be a burden on the monks. The guide assured me that I was indeed a welcomed guest and that all guests were welcomed in monasteries since it was a prescription of Saint Benedict's rule, a rule followed by most monasteries in the world. I remembered that the Greeks had a similar understanding that one had to welcome strangers and visitors because one never knows if a stranger is not an envoy by the gods. I thought that was a very good prescription.

The guide went over all of the steps of the day with me instructing me how to pray, how to and when to meditate, how to instill silence into the soul and how to abide by the rule of the community. First of all, he told me, one must be open to the spirit of humility and obedience to the rule. Then, one must accept the full spirit of brotherhood of community living. "You must renounce all the pains of pride and vanity that are locked inside of you in order to start anew as a child of the Christian faith," he told me.

"The pains of pride and vanity?"

"Yes, pride and vanity cause pain and must be rooted out in order to make room for self-discipline. It's a spiritual pain not felt by the body but by the soul."

"I see."

"You must also take stock of your failures and sins and open them up to confession which is a sacrament, a sacrament of forgiveness and reconciliation."

"Oh, my God, I haven't been to confession in years."

"Don't fear it but rather invite it and accept it as a grace and an opening to the wiping away of all that harms the soul in its pursuit of peace and graceful tranquility."

"I'm willing to do whatever is prescribed to me while I'm here."

"Good, then you will be able to fit in very well with us who are your brothers in Christ."

"But how do I do this?"

"I will show you how and later on you will get a spiritual director to further instruct you in the many paths of monasticism."

"You mean that you will stop being my guide?"

"Yes, but I will always be with in prayer."

"Thank you."

After a few days had gone by my spiritual director introduced himself to me and said that his name was Father Bonaventure Lalande. He told that he had been assigned to me by Abbot Jean-François Gaulthier and that he wanted to make sure that I got the best of direction both physically and spiritually but especially spiritually during my stay at the Transfiguration Abbey. I told him that I was very grateful to the Abbot and that I was looking forward to meeting him during my stay. I found that everyone at the abbey was mindful of courtesy and concern for the person. Personhood was an important factor in human relationships and I had studied that in college as part of my liberal arts curriculum.

Father Bonaventure began by instructing me in the history of monasticism and its development over the years. He said that it would be good for me to understand the rich history of monasticism and the reasons behind its development. He would also teach me the Benedictine rule, the protocols and the everyday prayers and devotions of monastic life. But especially so was how I would adapt to all of this during my stay with them and how I, myself, would develop as a person in search of my identity and my calling in life. I told him that I was at the abbey for that very reason. I found him to be gentle and kind in his dealing with me. I was learning how to put to rest my anxiety, my fears and my desires to become some kind of celebrity in life. I wanted to succeed and to flourish like other people my age do. I also wanted to make money for money was the key to all things, I thought. Well, he put to rest also the question of money for he told me that money was the root of all if not most evils in the world. Too much money breeds greed, he said and money engenders the passion to make more money. There's never enough to satisfy the hunger to be rich and have things. But things were things and provided none of the satisfaction that the human heart needed to thrive and grow. That is the reason we have the vow of poverty in our institution, he told me, not to be poor and especially indigent, but to detach ourselves from all that corrupts the mind and heart. Money thwarts the person from all that is good and fruitful, he said. Of course, I did not have to worry about money since I had none. However, he said, the desire, the hunger for money is just as devastating as the power of having it. It makes the person want to gain wealth and oftentimes step over people in order to gain money. The power of money and things, he told me, is a corrosive tool of the devil and it drives the human being to self-destruction with time. We here have no problems with money for we are detached from it and we let the bursar handle it. Still, I was in my heart longing for the opportunity to make money and enjoy the fruits of it. Also lodged in my heart was the haunting desire to make music my life. Music was my calling, I thought. When I told Father Bonaventure that he smiled and looked at me with soulful but gleaming eyes, and said, "That's a good and beneficial thought, François, for you have a calling in you and it will emerge more and more with time, but first you have to develop and nurture your spiritual life." I told him that I concurred with his thoughts on it.

"François let me tell you about monasticism and its history before I tell you about its development and its true meaning in our lives, we who are monks. It will help you to focus on the reason why you are here."

"I appreciate your time and effort in instructing me for I'm not an important person to you and the monastery. I know my limitations and my failings."

"It's precisely the reason I am here instructing you, my friend, because you have come with your burden of worries and failures to seek refreshment in your life. That's precisely what the gospels teach us based on Jesus's teachings that he, the Son of God, was here on earth not to glorify himself and the rich and powerful but he came to the aid of sinners and those burdened with failures in life. Those are the ones who most needed him, and he was very convincing in his teaching about the poor, the lonely, the abused, the disenfranchised and all those who suffered the miseries of alienation and discrimination. The poor widow's mite was worth more to God that all of the surplus money the other contributors put in the till. So you see that money is not important, it's the way people handle it and how they distribute or not distribute it to those in need. Thank God that I do not need to concern myself with money."

"But you need money to live and to do the things that are necessary in life."

"Yes, but you must not let it manage you and overpower you to the point of overpowering your life and making you miserable because you never have enough of it."

I'm sure that Father Bonaventure detected in my face the concern I nursed in my heart about money and success. I could not prevent my concerns about all of this from showing in my eyes and lips as well as my entire physiognomy that could not be changed overnight because some monk was telling me about the corrupting power of money. Money was the key to most everything and he had to learn that, I thought without expressing it. He read me very well when he said that he knew about my concerns and that things do not change in an instant but he hoped that I would be a good student of the Lord and of those in whom was entrusted the message. "The message is the key to all," he told me, "and I have come to bring you the message through the good will and command of my abbot."

I thanked him and told him to begin his instructions. He then began by telling me that he would not dwell too much on the historical part of monasticism, only the bare essential for me to begin to understand its history. "Besides," he said, "you can read about it. There are many books on the history of monasticism in our library."

First he told me about the difference between the Eastern Orthodox Church and the Western one. That the basics of their faith was the same but through some schism of the past they had split into two distinct churches. He told me that the whole story about the great Schism was too complicated for me to begin to understand and not worth the time to get into it. I thanked him for sparing me from all of the details that I did not want to hear anyway. He then proceeded to tell me about the basics of monasticism and how it was practiced at his monastery, The Transfiguration Monastery.

"Monasticism is basically a truth about our faith meaning that the monastic life is one of prayer, fasting, meditation and contemplation, and sacrifice. The first premise of the Orthodox faith and for the Christian is one of salvation through the works and inspiration of the

Holy Spirit. Christian life becomes a spiritual pilgrimage, not simply a journey, in which each person, through the imitation of Christ and *hesychasm*, or *Hierotheos,* cultivates the practice of unceasing prayer. So you see that prayer is an all-important element in monasticism. Monks live in a community hence the word *coenobitic*. They all follow a common rule. There are no religious orders in Orthodoxy although some monastic centers such as Mount Athos are highly influential."

"Can we talk about Mount Athos?"

"Not yet for I have other things I want to talk to you about. Mount Athos falls into a different category. You don't mind?"

"No."

"Everything in the Orthodox Church has a purpose and a meaning revealing God's revelation to man, hence the symbolism in our Church. Supreme in our faith is the Blessed Trinity and Jesus Christ the Savior followed by the Virgin Mother, the Theotokos, the God-bearer, for in Orthodox theology the Theotokos is the fulfillment of the Old Testament in that she carried the New Covenant in the person of Christ. Many icons exist showing Mary as the Theotokos such as the one by Vladimir, one of the most venerated icons. We have a copy of this icon in our chapel."

Then he talked about the Divine Liturgy which is the celebration of the Eucharist, the divine banquet. It is usually celebrated between the Sixth and Ninth Hours, he told me. When I asked him about music and the fact that I did not see an organ in their chapel, he told me that prayers are sung or chanted following a prescribed musical form. He went on to say that because the human voice is seen as the most perfect instrument of praise, musical instruments are not generally used to accompany the choir. "We have eight Modes or Tones within which a chant may be set," he told me.

"But musical instruments are so important to help carry the voice and heighten the full delivery of the chant."

"But in the Orthodox Church they are not necessary. We depend entirely on the human voice, the majestic and ever pleasing instrument of the chant."

"But...."

"Musical are important for a concert or an opera, but not for us in the monastery."

"I find it difficult to accept a world without musical instruments."

"That's because you are not a monk in a monastery. It's even true of our brothers in the Catholic faith in their own monasteries since the Gregorian chant is most of the time without musical instrument where the human voice dominates."

"Be it as it may, I still find it hard. Do any of your monks ever listen to opera?"

"Of course, although we do not partake of the values of the world, we live in it and enjoy its God-given talents and performances."

"I'm, glad to hear that."

"Just go to our recreation room in the evening when the monks have recreation and you'll find someone listening to music and most probably to opera."

"Are you into opera, Father?"

"No, I'm not. I'm more into symphony and concerts."

After that session, Father Bonaventure decided that it had lasted long enough and that he did not want to tire me. "Next time, I'll talk to you about spiritual life and its manifestation in one's life as a human being," he told me before leaving me to my thoughts and prayers as he suggested. I was glad and felt liberated from all of that instruction although it was meant to be beneficial for my spiritual development. It was then that I truly began to think of my journey as a pilgrimage and that I would have to concentrate on that idea as I progressed on my journey. The bell rang and Father Bonaventure quickly got up and left.

The next couple of days were spent in reading and prayer. I was told that meditation was also very important and I was left to my own wits to meditate. I had meditated before but not concentrated on the exercise of meditation. Brother Alexis came to my room in early evening and brought me a book on meditation because he said it would help me find my way to meditate and concentrate on my inner self or inner life. "You have one," he told me, "and it needs to be cultivated." I thanked him and I felt that he was so kind and generous just like Father Bonaventure had been with me.

After a while I wondered if I was being left to myself and even somewhat abandoned since I had no one come to me to instruct me any further than what Father Bonaventure had given me several days ago. Was I Ieft stewing there in my own juices like a boiled plum or was I left to my own devices to create my own thoughts on meditation, fasting, and the other disciplines that went along with monastic life. I did not know. I felt a little perturbed and somewhat offended and I did not know why. I was so hoping that the old monster, *ennui,* would not creep back into my life. Thank God for the following day Father Bonaventure came to me and told me that he had come to resume his instructions. I told him about my worries and tried to console me saying that in everyone's spiritual life there are dry moments and that has to be overcome with prayer and contemplation.

"I realize you thought you were abandoned and alone in your moments of discontent and spiritual dryness but I was with you in my prayers and so was entire community. We know you are here with us as part of our community and we wish to help you in your search for self-identity and your calling in life. You have a calling but you have not discovered it yet. It takes time and more time for some."

"Yes, especially for me."

"Don't be impatient and don't worry for the Holy Spirit of God has not forgotten you. He's giving you time to think and to persevere in your pursuit of what is good in your life. Goodness if not just the quality of things but the quality of life as it is meant to be. God is all good and he wishes us to partake in that very quality with him. He cannot be otherwise for he is the creative and almighty spirit that elevates his created ones to a level of spirituality that will soar to the highest of human level for we are not made to decline but to soar, not made for the ditch but for the right and straight path."

"But I do I know which path to take?"

"You will know, you will know when you are on it."

"But how?"

"By adhering to the dictates of your soul."

"The dictates of my soul?"

"Yes, the dictates are the prodding of the soul telling you where and how to go and find the comfort of a soul in peace and tranquility. That takes deep reflection and sincere abandonment to the will of God."

"But how do I know the will of God?"

"It's in the commandments and the prescriptions of the teaching of the gospels. Don't you say the "Our Father" every day?"

"Yes, I do."

"Then the will of God is in there. It's Christ's teaching us how to pray."

"I know but what precisely is the will of God?"

"The will of God is what he has engraved in our soul at baptism. We follow it and by our actions and words we are in harmony with it if we follow the dictates of the soul. You must learn to follow these dictates, my son. Learn to listen to your soul. Too many people do not listen. They think they hear but they do not listen. They too often are busy and distracted by the noise around them and the demands of worldly desires which often lead to greed and deadly coercion from our sinfulness."

"But are you saying that we sin even though we don't want to or are unaware of it?"

"That's not what I'm saying. I'm saying the sin is an act of revolt against God and his commandments and sin is part of free will on our part. The Jews were the first to discover that. If we want to rebel and we want to reject any adherence to what God has commanded us, then we sin."

"How do I know if I sin or not?"

"You will know by your conscience. Unfortunately too many people have squashed or muffled their conscience to a point that they do not hear it for they have refused to listen to it for a very long time."

"I don't even know if I have a conscience."

"You have one. You're probably not aware of it because you do not listen to it attentively enough, but you have one, François Basil Spirounias."

"How do I know I have one if I don't hear it telling what to do or how to do it?"

"Listen very carefully with your heart and soul and you will hear it. You must cultivate your conscience and let it flourish within you then it will come alive and you will hear it."

"I wonder if my father has a conscience. He's so self-centered and mean, my father."

"Please do not judge others, my son, especially your father. You have to accept people as they are and not what we would like them to be."

"But, he's a very difficult person to understand and even live with. I don't know how my mother has lived with him for so many years."

"Perhaps out of love and caring and especially perseverance on her part."

"That's true, she is a patient being, my mother, and caring too."

"Patience is a virtue and too many people do not have it. They act out of pride and intolerance. And, they have a short fuse. Are you like that, François?"

"A little bit."

"More than a little bit, I think."

"You're right Father. I'm not always very tolerant of others and their way of being or doing things."

"Then you must cultivate another facet of your personality and learn how to not judge others strictly on appearances and their way of being. They are who they are and no one can change that."

"But sometimes I wish they would only listen to good reason."

"What is good reason to you may not be good reason to them."

"Well, they have to learn to be more reasonable, that's all."

"Are you always reasonable?"

"I suppose not."

"Well there you have it."

I stopped speaking for a long while until Father Bonaventure broke the silence between us to tell me about fasting and the monastic life.

"Fasting is a discipline and it's seen as a purification. We all need to purify ourselves and our ways of doing things. There are spiritual, symbolic, and even practical reasons for fasting. Fasting is not simply abstaining from food. It's a practice of learning to temper the body's primary desire for food and satisfaction of the senses. How did Christ begin his ministry? He began his ministry by fasting in the desert away from the tumult of the world around him. He was emptied as we all are but he was strong enough to resist."

"But he was the Christ, the Son of God. He was a special being. He had great gifts."

"And he had the same human nature as ours and the same weaknesses. He had to calm down his passions and live according to his Father's will."

"He had passions?"

"Of course, like all of us, and his greatest passion was to die on the cross for our salvation."

"He was like us then."

"Yes, except sin."

"Father Bonaventure, how do I go about fasting?"

"Well, you simply follow the community in its rule of fasting and follow the dietary regulations observed by all of us here in the monastery. Even the abbot fasts. Perhaps even more than we do. You know, fasting, as I said, is not only abstaining from food but from some of the pleasures we are so accustomed to. It's not a sin to enjoy the pleasures of life but we must refrain from allowing them to overwhelm us and our lives."

"Does that mean that I have to refrain from my music and operas?"

"Not at all. Just temper those desires and allow your soul to seek pleasure in prayer and meditation. It's all in *sophrosony* as the Greeks say."

"Yes, as the Greeks say."

"Listen François, I have been your instructor in matters of the spiritual and monastic elements in your life here in the monastery. Now comes the time to have a chat with the abbot, Abbot."

"But I thought we would talk about Mount Athos."

"I have not forgotten it and we will be discussing the *Meteora* in our next and final get-together."

"*Meteora ?*"

"Yes, it means "middle of the sky" and "suspended in the air."

"Oh, I get it. Mount Athos way up there in the skies."

That evening while I was enjoying a brief walk in the garden I overheard some music coming out of the recreation room. The windows were opened and I stood there listening. It was opera, an operatic aria sung by a splendid voice I did not know. I went inside and walked quietly into the recreation room and saw a monk listening to music on a phonograph. He seemed to be relishing what he was listening to. I dared not interrupt his concentration and I very quietly sat next to him without uttering a single word. He bowed to me and said very gently, "Do you like opera?"

"Yes, I do."

"Do you recognize the opera and the singer that I am listening to?"

"No, Father."

"I'm not a priest but a brother."

"I cannot tell the difference."

"That's alright because we are all equals here in the monastery."

"What are you listening to, Brother?"

"I'm listening to my favorite opera with Maria Callas my favorite dramatic soprano. It's **Andrea Chénier** by Giordano. She's singing the aria, "La momma morta." Listen to it with me for it's a heart-wrenching aria with music to churn the soul to tears. You may think I'm overly sentimental but that's what I feel and sense when I listen to such immortal music and singing. My brothers tell me that I'm overly sentimental and I believe them. Listen, listen to the strains of the cello and the violin in complete harmony with the voice or I should say the voice in complete harmony with the music. It's an amazing voice with a masterfully disciplined range."

I just sat there mesmerized by the sounds coming out of the player. I had never heard just captivating and gut-wrenching sounds in my life. I could see that the brother had tears in his eyes and was trying not to show it. Suddenly the bell rang and he stood up, shut off the phonograph and started to leave as I said, "What is your name?" He turned around with his right index finger to his lips and he walked away.

The following day Father Bonaventure came to my room to tell me that he had reserved some time for our discussion of Mount Athos and that I was to meet him in the garden early afternoon. It was a glorious day and the sun was shining brightly. The flowers were in glorious bloom and I could smell the sweet scent of mimosa and sweet grass. How all of my senses took delight in this natural setting and how I relished the moment. I was not inclined to fast at that given moment for I was going to enjoy completely and with gusto the delightful passion of the giving of oneself to beauty. I was out of my cave so-to-speak and into the bright light of the sun and I reveled in it.

"François, here you are."

"Yes, I'm enjoying everything that's here in the garden."

"That's good. It's healthy to enjoy the little pleasure that God had granted us through nature and her many offerings. Some people disregard them and often take them for granted. Look at that flower over there and gaze at one of its petals, why even Solomon in all of his glory could not match the splendor of a single flower."

"That's in the Old Testament, I know."

"Well, the New Testament when Christ says it to ."

"You see, I don't' know my Bible that well."

"It's sufficient to know parts of it and then get to learn more."

"When will I ever get to learn more?"

"Life is a learning experience not just what we learn in school. I'm here to talk to you about Mount Athos."

"Good."

"First of all there is the *Meteora,* one of the largest and most important complexes of Orthodox Monasteries in Greece second only to Mount Athos. The six monasteries are built on natural sandstone pillars in central Greece. I've been there and have seen all six of them. I was granted special permission to take this pilgrimage that I had so desired but not expressly asked for. It had remained in my heart ever since I was a teenager but I knew that I would never satisfy that desire. But, I did. I did because the Abbot granted me my unexpressed desire for he could read my heart and soul. He is such a clairvoyant. Oh, how I enjoyed the wonders of the *Meteora.* You should go there someday."

"I wish."

"Well, Mount Athos is truly high up in the sky, suspended there as if there is nothing holding it except the very pillars of stone that support it. There were no stairs, no elevator, no way to climb to that heavenly place in olden days. You had to be placed in a large basket and be hauled up by the monks above. But nowadays, there are roads and vehicles that go up the mountain. Only males are permitted to visit the territory which is called "Garden of Virgin Mary" by the monks .Laymen are required to have short hair and any non-cleric arriving on Athos with long hair has his hair cut. There are several sketes or communities of Christian hermits following a monastic rule allowing them to worship in comparative solitude. Fortunately Mount Athos was spared during World War II and very little destruction happened. It is now a UNESCO World Heritage Site. And is well protected against any endeavors to change it or even modify it. What is the most admired and highly acclaimed by all is the art and literary treasures of Mount Athos. The Athonic monasteries possess huge deposits of invaluable medieval treasures, including icons, liturgical vestments and sacred objects as well as codices and other Christian texts."

"Have you seen any of those treasures on Mount Athos?"

"No, for I have never been to Mount Athos. I have studied it and I have talked to some who have visited it but I was never privileged to go there."

"I only wish that someday I will be able to go there and spend some time relishing all of those treasures."

"You will need special permission to do so."

The bell rang and Father Bonaventure told me that I was to meet the Abbot and get to talk to him in the afternoon and in the meantime I was to gather myself in prayer and meditation in order to more fully enjoy the fruits of my monastic living with the monks.

After a brief lunch in common I was led to the Abbot's office which was down a long passageway facing a large window through which sunlight could be seen filtering through the frosted panes. I knocked and a voice beckoned me inside. I opened the large wooden door and saw a fairly large room with walls practically bare except for a cross and an icon. The furniture was sparse and very simple. Sitting at his desk was Abbot Jean-François Gaulthier. He wore a simple pectoral cross of pewter on his chest and wore a ring more like a band made of silver, I believe. He welcomed me and begged me to sit down. He looked at me with his intensely dark eyes that shone like agate. It was as if they were piercing my soul.

"Welcome, my son. I have heard good things about you."

"You have?"

"Yes, from Brother Hilarion who welcomed you, Brother Anthony who was your initial guide and from Father Bonaventure who has been directing you and even from Brother Theodore who enjoyed listening to music and opera."

"So his name is Theodore."

"Yes, Brother Theodore is a model monk who has adapted very well to monastic life. Although young he shows a certain maturity that sustains his vocation as a monk progressing on the path to salvation and inner strength as a person of quality and firm purpose. Myself and other priests are here to help mold him into the vessel of choice as ready to receive the graces of our Good Lord, Jesus Christ through the intercession of our Blessed Mother, the Theotokos. That is our collective mission here at this monastery, to form young people who come to us for transformation and solid discipline of self and especially of the heart and soul. If the heart is not in it, then the transformation will not occur. You probably have witnessed some of this during your stay with us."

"Yes, Father Abbot, I have and I've admired some of the monks who are so given to prayer and contemplation. It shows in their eyes, their composure and their disposition."

"I know. You have been with us for almost eight weeks now. Has it all been fruitful in your life?"

"Yes, it has and very much so."

"Good, I'm pleased. What do you intend to do with your life? I'm sure that you are well aware that you do not have the vocation of a monk."

"You are very perspicacious, Father Abbot."

"That's my job and my duty. Well, what do you intend to do and where do you intend to go when you leave here?"

"I don't really know."

"Well, you must have some inkling of what you will pursue in life."

"Very little. I know that I love music and opera and I am developing a strong sense of the art of the opera and I may want to pursue that path."

"God has given you talents for you to develop and nourish and you must ask for guidance and I know you will receive it for the Good Lord will not leave you just hanging there high and dry. But, you must ask for it, you must pray to receive it for it does not come cheap. It requires prayer and sacrifice and even fasting."

"I know for I have been practicing all that was required of me here at the monastery."

"Well if we have taught you anything we have, at least, taught you that."

"I trust that I have been a good disciple."

"What I really want to talk to you about is that I believe you are still in the dark as to your identity as a person of God and your talents given to you as a gift from him. You probably have not realized this but I see you as still being in the platonic cave searching for the sunlight of truth. And you have not found it yet."

"But I thought I already had."

"You thought but you have not attained it yet. It's good to be searching and to be on a journey in order to determine which path to take, but searching endlessly must not deter you from attaining your goal."

"But how do I know when I attain it?"

"You will know when you have. In the meantime you must discover the self that is you, the real self."

"But, I am not much, Father Abbot. I'm really nothing in the sight of God. Sometimes I believe that I'm worthless and not worth very much to myself and to others. At times I even think that and feel that I'm junk. My father has never once assured me that I was worth something. He was always there to criticize me and what I was doing. Never did he ever hug me or even kiss me. That was his Greekness in him, I suppose."

"No that's not it. That was probably because he himself never experienced fatherly love. I want you to do something for me before you leave us. Furthermore, God does not make junk. Do you understand that, my son? If he did then he would not be God."

"Yes, of course."

"I want you to take your Bible and read Psalm 138 verses 9 through 19. There you will encounter that you were wonderfully made by God the Creator. Need I say more?"

"No. I will do it tonight in my cell"

"Then go, my son, and I will see you again tomorrow before you leave us."

I got up, turned around and before leaving his office, I turned towards him and bowed in reverence for he truly was a clairvoyant and humble man.

That evening when I found myself alone and tranquil in my cell, I picked up my Bible and turned to the page where the psalm that I was to read appeared. I then started reading the excerpt indicated:

If I take the wings of the morning/ and settle at the farthest limits of the sea,/even there your hand shall lead me,/and your right hand shall hold me fast./If I say, 'Surely the darkness/ shall cover me/ and the light around me/become night.'/even the darkness the darkness is not dark to you,/the night is as bright as the day/for darkness is as light to you.

Yes, yes, I said out loud, darkness reigns in darkness but not in pure light.

For it was you who formed my inward parts;/you knit me together in my mothers' womb./I praise you, for I am fearfully and wonderfully made.

There's that line that the Abbot quoted me and it's must be true. It has to be true. I am not worthless; I'm not junk. I'm somebody and that somebody, God has made with worth.

Wonderful are your works;/that I know very well./My frame was not hidden from you,/when I was being made in secret,/intricately woven in the depths/of the earth./Your eyes beheld the unformed substance./In your book were written/all the days that were formed/for me,/when none of them as yet, existed./How weighty to me are your/thoughts, O God!/How vast is the sum of them!

So true, so very true. I cannot fathom your existence nor your depth of thought and action as Creator blest. I cannot hold in my hand nor my heart and certainly not in my soul what you have designed me for, and I'm still searching. When shall it cease? When does the longing to be cease or does it ever? I am and I am not. Yes, I was knit in my mother's womb, but is the knitting done? Where will I find my happiness, my contentment in life? How do I find it? When will this pilgrimage of mine end so that I know that I found my niche in life? Do I have one? I must have one or else I am rootless and purposeless. Will I keep staying in my cave or will I ever step out of it for real? Please God, I don't want to be my father. I do not want to wallow in the muddy waters of decay and self-inflicted uselessness. I want to be somebody. I want to be me. And I could feel tears coming out of my eyes close to sleep but still half open in the darkness of night with no candle burning, no glow of any light. I felt I was truly in a cavern and there was no glow bright enough to sustain me and to give me light. I fell asleep and woke up early before dawn.

I felt that I had a restful sleep and I was ready to face a new day. I went to the chapel to join the community and to recite the hours. When came time for breakfast, I went into the dining hall and suddenly spotted Brother Theodore. I suddenly without thinking blurted out, "Brother Theodore!" He turned around and put his index finger to his lips and then I knew I had broken the sacred silence of the monastery. I just stood there and I could see that

Father Bonaventure was not smiling but not in a deprecating way. He motioned me to come close to him and then he whispered, "You have to do penance for your infraction, you know." "I know," I replied. "You will go to every monk here in the refectory and kiss his feet humbly and with kindness." "That's all?" "That's enough for now." So I went to every monk and knelt down so that I could reach each one's feet under the table and started to kiss the feet of the monks. When I finished my penance I looked at each one and there was generosity in their eyes and in their smile. I felt wanted and part of their community. I felt light shining through my miasma of pride and lack of self-confidence that I had been nursing all along. I felt free. I looked at Brother Theodore who was slowly eating his bread and drinking his coffee and as he glanced up at me I detected a warm feeling of understanding and even joy on his part. Perhaps even a twinkle in his eye. I was ready for the music to begin once more.

The rest of the day was spent in contemplation and meditation as well as in prayer. I was relishing the quiet moments of silent prayer when the soul speaks and especially when it listens. I had not yet learned to listen to my soul and I was gradually learning how. It's a welcome thing to be heard and the process of listening is even greater than hearing.

The following day, I woke up early again and decided to spend the rest of the morning in my cell preparing for my departure from the monastery. I was going to miss this quiet and sacred space, so tranquil that I could even hear myself think. Early afternoon, I went to see the Abbot who had summoned me one last time. I went to his office and he was not there. The porter came to see me and told me that Father Abbot was waiting for me in the garden under the oak tree. I welcomed the site rather than a rather bare office space. I found him sitting there reading his book of prayers. When I approached him he looked up at me, smiled and said,

"I learn that you had an episode yesterday morning at breakfast."

"Yes and I'm not surprised that you know about it."

"Yes, the walls have ears you know," and his eyes glowed.

"I was not thinking when I hollered our Brother Theodore's name. I should have known better."

"You're still new to our way of life. It takes time to learn and to practice it. But everyone one is forgiven when there is infraction of the rule."

"I'm afraid that it would take me too much time and I would not turn out a good monk."

"That's why you are not saying on. Your path is traced for somewhere else."

"I know that now."

"Before you leave, I want to talk to you about the values and strengths of monasticism for these values will guide you in the future as you commit yourself to your calling and find your destination in life. First, I want to talk about Eastern Orthodox monasticism as a joyful mourning. This paradoxical phrase denotes a spiritual state in which a monk in his prayer grieves for the sins of the world and at the same time finds joy in the forgiveness and resurrection of Christ. You see we as monks are closely tied to the world because we are part and parcel of Creation. We love our brothers and sisters in every part of the world and in whatever capacity they are to be found. You see we are very tolerant beings and we grieve when people grieve, find joy when people are joyful and we are sad when they are sad. We not only sympathize with human beings but we share in their humanity. We are all one in God's creation, saints and sinners alike."

"What are the essential qualities of monastic life?"

"Fervent and unceasing prayer and love, love for one another even though it's not always easy sometimes. You must remember loving is not liking. I do not always like the ones I love. Also, remember that the adoption of frugality, the shunning of idle talk and the call to show selfless love are not given only to monks but for all the faithful."

"I also like the silence and tranquility of the monastery. It's so unlike so many places I've been before."

"Orthodox monasticism has always been associated with stillness and or silence, which is seen primarily as an internal rather than external state. You have to seek external silence in order to attain internal stillness of mind and soul more easily. This stillness is not inertia or inaction but awakening and activation of the spiritual life."

"I understand."

"Do not forget that there will be successes and failures in your life, but that's how things work. That's part of being human. We are not perfect and we who are monks realize that so very much. That's why we rely on the mercy and grace of God. Don't be afraid to seek help in your venture in order to find consolation and mercy in all of your endeavors. Failure is not a crime nor is success a right for all. We do fail at times and all of our endeavors are not successful. Please, please do not allow yourself to measure success with wealth and money. That's not real success. It's attainment that can easily deceive. And above all please avoid at all costs the inexhaustible pursuits that never satisfy. The heart can only find solace in the Creator and his grace. Remember also that you are the clay in the potter's hands, *l'argile de ta spiritualité,* and let him fashion you into a vessel that can hold his grace. It's a gift. The vessel can easily be broken but it can also be put back together again, so no matter what, you must endure."

"I'm beginning to see that more clearly. I can break but I cannot be broken."

"Well said, François Basil Spirounias. Farewell and may the Good Lord bless you and guide your path to everlasting life. That is my wish and blessing for you. I will not see you again, my son, but my prayers will always be with you."

With that he blessed me with his hands and gave me the kiss of peace, a kiss that I had never received before in my life but a kiss that I craved for and cherished. I was ready to leave and I wanted somehow to say farewell to all of my monastic brothers. How would I do this? I asked myself.

The following morning at breakfast just before I was about to tell the community farewell the best way I could, they all broke silence and said a fond farewell. I was touched by their gesture and their sacrifice for I knew that each one would have to do penance for their breach of the monastic rule. The sacrifice of breaking silence for a lesser confrère felt great.

13. Dekatria

As I came out of the gate of the Transfiguration Monastery, I truly felt like I had been, for a single moment, the witness to a transfiguration, the transfiguration of a Christ that I had not known before. The entire community was the manifestation of the transfigured Christ, all arrayed in bright light. I felt that I was now out of the cave and into the fullness of the morning sun. It felt great. I was on my way. But, where was I going? I asked myself. However, I did not feel as insecure as I had been before entering the monastery. I had gained some self-confidence and I knew in my soul that I was not God's junk. That was indeed a very good feeling. I left with twenty dollars in my pocket that he bursar had given me as travel money. I owed those guys, I owed them big time.

I took the bus to New York and I went to see Alexander. He was still working at the Hotel Empire. He was surprised to see me. I told him about my stay at the monastery after I had gone to see my parents. He asked me about them but I told him that I did not want to talk about it.

"Are they still as bad off as they were?"

"Not my mother but my father is completely demoralized and he lives in his own dark world. My mother is fine. She's the same as she has ever been, for as long as I've known her. She endures."

"But life is not meant to endure."

"I know, but what can I do? I can only endure myself, endure and not complain."

"You must have been frustrated with the situation."

"I was but I'm used to it. I then went to an Eastern Orthodox monastery for a reprieve of eight weeks. It did me a lot of good. Now, I want to get on with my life and live, listen to music and go to the opera. But first I have to find a job."

"Before I forget, my old uncle Konstantine is gravely ill."

"Where is he?"

"He's out of the hospital and is at home with a friend who's taking care of him."

"Can I go see him?"

"Yes, but not right now. He had a very bad spell. It's his heart. We almost lost him. Wait a few days."

"But he might die in the meantime."

"I don't think so but if you insist we'll go tomorrow."

"I'd like to do that."

The following day, early afternoon, Alexander and I went to Mister Kapalodous' house to pay him a visit. His old friend, Mister Agnosistos, opened the door and invited us in. He then led us to the sick man's room. I was so glad to see Mister Kapalodous again that I rushed over to squeeze his hand.

"Please be careful for I'm not too strong, Basil."

I could see that he had tears in his eyes. Either his eyes were moist like most elderly whose eyes are ever teary or else he had tears in his eyes at seeing me again.

"How are you, my dear friend of the opera?"

"I'm fine except I have no more strength in my body. I can't even walk straight, can't stand up and I can hardly speak. I'm on my last leg, Basil."

"Oh, don't say that. You're good for another ten years if not more. You're made of good Greek stock."

"Even Greek stock gets depleted and dies."

"Not you."

"Listen, Basil, I know I do not have long to live and I must put my affairs in order. I still have my subscription to the Met and I want to transfer it to you."

"Why not Alexander."

"No, it's you I want. Alexander can get his own if he wants."

Alexander looked at me and smiled.

"If that's what my uncle wants then you must accept it, François."

I turned to Mister Kapalodous and saw that he had fallen asleep or was in some king of stupor.

"It's time we leave for we do not want to tire him and annoy his friend here," said Alexander.

"I wanted so much to talk to him and share my experiences with him. He's such a dear friend."

"I know, François, but later perhaps."

I returned to see Alexander the following afternoon and saw that he looked morose and a bit under the weather.

"I wanted to get in touch with you but you were not in your room this morning."

"I was talking a walk in Central Park."

"My uncle Konstantine passed away in the night. He left this world very peacefully his old friend told me. He did not suffer nor did he fight for life. He just let go and slipped away like a good Greek does when the time has come to surrender to one's fate."

I was stunned. I could not move nor utter a single word.

"What's the matter, François, didn't you hear me?"

"I heard you but I couldn't say anything. My words were caught in my throat and I couldn't get them out."

Then I started to cry. I couldn't help myself, I just sobbed like a child who has just lost his father.

"I'm sorry. I cannot help the tears for such a good friend that I got to know for a brief period of time. It was brief but I truly enjoyed it and it was rich in friendship and love. I loved your uncle, Alexander. I truly did."

"I know. I only wish I could have entered into that love that you and he shared even for a brief period of time."

"But surely you did have your uncle's love and closeness that an uncle has for a nephew."

"Yes, but I did not have the closeness that the two of you had. He was truly like a father to you and he accepted you as a son."

"Yes, the fatherly closeness that I never had."

With that Alexander handed me a large envelope with my name on it.

"My uncle wanted you to have this."

"I can't take this, this belongs to you, his nephew."

"No, it's yours. He wanted you to have it, not me."

I put the large envelope in my breast pocket and thanked Alexander for his courteous gesture.

"Don't thank me. Thank my uncle. He left me cash and some stocks and bonds to my mother, nothing of great value. It was simply as a token of fidelity to family ties. My mother and my uncle were never really close."

The funeral was small, just a service for the immediate family which was small. I was included because, as Alexander told me, I was part of the family the way Konstantine Kapalodous would have wanted it. I was so glad that I could be there and share these rare moments of farewell when the heart cannot openly express its feelings but the presence can translate them for all to see. The funeral was held in a small Greek church and the burial took place in a family plot in a Greek cemetery off the center of New York. I could not tell you where. My grief was so strong and evident that the family saw it and expressed their empathy to me by their gracious gestures and soft words. I just could not think straight at that moment nor could I set to memory the spaces and locations that I had been part of. I felt numb. Alexander kept looking at me and smiled his soft smile that consoled me in some fashion. As we were leaving the plot which we had just surrounded all dressed in black, I went over and plucked a white carnation form the spray on his coffin and left to go with the others in one of the limousines. We then proceed to Mister Kapalodous' friend's restaurant, "Plato's Restaurant," he called it, and we had a lovely Greek meal.

I arrived at the hotel late in the day and threw myself on the bed before undressing. I felt drained and lonely from the all the sadness I had experienced that day. As I was taking my suit coat off I felt the envelope in my pocket and took it out so that I could open it and see what was inside. I saw ten crisp one hundred dollar bills, his subscription to the Met and attached to it was a signed note transferring the subscription to my name. There was also a note written by an unsteady hand, all wavy-like but legible, in which he begged me to continue to love my music and explore opera for there was much to gain from those discoveries that charmed the heart and soul. "Let opera be your path to your passion in life. It's your calling, Basil," he wrote. Then in the envelope there was also a key to a safety deposit box at his bank. Another note explained that the box contained some Playbills, some Opera News, and some old treasures, as he called them, that he had collected over the years. I could not get over the fact that he had entrusted all of that to me, a friend that he had only known for a very brief period of time. I could hear his voice from beyond the grave, "Basil, don't let the bad times get to you and don't ever forget to take full pleasure in life the way a Greek man does...like Zorba." I put everything on the desk and went to bed.

The morning after the funeral, I took a long walk to the Met which was very far from the hotel and I simply stood there glancing at the tall majestic windows and the fountain gurgling and spraying in front of me. I tried to soak in the atmosphere I had enjoyed when I first stood there waiting to go inside with Mister Kapalodous. It had been a joyful experience for me what with the building itself, the interior splendor and the performance of the opera, **La Bohème**. I could still hear Pavarotti's voice pronouncing that lyrical Italian that he knew so well in harmony with the lyrics and the music by a master composer. That could never be taken away from my memory as long as I lived. I was overjoyed with the fact that I could stay on in New York and attend the operas of my choice since I now possessed a subscription. I had money, I had a reasonable hotel room and I had all of New York City to delight in. But, I had to get a job. I just could not stay idle like a street bum as my dad would say. Then I decided to go to Mister Kapalodous's bank to look at his safety box to find out what was in there since I now had the key in my possession. I entered the bank and asked for the safety deposit box that I intended to retrieve. I showed the clerk the key and Mr. Kapalodous' note. A man came over and led me to the vault where the boxes were stored. He went to get the appropriate one and asked me to open the box after he had inserted the bank's key. I took mine and inserted it in the other lock and then the box was open. The clerk left and I was able to look inside Mr. Kapalodous' box. I found some old photos, some papers related to his family, some Playbills and a few Opera News. What I was anxious to look at was his "treasures" that he mentioned in his note. What I did find were gold cuff links, an onyx ring of some value, I'm sure, and a wedding ring tied to a note saying that this ring had belonged to his wife years ago. It was a private civil ceremony and no one of the family was in attendance. The family had strongly objected to the marriage since the bride was not Greek and had no religion as such. It ended up with an annulment. "Sophie gave me back the ring for she had no use for it, she told me. Sophie was a member of the chorus at the Met. She had a pretty voice. I'm sorry that I had no backbone to thwart the family's objections and gave in to their threats. They cut me off anyways. Poor Sophie, I felt that I had abandoned her. All I know is that she died in childbirth not too long after we separated, my child. I never knew what happened to this child of mine." I was so surprised that Mister Kapalodous had never mentioned this to me when he was still alive. I closed the box and took the contents with me.

I got a job in a restaurant called "The Sirens of Greece." It was a seafood place and it was owned by a friend of Plato Throuvincios, Mister Kapaloudos's friend who owned the restaurant where we had gone to when we first went out together. It was a good job but it exacted hard work as a waiter. I was ready for it and I wanted to do it since it gave me the opportunity to meet people and provide a steady income with tips that amounted to hundreds of dollars a week. I was amazed how much one earned in tips in a single week. I imagined New Yorkers to be generous but not that much. Most of them were not stingy although there were some who pinched pennies and only gave you the bare minimum much less than the ten percent, if not required, at least expected. I knew I could save some and build up my savings so that I would be able to travel later on. One day, this opera star came to the restaurant, I don't remember his name, but he left me a fifty-dollar bill as a tip. He had had champagne, hors d'oeuvres, lobster bisque, a seafood casserole, and an extravagant dessert. I told myself that if this continues, I'll build up a savings account worthy of King Midas.

All I had to pay was my hotel room on a weekly basis, some of my meals since I took most of them at a discount at the restaurant where I worked, my ordinary expenditures like toothpaste, socks and underwear, and, of course tickets to Broadway plays now and then, in a particular play that interested me. Moreover, I knew that I had a free ride at the opera and I would certainly take advantage of that as long as I could, thanks to my benefactor.

I started looking at the program of upcoming operas and I found an opera that I knew I would really love. We were now in the 1969-1970 season. It was **Aida** with Leontyne Price and Richard Tucker. Unfortunately the opening of the opera season was delayed and the season almost cancelled due to prolonged labor-management negotiations. I kept looking at local headlines to make sure that opening night at the Met would not be cancelled or postponed. But it wasn't and on the evening of December 29, I was at the door waiting to be ushered in for Verdi's masterpiece opera. I had read much about it and I felt that I was well informed enough to be able to enjoy this epic presentation of an Egyptian drama set to majestic music. I had read so much about it that I couldn't wait to hear the "Celeste Aida" aria and especially the forceful splendor of the Triumphal March. I was on edge and at the same time tingling inside. It would be the first time that I attended an opera by myself without the help of a companion. I thought of Mister Kapalodous watching me from his box somewhere in the heavenly spheres. "Mister Kapalodous, I am here ready to enjoy **Aida**, I said to myself. I entered and was seated. At exactly eight the curtain rose and I watched the audience in the most of whom were elegantly dressed, settle down to enjoy the start of the 1969-1970 season with an opera that had had in the past a most glorious acceptance by the public. Verdi would have been pleased, I told myself.

I was excited and eager and it showed in my face, I'm sure. When I saw the splendor of the set and the costumes, I knew that this would be an extravagant show. I sat through the entire performance and marveled at the performances and voices of Leontyne Price and Richard Tucker. The "Celeste Aida" touched me greatly and, of course, when it came time for the Triumphal March, I could not believe that the stage could handle so many people and so much paraphernalia, even horses and large carts pulled by two donkeys. For a moment, I was distracted by the show of extras, the chorus and the many other details of the marching contingents. It was truly a spectacle. I enjoyed all of the four acts and felt relieved when the opera was over since I was all tensed up and still reviewing in my mind Verdi's music. I felt like singing out loud but, of course, refrained from doing so. I went out in the cold night and headed straight to my hotel without the usual *souper.* The next morning, I hurried to but the newspapers that would certainly carry the reviews of the opera. I picked up the New York Times and thumbed through the pages and found Harold C. Schonberg's review. I read,

"The curtain may have lifted three and a half months late, but nevertheless there was the feeling of a grand opening last night at the Metropolitan Opera...No new insights were cast on Aida... and none were expected. Each of the principals was in good voice. Richard Tucker was a Radames with a manly, ringing voice. He was determined to sing, and sing he did. He even refrained from mouthing the words at the end of the second act, and his voice could be heard over orchestra, full chorus and the other principals."

Yes, he certainly did ring out so loud that I almost rose from my seat to applaud, but I knew better than to not follow the listening audience. Continuing the review, I read,

"Leontyne Price, too, used her big voice effectively, and also with a good deal of nuance. Her pianissimos and pianos on phrases like "Numi, pieta" or the end of "O patria mia" were in the tradition stemming from Rethberg and Milanov, and were as well handled as any soprano today can manage. Occasionally her tone veered to a near-stridency in full-voice passages, but never, at the expense of expression. There was an immense vocal authority to Miss Price's Aida."

I agreed with the critic's call on both counts that Miss Price had a powerful voice and I might add lusty, and that she sang very well. I didn't know about the tradition of the sopranos he mentioned, and I wondered about his use of critic's jargon about the tone veering to a near-stridency. I let that pass by me. Who was I to dismiss and even oppose Harold C. Schonberg's claims? I was not a critic and I certainly was not educated enough in opera to analyze the music and the delivery in any opera. All I could do was to enjoy it and to build upon every opera that I would see and hear so that in the future I would be better prepared to be a critic myself, not that I wanted to.

Prior to going to the opera in December, I went to see a musical play called **Coco** based on the life and career of Coco Channel. The main role was held by Katheine Hepburn. Although not primarily a singer, she held her part very well, I thought. After for, she was a fantastic actress. I did not know much about Coco Channel except that I knew a bit about her perfumes, especially Channel No.5 that sold at a ridiculous retail price. The play was entertaining but not at all as much as the opera **La Bohème**. That's why after this musical, I decided to go to the opera next time.

I kept on living at the same hotel and kept my job as a waiter. It paid well. I kept putting money into my savings account. I knew that someday I would want to travel and go to Paris. My mother would have been proud of me and my thriftiness. I still had not heard from either my mother or my father. There was dead silence in the air a far as I was concerned. I knew that I should go and see what was happening up in Maine, but I just could not bring myself to go up there and face the strange and frustrating foolishness of my father in his cellar. However, I owed it to my mother to go and pay her a call. I kept postponing it.

Sometimes in early February, I decided to go back to my village and see my parents. I did not know if I should call beforehand or simply surprise them. Of course, that would not in any way affect my dad. He was beyond feelings and reactions, I knew that. What a miserable existence, I thought. When I got there, I could see that the small house had been abandoned in some fashion. I was terribly puzzled by this. I hurried to the neighbor's house and knocked on the door. Madame Villandry, a widow of many years, opened the door and was surprised at seeing me at her door. She told me to enter and quite suddenly she started explaining to me why our home looked abandoned. She told me that my father was taken ill and had been transferred to a local nursing home and that my mother had had a stroke and was unable to speak. Madame Villandry told me that she had tried to reach me but that she did not know my address in New York. My father was helpless and my mother too. Why hadn't I tried calling my parents was the question that seem to linger on Madame Villandry's lips. I did not try to explain the situation to her. I rushed to the hospital where my mother was and asked to see her. They told me that she had been transferred to a therapeutic and rehab center some twelve miles away. I got the directions and hastily set out to go and see her. When I got there I was led to a room that was almost bare and where the white lusterless walls felt like everything had been whitewashed in consonance with the ambience of the institution. When I stepped into the room where my mother was, I saw an emaciated, almost lifeless woman whose eyes were sunken and whose cheeks were hollow. She appeared to me to be beyond recognition. I felt a great lump in my throat and I tried desperately to keep my eyes dry and my composure steady. I got closer to her and bent down to look at her face when she recognized me and tried so very hard to speak. I knew that she was grasping for words, words in French that would not come out. She tried desperately to form the Fr of my first name and all I could see was the effort that she was putting into it. I squeezed her right hand and she responded to my clasping. I stayed with her for a while until she fell asleep. I was told that she was on morphine and that her days were numbered. I went to the office with the charge nurse and she told me what there was to be told about my mother's stroke. The hospital and the rehab had tried to convey whatever message to my father, but there was no use, he was totally out of it, were her words to me. I told her that I was going to stay in town for a while and visit my mother every day to see if there was going to be any improvement. She then told me that I had better stay close since they did not give my mother much time to live. I could not speak, not a single word for my throat was locked tight and my heart was pounding. I felt like fainting. The nurse went to get me some water and had me sit down. What was I going to do now? I wanted to go and see my father but I realized that mother was in a much worse condition and that she need my immediate attention. I spent the night at the rehab center and the following day I went to Madame Villandry's house to tell her the news about my mother. She had tears in her eyes and she pitied me for having such bad luck with my parents. She asked me if she could do anything for me, and I told her, no. "Pray for me, pray for them," was all I could say to her before I left.

When I got back to the rehab center, the charge nurse took me aside and told me that my mother was in a coma and was not expected to live much longer than the afternoon. She passed away around four that afternoon. I was with her and saw her peacefully breathe her last breath. She was gone. How could she without telling me goodbye? How could I have not known about her ailing condition? Of course, a stroke comes suddenly without much warning signs. How could she go like that? Why didn't she have time to enjoy life a bit? Where was my father all this time? Of course, he was in his cave, damn him, damn his darkness and his burrowing like an animal. I was through with him and his stupid behavior. Done.

For the next few days all I could think of were the words "La Mamma morta" from the opera **Andrea Chénier** that I had heard a long time ago and that had struck me with not only with the lyrics but especially with the heart-throbbing music. The funeral was held at the local chapel. There were hardly anybody there except for the priest, Madame Villandry and another neighbor, Madame Fortin. I tried to get my father to come and had enlisted the support of the staff at the nursing home, but he screamed and he fought the four of us and we could not force him to leave his room. All the shades had been pulled and he was living in perpetual darkness, I was told. That's what he wanted. Of course, I could not reason with him and tell him that mother had died and that we were trying to get him to the funeral. That would have been in vain. Once mother was interred at the local cemetery, I went back to the house and tried to straighten things a bit. I collected the necessary papers that seemed important to me. There was a large manila envelope hidden in my mother's bedroom that I grabbed, and without looking inside, I shoved it into the large pocket of my winter jacket. I shut everything off and went to the local realtor and put the house up for sale. Before leaving town, I went to the cemetery and put some flowers on mama's grave. I wanted to do that. It made me feel good that I had been a good child and that mama had been a good mother.

I left town without going back to see my father in the nursing home. What good would it have been? I never saw him again nor received any word from the nursing home probably because I had not left a forwarding address with them. I didn't care. He was probably buried next to my mother and I did not want to know about his passing nor his final resting place. His bones must be rejoicing in the still darkness of the earth.

I went through a brief period of mourning, for my mother, of course, and even for my father with whom I had never been close and who had never ventured to allow me enjoy his Greekness although I had craved for it all my life. I suppose that I mourned for the Greek character in my father and the fact that he had refused to live his ethnic identity. He was no Odysseus no Priam no Greek father for he had no tears, no compunction of having none either.

On February 13, I went to see the opera **Turandot** with Birgit Nilsson and Plácido Domingo in the title roles. It was another of Puccini's masterpiece of music and exotic story. I was looking forward to it and I was indeed enjoying Mister Kapalodous's subscription for the season. I felt blessed with a godfather who had insisted that I go to the opera and enjoy my education in opera. I was fortunate indeed. Learning about cultural events and the culture of music, dance, drama, the stage and its settings, as well as the entire magnificence of international exchanges of singers, actors and musicians were all, tome, and exciting venture into the heart of New York City and it's venues. I relished it and I swam, yes, *j'ai nagé* into its vast treasure of Broadway, its museums, the Met, the parks and even its luxury hotels where people from all over the world came to partake of the treasures to which I had become accustomed. As far as **Turandot** was concerned I enjoyed it but not as much as I had enjoyed **La Bohème.** Probably because it was my very first incursion into opera and into Puccini's world of music. Although I did like Mister Domingo's performance and his voice was superb as far as I was concerned as an amateur.

My next venture in opera was the much heralded offering at the Met on March 3. Bellini's opera was known to offer many challenges and what may be called pitfalls for the singers if they are not prepared for them. At least, that's what I heard in the restaurant where I worked from customers who were opera buffs and could not help themselves from expressing their views on singers and composers and even review critics. The principal roles went to Joan Sutherland as Norma and Carlo Bergonzi as Pollione. The conductor for the evening's performance was Richard Bonynge, well recognized as a knowledgeable musician and capable conductor. It was, I was told, a new production and people were looking forward to it. It was also the debuts of Marilyn Horne as singer and Desmond Heeley as designer. I must say that over the years I have grown to admire the voice and personality of Marilyn Horne. She's a splendid opera star.

I need not go into the details of the story of the Druid goddess and her plight. I'm sure my readers know as much as I know about it. What is truly interesting is the long review written by Winthrop Sargeant in the New York Times. It's entitled NORMA RECONQUERED. The critic begins his review with the past history of the opera **Norma** and its various coloratura sopranos like, Lehman, Ponselle, Cigna, and Milanov branding the Cigna's performance as "a defeat." What truly captured my interest was what he said about Maria Callas' and her voice quality in her 1956 performance at the Met. You might have been wondering when was I going to introduce Maria Callas in my story since the title leads one to believe that it's all about her and her career. Not true. Well, not entirely true. What you will discover is that this is not about her entire career, nor is it about her mother, nor her father, nor her husband, nor he great triumphs, but about her burrowing herself in that Paris apartment, having lost her voice is what she said and her deep desolation and deeper than deep isolation that she created for herself. That will be my story of Callas, the final times, the final moments of her glorious career as a diva. However, this is what Sergeant wrote on wrote on March 4:

"In 1956 Maria Callas entered the arena. Miss Callas may be marked up as a near winner. Her musical style was impeccable, her agility tremendous, her breath control in long vocal lines admirable, and her treatment of ornamentations immaculate. The only thing she failed at was vocal quality. Her voice was already on the decline and had assumed a reedy, nasal sound. Except for this, she was magnificent, and there was the unforgettable Callas stage presence, which did a great deal to enhance the credibility of Bellini's musical drama."

Wow! I said. This is quite an accolade to the great soprano. However, since I did not see nor heard the performance, I could only take the critic's word for his criticism of Callas' vocal quality. I suspect that he might have been right, but I just could not swallow the thing whole. Did Maria Callas' voice begin its decline in and before 1956? I wondered. We shall see, I said. Then he went into his review of the Sutherland performance,

"Last Tuesday night, Joan Sutherland joined this succession of gladiators, in a new production of the opera. Miss Sutherland, as everybody knows, has already been acclaimed a champion at lesser events, and there was much curiosity about what she would do with this role, as well as a fairly settled conviction that she would at least conquer its technical aspects. She is a dramatic coloratura soprano (unlike Beverly Sills, who is a lyric coloratura), and that is the kind of soprano that **Norma** requires---a heavyweight capable not only of singing all of the "fioratura" but also of heaving great quantities of sound across the footlights."

I kept on reading the review with great delight since I had enjoyed what the critic had also enjoyed.

"Miss Sutherland's performance was, as might be expected, a triumph of coloratura singing. Her control of the long lines of "Casa diva" was impressive, and her agility elsewhere was very nearly flawless. There were other elements in her singing that were les pleasing, although quite familiar. Here is a cold coloratura voice, without much emotional coloring, and she has a way of bunching her ornamentations together and hurling them out rapidly. In these matters, Miss Callas was her superior."

Now I see the richness of Maria Callas' dramatic quality and her startling emotional coloring, to which Mr. Sargeant alludes. Maria Callas was and is indeed a superior performer from what I can see. Following this, Mister Sargeant continues to compliment Miss Sutherland's performance while criticizing her diction when he says,

"Then there is Miss Sutherland's peculiar language, which is certainly not Italian though it resembles it here and there as it emerges through her faulty diction. Nevertheless, the vocalization of the role was thrilling. She hit the bull's-eye neatly with all her high notes, and her scale and arpeggio passages were, except for a couple of descending chromatic scales, brilliantly executed."

He then goes on to say that this was a first-class **Norma** and he extols Miss Sutherland's ornamentations. What I liked about this review was not only what he said about Joan Sutherland and Maria Callas, but what he said about Marilyn Horne.

"The Adalgisa of the evening was Marilyn Horne, who was making her Metropolitan début. It was high time this début occurred, for anybody who has been around singers knows that Miss Horne is, and has been for some years, one of the world's most spectacular mezzo-sopranos. From time to time, with her younger and more expressive voice, she even stole the show from Miss Sutherland, and their duets, which they had sung together many times before in other opera houses, were beautifully coordinated—particularly the finest of them, 'Mira, O Norma.'"

I was so pleased with Mister Sargeant's comments on Marilyn Horne since I truly believed that she had a most beautiful range and color for a mezzo-soprano, rich in quality and superb in delivery. I was indeed learning about opera and its singers and now I felt I could give my own comments, if only to myself, about opera.

In all the excitement about opera, I forgot to mention the large manila envelope that I found in my parents' house that was left by my mother for me. I had it in the pocket of my winter jacket and I only found it a few days after the funeral. When I opened it, there were several fifty dollar bills and some stocks and bonds with my name on them. When I got back to New York, I went to my bank and showed them to my investment counselor, Mister Putnam. He told me that those were worth about fifty thousand dollars and that I should keep them as investments. All of that, along with the sale of the house in Maine, I was worth around one hundred an seventy thousand dollars, a small fortune for me, not to mention the savings that I had accumulated. I was now free to travel and to continue my subscription to the Met as well as purchasing theater tickets. I left the hotel and got a small apartment on the seventh floor right on East 67th Street. I kept my job at the restaurant while deciding what I was going to do the rest of my life. Was I going to stay in New York City or was I going to move elsewhere? I would have to think about it since New York, for me, was a great city with great cultural opportunities.

I had been out of touch with Alexander since he had not tried to touch base with me. Strange how some friendships simply seem to evaporate with time and lack of closeness. A new episode was starting in my life as François Basil Spirounias, and I wasn't going to let it slip out of my grasp. I was going to enjoy it and create for myself new windows of opportunities. I was still in the process of learning and accumulating more and more facts, knowledge, and appreciation about music and opera. Mister Kapalodous was right in granting me the power of enjoyment or, at least, making me discover enjoyment in life. Enjoyment was my main goal from now on. Enjoyment of myself as a person, enjoyment of my newly found or rather, renewed spiritual life, enjoyment of little things in life such as, nougats, divine Belgian chocolates, walks in the park in the morning, meeting new people while serving tables at the restaurant, and knowing that I was getting closer and closer to understanding and relishing the experience of Maria Callas as an international diva *hors pair*. Finally, I was reaching the level of my next adventure, that of pursuing my dream as a knight on horseback reaching out to his lady on a pedestal who was put there by her fame and masterful talents as an extraordinary soprano who had initially learned how to sing by the canaries that she had in her youth in Athens. That much I found out and I was going to pursue my study of her life and career if I was to do justice to her great talent as an artist.

14. Dekatessera

Maria Callas, what can be said of her that has not already been said? I don't really know. But, I was going to try and find out as much as possible about her, her life, her career and especially her voice. I got serious about it and I went to several libraries to find whatever materials I could get in order to pursue my quest. The more I read, the more I discovered different facets of her life, first as a teenager with talent, her plump if not obese physical condition, her voice in development, her dramatic flair learned from her mother who was quite the sensuous and explosive woman, and so many other details about the girl who fell into womanhood unbeknownst to her and who was known as Maria Callas. I read books, magazine articles, newspaper articles, reviews, commentaries, and I just could not stop reading whatever was presented to me about Maria Callas. I was voracious as a reader of Maria Callas' fame and eventually her fall. I had read reviews about the decline of her magnificent voice but I did not know how true they were. I had not had the chance to attend any of her previous performances during her glory days. After all, I was from a small village in Maine, I was poor, and I did not know of anyone who could introduce me to opera… until I met Mister Kapalodous. I was so ignorant about the whole of opera that I did not even know the difference between a coloratura soprano and a lyric soprano. I knew very little about music, in general, only what I enjoyed and perceived I knew through concerts and recordings. At Berklee, I studied on the fringes of music and music appreciation, but gained very little from my limited studies. I got to know Ange-Aimée and, later on, Katerina---a bad experience for me---but I got nothing of substance as far as the knowledge and appreciation of music. New York City was the gate of cultural paradise for me. That is why I was serious about plunging into opera, learning all I could about Maria Callas, and eventually traveling to Paris to attempt to meet her, if only I could. It would be terribly difficult, I knew, but I had to try. I insisted on it. Maria Callas, I was told, had burrowed herself in a luxury apartment and very seldom went out. She lived with her poodles, a maid and a servant. She did not even receive her mother who was so mad about it, or her sister, Jackie, who lived in Greece. Cut off. Completely cut off from family, friends and fellow singers, except for a very few intimate friends like Franco Zeffirelli, who soothed her broken pride and her broken voice. I had to try and I would put everything in my pursuit so that I would be able to say, I tried to meet la Callas.

As I have said before, my adventure in Paris and the meeting of Maria Callas was not meant to be a biographical venture nor a critical analysis of her craft and her amazing career. It would be simply my personal experience of gaining some knowledge of this superior talent and getting to a point of perhaps befriending her in some way. How was I to do this since she lived in a fortress shielded from the gaze of outsiders and sheltered by her own distress of loneliness and depression? I was going to attempt to go around her and get to meet people with whom she had contact and whom she trusted to enfold her in their pride of being close to Maria Callas. But how?

Prior to going to Paris, I continued to go to stage performances on Broadway and, of course, attend operas. Between 1970 and 1974, I saw several operas and some Broadway musicals. In January of 1970 I took advantage of the new productions of **Cavalleria Rusticana** and **Pagliacci** usually given at the same time, I was told. I wanted to hear Franco Corelli about whom I kept hearing at the restaurant where I was still working. He sang the part of Turridu in **Cavalleria** with Grace Bumbry as Santuzza. In **Pagliacci** Canio was played by Richard Tucker with his magnificent voice still in perfect pitch. Lucine Amara sang the part of Nedda. I had never heard of her. This was a new experience for me and I truly enjoyed these two operas. I especially enjoyed the set decorations and the vivid colors of it all. When I got the Wall Street Journal the next morning, I hurried to read the review by John J. Conner and I saw that he had really enjoyed the performances and particularly the new productions. He bubbled with joy in his review at their complete success referring to that "fantastically sumptuous mounting" of the duo operas. Here's what he said in part:

"The point is that when the Met is good it can be very very good indeed. The problem is that, considering the huge outlays and seasonal deficits, it is not that good that often. Still, when something as successful as this "Cav" and "Pag" comes along, the inclination, no doubt short-lived, is to shout: Damn the expense, full speed ahead… The hero of the piece is Franco Zeffirelli, the Italian director already represented in the Met repertory with the magnificent production of Verdi's **Falstaff**…The result, from any angle, is one of the most visually exciting and intelligently staged productions on any stage."

Given this part of the review, one recognizes that the critic is enchanted with productions that are well staged even though they cost a lot of money, "Damn, the expense" he says, that coming from a staff member of the Wall Street Journal. When it comes to the singers he said this:

"Richard Tucker, celebrating his 25th year at the Met, is surprisingly enough singing the role of Canio for the first time, and it is one of his better acting high point."

Conner doesn't say too much about Grace Bumbry's performance except to give her high praise for her brilliantly acted and sung entrance scene, nor does he say much about Franco Corelli's performance, and that truly surprised me. I thought that Mr. Corelli's performance was excellent and merited some much merited praise. Oh, well, so much for critics and their reviews. However, I have to add that at the very end of his review John Conner does give this operatic offering a rave final spin when he says, "All in all, the Met has come up with a winner, a super prize for anyone interested in opera, or for that matter, theater." Agreed. Opera is theater at its best, I think. Of course, when it's well performed and well designed and that's when true artists are put to their test and come up stars.

My next night out for entertainment in the great city of New York was a much heralded musical called, **Applause** with Lauren Bacall. I had heard so much about this production that I simply could not afford to ignore this Broadway play. I wondered why Lauren Bacall had been selected for the title role since she is not known for her singing, but I supposed that they offered it to her for her acting skills and renown as a Hollywood actress. As for the singing, I said to myself, they will do something with that and her sultry voice. She can always mimic singing in one way or another. I had seen it done before with actors who had no or hardly any singing voice. After all, actors and actresses are well trained in their profession to take whatever challenge and succeed in doing so.

It was on a cool September evening of 1970, that I walked over to the Palace Theater with theater tickets in my pocket. I was to meet a new friend of mine, Lawrence Cochrane, who happened to be one of my customers at the restaurant. We had talked about the theater and he explained to me the intricacies of getting theater tickets when it happened that the show a smash hit like **Applause**.

"It's practically impossible to get theater tickets when the show gets to be so popular that everyone wants to see it and then the reason behind scarcity of available tickets. You can but some from a scalper, or you can gamble and find someone who knows someone who has a friend who can get you tickets but at a very high price."

"How long do you think **Applause** will last on Broadway, Larry?"

"I don't really know but it's been getting very good reviews. I suppose the name Lauren Bacall attracts patrons. Her photo is already on the cover of some magazines. That helps a lot. Good publicity."

"It opened six months ago and the musical doesn't seem to diminish in popularity. It could go on for months and even years."

"Really?"

"Really, some shows go on for over a thousand performances. I'd be willing to bet that **Applause** will go at least 800 performances. It's that good. I can't imagine the profits such shows bring in. Can you, Larry?

"That's what producers want, especially those who invest in them. They want a good solid return for their money."

"I suppose."

"I just wish I could get my hands on some tickets before the show closes."

"Listen, what if I told you I could get us theater tickets to **Applause**?"

"How? It's impossible, I tell you."

"Let me find out."

Well, I did find out. I got to know a friend who knew a friend who knew somebody unnamed who could get me theater tickets. All I had to do was to keep my mouth shut and pay the price. I did both and got a pair of tickets for the acclaimed performance of **Applause** with Lauren Bacall. It was so nice to be able to afford theater tickets at an inflated price. Money does speak and it does get you theater tickets.

We walked into the theater through the glass doors and handed our tickets to the usher who was standing there looking like an upright, stiff, unsmiling robot dressed in a dark suit, bow tie and starched shirt that seemed to irritate his large neck all the time getting redder and redder. We took our seats and chatted in a low voice for a while until the house lights were dimmed. I looked at Larry and Larry looked at me and we blinked our eyes in consonance. The theater was huge. It had served the vaudeville entertainers well in the past, for if you played at the Palace, you had arrived, they said. But, that was of another era and before my time. I was here at the Palace now to enjoy a musical and get my fill of song and dance as well as a show that was Broadway at its best.

It's the story of Margo Channing and her assistant Eve and the eventual rivalry between and older woman and a young *parvenue* who will do whatever it takes to get ahead in the theater. I knew it was based on the movie **All About Eve** so I had a pretty good idea what the story was all about. I loved the music and the dancing and Lauren Bacall was fantastic in her role, and she sang and danced very well, better than I had expected her to. I especially liked the song, "Fasten Your Seat Belts" by Bacall as Margo who warns her immediate audience as well as the audience in the theater seats to be prepared for a showdown. Overall, Larry and I really enjoyed the musical and we were like the gypsies in the show singing "Applause, Applause." Of course, everyone knows that the show won a Tony Award for best musical of the season and Lauren Bacall won as best actress. Although I loved **Applause** I felt as if I was missing something and that something was opera. I had developed a sense of opera that lingered in me and lodged in my soul. Not that opera was spiritual in the way that transcendental thought and inspiration are inculcated, but there was something spiritual in opera, something that nudged your soul into a higher plane of esthetics and pleasure. I don't know if I could explain it to you but that's the way I felt and that's what opera did for me now that I was fully implanted in opera and its magnificence when it's well delivered by every artist involved with the show, for it was a show indeed, a show that captured my imagination and my deep sense of music.

And so, I went to the Met to see **Tosca** with Renata Tebaldi who, supposedly, was Maria's Callas' arch-rival. There was talk about the tensions drawn between the two of them. I didn't know if it was all trumped up by the press or did it have some merit to it. It was said that Maria Callas once said that in comparison to Renata Tebaldi, her signing was champagne to Tebaldi's common wine. I didn't know if was true or not, but it sounded a bit petty to me. Whatsoever was the case of the talent of either divas, all I knew was that Renata Tebaldi had a great voice and she would make a wonderful Tosca. It was January 10, 1970 at the Met and I had gotten tickets for myself and for Larry since he had become practically my constant companion for theater and opera. We both liked it and it gave me a chance to share my passion with him. Besides, I could afford to buy the tickets and he could not.

The sets were not too good, mediocre by some standards, and the orchestra led by Francesco-Molinari-Pradelli was not always what it should have been, I thought. I even heard someone behind us saying that the music was not reaching any stupefying dynamics. The "Te Deum" procession filtered haphazardly, partly unnoticed, partly out of step and, as someone later said, "sloppy" was the word he used. The second and third acts sets were alright but not spectacular. It was Miss Tebaldi's singing that warranted time and money as an investment on my part. I was delighted to have the chance to hear her marvelous, well-disciplined and nuanced performance. The "Vissi, d'arte" she sang that night was superb and well received. I could easily understand why her fans went everywhere and anywhere to hear her and to see her in whatever opera she undertook. I understand that her musicianship was totally inviolable in her capable hands as an artist with great control of her delivery.

The role of Cavaradossi was interpreted by a tenor I did not know or had seen before, Sándor Kónya. His delivery in both lyric and dramatic aspects was superb, I thought. All in all, the entire performance of the singers was worthwhile and deserved high merit, although some complained about the décor and the settings as being cheap and time worn. Larry did not complain about the opera and he shared his high praise for the performance with me. I didn't know if it merited high praise, but I recognized Larry's ignorance of the details of an opera. He had not been treated to opera for a very long time and I had gotten to a pint where I was getting to be not only the amateur but the connoisseur, I might add.

Finally on April 16 of the same year, I decided to go to the Met for a performance of U.Giordano-Illica's fine opera, **Andrea Chénier**. Ever since I had heard the splendid aria, "La Momma Morta" I had kept in my heart and even my soul the remembrance of the poignant operatic rendition of heartfelt and soul-touching emotions whose music could only have been composed by someone who was an artist at putting together such tender and vibrant music to be sung by a disciplined soprano. I did not know much about the opera **Andrea Chénier** but I wanted to get to know more about it by attending a

Met performance. The main role was sung by Carlo Bergonzi and that of Maddalena by Gabriella Tucci. I was not at all disappointed by the performance that evening and I cherished it for a long time to come. As I walked back to my apartment, I could not help but to call to mind by the strains of "La Momma Morta" the cruel death of my mother. She had not deserved that but that had been her fate as the Greeks would say. True my mother was not one of the greats in Greek history and drama, but I would compare her to the faithful and wise Penelope of the **Odyssey**. Papa would not, but I could. I could compare my mother to Madame Hortense, Zorba's friend in the movie, for my mother also craved for love from a husband who had lost all inclination towards affection. Death is such a cruel companion but it's also a deliverer from pain and disaffection.

About that time as we moved into 1971, I heard about the Master Classes at the Juilliard School of Music and that Maria Callas was scheduled to teach there. How I would have loved to participate in one of her classes but they were restricted to advanced music students from what I could see. To learn from one of the greatest sopranos in the world would be a dream, *un rêve réalisé*, for me. At least, I knew that she was still in voice and that people still wanted to hear her and learn from her although I did not hear too much about her future performances at the Met. Larry came to see me one day and told me that *la Divina*'s career as an opera star was almost over and that her voice was practically gone.

"Where did you get that terrible news, Larry?"

"Well, everyone knows that. You can hear about it in the news media."

"In the news media?"

"Yes. Look for it."

"But where?"

"It's there if you want to find it. They don't want to blast it for fear of hurting her career and especially for fear of slander, but it's there."

"It must be a rumor."

"Rumor or not, she's done."

"Don't say that. She's not done."

"But, my dear François, rumors or not, it's the truth and the truth has a way of turning up want to or not."

I was devastated for I did not want it to end, not the dream of going to one of her operas. She was a mature woman but not an old lady who was done for. It could not be. I just could not convince myself that the news was real and that Maria Callas' career as an opera star was over. It just could not be, I told myself. Her career might be slowing down but she would always remain an artist. An artist of the highest quality. After all, she had totally dedicated her life and even her soul to her art. Totally. *Totalement et absolument*. Why, to some, she was Callas *assoluta*. No one else could and would ever replace her. Her dramatic skills, her intense devotion to music, her unbelievable range of voice, and her absolutely perfect pitch at the height of her brilliant career were unbelievable and irreproachable, if not absolutely unattainable by any other operatic artist. I knew that and I totally believed in it. Her dynamism and her dedication to her art had been the hallmark of her career. So, how could she just fade away? No, it could not be. However, I had to start believing the news when I kept hearing that she was thinking of retiring and leaving New York for good. Why, she had been born there and had been an American citizen all her life. I knew that she was Greek through and through and a proclaimed citizen of Athens, the cultural mother of people like Miss Callas. Then there was the question of the Onassis affair.

The Aristotle Onassis affair was like a wart on Callas' life, an ugly, pernicious, and unfavorable wart. How could she fall for such a man? Yes, he was very rich and very jealous of beautiful women especially beautiful and famous women. I read that he wanted them like a man who wants to collect things, beautiful illustrious and hard-to-get things. But, I'm sure he thought he could get anything he wanted since he had money, a yacht, plenty of cargo ships, a reputation as a wheeler-dealer, and, above all, a manipulator extraordinaire. I thought he was a gnome, a dwarf, a fat little man who exploited others and got what he wanted with money. Yes, money talks and it talks very loudly when applied at the right time and in the right places on the right people. Yes, the politics of money for those who have too much and for those who grab it with their greedy hands. I'll have to talk about this later on because right now I really don't have the heart and the guts to do it. You could say I'm disgusted, *dégoûté, absolument dégoûté…point final.*

The next bit of news that I got was that Maria Callas had been convinced by her friend the acclaimed tenor, Giuseppe di Stefano, to make a comeback and to do it with him. He would organize things and make sure that they would have a welcoming audience wherever the concerts would be held. Apparently she believed in his enthusiasm and in her own self-confidence only because she wanted to it and prove to herself and to people out there that Maria Callas still had the voice. After all, her voice was what kept her alive and kept her from giving up on herself. My God, what would happen if she ever lost her voice completely, *totalement perdue, absolument égarée, serait-elle*. God gives and God takes away, but Oh, God, never ever leave me without a voice for singing, she would say, I'm sure. For Maria Callas as an Orthodox Christian believed strongly in God and the Virgin Mary and sought their intercession. We are told that before a performance she would sign herself and when she was at La Scala performing, she would go to the Duomo of Milan and kneel before the statue of the Virgin to pray. Her pride, her sense of dignity, and her courageous self-confidence would fritter away without the power of the voice. A singer without a voice is an artist without a soul. She becomes dull, mortified, and filled with *ennui*. There goes that cruel word again. Losing one's gift of a singing voice is disastrous and totally unthinkable to an opera star. *On ne peut penser à ça car ça nous rendrait absolument fou. Impensable, inacceptable, impardonable même.* Yes, nuts. Unthinkable, unacceptable and even unpardonable.

The series of farewell concerts began in Hamburg on October 25, 1973 and ended with the Sapporo concert, November 11, 1974, six months before I first arrived in Paris. She and di Stefano did come to the States but I missed the concert in Boston at Symphony Hall on February 27, 1974. I don't know why I missed it but I did. I had learned about it too late to get tickets. I heard that Maria Callas did not like the series to be called the Farewell Concerts and I suppose she did not agree that it was veritably her farewell to singing. However that may be, I read that the concerts were mildly successful to say the least. Maria Callas thought it was a fiasco. The concerts were considered to be a personal triumph but an artistic failure for the once glorified Divina. The audience loved Maria Callas and her energetic comeback but the critics and their reviews did not. They expected Maria to sing as she had always sung, that is, in her very best form, but she had aged and her voice had declined. An artist's voice like Maria Callas' cannot go through the strain and wearing our process of the years without some damage. The tension builds and then the vocal chords stiffen and lose their suppleness and vigor they once had. The human voice is not something indestructible; it's an instrument and instruments wear out.

Now comes the total hibernation of a fallen Divina in her plush apartment in Paris. She was not ever to come out of it. Unlike the animals that go through a natural process of hibernation in the wintertime, Maria Callas would not emerge from her frozen state. She had lost her voice, she said, and lost her friend/lover, if ever he was one. She was frozen emotionally, physically, and especially artistically as a singer. *Elle était transie par la froideur de sa passion inerte*, totally frozen in her inertia. This is the stage of her life that fascinates and disturbs me and I wanted, from the start, to explore this stage in Maria Callas' life. Could I do it or rather would I be able to penetrate the hardened core of the Divina's somber life now that she was a recluse and a fragile creature in her emotional and physical depression. I'd have to find a way somehow.

I planned to go to Paris when the time was ripe for me and I had accumulated sufficient funds. There was an interlude between 1972 and 1974 when I decided to get better acquainted with Maria Callas' singing and her celebrated performances. I knew that I couldn't do it live for the height of her performances had occurred in the 1950's and 1960's. So, it had to be done with recordings. I bought the one done in Mexico City in 1951. It was **Aida** with Maria Callas, and Mario Del Monaco with Oliviero de Fabritiis as conductor. Maria's performances in Mexico had been cheered and much appreciated. Then I purchased another **Aida** this time with Callas, Richard Tucker, and Tito Gobbi with Tullio Serafin as conductor, just to compare each version to one another. Then I bought **Lucia di Lammermoor** with Maria Callas, Giuseppe di Stefano, Tito Gobbi with Tullio Serafin as conductor, recorded in 1954. I isolated myself for an entire week that I had taken as my vacation time, and listened exclusively to opera. I had become an opera freak of sorts and I marveled in it. I did not shave, I took very little food, and I slept very well at night. Rising in the morning, I had breakfast and then I went straight to my operas and listened very attentively to Maria Callas, the greatest voice in the world as far as I was concerned, and for that matter, for so many hundreds of thousands of people across the world, I'm sure. It was opera heaven for me. I had learned so much beforehand either in reading and going to live performances at the Met that I felt comfortable in being my own judge of Maria Callas and opera. It was like graduate school in Maria Callas' performances for me. *J'allais approfondir mes connaissances de Maria Callas et sa* merveilleuse *voix, cette divine voix.* Yes, I was going to venture deep into my knowledge of Maria Callas' marvelous and divine voice.

First, I listened to the recording of the 1951 Mexico performance of **Aida**. The recording was live and overall I found the quality to be moderate to inferior. I could hear voices in the background and the orchestra performance was not of deep, rich and melodious sounds, as far as I was concerned. The opera **Aida** is supposed to be bold, highly forceful, and royal in scope. The only real thing I truly loved about this rendition was Maria Callas and her tremendous capacity to deliver a dramatic performance. Aida's strong feelings for her father and her country are sincere and convincing. I could feel the pain and anguish in Callas' delivery as she sang *O patria mia* and the voice control, her modulations were superb. Her high notes reverberated with passion and depth and they were clear and glorious. That's the only way I can express it. The highlight of the opera, for me, was when Callas sang *O patria mia, non ti vedrò...mai piu*. The repetition of the last two words, *mai piu*, nevermore, had so much feeling in it, conveyed so much sorrow that I felt it deep inside me. Her dramatic ability and her talent to translate strong feelings through the channel of her voice, is absolutely astounding. I am told that the remarkable thing about this performance is that she was able to reach a high flat "E" in the Triumphal Scene which is incredible. Nobody or very few can do that. Now I know why people say that she's sublime and her voice is superior to many, many others. She's the Divina. I realize that she loved the audiences in Mexico City and that she was possibly very close to the very height of her operatic capabilities, but I would have loved to hear her sing at the Met, or possibly at the Opéra de Paris or even at La Scala. Be it as it may, I am privileged to be able to hear some of her recorded performances that will live on for a very long time, I'm sure. That's why after listening to the Mexico City performance I wanted to listen to the same opera but with a different conductor, the much revered Tullio Serafin, and with a different tenor voice, that of Richard Tucker as Radamès. There exits many other recordings of the same opera, but I chose this one. This one was done in 1955 when I knew so very little, if none, of opera and Maria Callas. I was on my way to become somewhat of a knowledgeable judge of opera and of Maria Callas if I pursued my path as a veritable amateur as Mister Kapalodous had instructed me. I wasn't perfect in my attempts to get to know opera fully and masterfully like opera critics do, but I was sincere and I loved it the more I got into it. Opera was my way of expressing my love of music and my interest in drama. Some people do not like it, but I do and I intended to pursue this marvelous adventure of mine, quite possibly the pilgrimage of my soul into the transcendental vistas of music and voice. I'm sure that some people would think that I was mad for linking the two, opera and pilgrimage, but I was convinced that I was on the right path to my plenitude as a human being. Furthermore, all of this was perfectly linked to my liberal arts past and my sense of creativity as well as my conviction that music is the voice of the spheres and eternal presence of the Great Creator. Good music, excellent music, superior music stemming from the creative soul of a human being has to be part of the process of divine creation. I can't imagine the Creator creating man and woman without the intrinsic quality and ability to make music. Some are very good at learning how to play an instrument, mastering the strings of a violin or the keys of a piano, but the very best instrument is the human voice, in my book. Of course, there are those endowed with excellent to superior vocal chords, and when the voice is trained and disciplined with the right power to exercise the disciplines of mastery and control, then the voice can rise to very high notes or in the case of baritones and especially basses, down to splendid notes that seem to reach the very resounding bottom of the scale. I imagine things and very often they turn out to be right. Think what you think, and I'll think of what I want to think. I call it freedom of right thinking.

First of all, **Aida** in the capable hands of Serafin as conductor, becomes a masterful orchestration that is delivered by talented musicians who know how to be led by an artist. To me, the sounds I heard and felt so deeply in my guts as a listener were sounds of melody intertwined with a colossal sensuous vibration and deep sense of genuine artistry as Verdi would have wanted them to be. Serafin thus interpreted the composer's art and music colossally true. I could imagine Verdi holding Serafin's baton and leading the orchestra himself. I imagine things, you see. The second time around, I found the aria, *Ritorna vincitor*! by Callas to be captivating. I had not noticed this part the first time I listened to **Aida** but now I listened carefully to the soprano's delivery of touching words ensconced in the melody especially, *I sacri nomi di padre, d'amante* followed later on by, *Numi, pietà, del mio soffrir*! when I realized the complicity of high notes with the tenderness of softer ones all in the voice control as exercised by Callas. The plaintive quality was certainly there and I paid attention to the emotional rendition of *del mio soffrir*. That's what I realized throughout this performance, the voice control and the powerful high notes when exacted by the composer. And again, her *O patria mia* with the ending of *mai più* was delicate and yet forceful in tone all contained within the rendition of words and music by the soprano who, I am sure, had practiced her part for long hours. That's one thing I realized, opera singers, the good ones, the superb singers and disciplined ones must spend hours and hours at rehearsals in order to perfect their craft and the opera they're going to perform. Endless hours, endless effort with much patience and determination. Of course, talent has a lot to do with it, I'm sure. I knew that I would have to listen to more of Callas' performances such as **Norma, Lucia de Lammermoor**, and **La Traviata** among the many. However, I was busy working and trying to earn money for the Paris trip that I had proposed for myself. In order to fill in the gaps, so to speak, and profit from some of the highlights of Maria Callas' career of singing, I decided to listen to some of the very well-known aria's that she sang and remain to this day, favorites of the amateurs like me. First, there is *Vissi d'arte* from **Tosca** that's a standard for most sopranos and Maria Callas sings it so well. Then there's *La Mamma morta* from **Andrea Chénier** that I've mentioned before. It's really one of my favorites as sung by Callas. The high notes are superb. Maria Callas sings Bellini and Rossini and I'm thinking now of composers like them and how much talent they had and how great their music is. I tell myself that such talent is beyond description and one could never truly assess their great gift to the music world. I'm sure that Maria Callas appreciated their talent and their compositions and she rendered them with style and a musicality they would have appreciated as composers. I also listened to excerpts from **Rigoletto**, **La Traviata** and **Manon Lescaut**. After a while my ears were hearing sounds I had never heard before and I was enjoying them because Maria Callas was singing them with superb talent and mastery of her art.

The excerpt that I truly enjoyed as Myerbeer's masterpiece aria O*mbra leggera,* The Shadow Song, as sung by Dinorah in the so-called mad scene when she sings a duet with herself actually her shadow. Myerbeer injects drama and playful wit in this opera and I especially like Maria Callas' voice play with the flute when she mimics the flute and her voice is in such harmony with the musical instrument she hears and what the composer has written down that I marveled at such musical consonance. Perfect, I said and meant it. I read somewhere that a famous soprano named Adelina Patti considered the role of Dinorah as one of her favorites. She was a highly acclaimed 19th-century opera singer owing to the purity and beauty of her lyrical voice. Verdi himself described her as being perhaps the finest singer who had ever lived. I would say that Maria Callas could be compared to her for she faced the same challenges of the difficult aria *Ombra leggera* and conquered them with her dramatic agility, *drammatico agili* and her inimitable voice, .

In **Turandot** Act II, Maria Callas reaches the high notes of the aria *In questa reggia* and ends it with a powerful thrust of high notes that culminates the aria with dramatic force and musical vigor. I truly liked this one. Puccini's opera **Turandot** was well served by her ability to interpret an operatic role like this one, another demanding aria. I then listened to some French operas where Maria handled the arias superbly such as **Carmen** and the Habanera song by Bizet and conducted by Georges Prêtre. The swirl of the music and the lush tones of Maria's delivery had me in a kind of a tizzy. Saint-Saëns opera **Samson et Dalila** offered Maria yet another role and an opportunity to sing the aria *Mon coeur s'ouvre à ta voix* that resonates with sensuousness and dramatic pleading. Of course, I listened to Charles Gounod and Jules Massenet and found their music charming. I found Bellini and Maria's rendition of the often heard and very popular *Casta diva* from the opera **Norma** in the title role to be just captivating. Of course, I'm not an expert on analyzing arias and their musicality but I know what I like and what I don't like. I really like *Casta diva* . I also listened to Donizetti's aria *Regnava nel silenzio* and told myself that one day I would have to listen to the complete opera, **Lucia de Lammermoor**. So much to learn and so much to absorb in a being limited by his ability to do so as I was, and I could not do it. I would have loved to be able to have the talent that Maria Callas had with her voice and her incredible ability to learn the lyrics and the music of any given opera. I found her Italian to be perfect but what do I really know about the Italian language. Someday, perhaps. One thing I know is that I have to listen to the complete **Norma** since it's one that Marias Callas favored and performed on the stage several times. I believe as she sang once, twice and several other times after that, she gradually perfected the role and her delivery, not that the initial performance wasn't good, but there are certainly shades of differences in each performance. I'm sure that Mr. Kapalodous would agree with me.

After a while, I came to the realization that I could not do justice to Maria Callas' singing career, to her voice, to her many performances throughout the world since there were so many people who had either seen or listened to her operatic performances and so many critics who had done reviews of her work besides the authors who had written books and books about her. That would continue for years to come, I knew that. I did not want to listen endlessly to operas even though I recognized that Maria Callas had sung so many in her short life. All I knew was that I could simply enjoy Maria Callas' voice and her work in opera as an amateur and as one who could certainly progress in the path of his pilgrimage toward knowledge and enjoyment of her role as an amazing dramatic performer in opera. I would learn whatever I could about her and her voice and I would then analyze her style and her delivery the best I knew how. I did not need critics or world-renown disclaimers who had undertaken the role of professional know-it-all about Maria Callas' life and career as a singer. I certainly could learn from them as much as I wanted to but I did not absolutely need their opinions. Facts and historical details, yes, but not opinions that can maneuver or even distort the true judgment of any art form and its performers. Twisted opinions can only curtail the full understanding of opera and its delivery by a given artist. I would not judge and I would not base any judgment on someone else's opinions. They had a right to their opinions and a right to say whatever they wanted to, but I also had a right to my own opinion and my own enjoyment of opera. I discovered along the way that there were some who liked to demolish or discredit any performer who had reached fame and fortune. I know of one who did just that for Maria Callas but that comes much later in my pursuit of opera and Maria Callas, and I'm not ready to disclose that at this point in time and at this point in my novel. It's the fashion of contradicting what has been hailed as nigh perfection that other people see and hear, and is panned by those who disagree or wish to proclaim irreverence for the reverence attained in any career or facet of entertainment. I know that some people do not like the term entertainment when used with opera, but that's what it is in my book, good, solid entertainment, what one enjoys and goes to see and listen to any given performance. Opera is entertainment for those who like to be entertained and brought to the magic of a performance on stage live or recorded. It is another world, another sphere of the "splendor in the grass" as Wordsworth so aptly put it although he was not talking of opera. Imagination and creativity play such an important role in all of our lives that we must own up to them and be ready to accept them within the confines of human values and human endowments given to us by the Creator. That's how I look at it and I owe it to my liberal arts education for I will ever proclaim its value in my life. It's nice to be trained for a job but it's even nicer to be educated for education is a formation of the mind and soul and it teaches us to respect the power of independent thinking as the Greeks saw it and the power of the soul to engender spiritual journeys often called soul-searching. Transcendental thinking is so often ignored nowadays that it has become passé and seemingly antiquated, but I know in my own mind and in my own soul that it is ever present and forcefully empowering. I suppose that's the Greek in me and I'm proud of it.

15. Dekapente

Paris, the eternal city of life and the pursuit of pleasure and artistic wonderment, Paris, the artist's haven and the center of creativity where one can take its mud and turn it into gold, as Baudelaire once said, "*tu m'as donné ta boue et j'en ai fait de l'or.*" Paris where rich tapestries and vibrant paintings are kept in museums along with the memories of fallen artists and divas, and so Paris remains Paris throughout the ages. For a fallen Divina like Maria Callas, Paris becomes a refuge and a place where one's home has become a museum of personal treasures and accumulated things. Whatever money could buy at what pulsations of the heart, the Divina had at her disposition. But, things and museum treasures do not bring happiness in spite of their value. Love, friendship, emotional attachments, and reciprocal affection are what make the heart and soul function as they should. Without these balms of lasting healing, the heart and soul cannot absorb the miseries of life. And, without the spiritual regenerative balm of the soul, the soul cannot remain vibrant and attentive to its genuine needs. Inertia and stiffness of the entire being cannot nurture life; it can only breed survival. That was the case of Maria Callas in Paris in the last few years in Paris.

I felt stronger about all of this ever since I had been to the monastery for my retreat where I had done my own soul-searching. I recognized that my calling was not in the monastery but in the pursuit of music. Music can lead one to paths of glorious épanouissement as the French say, an opening up and a blossoming forth. My mind and my soul had been closed for so long that I kept running after what I did not know was my calling and my deep inner *penchant*, my leanings. I had rejected my inner probing that, although it kept telling me that I belonged on a certain path in life, it was kept at bay by my refusal to know myself and my inner truth, this Socratic truth. I had been waylaid by my struggle with my father and his ever daunted refusal to accept me as I was. He wanted me to be what I was not and could never be. I had to be liberated from his closed mind and his abject prejudices. I tried to somehow adapt to the father-son relationship that was given me, but I could not tolerate it, so I rebelled in my own heart and soul. It was an all out rebellion for I did not want to create and violence. Besides, I saw my mother trying to appease me while defending my right to be who I was and at the same time deflecting the many barbs of her husband. She was such an innocent flower that with time she wilted away. My father, well my father became the squirming being with a worm inside him that compelled him into darkness and total unawareness of soul. When I saw him for the last time, I realized that his soul had shrunken to a mere reflection of the spirit of life that keeps all of us from being reduced to matter, and I felt pity for him. I told myself that his life had been a downward spiral and that he wasn't at all my father but only my progenitor. *Un père manqué*. Failed.

I left New York for Paris in May 1975 with enough money in my pocket to be able to live, if not comfortably, at least not in need. Besides, I still had some of my investments given to me by my mother, dear soul. I told myself that I would live frugally and I was used to that. I got my passport and contacted a friend of Larry's whose name was Marcel Lavertu and who had lived in Paris for thirty years. He was a Québécois transplanted in Paris. He would be my source of information and contact resource. I was ready to begin my pilgrimage to my ancestors' country and to seek comfort in the knowledge that I was doing what my heart wanted me to do and had been doing so for a very long time. It would be a pilgrimage also since my soul would also been involved with seeking out a poor soul to try and help her out of her pain and distress. I knew that it would not be easy and chances were that I might not even be able to see her face to face and convince her to accept my aide. Would she or would she not? I was taking a chance, a very big one. Whatever happened, I told myself that, at least, I would try. It would not only be my pilgrimage of culture and soul searching but also a pilgrimage to my mother country as far as my native culture and language were concerned. I wondered if I would fit in and thought of the joy of returning home, *chez nous*, as we used to say. I had traced my genealogy on my mother's side back to Bouctouche in Nova Scotia and way back to France to find out that my ancestors had emigrated to Canada in 1687 from the harbor of Larochelle. They were farmers and owned a lot of land that they cultivated. Ultimately, their children's children became part of the Great Expulsion of 1775 and had been forcibly gathered at Grand Pré by the British troops and shipped away and scattered as far south as the Carolinas. Eventually some of them returned to Nova Scotia and remained there. My immediate ancestors moved to New Brunswick to find work and to prosper and dwell in peace. My maternal grandfather then moved to Maine and got married to Anne Valois and they had a rather large family of twelve children of which was my mother, Valéda Louise Arcand. I knew I had a rich history background but I had never traced it back to France until I recognized that it would be interesting for me to do so if I happened to go to France.

I met Marcel Lavertu at the train station and we began a friendship that was to last for several years. He was older than me but young at heart and mind. I got to know his creative soul and his deep fascination with music and opera. He was so creative that he always had a new idea on his mind even before he had expressed the one he had already formulated. He showed me around Paris not starting with the familiar engineering icon of the Eiffel Tower but with the Louvre. We spent days at that vast museum exploring artists and their marvelous canvasses. I especially liked David and Ingres simply because I marveled their sense of realism and details. How anyone could capture the finest of details on canvas was beyond my imagination. I was captivated by the Greek statues beginning with the Winged Victory of Samothrace at the very entrance of the Daru staircase at the Louvre. Marcel was more into Egyptian art and so we strolled along the many rooms and he taught me how to enjoy and analyze artistic painting. Of course, we enjoyed the many cafés that Paris had to offer and I sought meals that I could afford by going to the outskirts of the principal avenues and locating menus that were posted with prices outside the restaurants. At the insistence of Marcel, I went to the Cité Internationale Universitaire de Paris located on la rue Jourdain in order to find a room for myself. Once there, I decided to go to the Fondation Hellénique, the Greek pavilion. I did that because of my family name, Spirounias and because I did not want to cast aside my true identity as the son of a Greek man who had emigrated to the States and had somehow rejected his cultural identity. I knew that I was also in France to look into my French genealogy but that could wait. First and foremost, I wanted to be able to get closer to Maria Callas and possibly get to meet her in spite of the declared impossibilities. In any case, Maria Callas was not in Paris; she was on her farewell tours.

I visited Notre-Dame de Paris Cathedral because I had studied gothic architecture and wanted to explore with my own eyes this tremendously popular structure in the heart of la Cité. I was struck profoundly by its large stained glass windows from where emanated streams of colored light if you happen to be facing either one. Of course, the bright sun has to be out illuminating the windows and that's why the glaziers made them, just like the famous blue of the Chartres windows. I positioned myself directly in front of the one on the right, not too close and not too far, avoiding the stream of visitors going through the ambulatory and I stayed there mesmerized by such masterpieces of glass and color. I did the same thing for the one on the left. I felt transformed and elevated beyond my physical self into a total consciousness of the art and the magnificence of the interplay of light and color. People stared at me and my seemingly inertia and I did not care. I was enveloped not by inertia but by some kind of static metamorphosis of mind and soul. I guess I stayed there like that for at least an hour. The following Sunday late afternoon, I went back to Notre-Dame to listen to a free organ concert given by a well-known organist and I don't remember his name, but he played very well. The cathedral was filled with people everywhere, it seemed, even those sitting on the floor up to the level leading to the main altar. Again, I was totally absorbed by the artistry of the organist and the captivating ambiance of the Gothic interior. I was truly on my pilgrimage in the heart of Paris where the new and the old traversed one another. I wanted to take in so many different areas and varied offerings that Paris had in store for me. I could not absorb everything and I knew that all too well. Paris has to be absorbed in many gulps and in many instances. It cannot be absorbed by simply one gulp of tourism as so many people do. How many visitors proclaimed that they have seen Paris and that once is enough? It cannot be. Paris is Paris and the more you frequent her [the French feminize her] the more you find that you have missed so much or that you need to keep discovering more of her. The Eternal Paris, the Alluring Paris, the Paris of the deep soul, Paris with all its *bêtises* and all its artistic achievements, Paris and its unending paths to glory and fame, also, Paris *l'éternelle vacherie de sa poésie inédite*, yes the eternal bitchiness of its unsaid, unpublished poetry. *Paris je t'aime et je te hais.* I love you and I hate you, said my French teacher in college one day. Paris, for me, was a never ending labyrinthine puzzle and a mystifying presence in a world filled with creative souls at times lost at sea, a sea of churning waters and tempestuous skies ready to strike at your most creative moment in life. *C'est pour cela, Paris, je t'aime et je te hais. Tu es indéchiffrable*, says the Baudelairian man. *Tu m'as donné ta boue et j'en ai fait de l'or*, yes, because I could take your shit and make it out to be gloriously bright through the power of the flaming word, *la parole enflammée.*

I met this man, an older gentleman, at the Cité Internationale who came from Athens and who had settled in Paris for a few months. His name was Socrates Moustaka and he was there to do some research on the contributions of Greece to French letters, namely its drama and philosophy. He was a very interesting person with a particularly delightful lilt in his voice. He knew Maria Callas' parents and had a profound respect for Maria's father, the pharmacist, since he had worked with him in Greece until Maria's father moved to New York. He also knew of Maria the operatic singer with the marvelous soprano voice, he said. I asked him if he had tried to visit her, and he told me that this was an impossible task since she was well protected from the public. That she had become a recluse ever since Onassis had rejected her for the President's widow, the famous Jackie Kennedy. It had been in all of the newspapers, he said. However, he did know a friend of Maria Callas, his name, Roire. Mister Roire really knew opera for he had devoted practically his entire life to opera. Even as a young teen, he went to the opera with his mother and she explained to him the movements of the orchestras, the distribution of operatic roles, the highlights of each opera, the superb qualities of the voices heard, and the richness of tones and renditions of lyrics. She even outlined to him the dramatic quality of each opera singer, especially when it went from lyric to a more dramatic performance ass in the case of Maria Callas: the sopranos, the mezzo sopranos, the altos, the contraltos, the tenors, the basses, and the many ranges of the singing voice. The mother had always desired to become an operatic singer but her father had adamantly refused sending her to music school for he hated opera did not think that an operatic career was worthwhile. She took refuge in music in spite of the father's contempt for music, opera and classical. He loved jazz and show tunes but never did try to appreciate what his daughter called good music.

Now I'm taking over the story. It's my turn, after all I'm the designated narrator.

Well, Mister Roire had gotten to know more and more about Maria Callas since he bought every recording she had ever made and went to whatever opera she happened to sing in and wherever he could afford to go and see her live. He had received lots of money from his grandmother's estate when she died and he had been able to afford the luxury of opera going, as he called it. "I could write a book about it," he told François. And François could not be more delighted in meeting this friend and getting to know him in many ways, especially about opera. François could not believe how much he had learned about opera on his own and especially with friends with whom he had been able to connect. It was far from what he had ever expected in life, the life of a very simple background in a small and out-of-the-way place in rural Maine. What he could not believe was that in spite of his father's abrasive and beleaguered attitude toward François the son and François the humanities educated young man, he, François Basil Spirounias had blossomed into a sophisticated amateur of opera. Now that he was living in Paris and experiencing the life of a connaisseur of Parisian life and the lilt of meeting people who knew people who met people who had important connections, he was getting ready to move into Callas's life in her apartment on Avenue Georges Mandel. How would he accomplish that? Well, he would try to make some kind of contact with someone who was either close to the Divina herself or, at least living very close to her. But how? He would leave that to good fortune, he told himself. He was a great believer in serendipity and fully aware of its mark on all who believe in chance. *La chance de rencontrer Maria Callas, la chance qu'elle soit ouverte à ses avances amicales, la chance qu'elle partage un peu de sa vie et sa voix, et la chance qu'elle puisse dévoiler quelques faits de sa vie en tant que la Divina.* Yes, the chance of meeting Maria Callas, the chance of her being open to his friendly overtures, the chance of her sharing a bit of her life and her voice, and the chance of her revealing a few facts about her life as the Divina. It all sounded marvelously possible through the prism of the dreamer that he had always been. Dreamers take chances as they come, he told himself over and over again.

16. Dekaeksi

It so happened that on a Wednesday morning when François decided to go to the market to get some grocery items, cheese, jam and fresh fruits, he happened to go to the La Grande Épicerie in the Latin Quarter where he occasionally went to find what he wanted. He loved the smell of fresh cheeses in their large showcase, the stacks of fruits, oranges, apples, Anjou pears, big fat grapes, the kind he liked, the many rows of jams and jellies from which he had a hard time to choose and so many other delicacies for his palate. As he was walking through the aisles he met this old couple who was trying to decide which cut of meat they were going to buy. The man wanted the pork loin while the woman wanted the choicest portion of beef. They finally settled on the *poulet* for they, at last, had decided on a *coq au vin* since they much preferred the chicken to anything else, they told François as he stood next to them eyeing some chicken livers.

"*Excusez-nous, cher Monsieur, de partager nos petites inconvéniences avec vous sans vouloir le faire.*"[Excuse me for partaking of your little inconveniences without wanting to].

"*Ne vous en faites pas, je vous en prie.*"[Don't worry, please].

"Aren't you an American? I can detect your accent," said the man to François.

"Why, yes, I am. Don't I speak well enough to go unrecognized as an American?"

"Yes, but I can detect some form of accent in your speech, Monsieur."

"Well, you must detect my Acadian accent."

"*Ah oui, les Acadiens du Canada.*"

"But they also live in the Unites States and my maternal ancestors were Acadian."

"*Il est de souche française, Belle Amie,*"[His roots are French] he told his wife. Permit to introduce ourselves to you, Monsieur, my name is Olivier DesGrandforts and this is my wife, Alexandriana Poteau DesGrandforts."

"I'm very glad to meet you."

"Do you live here in Paris?"

"Yes, I've been living here since July of last year."

"Do you live far from here?

"A bit far. I live at the Fondation Hellénique in the Cité Internationale. I only wish I could find myself some more suitable lodging especially in the area of l'Arche de Triomphe."

"Why, we don't live too far from there. We are concierges, a concierge couple who takes care of the building for the owner. We are *concierges honorifiques.* That's what the owner calls us. We don't pay rent and we also render some services to a few apartment holders such as Madame Callas."

"The Madame Maria Callas?"

"*Mais, oui,*" responded Belle Amie.

"Oh....."

"Belle Amie is my wife of forty-seven years and I call her Belle Amie for that's my nickname for her. She is still beautiful just as the day I first met her."

"*Olivier, tu n'as pas besoin de lui dire cela* ."]You don't need to tell him that].

"I'm so very proud to have met a true Parisian couple like you. You sound so nice and so kind for you take the time to talk to a complete stranger like me."

"Not at all, Monsieur. We are a lonely couple who live alone with our cat, Misette, and we crave for company especially for conversation. We talk to each other all day long, Belle Amie et moi."

"You don't have any children?"

"*Non.* We were not blessed with children. We lost one during the war."

"Oh, that's too bad."

"Let's not talk here like strangers in a grocery store. Although we live in a small apartment, *au sous sol*, it's quite comfortable and we can receive somebody now and then if we have the good fortune of meeting someone who wants to share our *petit confort*. Would you care to come over someday? My wife makes a very good, no an excellent, *coq au vin*."

François looked at the wife and she smiled at him.

"Why, I'd be delighted."

The three of them went to the cashier and picked up their purchases and were ready to go when François offered them to carry their two filets. At first, they refused, but as François insisted, they both sighed a sigh of relief and surrendered their purchases. They then took the métro and went as far as La Porte Trocadero where they got off to reach their destination, Avenue Georges Mandel, au 16me arrondissement. They both insisted that François accompany them to their apartment for an afternoon coffee. At first, he declined but afterwards he accepted their invitation for he didn't care to spend another afternoon at la Fondation Hellénique alone. He had not seen Marcel Lavertu for weeks and was quite dismayed at his friend's absence for he had wanted to keep a close contact with him. François felt lonely and without friendly presence in his life. Besides, he wanted to move on in his project of getting to meet Maria Callas somehow. Perhaps the encounter with the DesGrandforts would give him the opportunity to open a breach in the hard wall of silence and aloofness that separated the Divina and people that she did not wish to meet. It was said that she had completely cordoned herself from almost everyone except a very few close friends and, of course, her maid and her butler. How was he going to cut that cordon and introduce himself into Callas' Parisian life, he asked himself. But, for now he was going to accept the offer of a possible connection to her and, of course, the company of two dear and sweet people. Olivier and Belle Amie were going to enliven his life right now and at the same time fray a path to the Divina who had shut herself up in an apartment on l'Avenue Georges Mandel. It was like living in a tomb, he thought to himself. She had lost her voice and especially her *raison de vivre*. What is life without a reason to live; what is life without the passion for art being extinguished slowly, ever slowly by *un coeur assombri par la misère du rejet et d'un amour totalement froissé.* Yes, what was life without a heart that was being darkened by the misery of rejection and a great lack of shared love, he kept thinking over and over again. That brought him back to his father and his terrible scorn of art and the great lack of compassion of a husband and father for his wife and child. That would never leave him, that would ever be part of his life and his memories. He had dared to step beyond the boundaries of the small rural village and beyond the smallness of crushing feelings that left indelible marks on the soul. François stopped himself from reminiscing about such thoughts and events and came back to the reality of finding himself and his quest for Callas that would lead him to the grail of the mystical and idealistic desire for art accomplished with the artistic phenomenon that was the sublime voice of "La Divina."

As the three of them stepped out of the métro and headed for the Avenue Georges Mandel where the couple lived followed by François who carried the two filets and his own to a new adventure for him. He was thrilled and could not wait to step into the fortress that was 36, avenue Georges Mandel, and this huge apartment building that exemplified for him the luxury of living. As the Olivier unlocked the huge baroque door and stepped into the large hallway, François could not help to notice the stairway and to the left a half-lift as Olivier called it, where one could view the magnificence of the building going up, as he explained. Olivier showed François a small stairway leading to the *sous sol* where they lived. The three of them went downstairs and Olivier hastened to unlock the door to their small apartment and ushered in his wife and François.

'Pardonnez donc l'apparence de notre petit apartement, Monsieur, car je n'ai pas pu faire le ménage ce matin. Nous étions un peu pressés."[Please forgive the appearance of our little apartment for I did not do the cleaning this morning. We were somewhat in a hurry].

"Oh, don't worry about the look the apartment, Madame DesGrandforts. *Ne vous en faites pas.*"

"I'm sure that Monsieur does not look at the life we live but at the place where he is greatly welcomed."

"Please, do stop calling me Monsieur. My name is François."

And the lady responded," *Oui, Monsieur François.*"

"No, François...*François tout court.*"

The three of them began to laugh out loud.

"So, it's Olivier, Belle Amie and François," said Olivier with an amusing grin on his face.

Madame DesGrandforts started to set the little table in the middle of the kitchen since they had no dining room, only one bedroom, a kind of a den with a sleeping sofa and two chairs and the kitchen. They had lived that way for seventeen years, they told their guest. They had met many people who came and went from the luxury apartment building. They acted as part-time concierges since there were people who took care of security and they were reliable. No one entered into the building without their permission and authority given to them by the *gérant* of the building. They told François that the most remarkable person they had met in the building was Maria Callas who had come to live there for some time now. François' ears perked up as he heard the name Maria Callas and he told himself that he would delve into this rich treasury of the Callas legend and story of her life in Paris later. Surely, they would be able to give him much inside information since they told him that they were friends of Callas' maid and butler/chauffeur. They even knew the two dogs's names, Pixie and Djedda. What a find, François told himself. That was exactly what he had been looking for, an entry into Maria's life in Paris. Would he be able to open the door and step inside the famous woman's fortress and her luxurious dwelling. He had heard about the luxury she lived in and wanted so very much to be dazzled by it. Oh, yes, he had lived in New York and had seen the rich and luxurious apartments of those who could afford luxury and that had stuck with him, poor little descendant of ordinary people of the rural country up north in Maine where the lap of luxury is non-existent.

The coffee was placed on the table with some *Madeleines* and the three of them sat down and started to chat as friends. François had a warm and pleasant personality that invited people to open up to him and he delighted in this gift of his. He told them his own story and how he happened to go from a poor milieu and how he had gotten an education that had transformed him into a more open-minded and cosmopolitan person. That's what the humanities had done for him, he told the couple who listened to him without interruptions. François just kept talking and talking until he realized that poor Belle Amie had her eyes shut and her head seemed too heavy for her shoulders. She was dozing off now and then. François, all of a sudden, realized that the poor lady was probably not listening too well and that her lack of understanding English put her at an inconvenient disadvantage. He stopped talking and kept quiet for a moment when Olivier told him to continue his story that he, Olivier, found quite interesting.

"Please excuse Belle Amie, for she had a bad night last night and she did not get too much sleep."

"I'm afraid it's my fault because I talk too much. My mother used to tell me that very often. My father, well, he just walked away."

"But I find you *sympa,* and I like to hear you speak."

Olivier nudged his wife and she opened her eyes and started to clear the table. Olivier went into the den and invited François to sit with him while Belle Amie took care of the dishes.

"Si je préparais le dîner pour ce soir, resteriez-vous avec nous, François?" If I prepared dinner for tonight would you stay?].

"Ah,non, Belle Amie. Ce serait trop, beaucoup trop de votre bonté gaspillée sur moi, chère Madame." No, please that's asking too much of you."

"Mais non..."

Olivier interrupted her to try and tell her that she would not have the time to cook her *coq au vin* and that François might have other plans for the evening. François replied that he would simply love to have dinner with them but that he did not want to impose on them and their gentle offer. After all, he told them, it was the first time they had met and that they needed more time to digest his presence among them and that he felt a bit ashamed of intruding on them like that. Olivier assured him that this was not an inconvenience nor an intrusion but a delight for both of them since they pretty much lived alone and had very little company to enliven their humble existence. François assured them that he appreciated their kind offer but that he could not accept their invitation for the moment. It would be too embarrassing, he told them. However, François craved very much their company and a fine dinner when he could talk for hours with such fine people, but he refrained from such advances for he thought of the right moment to establish a true connection with them when he would be able, no, find it most convenient, to talk about Maria Callas. Now was not the moment.

17. Dekaepta

A week went by and François was longing to meet up with the DesGrandforts for he missed talking to them while enjoying their company. He recognized the fact that he was seeking an inroad into Maria Callas's life here in Paris, but he did not want that to color unwittingly his relationships with people. Certainly, he was adamant about his project but he could always postpone it until the right time arrived. He felt within him a need to jump full speed ahead in his project but there was a certain restraint that caused him to slow down his ambitious plan to introduce himself boldly into the Callas project, as he called it. He had leaned over the years to minimize his ambition and to learn from past mistakes how to gradually and wisely promote his plans for whatever he proposed to do. He realized quite often that he had deliberately and unwisely jumped into a difficult situation and had botched the whole plan that he had made for himself. He did not want to do that with the Callas project. Moreover, he felt somewhat strange about calling his possible encounter with Maria Callas a project, as if this was a school project and even a graduate research study. He was not going after his Ph.D. degree and he did not have to write a doctoral thesis to get his credentials. He did not need a piece of paper with lots of signatures to tell him that he was qualified to be out there in the academic world. That was not the place he longed to be. He loved music and that was all. He had studied on his own and was now able to recognize arias, lyrics, movements of the orchestra, and so much more that he had learned while experiencing opera. His formal education was over and now he was learning on his own for, after all, learning comes with the passion for learning, he told himself. Professors were the leaders that brought you to the gates of disciplines and research. That is, good and excellent teachers who did not use students as research assistants and who did most of the leg work for some project that the professor had initiated but not followed up on. Of course, he took all of the credit and never thanked fully those who had done the work for him. That's how the game of promotion and tenure worked for college professors. Of course, there were some decent ones but they were far and few between. Oh yes, he could remember some very decent and some very good teachers in his journey to a formal education like Mister Kolomon and Mister Bistoff and they had truly inspired him, but how about the others? What others? He didn't mean to be so ungrateful towards those who had guided him in his attempt to learn such as Mister Kapalodous. Dear Mister Kapalodous, such a decent and resourceful man who carved himself a niche in opera and allowed François into his world of music in order to learn and especially experience the sublime music of opera. At least, that's what François thought of his dear friend from New York and the Met. Yes, the Met had been opened to him by this close friend and François was now enjoying the fruits of this encounter. New York was ever locked in his heart for it was there that he not only experience opera but Broadway musicals, concerts and other venues of entertainment that were recognized internationally. That's when François truly felt that he was on his pilgrimage of the music of the stars, the sublime music that transcended mere sounds and words. Such music made him wish for the stars themselves and the great experience of coming in contact somehow with the renowned composers and the famous singers who delivered the music with passion and dramatic flair such as Maria Callas. Yes, François was ready to finally meet her and possibly talk to her about her craft and especially her art. She was an artist indeed, an artist who had trained herself not to imitate other great artists but to build upon their craft as singers and interpreters of both music and lyric and push herself to heights that had not be known by other sopranos before her and even after her. Callas had put much energy, time and willpower into her music that it became her obsession and her *passion délibérée.* It had truly become a deliberate enterprise of strength and willpower. A passion wrought out of intense working habits and idealistic goals. François had read much about Callas and he now wanted to know if what he had read about her was true or just something fabricated to get a writer known or even worse, the stuff that paparazzi is made of. He told himself that he absolutely had to meet her and get to the very core of the truth about her and her music, if that at all possible.

The day following November 11th, Armistice Day, a much anticipated holiday in France and especially in Paris, François went to the Champs-Élysées to watch the military parade where the avenue was lined on both sides with people who stood there starry-eyed in anticipation of the military display of guns, tanks and other weapons, the mighty strength of the Republic, but most of them were there to get to see *le Président de la France,* in person, Président Valéry Giscard d'Estaing. François caught a glimpse of the huge Tricolore right next to the Arc de Triomphe where the Tomb of the Unknown Soldier lay. It was truly a day of remembrance for the French, the remembrance of the end of World War I and World War II. France knew how to remember and immortalize its patriots and soldiers. It also knew how to remember sadly all those who had been caught and shot by the infamous Gestapo. There were plaques on practically every building where these brave men and women had been executed. François told himself that war was even that much cruel and real when it happened to be in a particular spot where it had happened. France had suffered through so many wars, so many. The crowd went wild at the sight of the president sitting in an army vehicle with a general all decorated with medals when it started cheering, "*Vive le Président!*" The woman next to François looked at him a bit insulted if not angry when she did not hear him shout and that's when he began to chime in with the others. She then turned around to face the parade and whispered to her husband, "*C'est un Américain.*" The husband turned around to look at François and smiled.

When the parade ended and people started to disassemble and many headed for the vendors all along the boulevard, it was then that François recognized his friends, the DesGrandforts sitting on a park bench looking somewhat tired with their eyes a bit somber from the strain of looking over the heads of so many people who happened to be there almost surrounding them with their overwhelming presence. François hurried to go and meet them before they departed from their station. He managed to wind through the small crowds who had not yet fully dispersed and just stood there talking and gesturing like so many good Parisians often did. That was part of being not only French but Parisians.

François hurried as he elbowed his way to the park bench where the two friends still sat not saying a word to each other and only whispering, "*Allons nous en, c'est le temps.*" They had had enough for this holiday of cheering and vocal remembrance. As they started to get up and walk toward the métro, the Franklin D. Roosevelt, François caught up with them and to their great surprise, they kissed him on both cheeks and began their conversation chiding him for not visiting them for a very long time.

"But, I did not want to embarrass you with too many visits for you would get tired of me."

"*Mais non, mon ami.* We never get tired of you. You are our only friend with whom we can have a conversation. Without you, we would be left alone and we'd get very lonely. We need you in our lives. We are so old that we can practically not get around at all. We manage but it takes a lot of effort to do so."

"*Ah, oui, monsieur,*" said Belle Amie.

"But I did not realize that you wanted me around you frequently if not all the time."

"*Mais, oui,* François, but yes, cher ami. You are our very dear friend."

François felt somewhat guilty for not having visited them when they needed his company. He had stayed away fearing that he would overstate his welcome and drive the DesGrandforts to annoyance and probably despair. Of course, he knew better, but still he insisted that he was but a stranger to them and it would take time either to deepen their friendship or widen the distance between him and the two of them. He decided that he would make an effort to deepen rather than widen the distance. He would offer them more help and a greater affection to both of them. He remembered the wide gap between himself and his father that existed although he had tried in vain to shorten it and come to terms with the father and son strained relationship. He remembered kindly his mother who tried so desperately to tighten the bonds between father and son, but to no avail. She had constantly urged, pleaded and even threatened but nothing seemed to work. She was caught in the middle of a purported relationship that did not even seem to exist. She cried in heart of hearts many times but that did not relieve the tension that she felt for both husband and son. François even to this day, remembered her loss of strength and even her loss of appetite over this tension. He knew that she had died from worry and especially from despair.

It was agreed that François would call on them at least weekly. Olivier had insisted that it be twice weekly but François still wary of the situation of being too aggressive in his attempt to meet Maria Callas, settled for once a week for now. Late in November when the weather was unusually chilly and the chill in the air was accompanied by high humidity, so much so that it seemed to chill everyone to the bones, François decided to pay his friends a visit even though it was not time for it. The last visit was only three days ago. However, he felt that they might have need of him and he was going to try to help them in whatever way he could be it errands or anything else. When he got there, he found Olivier eating a cold sandwich all by himself. He seemed worried about something.

"What's wrong, Olivier?"

"It's Belle Amie, she's sick."

"Very sick?"

"More than just sick, she's in bed. She's been like that for two days now."

"Did you call a doctor?"

"No. He would not come anyways. The doctors are all too busy. I'm doing my best to take care of her. I went to the pharmacy and asked about some medications they could prescribe. They did give me some kind of cough medication but it doesn't seem to help. She simply has a bad grippe."

"But that can turn into pneumonia."

"I hope not, François. What if it does and she has to go to the hospital? I could not stand being alone here in the apartment without her. She does all the cooking, you know. I can't even boil an egg."

"I can help you. I know how to cook. I can prepare your meals and Belle Amie's."

"You can? That's *joliement fantastique.*

"Of course, I can and if you'll let me, I can also do the housework and whatever needs to be done."

"You would do that for us?"

"Why, of course."

"But it would mean that you would have to displace yourself every day from the Fondation Hellénique to here."

"That's no problem."

"Besides, it's getting cold here in Paris at this time of year."

"You must not forget that I come from the cold climate of northern New England."

They both started to laugh. All of a sudden, a cry was heard from the bedroom.

"It's Belle Amie. I have got to get to her right away. You want to come and greet her. That will most probably cheer her up."

François visited Belle Amie every day while she was still bedridden. He went to the pharmacy and spoke at length with the pharmacist about the conditions of a bad grippe and its most efficient remedies. He went away resolved that he had taken the right route in healing his friend who was diminishing in health and body. She hardly weighed fifty-four kilos. He treated her with the medications and with some home remedies that he had learned from his mother. She had taught him how to mix some herbs with warm olive oil and how to apply some warm compresses for a bad chest cold. He applied some of these compresses on Belle Amie's chest as he turned his head a bit sideways in all modesty for her. He even tried a mustard compress to enliven her breathing and make her feel better. It seemed to work because she stopped coughing incessantly and started to sleep better. Olivier was so very relieved that his wife was coming along well. Belle Amie's fears were allayed about dying and her worries by the thought of abandoning her husband to himself ceased. She now felt comforted by the thought that François' constant company could be relied on. He had become not only a friend but almost a relative, he was told. That pleased him very much since he recognized the fact that family relationships are so very important in French society. François kept coming every day until he saw a marked improvement in the health of Belle Amie. She ate better and was able to leave the bed and sit for a few hours with the two of them. Her complexion was soft and rosy and her eyes did not have that dullness that she exhibited during the worst of her illness. She wanted to go for a walk but Olivier and François convinced her that it was much too windy and cold for such a venture. She agreed with them and told them that it would have to be in the spring after *les fêtes.*

"Mais les courses, alors?"

Olivier told her not to worry about the errands and that François had been doing them regularly since she had been bedridden and that he, Olivier, had to take care of her and stay with her to see that everything was alright.

A few days after the recovery of Belle Amie and that things seemed to improve dramatically, Olivier and Belle Amie told François that they wanted to have a long chat with him.

"*Pourquoi pas?*" said Belle Amie.

François agreed but with some trepidation since he thought that he had done something wrong and that he was going to get a good chiding from both of them or that they were getting tired of him and wanted him to stay away for good. He didn't know what to think or expect. He was confused. He did not know what to say except, "*À votre goût.*"

The next morning after the three of them had croissants dipped in hot chocolate steaming it its large bowl, the desired conversation began its course.

"François *tu nous as beaucoup aidé surtout moi dans ma maladie. Et je l'apprécie énormement.*"[You've helped us a lot especially me when I was sick. I appreciate it enormously].

"She's telling you how much she appreciated your kind service during her illness and that she will never forget it."

"I know, I know. I understand what she's telling me, Olivier."

"Alors moi et Olivier nous voulons trouver le moyen de t'établir ici avec nous autres. Tu comprends?"

"Oui, je comprends, bien sûr. Mais comment ceci va se passer?" How is that to come about? You live in such a tiny apartment.

They explained to him that they knew how much he wanted to get out of the Fondation Helllénique for it had much too long living like a gypsy, they told him. That they would make room for him and the three of them would not live in discomfort. They would fix the den and he could have the divan for sleeping and they would make room in the den closet for his clothes and other belongings. He would also have the freedom of the apartment to come and go as he pleases. He would not have to do many chores except to help out now and then. They would not charge him a single sou, they told him. He told them that he would certainly consider it and that he would not live at their expense and that he was going to contribute his share and that furthermore, he would help out with the cooking and the preparation of meals for he knew how to bake and cook. They agreed and welcomed him "home" the following day. He did not have to think about it too long, overnight was enough. Of course, that would make François that much closer to la Callas, he told himself without wanting to express it out loud to them. He did not want them to think that he had ulterior motives. That would have been *paysan*. He certainly might be considered a peasant by some who did not really know him, but he did not have that temperament nor its pettiness. He was sure of that.

18. Decaoxtw

Once he was settled in, François made himself available for all errands and most of the cooking. He enjoyed it and felt like being back home again with his mother who taught him many recipes and many culinary tricks such as boiling green peppers before stuffing them since it takes less time to cook in the oven. He loved the traditional Acadian recipes handed down from family to family since years of settlement in Acadia now Nova Scotia and New Brunswick and now spread throughout New England. The *ragoût* and the *tourtière* were some of his favorites. However, his very favorite recipes were the Greek recipes taught to him by Mister Kapalodous' friends, the two restauranteurs, especially Mister Bastonides. He taught him how to slowly cook the eggplant before putting it in a casserole. But the first week he was with the DesGrandforts, François decided to make "Boeuf Bourguignon" for them as a kind of transitional dish from Acadian and Greek to French. He thought his friends would appreciate that. Then, later on he would introduce them to some of the Acadian dishes and later to the Greek dishes. That way, he would not only please his two friends but please himself since he loved all three ethnic culinary selections of food. First, he chose the beef dish that so many French loved and made almost everywhere in France even in the provinces. He knew that he would have to select the very best of meat, the best of vegetables and since he would not be able to find bacon in France, he would use what so many French recipes call for, the *lardons*, these very small pieces of pork that render exactly the taste needed and wanted by the chefs and all the women and even men, who loved to cook. Why, without the *lardons* mixed with the wine and other ingredients, it just would not be "Boeuf Bourguignon."

François went to the "Grande Épicerie" on Tuesday morning of his second week with the DesGrandforts to buy all he needed for this dish with fresh beef cubes as the main ingredient of the recipe. He talked to the butcher at the *boucherie* counter to make sure he was getting the best of the best of beef. The man assured him that indeed he was getting the very best and that la "Grande Épicerie only provided its clients with the very best in everything so as to guarantee perfect quality to those who loved to cook and those who loved to eat. Oh, that French pride of *délicatesse du palais* was indeed a prerogative of the French civilization, he told himself.

François rushed to the apartment that he now called home and wasted no time in the preparation of the dish he was going to serve that evening. When Belle Amie heard of what he was going to do, she marveled at the thought of eating one of her favorite dishes and could not refrain from insisting that her husband provide the exquisite wine that he had been keeping for a particular celebration and serve it in their crystal glasses that they had not used in a long time. There was joy in her voice and glee in her exclamation of anticipated pleasure that she had not known for a long time. Olivier shared that glee with her. François was himself happy to provide that moment of glee to them. The bonds of friendship were being cemented with every gesture and every promise of delight that François provided.

First, he placed the *lardons* in a large pot and let them simmer for a while and then he dried them. He then sautéed the *lardons* in some olive oil in a casserole and then put them aside. Then he took the pieces of beef and browned them slowly until they became nice and well -browned on all sides. He put them in with the *lardons* and sprinkled flour over the content. He then let the casserole stand in the oven for a short while until he added some beef stock to it and let it simmer, He added tomato paste, a crushed clove of garlic and let the whole thing simmer. While the meat was cooking he prepared the mushrooms and the pearl onions. It was at that point hat Belle Amie came to the counter where François was working and peered over his right shoulder to tell him that she appreciated all the work he was doing for them.

"*Ça sent si bon. C›est bien d›avoir une fraîcheur de cuisine encore dans l›apartement.*" So good to have the freshness of cooking again in the apartment.

"Oh, Belle Amie, it's good for all three of us."

She smiled and turned away so as not to get in the way. François told her that she was not in his way. Not at all, he told her almost reverently and indeed fondly.

"It's your apartment, Belle Amie."

"*Non, non, non....*" and he cut her off.

He then was ready to put in the nice red Burgundy wine to the mixture in the casserole and then place the *bouquet garni* in it since, he said, that's what gives it the flavor we need to sustain our "Boeuf Bourguignon." Finally, he added more stock and some sliced carrots, as thin as wafers for he did not want them to cook too long and become limp.

"The simmering is the key to the casserole dish", he told them. "Avez-vous faim?"

Both of them nodded their heads in agreement that they were indeed hungry. François then decided that a glass of wine would be just the right thing for this long pause before dinner.

While they were waiting for the casserole, Olivier set the table and Belle Amie helped him with the cloth napkins. They were lovely linen napkins with blue embroidery that she had in her fine oaken chest that her father had made for her a very long time ago. She kept all her precious things in there, she told François, all her mementos dear to her since they were like old friends that never die. In the process of placing the napkins on the table, she held out a piece of yellowed newspaper that she offered François.

"Take this, s'il-vous-plaît," as she handed him the piece of paper.

François was somewhat bewildered by this gesture but he took it from her and started reading it. It was about World War II and an incident in Paris in 1944. An incident related to the gestapo who had caught up with a member of the Résistance and who had been shot on the spot on la rue des Espions. François realized that the article mentioned someone name Alexis DesGrandforts and thought to himself that this man must have been related to his friends.

"*Mon fils*," said Belle Amie and then she could not go on because her voice started to crack.

"Yes, he was our only son, our dearest of dearest sons all over France who fought for all of us underground. But, he was caught right in the middle of Paris because someone hated him and was jealous of him because he was greatly lauded by General de Gaulle in one of his radio speeches across the channel. I guess that the General forgot that name of the Resistance members should not, no, never be mentioned in any circumstances. He should have known better but I guess he forgot. Anyway, he did come to us and apologized for his slip of the tongue and gave us Alexis' Croix de Guerre medal. Later on we received the decoration of the Légion d'Honneur presented to us by a special envoy from the Président de la France, Charles de Gaulle, le Grand Charles.

"Show him the medals, Belle Amie."

"*Pas maintenant, Olivier...plus tard.*"

"Olivier can you tell me a bit about the liberation of Paris. It interests me a lot."

"Why, of course. The liberation of Paris occurred on August 25, 1944. Great day, a very great day for us. You see, France had been occupied by the Nazi regime for four years. Four long years, how well I remember that, and will never, *JAMAIS*, forget it. We suffered a lot during those four years; all of France suffered tremendously. We all knew that the gestapo was at work sifting through archives and so much paperwork in order to capture those who resisted and those who were of Jewish blood, be it a tiny fraction of what they called impure blood. And, the terrible prisons such as Auschwitz-Birkenau, Belzec, Sobibór, Dachau and Treblinka awaited those who were pushed like cattle into freight trains that would take them to their final destination, and I mean final. What could the rest of us do? If we resisted too loudly and became outspoken to a point of being heard loud and clear, well, we would have been shot or tortured or whatever. I was a coward unlike my son who died for his country and its faithful citizens. I helped those in misery, those who suffered from hunger and those whose lives were on the edge of total annihilation by either disobeying the Nazi imposed rules or by outright murder on the streets of our beloved Paris. Horror filled our streets. We had very little hope of surviving. What could we really do? We gathered at times silently and we prayed hoping very much that God had not forsaken us. Some despaired and wanted to die. The enemy became our own selves when we gave in to despair. *Sans espoir nous étions plus faible que faible et totalement démunis, sans âme et sans esprit de corps. Absolument rendus au plus profond du gouffre de l'ennui. Sans espoir nous serions devenus rien.* Oh, yes, without hope we would have sunk into the oblivion of despair and nothingness. I tell you, François, it was the most cruel of wars and the most cruel lot for us Parisians, to be taken over by the Nazis. They were horrible and unbearably cruel. *On ne pouvait pas être pas Français car nous l'étions et dans le coeur et surtout dans l'âme gravé là depuis la création du monde."* Yes, we were French and could not be anything else for we had been French in our hearts and in our souls since creation."

"I realize that had to be the cruelest of all circumstances and the most cruel reversals of all, that of losing one's identity as a free people. *Vive la liberté!* Isn't that one of your most cherished values and trust, Olivier?"

Yes, yes, my dear friend. You Americans cherish the same thing, freedom. Freedom to be who you truly are as human beings."

"It is so true."

"Let me continue about the liberation of Paris since you ask about it. Paris was liberated by the French Second Armored Division and the U.S. Fourth Infantry Division. Fortunately for all of us who are French and those who cherish our identity and history if not our civilization, we were spared the destruction of Paris by a decent man, a well-educated and sensitive man of letters and science, who defied an order by Adolf Hitler to blow up Paris' landmarks and burn the city to the ground. I will always remember his name, General Dietrich von Choltitz. The rest is history as they say. I so remember General Charles de Gaulle leading a joyful liberation march down the Champs Élysées. I was rejuvenated then and decided never to leave Paris."

All three of them sat down for dinner and the "Boeuf Bourguignon" was simply delicious. They all ate well especially Bellle Amie who had two servings and did not leave a single morsel on her plate. She wiped he plate clean with her morsel of bread and drank two full glasses of red wine. She slept well that night, very well indeed. *Comme une bûche;* like a log.

The next morning François got up earlier than usual and decided to go for a walk along the Champs Élysées while Paris was still sleeping. He wanted to walk silently on the avenue and think about what Olivier had told him last night about the liberation of Paris. Paris always had been a very important city to him. She was the very important touchstone of history for those who stemmed from her bosom, her land and shores, all those who had migrated to a far distant land like America and had not lost a single memory of her. Although the memories were at times somewhat vague and diluted by time and distance, they were nevertheless there and vibrant. One's cultural identity is never really wiped clean by whatever incident or lack of interest. It is deeply entrenched in one's heart and soul so that recalling the memories of the past and one's ancestors only have to be scratched a bit to find its resiliency and authenticity like one who scratches the layers of paint and varnish from an old table and discovers the original wood. That is if one does not want to lose the essence of being who he truly is a as a person with a family history. François didn't really care about detailed genealogy and all of its research struggle. All he wanted was to belong and to be someone who had a history like the Greeks and the Acadians. He didn't have the citizenship of being French from France, but he did have assurance that his roots were in France and none could erase that fact. It was a question of accepting who you were and living with it.

If one negated the facts of genealogical roots, then he becomes *un perdu ou un mal-connaissant*, a lost soul or a badly instructed being. All he knew was that he was French by ancestry and by cultural values, and that was all he needed. He walked along the wide boulevard breathing the cool morning air when he spotted Marcel Lavertu, his old friend who had received him and guided him on his arrival in Paris. He had not seen him in a very long time. He crossed the boulevard and arrived behind him just as he was going to take the métro. He hurried to touch him on his shoulder and ask him where he was going. Surprised, Marcel turned around and saw François.

"Where do you come from and where are you going, Marcel?"

"I come from a very late party of revelers who stayed up thróugh the night and now I'm going home to my apartment to get some sleep."

"You stayed up all night?"

"Yes, and I'm terribly tired and completely exhausted from the all the drinking and partying."

"You've been partying all night?"

"Yes. It was a hell of a night. We were just a few friends together but we had a lot of fun. Every one of us came from outside of France, I from Québec, another from Brussels, another from Dakar, yet another from Berne, and another from Los Angeles. We all speak French."

"Even the one from Los Angeles?"

"Yes. His family is from Paris originally. They moved there and formed a business. Eventually they established a French-speaking co-op and founded a journal published in French."

"In Los Angeles?"

"Of course. Aren't you aware that many who came from France to live in the warm climate of California are now settled there permanently and their numbers have increased a hundredfold."

"I didn't know that."

"There are a lot of things you don't know about the Francophone world, mon ami."

"I know."

"Well I must go. I'm sorry that I have to leave you so quickly, but I'm *assommé* as they say in France, totally bombed out."

"Let's get together sometimes."

"Where do you live now? I checked at the Fondation but they told me you had moved out."

François did not want to tell that he was living with the DesGrandforts for fear of revealing too much that would not be good for himself and his two friends.

"I'm looking for an apartment around here."

"Around here? Why it's much too expensive."

"Well I know some friends from around here."

"Are they far from here?"

"They live on Georges Mandel."

"That's where Maria Callas lives doesn't she?"

"I believe so."

"You believe so? I thought you were pursuing her story and her music."

"I am but more of an interest that has fast petered out."

"You've given up on it?"

"Sort of."

"Sort of? That's too bad. I'd have something for you if you ever decide to continue your search."

"Like what, Marcel?"

"You know she's worth a lot of money. Some of us would like to get some of that."

"Like what? Steal from her? But how?"

"There are ways."

"Yes, but what? I would not want to associate with anyone who would be out to get her and her money and even do her harm."

"Don't be so squeamish, François. She's an ordinary person like you and me except she is famous in the eyes of some people especially the paparazzi."

"She's famous on account of her voice and her immense talent. Don't you know?"

"Oh, people like you over glamorize her to a point of stupid veneration, the veneration of a false idol, in my estimation."

"Why are you so much against her, Marcel?"

"I'm not against her. I simply don't understand the great razzle-dazzle that goes on surrounding her persona as a singer."

"It's not razzle-dazzle as you put it. It's talent lifted up to a real accomplishment in opera, a genre that she has mastered and that very few others have equaled."

"You're over reacting to my way of seeing things. I just know that she is ready for the plucking, that's all."

"Well, just don't try it. Don't even think about it."

"Why not?"

"Why not? I'll tell you why not. It's because I'd tell the gendarmes about such schemes and you'd wind up in La Santé."

"Oh, don't be so concerned about me and about your diva. Nothing will happen."

"It better not, or I'll see to it."

Marcel did not hear him say those last words. It must have been that he was truly bombed out or that he did not want François' company anymore. "Strange," François told himself as he continued his walk. "It's so strange on Marcel's part. I would have never thought that of him. He was such a nice fellow too. He must have gotten into a bad crowd of people, robbers and drug addicts perhaps. They rob to feed their obsession and terrible addiction. I don't think I ever want to see Marcel again if that's the way he thinks and acts."

François lingered a while until he came to the Arc de Triomphe where he stood silently next to the tomb of the Unknown Soldier. Who was he, this unknown man who died while fighting for his country? Was he a Frenchman, a French immigré, or someone who was gassed or even someone completely mangled by the war machines? Who was his mother? His father? Was he close to his father, I wonder. No one will ever know except the Unknown Soldier who will never be known. François thought that was the weirdest mystery ever but one that he could begin to understand since that way every dead soldier could be him, every man killed in action could be this unknown dead person under a slab of marble right next to the center of the Arc de Triomphe and where the so-called eternal flame kept burning as a witness to the fallen dead of World War I and II, Europe's great wars, the ones that were not supposed to happen but did happen. The wars that no one wanted they said. People said many things but things still happened no matter what people said. Craziness, thought François, craziness exists.

As François was getting back to the boulevard Georges Mandel he noticed a lady wearing sunglasses even though there was not bright sun. She was dressed very well with a coat that looked like fine wool and a scarf of the finest silk tied around her neck. She wore black leather gloves and had a diamonds bracelet dangling around her left wrist. She had a small dog on a leash and she walked briskly close to the apartment complexes making sure she was walking away from the curb as if she was far enough from recognition by other pedestrians. François crossed path with her and she went by him without uttering a single word not even lifting her head looking down on the sidewalk. Things happened so quickly all that François was left with was a whiff of her expensive perfume lingering behind her like an exotic scent that can mystify one like a charm. All of a sudden, she uttered in a low voice, "*Non Djedda, non ne vas pas là, reste avec moi, tout près de moi.*"[No, don't go there and stay close to me]. Then François realized it had to be Maria Callas walking her dog early in the morning when people are not yet awake and out walking. He was so stunned that he did not dare run after her to greet her. Besides, he did not want to break her privacy. He did not even turn around and stare at her. She simply wanted to be alone walking her little dog on a cold November day. François now knew for real that she existed and that she did live on Avenue Georges Mandel, the very same boulevard where he lived. She was indeed real and she lived in her luxury apartment with all of her memories and her treasured jewels and Biki designed clothes. That much he knew about Maria Callas since he had read up on her and her love of Parisian fashion. Would he have the good luck of getting to meet her one day and get to talk with her about her signing, that he considered a possibility in his mind now that he had seen her walking her dog. But how would that happen and by what miraculous good fortune would that encounter happen, he left that to serendipity or happenstance. Whatever.

19. Dekaennea

Several weeks went by and François was still concerned about what Marcel had told him about his Maria Callas' scheme. He did not know if Marcel was going at it alone or with others, but he was genuinely concerned. He did not go out much except for some errands and when Olivier asked him why he wasn't going out much, he replied that he thought it was too cold to go for a long walk. He did not dare share his concern with Olivier for fear of frightening him for nothing. He told himself that he was not overreacting and that he was simply being very cautious about Maria Callas' safety. He did not know what Marcel planned to do. Would he kidnap her? No, that would be too risky for him, probably near impossible too. Would he rob her apartment? But how would he be able to since it was well guarded. Would he harm her maid or her chauffeur? But how? One thing he knew for sure was that Maria's well-being was being threatened in some way. He was going to make sure that that threat would not be fulfilled if he could prevent it. François put himself on guard and was seen looking out of the window upstairs in the vast lobby several times a day. There were several occasions when he thought he saw a shadowy character walking back and forth in front of the building, but that did not last long. He was waiting for Marcel to show up for he would warn him about doing any harm to the great singer who lived as a recluse.

On a bright but wintry day in early December, François decided to make some hot soup for lunch and he thought of making the Greek S*oupa Avgolemono*, the lemon and egg soup that Mister Kapalodous liked so much and was so easy to make. All it took was two or three egg yolks, some broth and some lemon juice. Mister Kapalodous' friend had told François that the egg whites cook faster than the yolks and leave white strands in the pot, so he was told to avoid mixing them at first. Some cooks add the whites later when the soup is practically done but François decided not to use them at all and keep the rich yellow flavor and color of the lemon juice and the yolks. The *soupa* turned out smooth and tasty to the palate. Both Belle Amie and Olivier liked it enough to have a second bowl. François had made enough that there was some left after the meal. He put it on the counter to cool. Right after lunch there was a knock on the door. It was Maria Callas' maid, Bruna, who came to tell Olivier and Belle Amie that she was in the process of making lunch and happened to be short of flour and eggs and wanted to know if she could borrow some until she would replace the items borrowed.

"*Entrez, entrez chère amie,*" said Belle Amie.

"Je m'excuse mais je suis en panne. J'ai besoin de farine at d'oeufs. Pourriez-vous m'en offrir. Je vous les remettrai plus tard. Madame attend pour son déjeuner, vous savez."[I'm in a jam. I need some flour and eggs. Could I get it from you? I'll replace them later. Madame is waiting for her lunch].

François went to get the items required and gave them to the maid. Belle Amie introduced him to Bruna and she quickly responded with a broad smile. As she was about to leave, she remarked about the good smell of lemon and asked what Madame had cooked. She told her that it was François who had made the soup and that it was a Greek lemon and egg soup.

"*Quel beau parfum cette soupe,*"[My, this soup smells good] said the maid.

Belle Amie then offered the rest of the soup to Bruna who replied that it would be perfect for Madame Callas since she loved Greek food. And so, the maid left with François' Greek soup. He was delighted that he was able to connect with Maria Callas in some way if not directly at least by means of culinary offering. He hoped that she would truly enjoy the soup and that this would open the door to their first encounter in some way or fashion he hoped. However, he did not expect any acknowledgment on her part for he was afraid of being disappointed.

"Do you know this Bruna?" asked François.

"Mais, oui, nous sommes de bonnes amies, Bruna et moi."[We're good friends].

François then tried to elicit more information about the maid and even the butler/chauffeur, Francisco. Belle Amie filled the void that had existed in François' mind about the two servants. She told him that she quite often saw Bruna but very seldom saw Maria Callas and never talked to her. *"C'est une recluse,"* she told him. Belle Amie went on to tell François all about the two servants, that is, all that she had learned about them. She told him that the butler's name was Ferruccio and not Francisco. They did not receive any salary but were permitted to live in the apartment and eat the food provided by their patron. That both servants were entirely devoted to their mistress and that the singer rewarded them with gifts and sometimes with money especially around Christmastime and their birthdays. Bruna told Belle Amie about la Callas listening to old tapes of her singing late at night when she could not sleep and that's why the great singer had become a night walker who could not sleep. She had begun taking some sleeping tablets that were provided by her sister in Greece and by a friend, named Madame Devetzi. She was worried about her mistress but there was nothing she could do to change anything for it was her heart that had been affected and then there was her voice that had suffered too. She knew that and the only thing she could do was to minister to her needs and sympathize with the great Callas, she told Belle Amie. What else could she do? Belle Amie listened to Bruna and took everything in without judging her and her mistress who suffered the vagaries of time and aging. She told François that she believed that the great singer could not go on like that and that her years were certainly numbered since no one can live that way, lonely and cut off from the world. That the heart and soul of a person cannot survive in the darkness of the refusal to live. *"On ne peut pas vivre dans le passé et refuser de faire face au futur."* *One* cannot live in the past and refuse to face the future, she told him. *"Nous avons tous besoin d'avancer avec le temps comme moi je l'ai fait quand on m'a arraché mon fils, Alexis."* We all need to move on as I did when my Alexis was taken away from me.

One bright winter day in mid-December when people were getting ready to celebrate *les fêtes* as they called it, François decided to make a Greek dessert that he liked so much and he was sure his two friends would like it too. And, he would probably dare to offer some to Bruna for her mistress. François truly wanted to break the ice and attempt to get to meet la Callas in some way be it through her stomach and her penchant for Greek food. He realized that there were ulterior motives in his cooking Greek food, but that was the way things worked or did not work, he told himself. If he was ever to get to meet her, it was now or never. That was his idea on the project he had proposed for himself a long time ago.

As for the dessert, he chose to make *Karidopita*, a Greek Walnut cake. He liked this cake for its consistency and for the blend of walnut and many eggs with the entire recipe spiked with cognac. It was said, as Mister Kapalodous told it, that little old Greek ladies back in Athens society used to sit in their tea or coffee houses for hours and enjoy eating this rich walnut cake as an accompaniment with their tea and gossip. At least, that was the case for ladies who had enough time for leisure and not for those who worked hard all day long for the pleasure of their husbands and children. It was not hard to make and François discovered the magic of taste and palate coming together when putting a big piece into your mouth when the savor and alluring smell of the cake come into its full power of seducing any lover of delicious cakes.

François put all of the ingredients on the counter where he was working that included the walnuts both chopped and grated, the flour and sugar, the butter, of course, everyone especially the Greeks and the French love butter, and the eight, yes, 8 eggs, with some cinnamon and not to forget the cognac. First he whipped the egg whites into a meringue and then added it to the egg yolks. He placed this mixture with the other combined ingredients and stirred everything together. He could smell the cognac and the nutty smell of the walnuts. His mouth watered at the thought of savoring this dessert after dinner. Of course, he would spread syrup that he would make right on the cake to add moisture and sugary taste to it, just like the Greeks loved it. Belle Amie came and looked into the mixing bowl and told François that what he was doing was going to be magic as he always did when he made Greek food. She loved Greek food and thanked François for introducing her and Olivier to it. She told him that she considered his presence with them unimaginable if he were ever to leave them for she told him she would not want to live the lonely life of before. He smiled at her and her eyes sparkled.

When dinner was over that night, François decided to bring a piece of his confection to Maria Callas' apartment. He knew that she would love this cake for, in the past, she adored desserts and ate a lot of them. She probably had cast them aside totally, but he figured that he would lure her back to Greek dessert and it would bring her back to the joys of good eating. He climbed the stairs leading to her apartment, knocked on the door and waited a moment until the butler opened the door. He seemed surprised and a bit rankled at seeing this stranger standing there with a small plate with a metal cover on top. He was about to dismiss François when Bruna arrived and told Ferruccio that it was alright and that it was for the benefit of Madame Callas that this young man was there offering something that would certainly please her. François gave the plate to Bruna telling her that it was piece of Greek Walnut cake for Madame Callas. She took it and added that she could not let him in since it would most probably disturb Madame and she did not want to offend her by admitting a stranger in their midst. François told her that he understood and that he simply wanted to delight the woman who had the world's greatest voice, his idol of opera. Bruna smiled and thanked him. The door clicked shut and there was François standing that close to Maria Callas without seeing her or even talking to her. He looked at the tall ceiling, took a deep breath and slowly, ever slowly went down the stairs somewhat disappointed and certainly unabashed at having tried to meet the woman of his dreams and music. When he walked into his apartment in the *sous sol,* both Olivier and Belle Amie asked him how it went, this bearer of gift who was on his journey of getting to meet this world famous opera star, this Divina Callas but by his sallow look and somewhat sad countenance, they realized immediately that he was disappointed and that he had not even seen her. They knew how much he wanted to meet her and get to talk about her music, her career as an opera star and especially about her climb to the heights of opera. They said nothing and went to sit in the kitchen sipping their after dinner coffee. Maybe next time, they told him, maybe when the time is right and the stars are in their good modes of casting beneficial light on those who crave for good fortune for they believed in the power and influence of the stars.

Four days later, Olivier came into the apartment somewhat upset for he had seen a man hovering like a black bird around the property. He was dressed all in black and he had a small mustache that made him look like Hitler. Olivier thought right away that this man might be a prowler or somewhat of a *malfaiteur.* François thought right away of Marcel. He asked Olivier if the man was alone. Olivier answered him that he did not see anyone else but that he could be mistaken. He did not like to see people like that hanging around for he was worried about the safety of all residents in and around the building.

"We have to be very careful for one never knows who may be perpetrating a crime or not. Paris is not always safe for people with money and those who enjoy fame like Maria Callas," he told them.

François hurried to go out and see if the man in black was still out there. He wasn't. The following day, Olivier came in telling François that the same man asked about him and where he lived. Olivier refused to give him any information. François was truly worried and angry that Marcel would go to extremes to get what he wanted, François' collaboration in getting into the Callas' apartment in order to rob her of her jewels and or her money. Olivier told François that he personally would get in touch with the security of the house and even tell the gendarmerie of the 16me arrondissement about the possibility of a crime in and around their building. He wasn't afraid to speak out against criminals, he said. Belle Amie told him to be careful and to watch out for any kind of revenge on the part of these men who walked the streets in order to get what they wanted. They were dangerous, she said. François took all the necessary precautions to prevent this from happening, that is the criminal mischief of Marcel and his cohorts. The police had been alerted and everyone was on guard against anyone who might harm anyone be it during the daylight hours or at nighttime. One never knows. Well, Marcel Lavertu and his three cohorts were apprehended the following day attempting to crash into the building by way of a large window in the back. The alarm had sounded and the police were there almost immediately. François, Olivier and Belle Amie got all the details the following morning even before they had their *café au lait* with fresh croissants gotten at the corner boulangerie. François was relieved and he imagined that Madame Callas had already heard about the break in and that she had already doubled her security and even alerted her maid and butler/chauffeur not to talk to anyone about her and about her affairs. She then insisted that her status as a recluse be enforced by herself and by any other person that might be connected to her in any way. She wanted no one, absolutely no one to come even close to her and her property. That's what Bruna reported to the DesGrandforts the following day. François felt miserable about all of this since he now believed that his chances of getting close to Maria Callas in any way had been nullified by that Lavertu fellow once his friend. He did not sulk nor did he give up but he redoubled his efforts of finding a way to la Callas through her stomach and that was good food and especially good Greek food. He remembered a couple of movies that did just that in some fashion and that was flattering people's stomachs with good food. He remembered especially one, "Tom Jones" in which the hero eats like a glutton and with sexual gusto the many succulent dishes laid before him. There, food was a principal metaphor for human appetite. Human appetite can be satisfied in so many different ways. However, if François were able to gaze into the future he would certainly enjoy the film, "Babette's

Feast," a film that best exemplifies the virtue of good food not only satisfying the stomach but turning people around from straight-laced and austere persons to receptive and happy people. Babette spends her entire lottery winnings on choice food and wine in order to get to those people who belong to an austere sect and are ever so sullen and cut off from other people as if they're angry with themselves and the world, so conservatively puritanical are they. Babette gets to them with good food well prepared and well served with wine and good cheer. Why the Quail in Puff Pastry is out of this culinary world. Added to that is the turtle soup, the buckwheat cakes with caviar, the *fromages* with fruit and finally the Baba au Rhum with dry figs. What a splendid meal Babette serves them. Why, it turns all of the participants around and their stern and austere countenances into smiles, contentment and even a strong glimmer of love. That's what good food, good and well-prepared food ameliorates any situation. It's through the stomach that one reaches the heart and soul of people. François would try to get to reach la Callas with food that she would appreciate. That would most probably resolve his problem of getting to actually meeting Maria Callas. Not that she was conservative and austere but she had cut herself off from the world and even from her true self as if she was an outcast on a deserted island where there was hardly any music except some old tapes and no real enjoyment of good food. He would try to remedy that, he said.

The day after François offered Bruna a bowl of egg and lemon soup to give to her mistress, the maid knocked on the door and gave the empty bowl back saying that Madame Callas had truly enjoyed the soup and wanted to know who had made it. Bruna told her that it was a guest at the DesGrandforts named François and that he was a very courteous young man who lived with them and often cooked for them. He loved to cook Greek food, she told her. La Callas' response was that she would like to meet this courteous young man someday, but not now. That's what the maid told François. He was overjoyed that his little scheme was working. He would certainly wait for the day when la Callas would make her initial overture and invite him to her apartment for a conversation. Why, he might even be able to convince her that he would be willing to cook an entire Greek meal for her. Wouldn't Mister Kapalodous be proud of him, he told himself. God rest his soul, this man who never failed to teach François about opera.

For the holidays, François decided to make an entire Acadian meal for his friends one that would bring back memories for him, memories of joyful days with his mother. She was a marvelous cook, the mother, and she took delight in offering her small family the best of what had been passed down to her. First there was the meat pies, then the *poutine râpée*, the pea soup, the fine dishes of crab and lobster, the mussels and, of course, the desserts. He looked for the dried yellow peas for his soup but could not find any. He decided he was going to make turnip soup with pieces of potatoes. Then he decided to buy the mussels for he did not think he could afford either the crab or the lobster. For dessert, he would see. Most probably "une bûche de Noël" since it was Christmas and they were going to have the *réveillon.*

The day before Christmas Eve, François started to make preparations for the Acadian "souper" and for the "*réveillon*." It would be a traditional meal for both events. The "souper," as the Acadian called their dinner, would consist of the mussels and the *poutine râpée* while the "*réveillon*", served at midnight, would offer the traditional t*ourtière* or meat pie, preceded by the turnip soup. Of course, there would be the traditional *amarinades* or if he could not find something similar, he would serve *cornichons.*

If he remembered well, the *poutine râpée* was easy to make. It consisted of potatoes, mashed and grated, and salt pork to be substituted with *lardons*, of course. François mixed the mashed and grated potatoes and formed balls much like snowballs back home. He made a hole in each one of them and inserted the *lardons.* He then put the potato balls into a pan of boiling water and simmered them for two to three hours until all of the flavor was ready for tasting, just like his mother used to make. They would be eaten with butter, plenty of butter. His mother even had them for dessert; she had them with sugar and, at times, molasses. He preferred not to have them as dessert. Both DesGrandforts tasted them with some apprehension, but in the end, they both liked *poutine râpée*." They would not have them every day of the week, they told François, but it was a delightful *mets étrange,* they told him.

When it came to the *réveillon,* François had persuaded them to take an afternoon nap so that they would be able to stay up late past midnight, the *tourtière* was served. It was made of fresh ground pork with mashed potatoes and spices, cinnamon and what the Acadians called "le poivre gent", or coriander. Olivier and Belle Amie both loved the *tourtière, cette tarte acadienne,* as they called it and they both had two pieces of it. As the crowning point of the Christmas meal, the "bûche de Noël" was cut into nice slabs of chocolaty cake and placed in a fine china plate that Belle Amie reserved for special occasions. The "bûche de Noël" had been quite a feat for François for he had never made one before. Belle Amie had stood right next to him advising him, at times, how to blend in the ingredients and especially how to frost the jelly roll cake like a real log, including the small stump. She had added some tiny leaf decorations with red berries to it and it was deemed perfect. Belle Amie was so wound up after the meal that she said that she did not want to go to bed until she drank her cognac after a long pause at the end of the meal and promptly fell asleep in her chair.

The following morning, as it was Christmas, François decided to bring a large slice of the *tourtière* to the Callas apartment for both Bruna and Ferrucio so they might have a taste of Acadian cuisine. He knew that la Callas would not enjoy such fare. He simply wanted to please both servants on a bright holiday morning. He went upstairs, knocked gently on the door and gave the butler/chauffeur the dish telling him that it was for both himself and Bruna. As the door closed, François felt a bit regretful for not having anything for la Callas for, after all, it was Christmas. On New Year's Eve, Bruna brought down some expensive candies that her mistress had given her and telling her to share them with the DesGrandforts and that young man, the gentle one who cooks. François was excited that Maria Callas had thought enough of him to offer him some of the

Christmas candies. He considered that a gesture that precluded an invitation to her apartment. Not now, but later.

François thought that in order to celebrate the new year 1976, he was going to prepare an entire Greek dinner for "la Divina." It would be the best he could ever make and so well prepared that even the very best of chefs could not emulate. At least, that's what he thought about his refined culinary expertise. He had worked long and hard at it and now he considered himself a master chef of the Greek cuisine. Even his father would be proud of him, he told himself. Or would he?

François studied and tried several Greek recipes during the winter months up to the second week of May until he thought that he had attained the results he had hoped for. He tried some of those chosen recipes on Olivier and Belle Amie and they both marveled at his culinary skills and congratulated him on his efforts to offer the best of Greek cuisine. They knew that he was doing all of this in order to please Maria Callas and get her to open up to François, but they truly appreciated his sharing the Greek dishes with them.

"François you are truly an artist with food," Olivier told hold him one day when the lilacs were in bloom.

"*Oui, oui, François. C'est merveilleuxce talent que vous avez de faire la cuisine chanter avec vos mets si délicieux, assez pour satisfaire les anges là-haut.*" You have a marvelous talent with food enough to make the angels sing.

"*Merci, Madame DesGrandforts, vous êtes gentille.*"

"Look here, Olivier, do you think that I am exaggerating this thing about seeing la Divina? Am I too arrogant about it or simply stupid so as to think that such a world famous diva would even consider seeing me and even talking to me? After all, she has shut herself up in her apartment not to see anyone especially a stranger like me. Am I being foolish? Am I impudent and self-centered? I'm afraid that I have overstepped my boundaries in this affair with Maria Calls and that I will suffer the rest of my life for it. People will laugh at me and find me glaringly stupid and offensive in my deliberate steps to claim victory with Maria Callas."

"No, no, mon ami. I don't think you're arrogant, certainly not stupid, and by any means, not foolish and self-centered. You are a humble young man who uses his talents to please people and along the way you have developed a passion for music. Your Callas project, as you call it, is perfectly understandable and no one can blame you for pursuing your dream no matter if it is a difficult one and an unreachable one for many. You have perseverance and determination and that's worth a lot in my book. Go on dreaming that one day your Callas project will be realized. You're doing it from the heart and even your soul is captivated by this project. It has become not only your journey but your pilgrimage to the heights of music and opera. You cannot give upon it and you cannot let others betray your dream with their words and vile thoughts of jealousy. It's you who counts in all of this and it's you, you must satisfy or else your life will have been a failure at the end. I only wish I had the same courage as you. I would be able to climb mountains and sail the highest seas and even conquer my most lasting fears of failure. Believe me, François, I have failed in life, failed because I was too afraid that I would and could not succeed. I was so afraid of success that I failed even before getting started on any project. I gazed at the stars but never went for them. I called it the impossible dream, *le rêve irréalisable. Rien n'est impossible si ce n'est qu'un coup de coeur ou un élan d'âme.* "[Nothing is impossible if it takes but an effort of the heart and a thrust of the soul].

François looked at Olivier and did not stop looking at him until tears welled up in his eyes. How he wished his father had spoken to him like that long ago. That would have been the balm of Gilead, the soothing and healing touch that he so needed and craved for but never got.

20. Eikosi

Rumors had it that Maria Callas was very ill and that she was being transported to the hospital. She was at death's door, they said. Reporters gathered in front of the Avenue Georges Mandel apartment building number 36. In droves they came. Waiting. Whispering. Some shouting until a gendarme came to tell all of them that the rumors were false. All of a sudden, someone shouted, "Look up there, we can see la Callas peering through the curtains. She's not ill. She's there." The curtains closed. Then, Ferruccio came to the entry to try and send all of them away. Some of them shouted that they would not go until la Callas came to talk to them. Ferruccio said, NO, and many of them walked away. There was one reporter who remained standing there for four hours until nightfall. François came out in early evening and looked around. He saw no one and then decided to go for a short walk. He suddenly looked up and saw la Callas peering in the window with a faint light behind her. She quickly turned away. He was sorry for her. She absolutely has no privacy, he told himself. He felt sorry for her for Bruna had told him that Madame had not been feeling well lately and that she had a hard time to sleep. She took a lot of pills. That she knew. But now it had grown worst. She got up late and had very little or no appetite. She told Bruna she wished she were back in Athens for she would be able to eat what she wanted in Greek food. She missed that a lot. François then told the maid that he would fix that. She thanked him and walked away with her head down. He knew that she was despondent over her mistress' plight. She told François that if nothing is done about it Madame would find herself either confined to a hospital or that they would find her dead some morning. She did not want anything like that to happen so she pleaded with François to try and help her find something that would buoy her up and give her strength so that she would be able to live longer and better. Poor François told her that he had no guaranteed remedy for her and that she needed professional help, but he would try to think of something. That something was good food. Good Greek food that had in substance vitamins and all the nutrients she needed to stay alive. Besides, Greek food would have the power and psychological value of lifting her and keeping her on tract as far as nutrition and moral support were concerned. We all need that kind of support when we are young and even as we grow old, he told Bruna. She thanked him and she left the main lobby to take the lift upstairs. She never did that; she used to climb the stairs.

Well, if Greek food was the key to making la Callas feel better, Greek food it would be, said François to himself. He felt glad that he was playing a role, although not a significant one, in the potential recovery of Maria Callas. He remembered all the times that he was sick and his mother had made him special dishes, either vegetable soup, chicken with a very light gravy or *poutine râpée.* That with traditional home remedies helped the young boy to regain his energy and make him feel so much better. Of course, there were the long naps forcibly taken in the afternoons. What he had hated the most was castor oil and cod liver oil, one for the bowels and the other for strong bones. She also strongly believed in herbal medicines that she got at the drugstore Pellerin on South Main Street.

François began the day with Greek recipes that he sifted through in order to find the right ones for a splendid repast for la Callas. They had to be just right, the ones that would entice not only her palate but her desire to eat. Finally, he had decided on a menu: *Giko Koutaliou Stafili,* Greek Grape Spoon Sweet: *Melitzanes Papoutsakia,* Stuffed Aubergines; *Spanakopita,* Savory Greek Pie, and for dessert,

Galaktoboureko, custard-filled phyllo pastry. He would start with the Greek pie made with phyllo pastry stuffed with chopped onions, crumbled feta cheese, grated edam, crumbled Roquefort cheese, chopped fresh dill, fresh breadcrumbs, egg yolks, olive oil, chopped spinach and seasoning. He would serve that at the beginning of the meal. This is a very popular item for people who are hungry and cannot wait for the full course. He was sure that la Callas would eat at least one or two pieces of this or she could bypass it and go directly to the next item which is "Grape Spoon Sweet." This would introduce the entrée by helping to open up the palate with fruit. It consists of grapes, sugar, roasted almonds and lemon juice. Quite simple but it gives the eater a chance to savor a light fruit opening up of the palate.

The full entrée would be the stuffed *aubergines* that was bound to excite the Greek palate and give it the full flavor of Greek food. Those eggplants are food for the gods. François thought that his would certainly satisfy a hungry stomach accustomed to Greek food. He would do his very best to make this the *pièce de résistance.* He began by browning the ground beef and onions in butter, then added tomatoes with salt and pepper. Then he cooked covered for about fifteen minutes. Then he removed it from the heat. Afterwards, he added parsley, egg, cheese and breadcrumbs. He then prepared the eggplants by peeling an inch strip on one side from one end to the other of the eggplants. Then, he heated the olive oil in a large frying pan and placed the eggplants until they came out nice and golden brown. He then removed them from the frying pan with a spatula being careful not to damage them and placed them in a baking dish. He was ready to slit the eggplants in order to stuff them with the meat mixture. He then prepared the béchamel sauce enough to cover the top of the dish. He added a beaten egg and the remaining cheese and sprinkled with the additional grated cheese and the he dotted it with butter ready to bake in the oven. This would indeed be delicious, he thought. After a short while Belle Amie came into the kitchen because, she said, "*Ça sentait bon.*" While waiting for the main dish to bake in the oven, François prepared the dessert, the custard-filled pastry. This recipe is a real traditional one, one that la Callas would certainly recognize and appreciate, François told Belle Amie who was watching him at the counter. He told her that it was one of the most famous Greek desserts and that it's a delightful egg and milk custard wrapped in thin sheets of phyllo dough and baked in the oven until they come out golden brown. Then each piece is soaked in a lemony syrup and served warm. François ' mouth watered just thinking of this dessert for he like desserts like most Acadians. He told Belle Amie that he was reserving a piece just for her and she smiled with her eyes since she had run out of words.

François had alerted Bruna about the feast, as he put it to her, and had asked her when it would be an appropriate time to serve it to la Callas. She had responded, at first, with a sigh because she did not know when Madame would be ready for such a meal and whether she would like it or not. It was very hard to know exactly when shed would be ready for something she had not counted on. She told François that she would watch for the right time like a sailor watches for storms before setting to sea. She would watch for signs from her mistress since she knew her very well and had gotten to know her idiosyncrasies as well as her temperament. She knew her well enough to know how she would react to such an overture on the part of someone whom she had not yet learned to trust fully. That's the way she was and nothing would or could change her mind and her heart on things. She was a very strong willed person, Bruna said, and she would not budge on anything if she did not have her mind to it. Furthermore, la Callas was not well and she lived on pills, pills to sleep, pills for depression and pills for indigestion, and whatever else. Bruna did not know exactly. She had to measure her condition on an exact day and gauge her performance in the morning to see if her mistress would be able to bear the entire day without any physical disturbances and mental aberrances such as mood swings. Oh yes, Bruna could detect the slightest off the scale behavior on la Callas's part be it morning, noon or night. However, she was able to persuade her mistress on some things such as food and going for a walk with her dogs, especially Djedda. Lately it had been too cold to go for a walk even though it was mid-May. If the mistress walked in circle in the house patterned after her dogs, she would plead with Ferruccio to take them outside and walk them for at least a short while. She insisted that although she wished to go out herself and get some fresh air, she was determined to send the dogs out . They needed it, she told her butler/chauffeur. Ferruccio did whatever the mistress wanted and commanded, winter, fall summer and spring. He himself welcomed the occasions when he would be able to go outside and smoke since she did not tolerate anyone smoking in the apartment not even Aristotle.

The day that François started cooking what he considered the sumptuous Greek meal was the day Bruna had designated as the banquet day for that's exactly what she considered it to be, a banquet for la Callas. François would bring each dish at the appropriate time and Bruna would serve it to her mistress on lace tablecloth with embroidered linen napkins next to the fork. The cutlery was of finest silver kept polished by Ferruccio. The glasses were crystal and the plates, saucers and cups were of the very best china especially selected by la Callas. They were glazed with a beautiful wine color and trimmed with a gold band. In the middle of the plates was a large scripted "C", so elegant and so Callas. The hour had come to serve the dinner and la Calls had not changed her mind about the meal. She had asked several times if the meal would be truly Greek and if the cook could be trusted to make such a meal. Bruna had answered her that if she liked the egg and lemon soup, she would like this entire meal cooked to perfection, she said with strong affirmation on her part. La Callas yielded to her maid's words, and sat down to dinner on a nice early evening in May. Bruna had even placed one of la Callas's favorite flowers in the center of the dining room table, bold red carnations. La Callas had given Bruna a quick smile while her eyes twinkled with joy at anticipating an authentic Greek meal.

She was a bit surprised when Bruna put in her plate a small dish of *spanakopita* since she had not expected that. *"Ceci c'est un amuse-gueule, c'est pas pour le dîner." That's* for snacks," she told her maid. *"S'il-vous-plaît goûtez en un."* Then the maid served her a small dish of the "Grape Spoon Sweet" and la Callas refused to have it. It was for old ladies on a Sunday afternoon, she said. Bruna took it away. Finally, the maid came in with the main dish, the stuffed *aubergine*s and the mistress's eyes opened wide and said, *"Mais, c'est pas vrai, de la 'melizanes papoutsakia'. Ah mon Dieu, ça me rapelle du temps de ma jeunesse alors que je faisais la bouffe."* This reminds me of my youth when I ate so much. Bruna put some in her plate and la Callas asked for more. Suddenly, she got up and told Bruna, *"Je ne peux pas, je ne veux pas manger de ce plat délicieux seule. Vas demander à ce monsieur, le cuisinier, de me joindre ici à ma table."* [I cannot eat alone. Go tell the young chef to come and join me]. Bruna was so stunned that she stood there frozen without any words coming out of her mouth. *"Vas, dépêche-toi!"* Bruna quietly cried out in a low voice to Ferruccio to go and get François downstairs. He did not have to go too far for François was standing in the hallway waiting anxiously to see how the meal would be received by the great singer. Would she like it or not? Would she thoroughly despise it and not allow herself to take a second bite? When Ferruccio came to get him, he was totally and absolutely surprised of la Callas' invitation to join her at table. At last, his dream was being realized through the mystery and magic of Greek food. He had taken the precaution to dress well enough not to be thought of as a peasant.

Maria Callas was sitting at the dining room table elegant and wide eyed at seeing this young man, a stranger, sitting down at her table for a meal that he had prepared just for her. She welcomed him and asked Bruna for an entire setting for the young man who had spent much time and energy in preparing such a delightful Greek meal. François's face turned red and he did not know what to say until la Callas said, "Καλώς ήρΘαϯεκαι καʹΥϦϰληοϯτέρα," Welcome and Good Evening. François surprised himself and responded, "ΕυλαΡιστσού με," Thank you.

"You're not Greek are you?"

"Half Greek. My father was Greek. My mother was French Acadian."

"Alors, vous parlez français?"

"Oui, mais je suis américain."

"And you know Greek cuisine?"

"Yes."

"Where did you learn it?"

"In New York with restauranteur friends of a Mister Kapalodous."

"I knew a Mister Kapalodous once."

"He was a master at knowing opera. He was a genius of sorts. He taught me how to enjoy and appreciate opera."

"That was nice of him. Do you like opera?"

"Why of course, Madame Callas. I adore it."

"So do I but sometimes I get tired of it. It has drawn all of my strength and power to sing. I feel drained and now I cannot reach those high notes that I used to."

She stopped eating and Bruna brought her some wine to drink.

"I'm afraid that our dinner is over, Monsieur François."

"But you have not tasted the custard phyllo yet."

"I might have it some other time," and she stood up to leave the table.

Bruna helped her and brought her to her bedroom and then closed the door. She told François that she was sorry and that probably at another time Madame Callas would feel better and stay longer at her meal. She then told him that she would keep a piece of the dessert for later when Madame would certainly want to eat it. François just stood there disappointed that his first encounter face to face with Madame Callas had been cut short. He thanked Bruna and silently left the apartment without looking at the treasures that la Callas had accumulated over the years. He went downstairs to tell the DesGrandforts about the evening and the meal that opened the door to Maria Callas and her gracious invitation to join her at table. They both wanted to hear every single word said at the table and how Maria Callas reacted to the meal. Of course, he did not tell them about the sudden departure of the great singer. He kept that deep in his heart not wanting to surrender it to misfortune and disappointment. He was sure that another encounter was in the offing somehow. He was sure of it.

21. Eikosiena

Two days after the first encounter with Maria Callas, François decided to take a short vacation somewhere, probably in France, where he had never been. He did so at the behest of his two friends, Olivier and Belle Amie since they had been after him to take time off and travel. They wanted him to rest and get some much deserved time away from the kitchen. He told them that he did not want to miss the next occasion to make another meal for the diva. And, they responded that he could not wait for a call from Madame because that would be wasted time. Finally, he realized that they were right and that he did need some time away from all of this. He decided to go to Madrid or probably Lisbon.

The following day he received a note from Maria Callas handed personally to him by Bruna. He opened the envelope and read the note. In it she apologized for her behavior during the dinner and said that she had not been feeling well and was suddenly hit by a frenzy unknown to her and that she had to rush to her bedroom to recover. She said that it was not very polite of her to rush like that without an explanation and that she really enjoyed the Greek food that he had prepared and she wanted him to know that. Furthermore, she invited him to a dinner at a future date when she would be responsible for the food. She signed the note Maria Callas. François took the note and put it in his pocket thinking that he was going to keep it in a safe place for he wanted to preserve it as one preserves precious memories. He rejoiced at such a memento that he had not expected. He was going to tell Bruna about the content of the note and let her know that he was accepting the invitation and to tell la Callas that he was only too happy to be with her at dinner when he would receive the invitation with the time and date. Meanwhile, he would postpone his trip and wait for word from la Callas for he did not want to jeopardize his chances of not being around when she sent word. He was so excited about it that he decided to bake a birthday cake for Olivier whose birthday was the following day. He would make it a celebration and invite Bruna and even Ferruccio, if he wanted to come. He had never done this with his father for his dad wanted no fuss with his birthday and forbade the family to celebrate it not even with a birthday cake. It seems that every time François wanted to do something special for his father, Basil would squarely refuse. He preferred to celebrate with his friends at the tavern. His mother had cautioned François about any kind of celebration for his father, either, birthday, Father's day or his Saint's day, Saint Basil, for she had tried long ago to do it and it had not succeeded. François was ever so glad that he could now shower his good graces on Olivier who was like a father to him.

François baked a chocolate cake for Olivier liked chocolate over vanilla or any other kind and he frosted it with white and chocolate icing with letters that spelled birthday wishes to Olivier. He put candles on it and lit them when it came time to partake of it. Bruna was there as was Ferruccio for a short while since he did not wish to leave the mistress alone for too long. Both he and Bruna were very devoted and caring servants. For a birthday gift, François gave Olivier a pair of merino wool socks with a blue fleur-de-lys design. He wore them right away, proud of his socks and proud that someone like François had thought of him on his birthday.

A month went by and no invitation from la Callas. François was concerned about it and wondered whether the singer had forgotten about it or had reneged on her offer of having dinner together. He was beginning to wonder if his project was altogether coming apart and that in reality the great singer did not really want to bother with him. François often thought that he was not worthy of her so great was her fame and so deep was her grief over her lost love with Aristotle Onassis and the virtual loss of her magnificent voice. It must be hard to realize that your most precious and unique gift has dissipated and is gone forever, never to return as it was. That's why la Callas was substituting live voice with the voice recorded on tape since she could no longer perform the way it used to be. François had read about it but did not really believe that his idol had lost her voice. It could not be, he told himself, but Bruna reassured him that it was true however sad if not tragic it was for such a famous opera singer to lose her voice. She was not the only one, of course, but when it's you, the Divina, then it's that more hurtful and that more tragic. La Callas' life had been entirely devoted to her voice and her signing. It had taken her heart and even her soul and changed them into a Pygmalion-like transformation whereby, Maria Callas' life was solely music and her energies were given over to her art. Hers was not only a vocation but a passionate surrender to music, music lessons, music rehearsals, lyrics learning and perfecting and opera performances. Ever since she was a young girl in Greece, she had dedicated her entire life and voice energies to music, concerts and opera. And, she was both an idealist and a perfectionist. Her teachers said so, her tutors said so, the conductors said so, her peers said so and she said so herself. How could she be otherwise, she repeatedly said. That much François knew but he wanted to hear it from her, Maria Callas, the greatest operatic singer of her century, people said. Every time François thought about it, he felt that more humble and almost unworthy of any personal exchange with the Divina. Furthermore, what did he really know about music? About opera? About lyrics sung in many languages that la Callas had mastered? About the dramatic movements that she had given to her performances? About all of the nuances of style and modulations brought to her performances? About everything concerning the great Maria Callas? Very little, he admitted to himself. Notwithstanding his own doubts and trepidation, François still insisted on pursuing with determination his project to meet personally with Maria Callas and get her to talk about her music and her career as a veritable operatic artist. Would his project come to fruition? At least, he thought so and he would not have it any other way. If it's to succeed then the efforts put into it have to be strong and constant or else it's doomed to failure. François had the strong will of his father and the perseverance of his mother. How could he fail?

Bruna had fallen ill and could not perform her daily tasks, so that another woman was temporarily hired to fill in the gap that was created by Bruna's illness. Within three days, the new woman was let go. Ferruccio tried so desperately to replace Bruna as well as he could but discovered that what Bruna did was beyond his energies and way beyond his abilities to do the job that the maid did. And she did it almost to perfection and according to the mistress' wishes and demands. And so, François was asked to do the cooking for la Callas. At first he balked and said that he could not do both, cook for his own household and cook for the singer, her maid and her butler/chauffeur. Olivier convinced him that he could do it and that he needed to do but one meal each for lunch and dinner and that he and Belle Amie could very well take care of their breakfasts. François gave in and told all of them that he was willing to assume such a task but that they all would have to cooperate with him and his possible flaws in his cooking. They all said, including la Callas, that they would indeed welcome his work as a provider of meals and that they would more than tolerate his minor flaws as a cook.

I'm turning the narration back to François. I'm getting tired of talking.

I welcomed the opportunity of working for la Callas although I rarely saw her, but I did grasp the few occasions when I was invited to share dinner with her. For my first dinner for her I planned a French meal with lamb sautéed in wine and herbs, fresh green vegetables and wild rice. I wanted to open her palate with some lemon sorbet with a dash of orange juice that would enhance the flavor of the lemon. As for dessert, I thought of *crème brûlée* would hit the spot, as we say. I served the meal slowly and with few words on my part. My motions were deliberate and simple without too many gestures that would interfere with the flow of eating and digesting, I thought. She ate the lamb and rice but only took a sampling of the vegetables. She had a glass of white Chablis and looked at me and said, "*Merci, Basil.*" She apparently adopted my middle Geek name in addressing me. I told her that it had been my pleasure to cook for her and to serve her. She looked at me and her eyes meant it, those beautiful dark eyes that look at you with a glimmer of fire and intense depth of soul. She looked a bit tired so I excused myself and started to clear the table when Ferruccio came in and helped me. I asked him if he and Bruna had eaten yet and he told me, no. I then told him to serve himself and to bring some food to Bruna. As I was leaving, I saw la Callas sitting in the next room playing with her dog, Djedda, and she seemed to enjoy these playful moments. I stood in the doorway for her to see me waiting until she would address me. She looked up and asked me if there was something I wanted to tell her.

"Yes, Madame. I have heard that you have a special devotion to the Virgin Mary and that you often stop at some chapel to venerate her and pray to her for encouragement."

"Yes, I do. I pray to her to give me the strength that I need to live and especially to perform at the highest level of my God-given talent. I realize that it's a rare gift and that I need to nurture it and perfect it every day."

"Have you heard of *la médaille miraculeuse* ?"

"Somewhat, but I don't know it well. What exactly is it and what importance does it have?"

"Why it carries great importance for those who believe in it and know its history, that of Catherine Labouré and the apparitions she had right here in Paris on la rue du Bac."

"She had apparitions from our Lady?"

"Yes. You can visit the chapel where the Virgin Mary appeared right here in Paris. A lot of people from all over the world visit this shrine. There's even Catherine Labouré's incorrupt body under one of the altars."

"I did not know that. It's very interesting. I might want to go there one of these days."

"Well, I mentioned it to you because I have something for you and it comes from the shrine. It's the miraculous medal and I want to present it to you if you care to have it."

I stepped forward and placed the small gold plated medal in her right hand. She looked at it and thanked him smiling her charming smile.

"I will treasure it and keep it with me every day. I certainly need the Virgin's help since I..." and she stopped and turned around to go to her bedroom.

I felt a little embarrassed since he did not mean to make her feel sad and dejected by his offering. I turned around and left the apartment without saying another word. I went downstairs, quietly went to my niche as I called it, I got undressed and ready for bed. Both Olivier and Belle Amie were sleeping in their bedroom and I did not want to make any noise. I felt somewhat sad myself for I had seen the great singer's human side, I told myself, and that was quite revealing to me that la Callas had deep emotions outside her dramatic self on the operatic stage, feelings that were real and very human. I had read so many times that she did not have feelings beyond her portrayal of an agonizing Norma or a fearful Mimi or even a dying Violetta. These feelings were all for show, they said and that deep down la Callas was a fiery and hard-hearted diva. She had no real feelings for people especially for those whom she did not like such as Rudolf Bing and Renata Tebaldi. That's what people said all the time that la Callas was immeasurably without genuine human feelings. Especially when it came to her mother. But I did not want to accept that and was never to talk about it especially about her family and particularly her mother and the frightening story she had told Time magazine some years ago. I did not want to believe all the stories about a diva who had a heart of stone. I had seen it tonight, the glimmer of the human heart filled with emotions and refusing to lay it bare in front of a young man who was still to her a stranger. I closed the light and slowly went to sleep thinking of how to approach la Callas and ask her some important questions about her career as an opera diva. Sleep was a great balm of couching worries and questions about someone and store them in the back of the sleeper's mind but never erased from the windows of the memory.

Morning came and the sun shone bright in the streets of Paris where people went to work by taking the metro, the train, the bus, the taxi cabs or private cars, bicycles or they even walked to work. There was indeed a lot of hustle and bustle in the city where dreams and reality met especially for visitors who had long awaited their visit to the City of Lights and Wonders. I had stepped out of the apartment early in the morning. It was late May and everything smelled of spring and the renewal of plants, flowers, shrubs, burgeoning branches of trees, and even the pace of everyone's walk as they went their way had become more brisk and hurried except for those who had time to slow down and even stop to admire a blossom, a newly painted sign on a favorite *boulangerie or pâtisserie* of theirs. It seemed that the aroma of these shops was crawling through windows and doors as the shop owners opened them up to let the fresh smell of baguette, croissant, or coffee éclairs waft through any opening for the client to inhale with delight or even nostalgia. *Le temps de lilas* was fast making room for the *pivoines*, the *muguet,* and the tulips to name a few June blossoms. I enjoyed them all. I was happy to be in Paris where even in the dead of winter, flowers in flower shops were available to all who desired them, or to offer them to a beloved one, or even to have them in the home as joyful reminders of *le temps des fleurs qui est tout le temps*. Flowers are for all times of the year.

I walked up to the Arc de Triomphe and past the many sidewalk cafés where the morning *flâneurs* lingered for very long moments even hours simply enjoying what they were drinking and looking at people going by. I himself had done that many times. However, I had not done this in a very long time. I had been too busy with my cooking and other chores while constantly thinking of my la Callas project. It was coming to fruition, I told himself while hurrying to make sure I would be back to serve Olivier and Belle Amie their breakfast. I knew that they were persistent in their demand not to serve them breakfast, but this morning I wanted to do it as a special favor to them. I would serve them not only croissants with jam, but *oeufs brouillés,* the scrambled eggs with slices of potatoes cooked in butter and with a touch of garlic. They would like that. I liked to talk to himself especially when I was carefree and I did not have any preoccupations left from the night before. I thought of Madame turning away with a sad demeanor all because she was thinking of something sad, I thought, and I insisted that I was going to make her a dish for the next dinner that she would truly relish. Something new, and Acadian dish that she was bound to like although very new for her. I liked to challenge people's taste and offer them some delight of sorts. I realized that his idea of delights might not be the delights of others, but I liked to please people the best way I could. Just like my mother who always was trying to please her husband and her son. It did not always turn out the way she had intended but at least she did her best.

When I returned to the apartment, it was still quite early and the old couple was just getting up when I wished hem "good morning" and started to take out the dishes and pans I needed to make breakfast. Olivier and Belle Amie asked me what I was doing and I answered that I was going to prepare breakfast for them. The both refused what I proposed and told me that it was agreed that as long as I was preparing meals for Madame Callas, they were going to take care of their own breakfasts and lunches. No need to bother with them, they said.

"Let me prepare for you a nice breakfast for once. You deserve it."

"*Non,*" replied Belle Amie.

"Absolutely not," said Olivier. "You are not going to get out of your way and create more work for yourself. We'll do it as we have been doing it for the last few days. We just don't want to keep imposing on you, François."

"But you're not imposing. I want to do it. I need to be with you once in a while having breakfast together."

And so I prepared breakfast for my two friends and they both enjoyed having me sitting at the table with them in the morning.

Belle Amie relished the soft scrambled eggs with the delightful potatoes cooked just right in delicious butter, she told them. Then afterwards, she dunked her croissant in her *café au lait* for she told me that one simply could not start the day without *un bon café avec un bon croissant. "Que font les gens qui n'ont pas la chance de se plaire comme ça?"* [What do people do who don't have the good fortune of pleasing themselves].

I went upstairs later on to check on Madame's taste for dinner that evening and to also check on Bruna's health and see if she was back *en forme*, as they say. It was Bruna who answered the door and flashed a good morning smile. I was surprised to see her and in such good health.

"But you look great, Bruna. How is Madame Callas feeling this morning?"

"Madame is still sleeping. She had a bad night and took many pills. You know, pills that make you sleep that her sister send her from Greece. She can't get them here in France."

"Oh, I didn't know that."

"*Oui, Monsieur.* I wish she wouldn't supply her sister with those awful pills. They're absolutely poison to her. She tries to hide them but I find them now and then in her bathroom or hidden under her pillow. She gets desperate sometimes, I know, but how I wish she would stop taking them. They're going to be her downfall someday, I know. Poor Madame Callas, poor her and her sad condition all because she's losing her voice, she says, and because of that lousy Greek man who left her flat like that. I'm sorry Monsieur François. I'm not supposed to talk about it to anyone, but sometimes I simply burst out with rage inside of me that I keep holding back but I have to let it out sometimes. Ferruccio chides me for doing so but I tell him that I care for Madame and I don't want her to be hurt by anyone, certainly not by people like that Ari, not by anyone anymore. I'm sorry, but it just came out and Madame would not want me to talk about it you understand. Don't you?"

"Yes, I understand and I sympathize for Madame and sympathize for you too who must bear the hurt of Madame. Don't worry, I won't say a single word to Madame, trust me."

I left the apartment knowing that Madame would not be having dinner tonight but that Bruna would be serving her a light meal of soup and a piece of this morning's baguette. That was all she wanted, Bruna told me. I, in turn, told myself that I was going to make up for it by preparing for her a wonderful meal on which I had been pondering for days.

Two days later, on Bruna's wishes, I started to place all my needed ingredients for a superb dinner on the counter next to the stove. There was ground pork, fresh and lean, a couple of potatoes, some spices, and other items that would provide me with the necessary ingredients for a fine Acadian meal. I realized that the palate of la Callas had been tamed and *gâté,* to say the least, with Greek, Italian and French cuisines, but I was going to try and challenge it with a new kind of cuisine, that of the Acadians. I was going to make a *tourtière,* originally made with black birds by the settlers in the olden days, I was told, and later made with pork that my ancestors had substituted in the process of farming and cultivating large gardens for their everyday needs. If la Callas wanted to hear more about the Acadians, then I would tell her about the *Grand Dérangement de 1755* when the British expelled the Acadians from their land and put them on ships and sent them far away so that they would never return to claim their confiscated land. I, Fançois Basil Spirounias was a descendant of these people who had suffered much hardship at the hands of cruel, unjust and greedy people who were ethnically insensitive to cultural values. It would be a meal of good food and sound history of poor people, exiled people whose heritage still resounds today. I would not only feed her pork pie but also tempt her with a delicious Acadian treat, la tarte *à farlouche,* a sugar and molasses pie. I was willing to try and delicately tease if not challenge her palate as well as the taste buds that had certainly accepted and adapted to so many things that had been offered them. Acadian cuisine was by far the very best according to those who preferred it to continental cuisine or even American fare which so often replicated the continental one. In any case, I, François

Basil was going to try and offer la Callas some different kind of food that she was bound to like. I was sure of it. If she did not like it and refused it, then I would have done his best to offer her something that was not only palatable but really good. I sure hoped so.

I started to prepare dinner for not only la Callas but for everyone, Bruna, Ferruccio, Olivier and Belle Amie. All would have the chance to enjoy an Acadian feast. Of course, both Olivier and Belle Amie had had Acadian pork pie but not the entire panoply of great food à l'Acadienne. Bruna came to tell François that today was the day to offer Madame a good meal and that she was feeling much better. She had not taken too many of her pills, she said. I was consoled by the fact that the diva was able to enjoy a full meal and a different one at that. My *tourtière* would be spectacular to say the least, I told myself, just because I was doing it with my heart and soul, just like my mother did when I was young and dreamed of far distant shores where I would enjoy the rest of my life playing in the sand and listening to music. The distant shores had vanished from my dreams and the sands evaporated, but the music was still there and even better now that I had matured into opera.

First, I prepared the pie dough that would serve as the crust. Then I set it aside and began putting together the meat that I had cooked, the mashed potatoes, the spices. I blended them into a nice spongy and not too dry so that the entire blend was moist and delicious to the eye and to the taste. I then rolled half of the pie dough and put it into a large pie plate and formed it into a bottom shell with a fluted edge. Then I placed the meat mixture into it ready for the top crust and crimped it all round. I spread some melted butter on top and it was ready for baking in late afternoon, a few hours before dinner.

Next, I prepared the vegetables and told myself that it was too bad that I could not find in Paris the green fiddle heads that the Acadians serve with a meal. However, I did find some buckwheat flower and was ready to make *ployes* that the Acadians preferred over regular bread. As for the dessert pie, I got the ingredients ready, sugar, molasses and milk with a cube of butter and mixed these together ready to place in the pie plate covered with pie dough. Once I had covered it with a layer of rolled pie dough, I was ready to put it in the oven for baking. The Acadians loved these recipes handed down from generation to generation. It was part of their tradition and they loved tradition enough to make it their ethnic calling. The hard and fast saying among the Acadians was we shall never die, we are part of the soil we cultivated with our hands and part of our souls is buried in this land and our heritage for we are Acadians and Acadians never ever give up.

I did not really know if la Callas would like all of this, this newness of the culinary art enough to really taste it and let her palate enjoy both the food and the history of Acadia. I told himself that I was doing my best to introduce her to something with what she would not be familiar. At least, it would enliven the evening meal and offer some history behind the meal served to her. I had served her Greek fare, my father's legacy although refused, and now I was serving French Acadian food, my mother's legacy totally embraced by her and passed on to her son, François.

The afternoon went by very fast and then it was time to put the *tourtière* in the oven until it would come out nice and golden ready to eat. I had made arrangements with Bruna to make sure that Madame would eat on time and be ready for the new culinary surprise. I went upstairs to her apartment and knocked on the door. Ferruccio opened it and let him in. First I would serve some lemon sorbet to open up the palate for the genuine taste of the food served. I had learned that from a chef in New York. No smoking, no hard liquor before a meal, he had told me, for you don't want to anesthetize the taste buds before relishing a good meal. I checked to see if Madame was sitting in at the dining table. She was. She smiled at me and told me to go ahead and serve what I had prepared.

"Bruna tells me that you have been toiling at the oven practically all afternoon. Is that right?"

"Yes, Madame. It was well worth it, first for you and then for the others. I made enough for all."

"Well, what are you going to serve me, I mean us?"

"To begin with, I will offer you a wedge of Acadian *tourtière* with some kind of buckwheat pancakes that the Acadians call *ployes.*"

"That sounds good. Similar, perhaps to Greek food. Am I right?"

"You could say that. The Greeks love to eat and the Acadians likewise."

"I love them already and I'm going to love their food, I'm sure."

I was glad that Madame was in good spirits and was in the mood to have fun with the food, the cook and the way food was prepared and served. That flattered my spirit and my *joie de cuire.* I served a rosé wine with the meal not truly knowing what to serve with Acadian food for they drank their own brew, so to speak. Madame ate everything that I put in her plate and she did not refuse anything. Bruna helped me with the food and the wine. When it came time for the dessert, I somewhat warned la Callas that this dessert was very sweet but insisted that she, at least, taste it. She did not refuse. However, after the second bite, she pushed it aside saying that it was indeed much too sweet for her and that at one time when she was much younger she would have eaten the entire pie. Then she laughed.

"You see, *mon cher François*, I was a glutton and my waist was proof of it."

"I'm sure Madame was comfortably plump then."

"Comfortable, no, but I suffered later for those excesses."

"You look great now," And I blushed a bit saying that.

She smiled and then told me that she was now comfortable enough to have that conversation with me, the one I had so wanted but never expressed. I beamed with joy and turned everything over to Bruna who smiled that benign smile of a maid and then left for the kitchen. Maria Callas and I went to sit in the spacious living room where comfort met the joy of conversation. Finally!

As both of us sat there, Madame looking directly at the person facing her, the other, me, casting short glances at the luxurious ceiling, then the paintings on the walls, the gorgeous lamps and the richness of the furniture, while the interlocutor waited for me to ask the first question, the mood of calm anticipation settled in like a warm blanket that one covers plants and flowers in the quiet softness of winter.

"I want to tell you something, François Basil, I refuse to entertain any questions whatsoever about my family and about that Greek man in my life to whom so many people refer and want so much to get answers from me. That is off limits, you understand. I don't like personal questions either. Let's restrict the questions and answers to my career as an opera diva."

"I quite understand, Madame and believe me, I will not intrude in your personal life. I'm not here to do so. All I want is some information about your singing, your depth of knowledge about music, arias, lyrics and whatever makes you the star that you are today."

"I'm not a movie star, I'll have you know. I've only acted in one film and that was Pasolini's **Medea**. I was practically forced into it because I did not want to play a role where there was no singing only words and then only a very few words. Have you seen the film?"

"No, not yet."

"Well, don't. It's not worth it. I'm not at my best in it. Pasolini is *un cinéaste* and he's very good at it, but that's not my line. I'm an opera singer and a very good one if I may say. I've worked extremely hard at it. Unfortunately, my voice today has diminished in volume and strength and I may add tone. At the height of my days in opera, I was quite good, even radiantly superb, I thought and so did many people who followed me wherever I sang, Mexico, Milan, Rome, Vienna, Paris, London, Lisbon and so many world capitals and cities as well as American cities."

"I know. You became an international diva. People cheered you, they applauded you and gave you accolades not received by many other operatic singers."

"Yes, those were the days of glory for me and I relished them. My voice was truly well trained and I vocalized often enough in order to keep it sound and on key. I stopped counting the hours spent on it and the many hours spent at rehearsals. Most of the time with the very best conductors. I as passionate about my singing, my career and those who accompanied me in any given performances. If I did not like a certain note that was sung without the clear and just sound that the composer wanted, I had them whoever they were, start over again and again and again. Many thought I was crazy with my sense of the idealism and perfection. I must admit, I am a perfectionist. I cannot stand mediocrity."

"I'm awed by your sense of truth and justice when it comes to music and opera. You demand to be faithful to the composer's truth and justice to his music, his creation. After all, creativity demands a knowledgeable and sensitive composer/creator and a performer who can capture the essence of his work."

"Where did you learn that, François, not by listening only for sure?"

"No not only by listening to music, great music, but I went to school also, Berklee in Boston. I also had a great friend, Mister Kapalodous whom I met in New York, and we often went to the Met. Why I was there when Pavarotti first sang at the Met. It was his debut in **La Bohème**.

"You were indeed quite fortunate in meeting this Greek gentleman. I remember my debut at the Met. It was both exciting and filled with tension for me. My nerves were on edge all the time."

"When did your very first operatic success occur and in what opera?"

"Why it was as if it happened only yesterday. The way time just crosses our paths in life and makes us see things as if we live in a kaleidoscope, that's the way I see my life and my career as an artist. The pieces of glass drop and a new image appears, just like my moments in life and my episodes in my operatic career. There were good images and others not so good. Some were awful and we let those pass by as we forget them in the abyss of bad memories."

"Do you have bad memories?"

"I certainly do, but I do not linger on them."

"Like those about Rudolf Bing and the Met?"

"I'd rather not talk about that Prussian corporal as my husband called him. I never did anything to him except to make him realize that I could not take on two different roles in two different operas in such a short period of time. I never met a man who was so very unreasonable. We Greeks respect reason for our philosophers taught us to deal with it and respect its values as well as its constant directives of thought and harmony."

"Yes, Socrates, Plato, Aristotle and so any others who taught us how to think about ourselves and our universe."

"They also taught us about art in our lives."

"You mean the philosophers?"

"In part yes, but especially the great sculptors and architects. What tremendous achievements that still live in our day. What we don't have in our museums we imitate and duplicate because we love the beautiful harmonious lines and perspectives."

"I just adore Greek sculptures. I love the one of the Discus Thrower.

"Tell me, how did we get on that subject and away from opera my career as a singer-diva?"

"I suppose they all intersect at some point and come to a harmonious whole of art and culture, don't you think?"

"I suppose so. But let not other things lead us astray."

"No, not at all. It's just that I love to have that kind of discussion with an intelligent, sensitive soul like you, Maria Callas."

"Thank you, but I am first and foremost a singer and although I deeply respect philosophy, it's not my first love and certainly not my expertise."

"But you are Greek and that makes you part of the great classical philosophers and their philosophical ideas."

"Now you're reasoning like a Greek. It must be that half of you that's Greek."

"I suppose so since my *logos* is fine. It's just fine. That's the part of me that my father did not understand. He never did."

"But not everyone understands logic, François. Not everyone is out of the cave."

"Yes, the cave of darkness and stupidity. Your Rudolf Bing certainly did not."

We both started to laugh. Bruna came into the living room to remind Madame of her early morning master class at the conservatory."

"You're still teaching, Madame Callas?"

"Only when I feel like it and I have very good if not superior students. You see, I simply cannot get away from music and teaching music is my recompense for years of experience and hard work."

"Besides, it's very good for her," added Bruna. "It's like a tonic without pills."

La Callas looked at her with distressed darting eyes and did not utter a single word. She left all of a sudden asking me to excuse her.

"I had a wonderful evening, François. *Merci.*"

The curtain had fallen on this part of the conversation. I could not wait to tell Olivier and Belle Amie about his evening with Maria Callas and the remarkable conversation we had together. "It was memorable, enough that I will not be able to sleep tonight," I told them.

Now I'm turning it over to the narrator.

22. Eikodyo

As Bruna was mending each day and her health grew better and her strength was regained, she returned to her daily chores and served he mistress breakfast and lunch although bot dinner, since Madame wanted to have François continue making her those special meals of his. François consented and Bruna was pleased to have Madame back as she was before her depression had taken hold of her. At least, she was eating better and her appetite gave her the impetus to do more and to stop taking more and more pills. Bruna was against those pills that Madame received in the mail from her sister in Greece. Even her friend, Vasso Devetzi was giving Madame some pills. She had told Bruna that if Madame wanted them to give them to her. Bruna did not like this woman for she found her bossy and oftentimes cantankerous. She took over the household and had Bruna and Ferruccio and even Madame at her mercy when things did not go the way she wanted. Bruna called her the little dictator under her breath while Ferruccio stayed away from her as much as he could. François did not take a liking to her as soon as they were introduced. He found her cold and as sly as a fox, he told himself. She showed a great devotion to Maria Callas while dictating to her what she wanted done and the manner in which it had to be executed. She was devious and envious, thought François. Devious in her way of managing Madame's affairs and envious, he figured, of Madame's fame and money. Not that Madame informed François about her friend and the way she ran her, but François detected by her mood spells and her words, that this friend was not truly her best friend, as she called her. Best friends often turn out to be one's worst enemies, he told Bruna one day as the two of them were sharing views about "the wicked witch of the west" as he called her. "But Madame likes her," said Bruna. François added, "She may like her but she will soon discover that liking her does not mean that the friend is out for her best interest. She makes Madame like her by telling her soft words and offering her more pills but that will not always work, believe me. Madame is sensitive to truth and she will soon detect that she is not being given the full truth by her close friend."

"But Madame is not always in the proper state of mind, I mean in her healthy mood, to detect such deviousness."

"Time will tell, Bruna, time will tell."

François told Olivier and Belle Amie about the continuing arrangements for the evening meals for Madame Callas while Bruna was sick, and that he would continue to prepare their dinner as he had been doing. They encouraged him to do so and wanted him not to feel any pressure in accomplishing his tasks as provider of meals. After all, they told him, he also had to do the shopping for provisions and go to certain markets for special items that certain recipes required. He told them not to worry that he was used to it and that he found joy in the market errands and the preparation of dinner. His next preparation would be a Greek dinner. That's what la Callas liked the most, he told himself. It would be an elegant meal what with candles on the tables, flowers, and a regal spread that would fill la Callas with delicious pleasure. However, he learned later that Madame did not like candles that were lit for she feared fire. Then, he would not have any. It was as simple as that, he told Bruna.

On a bright summer morning in late June, François decided to go the "La Grande Épicerie" and gather the provisions he needed for the dish called "The Greek Summer Feast" that he found in an old cookbook that he bought in one of those *banquettes* along the Seine not far from Notre-Dame Cathedral. He loved spending hours upon hours in his leisure time just looking and thumbing through that many books and magazines available there.

First of all there was the Ouzo that the Greeks loved traditionally accompanied by savory small plates and appetizers known as *mezethes.* The first dish would be the flatbread with two toppings called *Laganes* . He would make his own flatbread and that would take time. That's why he would start this summer feast the day before serving it to Madame Callas. Then he would marinate the pork for the Pork Kebabs with Cucumber Mint Yogurt Sauce, followed by the preparation for e Shrimp with tomatoes and feta called *Garides Saganaki* . Then he would have the marinated sardines called *Sardeles Ladolemono.* He wanted to include a salad called *Horiatiki* with tomatoes, red onions, cucumbers, bell peppers, crumbled feta cheese, Greek oregano, extra virgin olive oil, and green Cretan olives. And, of course, the stuffed grape leaves, called *Dolmades.* He would end he summer feast with the well-known and well appreciated *baklava*. It would require a lot of effort and many hours but he was willing to treat his famous guest as well as the other four partakers of the meal to a true summer feast so well-known to all Greeks who enjoy a summer Greek fare that delights and cools every appetite.

Once François had purchased all of the items he needed for his Greek feast, he began the preparation of the pork kebabs by marinating them the night before. He then prepared the mint yogurt sauce with the cucumber. The stuffed grape leaves he purchased at "La Grande Épicerie" since they looked so good and fresh that he could not make them to look that way, he told himself. Besides, he could not do everything all by himself, not right now. The sardines were plump and fresh from the fish counter and he marinated them ready to be served with the lemon sauce. He loved sardines. He had to take one and taste it for they looked so good marinated and put in that lemon sauce that the lemony taste gave the sardines the right summertime flavor needed. That's why the Greeks loved lemons and its smell and flavor added to so many dishes. After the flatbread had risen, he prepared each and every one of them with two toppings. They smelled so good just like bread coming out of the oven with its bread -with-golden-crust aroma. He then made sure he had enough Ouzo. After all, a summer feast could not be had without the anise-flavored silky liquor. Why, it does go down like silk gliding on a banister. François made sure he had printed by hand the menu *du jour* and had given three to Bruna as well as one each to Olivier and to Belle Amie. He wanted them to anticipate joyfully this summer fest he was preparing for them. He felt a little giddy about his culinary project. He had butterflies in his stomach and bees in his head whirling and buzzing around. How could he not feel that way since he was preparing the best Greek feast ever, and Maria Callas was going to share in it, in Paris and in one of the finest and most luxurious apartment ever, he reminded himself. "It's just like a big banquet scene from one of those operas," he told himself. "It's going to be a glorious feast for everything shouts summertime and summer fun and games when people are free and sing freely with gusto and pride." He told Olivier and Belle Amie before leaving to carry upstairs the various plates, "It's a holiday, my friends. Enjoy and be glad!" They smiled and thanked him for such a good summer feast. Their faces had turned red with flushing pride and contentment for themselves and for François the master cook.

When he arrived upstairs, the door was opened and Ferruccio was there holding the door for him as he said very politely, "*Bonsoir, Monsieur, bienvenue à notre demeure et surtout à notre table.*" François gave him a great big smile and said, "*Mon grand plaisir, mon cher Monsieur, mon très grand plaisir.*" When he stepped into the dining room, Madame was waiting for him and said with some trepidation, "You're not going to make me eat all that's on the menu you gave us, are you?"

"Well, Madame Callas each item will be served in small plates so that you don't have to eat large portions, you see. The summer feast is a traditional custom in Greece, you know."

"Yes, I know, but I have not eaten it in so many years. I have learned to tame my appetite."

"But for once, please try it. I'm sure you'll enjoy it as a return to the days *la flatterie du palais grec.*"

"You're teasing me, François. You're a flirt of the kitchen."

"I suppose so Madame Callas."

"Well let's see what you have. I'm sure I'll enjoy each culinary item with delight and nostalgia for I remember so well the summer feasts back in ."

Bruna helped him serve Madame and replaced each empty dish with another. François could hear the barely audible words of delight each time la Callas tasted a new dish, the soft exclamations rising in tone each time. The sardines were superb, she said, while the stuffed grape leaves were just like those her old aunt used to make, and the *horiatiki* out of this world, she said with a gleam in her eyes. François was so glad that things were turning out right. The Ouzo had been flowing although the diva was not accustomed to drinking the liquor in large portions. But, it went well with the feast, François told her. Later the traditional *baklava* served that Madame refused at first but took a small piece just to satisfy her craving, she told François. Madame then asked Bruna to serve her and François some rich black coffee in the living room without spilling a drop over her expensive carpet. Bruna looked at François with a look that translated her thoughts "as if I ever do."

Both la Callas and François settled in the living room ready to begin another conversation about the diva and her famous career. The warm night air was seeping through the slightly opened windows and it gave the feeling of being in a Persian garden where the exotic smells and sounds of summer were surrounding them.

"I feel that being well-fed is an overture to good conversation and good thoughts about music, don't you think?'

"Oui, Madame. I fully agree with you."

"But you did not eat a bite."

"Oh, I did. I ate with you with my eyes and my heart."

"You're being romantic, *Monsieur au coeur joyeux et pur.*"[Man of the joyous and pure heart].

"Just like the knights of olden days, Madame?"

"I suppose. I've only sung one opera about knights and ladies of the court. It was *Parsifal* by Richard Wagner. I sang the part of Kundry."

"Yes Perceval and the holy grail. It's part of the Arthurian legend and Chrétien de Troyes's was a master of Medieval romances that have all the drama, adventure and courtly love one can find in literature. Have you read any of them?"

"No, but I have heard of them. You see my education was in music and totally axed on music, librettos and operatic performances. I need to go back to school and learn about other great academic pursuits."

"But you have the master classes where you can guide young singers by forging new paths for them by giving of your experiences in operatic performances. You are the master, you are the diva, Madame."

"I know, but although these students show much talent, they have much to learn. I cannot give them what they don't already have, that is, great talent and receptivity to a sense of drama and a deep sense of music. You know what I mean?"

"Somewhat but no exactly."

"Well then, I mean when a singer has a voice but no great talent for creativity, no great talent for expressing emotions or passion, then I'm afraid there's something missing. The voice is not everything."

"I understand. But how about an artist who has talent and a voice and she fails to touch the heart and soul of those in the audience, then what?"

"Failure to connect music, voice, libretto, the conductor and the composition along with the composer and give it as a harmonious whole to each and everyone listening to her. I'm adamant about this. Some people claim it's my wayward passion and my strong sense of idealism and perfection, but I insist on it. There cannot be a good, no an excellent opera singer without that. And that's what I teach. Otherwise I would not teach and I would not be a good teacher and singer."

"*Vous avez raison, Madame.*"[You're right].

"Merci."

"Madame Callas who was your favorite composer and your favorite conductor?"

"Well, that's not an easy question, *mon ami* . I have many who are very good and a few who are excellent and a very few whom I admire and respect highly."

"Like whom?"

"You really want to place me in a tight corner, don't you?"

"It's your corner and you made it."

"Sly fox, François."

"I know that you really like Tullio Serafin who conducted for many years at La Scala."

"Oh, yes. Serafin the master's master. He's the one who guided me to become a true operatic singer. He became my tutor, a beloved tutor who spent time and energy on my singing in order to show me the passion of drama and interpretation. He was my brilliant guiding light throughout my career. I always deferred to him when it came to interpreting particular lines in the libretto. 'The composer wrote it this way, Maria,' he would tell me, 'and the composer is always right.'"

"Did he ever make the slightest of mistakes?"

"Serafin? NO! He was a 'singer's conductor.' Tulio Serafin understood the human voice and its artistic application. Most of all he had an unfailing consideration for the singer, for me, and I appreciated that tremendously. Besides, his wife Elena Rokowska, a former soprano, became my greatest champion. I love her. Such an elegant and charming lady."

"Anything else about Serafin?"

"He was a sly fox, one of a kind, I might say. We were at a stage rehearsal of "Parsifal" one day and I was supposed to kiss the handsome, Hans Beiter, the Parsifal, with a prolonged kiss on the lips. Being twenty-five and very shy, I skipped the kiss. The maestro stopped the rehearsal, walked on to the stage and gave Parsifal the required kiss, pretending to ignore me. Then he said to me in a rather mock tone 'Listen, Maria, if I can kiss him surely you can too.' Everybody laughed. That's the kind of person and conductor he is. He will always be my idol in many ways."

"How about Toscanini and Georges Prêtre?"

"Toscanini was a marvelous and gifted conductor. He was very adamant about diction and the words written and sung on stage. He told a friend of mine once when we were in rehearsal that opera was not a concert and that my diction was not clear and precise enough. I agreed with him. I resolved then and there that I would redouble my efforts to learn and vocalize the words written in that particular language. Any language has a very specific cultural tone and vocal sound to it. One must learn to master them. I have tried and am still trying to do just that."

"But you have mastered many languages and you sing very well in all of them."

"Maybe, but I had to give myself time and extra effort to do so. It did not come easy. I know when the sound of even a single vowel or consonant is wrong. It upsets me and upsets the integrity of the libretto."

"You are that particular about language?"

"Why of course. It's most important. It's opera. It's just not the music but it's also the words sung precisely and accurately in the particularities of that language."

"That's why everyone says that you are a stickler and a perfectionist."

"They're right, you know. I did not spend most of my life studying, rehearsing and performing just as a job or a frivolous activity of mine. Not even for fame and money. They do not mean all that much to me. That I have learned over the years. Sure, I wanted glory and some acknowledgment from people who knew about opera and its glorious possibilities. Did I ever reach the glory? I do not really know. Some phase of it, yes, but not its full extent. I do not really know if I ever will and I do not truly care. All I know is that at this point in my career, I will never be able to reclaim the glory of my best years."

"What about Georges Prêtre......"

"Let's stop here, my friend, I'm getting very tired."

Madame Callas stopped talking and then she looked at François with an exhausted look that revealed a sense of repressed anxiety.

She had said what she had wanted to say for the moment and now she was ready to sleep on it.

"I'm anxious for all of this to end."

"End what?"

"The anxiety of my doubts and sleepless nights."

As she closed the door to her bedroom, François thought of how many nights were spent sleepless and troubled with thoughts of failure. For surely la Callas had her share of worries and anxiety about what the future held for her. It must have been a terrible thing to even think of failure after such an illustrious career as one of the world's greatest operatic and concert singers. I couldn't imagine the inner struggle and tensions that affected her composure and stability as a person who had become a recluse in Paris, the city of openness to light, pleasure and socialization. What was Maria Callas's strategy for sanity, he asked himself. He certainly could not cope with what she was going through and retain his sanity. He was not as strong nor as courageous as her. She was a model of inner strength and determination. That's the way he saw her and understood her in his limited if not growing knowledge of her.

Now I will turn the story over to François.

I did not see her for several days since she was entertaining a close friend of hers named Stelios.That's what Bruna told me. She had few close friends but this one was Greek and they got along very well. She said to Bruna that she welcomed Stelios because she needed a true friend in whom she was able to confide certain things that often troubled her. "Better than pills, I tell you," added Bruna to me. I did not fully understand the problem with pills and the diva, but I knew that it must have added some constraints on her ability to reason things through and sort out her next moves as an artist.

One day in early July, it was mid-afternoon and the temperature was quite high enough to make you sweat doing nothing, Bruna came down and knocked on our door. She wanted to know if I could go to Berthillon on l'Île Saint-Louis and get her some of Berthillon's famous ice cream for Madame. Madame loved ice cream and wanted some right now to cool her off and give her the pleasure of real fruit and delicious ice cream. Everyone knew that Berthillon made their ice cream with real fruit. I did not know that la Callas enjoyed and craved for ice cream or else I would have served her some a long time ago. Here was another opening for me to talk to her besides my serving entire meals.

I took the métro and went to Île Saint-Louis and found there a very long line in front of the famous Berthillon. I did not want to disappoint Madame so I waited an hour to purchase some ice cream. I bought a combination of vanilla and strawberry. It looked so good. I was just hoping that it would not melt along the way. I hurried and got to the apartment in less than fifteen minutes since I took a taxi to go back. I didn't want the ice cream to melt. When I got there Bruna was waiting for me as she hurriedly went to the kitchen to scoop out some of the much anticipated ice cream for her mistress who was waiting in the dining room with her dog Djedda laying at her feet. Later on, Bruna told me that la Callas had a real treat and had thanked her profusely for having satisfied her craving for ice cream. I was glad to have been the instrument of the ice cream satisfaction or the *délices délicieux* as la Callas called it. Afterward, Bruna told me that her mistress had insisted on telling me to serve ice cream more often as a dessert. I did.

Several days went by and I hardly saw la Callas since she was feeling low and did not sleep too well, reported Bruna. She had lost her appetite and did not like the heat of August. She stayed in her apartment reading and listening to her tapes. I decided to do the tourist excursions and enjoy my free time. Olivier and Belle Amie were fine and encouraged me to relax and do what most French people did in August, enjoy *les grandes vacances.* At first I thought of London, then Lisbon but I decided to go to Venice because Belle Amie urged me to go there. It was her favorite site for a vacation, she said, and the canal with its gondolas were so romantic. And, what she truly liked about Venice was its Venetian glass. Well, being romantic at heart, I decided to go to Venice and explore this dream-like site. I took the train at la Gare de Lyon as far as Milan then took a connecting train to Venice. It was a delightful ride and I did not have to worry about cooking meals, running errands, and making sure that everyone was well.

When I got to Venice it was early evening and the sun was slowly setting. I could see the rose and violet colors on the houses and on the canal. I went straight to the small hotel room that I had reserved and found it comfortable an elegant in its own way. I left the hotel right away to go to Saint Mark's Cathedral and its vast piazza called the Piazza San Marco where people congregate and sit having a drink. They just linger there and talk leisurely and without any concerns about those who are looking for a place to sit. I looked up and stared at the tall Campanile as it stood erect and watchful for years. I then went to the Doges Palace and stared at the *Lion of Venice* on the eastern column. It was a large winged lion most probably representing the Evangelist Saint Mark who is often depicted with a lion. The lion of courage and strength, virtues that I did not possess and wished I had. I knew I was timid and shy at times, but I did have perseverance in most things, I told myself. I also had the talent for music and for cooking. I didn't know if that was a harmonious complementary combination or not but that's what I had and what I exercised in my own simple way. I knew that I was not a complicated man, just a simple one, and simplicity was a highly admirable virtue someone told me one day. I accepted his assessment of my quality as lover of music, I was not truly a musician, just a love of good music, and a passable cook because I loved cooking and creating dishes that looked great and tasted even better. That was *MOI* and I had to live with it.

I slept very well that night and woke up to a sun-filled morning that beckoned me to have a quick breakfast and then go for a long walk exploring Venice. After all, I did not come to Venice to sleep and have lavish meals. I came here, I told myself, to enjoy fully my vacation and take advantage of the architecture, art, shopping and mixing in with the crowd. And, most probably there would be music. I had brought with me my copy of Mann's "Death in Venice" and planned to read it again on the long train ride. However, I had not turned a single page on my way down. I was so tired and worn out from all the activities of the previous week that I dozed off repeatedly without even wanting to read a single page of the famous novella. I had no taste for it. I remembered writing a paper on it for Mister Warren in the Classics in Translation class and had gotten an "A". I wrote on the connection of erotic love and to philosophical wisdom traced in Plato's *Symposium* and *Phaedrus.* The idea was suggested to me by my professor and I had gotten a good graded for it. Oh, the delight of following your teacher's suggestions.

After breakfast, I took to the streets and made my way through the alleys, the bridges, and the many here's and there's of Venice. I encountered many people apparently doing the same thing I was, I called it snooping around. At the corner of a long alley I saw leaning against a post, a young lad of about fourteen who was staring at me. He had the most startling green eyes I had ever seen on anyone. I said under my breath, "Tadzio!" He asked me "American?" and I answered, "No." "Dollars?" and I said "No." He lowered his eyes and then turned his head away from my gaze. I had met Aschenbach's fascination with beauty, I told myself, but unlike the old writer with writer's block sitting on the beach watching and waiting. I walked away.

I spent the better part of my week's vacation walking and looking around. What I enjoyed the most were the free concerts in some churches or gathering places where people came to listen to musicians who gave these concerts just to be able to play their instruments be it a saxophone, a violin, a cello or any instrument. I especially enjoyed this one musician who played Bellini's "Casta Diva" on the violin. He was so talented and so very sensitive to the notes he was playing. I could feel the vibrations of the notes on the hairs of my two arms. I never got to know his name for as people started applauding him he hurried off and taking his violin fled from the crowd. Everyone wondered who he was and why he had left so quickly. I overheard from this Belgian couple "*Mais c'est un inconnu remarquable et étrange. Il joue comme un génie consacré mystérieusement à sa musique.*" [What a remarkable and strange unknown. He plays like a genius mysteriously consecrated to his music.] I had to agree with them. Afterwards, the three of us had a drink in a small café called "La Gioconda" and we talked about music. That night I stayed up until two in the morning so mesmerized by the unknown musician who played so daringly well the strings of his violin. His bow must have been his magic wand as he wove his magic on me and captivated my ears and my soul. That's what la Callas does to people, I told myself as I fell asleep wondering what would happen to her in the future. Would she mysteriously flee from everyone and everything never to be seen again?

The following morning after a leisurely breakfast sitting under a canopy and sipping my coffee, I decided that I was going to buy some Venetian glass for Belle Amie and for Maria Callas. Something nice, not too big but captivating for its color and radiance from the light. Nothing too expensive for I had a limited budget and had to keep some money to pay my hotel bill and get back to Paris. I went to an area where there were several shops dealing with Venetian glass and found this small shop that offered nice enough and affordable pieces. I knew that I could not afford the beautiful Murano glass gifts but I would buy something that captured the essence of Venice and its beauty. I bought a small hummingbird for Belle Amie and for la Callas, a small rounded bird, *bombé,* as we say in French. It had a violet-rose color to it and it captured the light well. "That's the piece I want for her, that's the one that imitates her feminine elegance as well as her solid presence as an artist," I told myself and the clerk knew that was the one I wanted and needed for whoever I planned to give it to. He saw it in my eyes.

When I left Venice, the sky was somewhat cloudy but with a tint of violet that gave the sky a somewhat eerie look, a look of mystery and suspense, I thought. I was always prone to make up things when I was a child and even as a teenager I had a vivid imagination. I believe it was carried through my mature life for I still made things up and imagined things when I saw unusual colors or what I called mysterious things in nature. Now I was seeing lilacs and roses in the light of the day. In Venice.

When I got to the apartment in Paris, I hurried to tell Olivier and Belle Amie that I was back and that I had missed their company.

Belle Amie threw her arms around me and kissed me on both cheeks so excited was she at seeing me once more. Olivier did the same thing and I could see that both of them had truly missed me. I was touched by that. I had no relatives, no more parents and only a very few friends, if I had any. But the DesGrandforts were my friends and they had accepted me as one of their own. That was truly comforting. It was as if I had been adopted by a couple who were now my parents. That filled me with contentment and pride since not only did I have a mother but also a father.

"How did you enjoy your trip to Venice?" asked Belle Amie.

"Oh, it was lovely, simply lovely and relaxing."

"Tell us all about it."

"Right now I'm very tired. I had a long trip, a very long one."

"Let him get some rest, Belle Amie and he can tell us about his vacation later," said Olivier to his wife.

"*Mais oui, mais oui. Je faisais ma folle en le voyant. C'est tout.*" (I know, I know. I was being foolish. That's all.)

"Are you hungry, François?" asked Olivier.

"No, just tired. I'm going to lie down for a while then I'll have something to eat with both of you."

I'm back to narrating as narrator.

When François got up after two hours of much needed sleep, he looked around the apartment to see how much food there was. He looked in the cupboards, the refrigerator and the spare closet, but found very little. What had they been eating? he asked himself, or have they been eating at all.

"What did you eat while I was gone?"

"We ate well, François, we ate well every day," replied Olivier.

"But what did you eat? Nothing much I'll bet."

"Olivier could not go to the market because he had to take care of me. *J'ai été malade.*"

"Bruna brought us some food and we ate the rest of the cereal and the canned tuna. Besides, I did not want to tell you that I was running low on money. I had so many expenses this past month."

"Olivier, why did you not tell me?"

"I did not want to worry you. Besides, I was afraid you would have canceled your trip. You needed that vacation."

"If only I had known. If only..... I'm going to the market to get us some food and I'll cook you something good, you'll see."

And so François, Olivier and Belle Amie had a good meal and they all ate voraciously, for even François had not eaten all day.

Things were back to normal in the household now that François was back and Olivier and Belle Amie were able to sigh a big sigh of relief. Bruna came to pay a visit and told François that Madame was feeling fine after having had two episodes of depression and two terrible sleepless nights when she walked all night long worrying Bruna and giving her a terrible fright after Madame had told her that she did not want to live like that anymore. She told François that Madame was taking more and more pills and that she was sleeping late almost every morning. She was also eating less. Bruna was terribly worried about her and she had a mind to call the doctor but that Madame Devetzi would not like it.

François reassured her that Madame Callas would start feeling better once she had a good meal inside her. That made Bruna really happy. After all, her concerns were genuine and they were serious.

23. Eikotrito

It was a cool day for early September cooler than usual and quite windy but François decided to go to the Grande Épicerie and get provisions for the meal he planned for la Callas. Bruna had told him that Madame was regaining her appetite and was glad to hear that François was planning an evening meal for her. It would consist of Italian dishes with all of the embellishments he could come up with. He had found good recipes in Venice and was eager to try them out. When François stepped out on the Avenue Georges Mandel he realized how cold it and windy it was. People were wearing their winter hats and coats. "Already?" he exclaimed. He rushed to catch the metro and he felt comfortable once inside. He had a long list of provisions he would need and he thought of how he was going to prepare all of the food he intended to bake and cook. It was going to be a banquet-like meal and it was certainly going to impress la Callas and revive her appetite. Furthermore, he was looking forward to resume their conversations about the diva's career and about conductors that they had already broached. Good food, he told himself, was certainly the door to good and lively conversation especially when it came to Maria Callas and her career as a diva.

The dinner was planned for Wednesday evening the day after tomorrow and he wanted to make sure he had everything necessary for the sumptuous meal he was planning. The menu would consist of stuffed duck, *bigolli,* chestnut gnocchi with pesto sauce, risotto with saffron, *pollo alla Cacciatora*, and for dessert *panna cotta*, a milk and caramel pudding, and for special crowning effect Italian gelato.

Both Olivier and Belle Amie were sitting in the kitchen watching silently François organizing himself for the sumptuous meal he was going to offer the following evening.

"I'm preparing a meal that will knock Madame Callas' socks off."

"Her what?" asked Olivier.

"Her socks, *ses chaussons*."

"What does that mean?"

"It has nothing to do with socks as such. It means it's going to astound her and you as well."

"*Mon Dieu*" exclaimed Belle Amie.

"I'm going to start with the duck and the stuffing and then put it aside until tomorrow when I will put it in the oven early in the afternoon. Then I 'm going to prepare the gnocchi and set it aside, after that comes the risotto with saffron, a dish that's very popular in Northern Italy especially in Milan. As for my thick spaghetti, the *bigoli*, I'll wait until tomorrow to cook it with tomatoes and olives. The pudding, I will make it tonight. Olivier, you can get the gelato for me at the corner shop tomorrow, if you please."

"Of course, I will, *avec grand plaisir*."

François told them that traditional characteristic of Venetian cuisine is the use of the finest of spices. The only pasta the Venetians use is the thick and coarse spaghetti called *bigoli. As* for their stuffed duck, they usually have a sweet and sour stuffing made with duck breast. He told them that fresh fish was a main ingredient on their menu, all kinds of fish including sardines and dried codfish. He was not including fish on his menu because it would have been too much food for one evening. Finally, François told them that a glass of **spritz,** the Venetian local apéritif would be served since he had brought a bottle with him from Venice. So, tomorrow's dinner would consist of dishes from two parts of Italy, the Northern and the Southern parts including Venice.

As he got ready to begin the preparation of the first dish, the stuffed duck, he got the duck breasts from the refrigerator and took off the skin. Then, he cut them into small strips and added the necessary spices and sweet and sour ingredients to them in the skillet. When they were done, he then diced them and placed them to one side while he prepared the whole duck, it was a small one, and once he had rinsed it and inspected it, he placed the stuffing in the opening and sewed it tight. He then put the duck in the refrigerator.

Then came the gnocchi. He prepared the potato dough with unpeeled mashed potatoes. Then he added two kinds of flour, white and chestnut flour (he had a hard time finding chestnut flour but he did get some at a small specialty shop). The egg was added to the dough and rolled out the dough into thick strings. Then he cut them in small pieces and placed them on a floured tray. He then cooked them in salty boiling water. They're done when they rise to the surface, he told his two friends who were still watching him intently. Following that, he prepared the pesto sauce so that he would have it for tomorrow when he would be ready to pour the sauce on the gnocchi.

As for the risotto with saffron, he put the ingredients one by one in a saucepan starting first by dissolving the saffron in some chicken broth. He then sautéed the onion in butter and then added some white wine until it evaporated. Then came the rice with the broth added gradually and then the last step, adding the dissolved saffron. It began to look like paste but I knew that it was supposed to look like that and that it would be good to the taste. He then started to prepare the pasta sauce of diced tomatoes, garlic, chopped anchovies, capers, Italian parsley, black olives and red pepper not to forget the extra-virgin olive oil. The whole mixture simmered on the stove until the entire apartment smelled like an Italian kitchen filled with the splendid aroma of Italian cuisine all in one preparatory sauce. Olivier and Belle Amie sat there mesmerized by the hefty aroma of tomatoes, anchovies, olives, parsley and garlic all cooked to perfection so that the mixture invited all nostrils and taste buds to acclaim this sauce. Every Italian man, woman and child cannot truly live without pasta sauce like that one, François fondly proclaimed. What not to love when one craves for spaghetti or any kind of rich pasta sauce. One never finishes eating pasta without licking the plate with a piece of crusty bread.

Olivier asked François if he wasn't tired. He answered, no, and told them it was time for a glass of wine before he got started on the *pollo.* The glasses were filled with a Riesling, the wine Belle Amie loved, and the glasses were lifted in the joy of good food and a good cook, said Belle Amie, *une bonne bouffe et un très bon cuisinier...non, non chef.*" Following the drinking of wine and the good cheers, he began his final dish. He then realized that the duck and the chicken would make too much of a similar dish and decided that he would keep the chicken for another fare later on, perhaps *poulet à l'estragon.* He then started to put everything away and enjoy another drink. He would do the dishes tomorrow morning since Belle Amie insisted that he go to bed and that she would help him after breakfast. Sleep came quickly to François and then morning soon followed for he realized that he had gone to bed way past two a.m. Both Olivier and Belle Amie had been in bed for some three hours. He had finished the bottle of Reisling and then opened a bottle of Chardonet. The bottle half empty lay on the floor next to his bed.

Right after breakfast, the three of them did some chores, Belle Amie and François did the dishes while Olivier did the sweeping and dusting. Later that morning Bruna came knocking gently at their door. She wanted to confirm the dinner for that night and that François would have everything ready for Madame. He told her, yes, and she hurried back upstairs taking the lift. Belle Amie asked him if there was anything she could do to help finish preparing the dishes for the dinner. He told her that everything had been well prepared the night before and that all he had to do was the cooking. He would do that himself. First came the stuffed duck and the sauce he would make at the last minute. Then the gnocchi with the pesto sauce that he would warm up before serving them. The risotto was ready for the serving once warmed up and the pasta sauce would also be warmed up after the bigoli had boiled and ready to serve. All he had to do now was to make the milk and caramel pudding. It was an easy dessert to make, cream and gelatin topped with fruit. Come late afternoon early evening everything was ready to serve and François was keeping things warm. He would ask Bruna to help him carry the dishes upstairs when the time came for serving dinner. She had already told him that she would help once Madame was ready for dining awaiting this sumptuous meal as François called it. It would be a feast indeed and he was sure la diva would relish every spoonful, every bite and every palate pleasing morsel that came into everyone's mouth be it la Callas', Bruna's, Ferruccio's, Olivier's or Belle Amie's. He was sure of it. Tonight would be this magnificent adventure into Italian eating, he told himself. He sure hoped he would not disappoint anyone especially Madame Callas. What he looked forward to was the conversation after dinner with the diva. He was excited about that more than the food.

When every dish was brought upstairs and placed in the kitchen ready to be served and Madame was seated at the table, Madame told Bruna when she came to ask her if she was ready to eat, to please ask François to join her at the table since she did not want to eat alone. He was so surprised by her invitation that he was tongue-tied and simply nodded his head in the affirmative. Thus he had his first meal with the diva and Bruna served every dish and waited on them throughout the entire meal.

"François, the duck is superb and the stuffing goes so well with it, so rich in taste and the *soupçon* of the sweet and sour is just right. It brings me back to my days in Italy, Milano, Roma, Venitia."

"Thank you, Madame Callas."

Later on, "This risotto is marvelous. I really like it. Did you make it yourself or did you buy it? I love the hint of saffron."

"Thank you."

And then, "Oh, the *bigoli* and this sauce is out of this world. I know it's a Venetian specialty but I did not know you knew how to make it or even get that coarse pasta. But the sauce makes everything delightful on this dish."

"I'm glad you like it."

"Like it, I love it. I shouldn't be eating so much but everything is so good and so very perfect that I cannot help myself. I just hope

I am able to sleep on such a heavy stomach. You are a wizard with food, *mon ami*, truly you are."

"I simply love to cook. I enjoy making pleasurable meals for people who appreciate good food. I suppose it's my calling in life."

"I'll have to stop eating now. I cannot take another bite, another taste of anything as good as it is."

"No dessert? I made a lovely cream and caramel pudding."

"No."

"Not even gelato?"

"Well I suppose just a little in a crystal dish."

After they had completely finished our meal ending with a spoonful or two of gelato, they agreed to get back to the conversation about conductors that they had started the last time. After another glass of **spritz**, Madame offered François *une flûte de champagne* which he did not refuse. It was extremely good champagne.

"Well now, where were we, François? Oh, yes Toscanini, Serafin and I believe Karajan?"

"No we did not get to Herbert von Karajan. I was on the verge of asking you about Georges Prêtre, remember?"

"That's right. Georges Prêtre, let me see. He's one of my very favorite conductors for he is open and above board in all things. He's a very dynamic musician and conductor. I loved every minute being with him at rehearsals and during the performances. He knows how to interpret the composers' every note of music along with each libretto."

"I remember his conducting **Carmen** by Bizet, an opera that you sang and recorded with him in 1964, I believe. I listened to it and although I knew nothing about opera, I truly enjoyed it, especially since it was sung in French. Your voice then captured the dramatic intonations of the passionate gypsy that was Carmen and your voice, I thought, hit some of the mezzo soprano's range so guttural was it. You rendered the fiery, volatile, infuriating and seductive gypsy real with your voice and gestures that I could not wait for the unfolding of the opera at every act. And when the last act comes and when Carmen provokes Don José and tells him '*Laisse-moi passer,*' that was truly bold and provocative, capturing the essence of why the composer wrote this opera of dealing with *la fatalité des gitanes*. Anyway, that's what I thought at the time. And I remember loving George Prêtre's rendition of the music and how he conducted his musicians especially in the song "Les Tringles des Sistres tintaient" you know the "Gypsy Song" and its whirling almost frantic music. He gave it a dynamic and most spirited accompaniment to the lyrics."

"Oh, yes, that was quite a recording. It did capture the dynamism and the thematic qualities of the opera such as the one dealing with death, '*La mort, toujours la mort,*' says Carmen while dealing her tarot cards. The conductor knew how to render musically such themes that Bizet had placed in his splendid work."

"And there was the splendid voice and presence of Nicolai Gedda. You two sang and played your parts extremely well and you complemented one another with such harmony and vitality."

"Yes, I've always loved Nicolai. His voice was elegant and resonant as a tenor. Most of all I enjoyed his beauty of tone, his vocal control and especially his musical perception. There are many tenors in the world of opera but Nicolai Gedda is one of a kind."

"Do you see him once in a while?"

"Not since I retired from the stage."

"You never did play the part of Carmen on stage did you?"

"No, I never did and I have reasons for it but I will not get into it now."

"Can you tell me more about Georges Prêtre?"

"Not much more except to say he was and remains one of my favorite conductors. Probably because he's French."

"How about Leonard Bernstein?"

"Now there's a man full of vitality, a conductor who gets to the core of the music and leads the orchestra and the singers with dynamism and strength of willful talent. He was principally a composer, you know, but he knew how to conduct, and masterfully so. I only had him for one opera, **Medea** at la Scala and he displayed his enormous talent for conducting with fire and determination. I really enjoyed this talent of his because I sensed that he understood me as a singer and he respected my talent as a dramatic opera diva. It was at my insistence that Ghiringhelli got in touch with him and offered him a contract."

"Ghiringhelli the manager of la Scala?"

'Precisely, Ghiringhelli the businessman who did know or understand a note of music, the circus master, as some people called him."

"That's funny."

"Funny but sad. Getting back to Bernstein, we only had five full days of stage rehearsals but Bernstein did wonders with the orchestra and the cast. I admired his talent, as I have said. Why, I even had a ten-minute standing ovation after my first aria and I could see that Bernstein's face illuminated with the broadest of smiles. It was after the performance that someone reported to me that Leonard Bernstein had said about me and my performance of **Medea** that night and had said enthusiastically, 'That woman generates pure electricity on the stage. In **Medea** she is a power-station.' Isn't that great? I love that man for he understood me and my voice much like Serafin did."

"Wow! That's quite a compliment."

"It is. I have never forgotten it."

'I knew you were the greatest singer in the world, yesterday, today and tomorrow."

"I don't know about today and I know about tomorrow since I will have most probably lost my voice entirely."

"Don't say that, Madame Callas, the Divina Callas."

"I know, François and the world knows that God-given talent is still in me but I have exhausted it and my voice is going downhill. It doesn't have the vitality, the power and the strength it had before. *Je l'ai abusée, rendue à l'extrême...usé jusqu'à la corde, comme le dit parfois Bruna.*"[I abused it to an extreme…used it to the very end].

"*Il ne faut pas dire cela, Madame, jamais le dire à moi, jamais.*" [Never say that especially to me].

"Merci. But I know when the signs are there, I know. Listen, François, you gave me a medal some time ago, a medal of Our Lady who appeared here in Paris."

"Yes, the Miraculous medal of *Notre-Dame du Bac.*"

"Well, I'd like you to take me there, at the shrine where this Catherine saw the Lady."

"That's Catherine Labouré. You want to go to la rue du Bac, that's it?"

"Yes, François, I want to go there. Can you make the arrangements for the two of us to go and visit this shrine?"

"Yes, of course. When? Remember, this site is usually full of devoted believers, crowds sometimes. We cannot go in the morning since that's when they have masses, probably in early evening?"

"You make the arrangements and I'll go. I want to go. I have to go and plead with Our Lady for my health. My insomnia is getting worse, François, I'm afraid I will lose my sanity and like some of my heroines, I'll go mad."

"No, absolutely no, Madame Callas. You will never go mad. You're too intelligent for that."

"Intelligence has nothing to do with it. It's my destiny, my fate or as we Greeks say, *moira*. There are certain things we humans cannot change and that is birth and death, but at the center of it all there's the evolving of our talents and dispositions. But, more important there's the physical impediments and aging factor that come to cut short these talents and dispositions and that leaves one at the mercy of fatality. What good is my talent if I gradually lose my voice? What good is my entire life's work if I slip gradually into some kind of incapacity? Then I know I am frail, inconsistent, inadequate, and immeasurably limited and I may go mad...I can go mad...I am human. Furthermore, I cannot reconcile myself to the casualties of emotions and particularly the need to love and the confrontation of unrequited love."

"But you did love once. Is it the other love affair, and I do not want to mention his name."

"Please don't, I told you before that I did not want to get into that at all."

"I'm sorry."

François left the Callas apartment sad and deeply concerned

about the Divina for he would have never thought that he would see her in such a sorry state. She was a strong, willful, vital woman not a person who succumbs to frailty and even debility. He could not bring himself to believe that. When he got to the apartment downstairs, he went to bed fully clothed and tried so very hard to contain his tears that were burning upwards from the heart.

24. Eikositessera

I'm now going to let François resume his story while I step back as narrator.

The following morning after I had washed and shaved, I started to prepare breakfast for Olivier, Belle Amie and myself. Both of them barraged me with question about last night and my serving dinner to Madame Callas. I told them about my being invited to join her for dinner and the wonderful conversation we had about conductors. Of course, I did not dare mention her revelations to me about her health issues. I simply told them that Madame wanted to go to the rue du Bac to visit the Miraculous Medal shrine.

"*Mais c'est une chrétienne et elle a une grande dévotion à la Sainte Vierge.*" I told them. [She's a Christian and she has a great devotion to the Blessed Virgin].

"Vraiment?"

"I'm simply going to make some arrangements for the two of us to go there and she can spend as much time there as she wants. I'm doing her a favor that she deserves. I owe her that, at least."

That very afternoon I took the metro and got out at Sèvres-Babylone and walked over to the rue du Bac and entered the courtyard that opened up to the entrance of the chapel. I entered and there were people praying in the pews and others kneeling at the altar rail.

Some came to deposit flowers that some nun came to pick up later. I could see there was practically a constant flow of people in and out of the chapel. I realized that it was a very popular place of worship. I would try to bring Madame Callas at a time when there would be less people. I'm sure that she would certainly be somewhat apprehensive of the traffic here fearing to be recognized. She was so protective of her privacy. But, she did want to come here and I would make sure she would be able to come here and offer the prayers for her health that she so wanted. She wanted to take the risk of being recognized hoping that not too many people would insist on pressing to answer their questions. She certainly not be in the mood for that. I knew that she loved her opera fans and in the past she was delighted to talk to them and answer their questions, but for now she was not in a frame of mind and heart to do what she used to with people gathering around her. She truly had become a recluse and wanted it that way. In any case, I simply wanted to comply with her request to visit the shrine on the rue du Bac. It would be a challenge for me since I could feel her pain and her fear of people, but she had to face her situation and go beyond it if she wanted to do certain things like stepping out of her reclusive environment that was the Avenue Georges Mandel and her confining apartment. I would help her to that.

The visit to the shrine was planned for a Tuesday in mid-October in the early hours of the evening hoping the weather would cooperate and the thunder storms, if they occurred, would not deter her from going there. Ferruccio would drive us to rue du Bac and he would come to pick us up a half hour later which would allow Madame sufficient time to pray and possibly meditate. She agreed to the plan and I was ready to accompany her. Being Friday, I knew that I had time to prepare lunch and dinner for the three of us, Olivier, Belle Amie and myself and be able to spend the weekend reading, taking long naps and just not doing much of anything. That would be my leisure time for la Callas did not want to be disturbed with planned dinners as was my habit of doing in the last couple months, at least for the time being, she told Bruna and she told her to tell me. So, it was my culinary break so-to-speak. Of course, Olivier, Belle Amie and I ate well enough but we had no elaborate meals that I loved to prepare for la diva. I missed that but I knew that I would resume those in the near future since Madame would eventually crave for good meals. I was sure of it.

Tuesday late afternoon came and I was ready to accompany Madame to the rue du Bac when Ferruccio came downstairs to tell me that Madame was indisposed our visit had to be postponed. He told me that she was sorry about this and that she would inform me when she would try again, perhaps the following week. I asked him if there was anything I could do, and he told me, no. I was caught by surprise, of course, but I realized that such things could happen with Madame Callas. I went back to my leisure time not doing much of anything except I did listen to some tapes of la Callas' Master Classes at Juilliard.

I discovered in the Master Classes evidence of Maria Callas' extraordinary talent for resiliency and composure under stressful situations like her realization that her voice did not have the same capacity to reach certain high notes. That must have been devastating to her pride as an accomplished singer. She had spent so much time and effort to polish and strengthen that voice of hers. Of course, it was a natural gift but she had to work terribly hard to refine it and, as an opera singer, polish her dramatic skills as well as learn the language a given opera be it Italian, French or German and the exact intonations and accents required. That is not easy. Everything had to be energized and harmonized into a whole, song, language, music and gestures as well as the emotions that render any performance real. She had mastered all of that and now at Juilliard she was imparting her skills and talent to some two dozen students she had picked out of three hundred applicants and she did it, from what I can see, with genuine understanding and the knowledge of how beginners feel and how they try to perform as well as they can a great piece of music. Can you imagine being in the presence of the world's greatest operatic singer and giving what you consider your best in trying to reach those notes that are a challenge to you? I can't. There must have been many a frayed nerve in the process. However, Maria Callas' awesome experience, her countless performances at the best opera houses of the world, her knowledge of music and especially of any given composer's words and music as well as her keen intelligence that provided her the thirst and passion for that knowledge, were all instruments of the craft of singing opera for Maria Callas. I say craft because it is a craft, a definite skill that one must learn and exercise in order to perform with excellence and perfection. Besides, Maria Callas had learned elegance in both fashion, decorum and the performance of on-stage delivery. Assuredly, Hidalgo, Serafin and a few others had helped her refine those skills but she is the one who had to work constantly at it and ever persevere. That was one of her virtues, perseverance. I found out about all these things by reading up on Maria Callas and especially by listening to her recordings and for me it truly began with dear Mister Kalapodous in New York who was so knowledgeable about la Callas and her operatic performances as well as her musical perceptions and great talent to connect so intimately with a given composer's work. All I know is that Maria Callas, the Divina as she is known, never stopped thinking of and aspiring for perfection. And perfection is earned not given. Besides perfection, true perfection is never fully attained; it can be reached to a level of approximation but never fully attained. Not on this earth.

I listened to all students of the Juilliard Master Classes on the EMI recording. There were nine of them and they represented and array of arias and one young man singing *Cortigiani, vil razza dannata* from **Rigoletto**. Callas displayed not only her singing skills but her teaching skills which were phenomenal as far as I was concerned. I planned to discuss all of them with her next time we meet and have dinner together. Of course I was going to prepare it and it most probably would be a French cuisine meal. That would be one, I mean a discussion, that I would certainly look forward to for it deals with the next generation of singers. My generation, if you please. I read that the Juilliard Master Classes were held between October 11, 1971 and March 16, 1972. Callas, I was told, was still in a self-imposed exile from the operatic and concert stage that had lasted six years. She was trying to regain her sense of purpose we were told. But I feel that she was truly attempting to find her way back to her heydays when her voice was supreme. However, would she ever find it or not that was left up to her capability to reinvent herself but most importantly overcome her fears and physical adversities pertaining to the quality and resiliency of a voice that had been used over and over again if not abused, as some people say. A singer can only push his or her voice so far before it begins to show signs of depletion and overuse. I did not plan to tell her that for I'm sure she knew it, but I thought I might just test her a bit about the evolution of her voice without inferring that she was on the verge of losing the great gift that she had, if not losing it at least risk damaging it somehow. I don't know since I'm not a voice master and I cannot judge the qualitative capacity of a singing voice. I'm just a listener and a sincere fan of Maria Callas and her inimitable voice.

First and foremost, I had to find out if la Callas still wanted to pay a visit to the Miraculous Medal shrine. That much I felt I owed her. I asked Bruna to ask her mistress if she still planned to go to the rue du Bac or not and when. Bruna came back to tell me that Madame indeed wanted to go and that she would plan on the following Monday for her visit with me and she wanted me to make all of the plans for it. Knowing that the chapel was filled with worshipers and devoted followers of the Miraculous Medal and Out Lady during the daytime hours, I thought of bringing la Callas in the early evening hours when the stream of followers was not as dense as in the mornings and afternoons. I was going to take a chance that I was right. I only wanted to protect la Callas from too many people recognizing her and rushing to get an autograph or a photo and who knows what. One never knows with celebrities.

So the following Monday around six o'clock in the evening Ferruccio was waiting outside ready to take the two of us, la Callas and me, to the rue du Bac. She was wearing simple clothes, black all-weather coat and a dark but expensive scarf, probably a Chanel or a Rochas on her head. She wore very little jewelry as far as I could see. It was late September so it was getting dark outside but she wore dark glasses possibly to hide her identity or at least discount it. She was going on a pilgrimage not on a tour or a premiere. When we got to the entrance of the shrine chapel, Ferruccio deposited us and was told to return in a half hour. There were not too many people there on the sidewalk. We walked briskly to the entrance leading to the chapel and I opened one of the doors. The chapel was not full but there were many people praying and meditating in the pews. Others were kneeling at the altar rail facing the large statue of Our Lady with golden rays streaming from her hands. On the vault of the sanctuary were written these words, " *O Marie conçue sans péché priez pour nous qui avons recours à vous*". O Mary conceived without sin pray for us who have recourse to you. And that's what la Callas saw up there right in front of her eyes once she had taken her dark glasses off. We went to the left side of the chapel, the side where Catherine Labouré's incorrupt body lay under the altar and we sat in a pew. She went in first and I sat next to the aisle. Everything was quiet and the entire chapel truly felt like a fervent abode of prayers and petitions. A little later, a gentleman in a trench coat came to sit next to me pushing me and la Callas. He then whispered in my ear "Is that Maria Callas?" I looked at him and said "No." "It sure looks like her," he said. "Well I'm telling you it's not her." That's when la Callas looked at me and I could see nervousness in her face if not panic. I excused myself and asked the gentleman to let us out of the pew. He looked disappointed and a bit angry at me for not allowing him to pursue his question about Maria Callas. I took la Callas's arm and we walked away and went directly to the front entrance hoping to meet Ferruccio there. Sure enough, he had been waiting for us for ten minutes he told us. The gentleman from the chapel was there staring at the three of us probably hoping to follow us to our destination. Ferruccio knew his way round Paris and he got us to Avenue Georges Mandel safe, sound and without anyone following us. Once in the car, la Callas thanked me for having brought her to the chapel and she assured me that she had had time to say the prayers that she wanted to say about her health and especially the favor that she requested from Our Lady about her insomnia. I told her that I was glad that things had worked well for her without any inconveniences. "Oh," she said, "You mean that gentleman, *cet homme ennuyeux qui voulait me voir?*" She took the lift up and I went downstairs to my apartment. It had been quite an adventure, *une aventure de pèlerinage.*

25. Eikosipente

For the soup I chose a lemon chicken soup that would be light and delicious to the taste right before the main course. It was early October and the cool weather had settled in. A good warm soup would be just the thing for us. Then I would make lamb with mint jelly, some kind of wild rice with saffron, and some stuffed grape leaves just to make it truly Greek. For the dessert I chose to make a delicious honey walnut cake with a not too sweet syrup that would make it moist and delicious to the taste buds. We would end the meal with a demi-tasse of black coffee *juste pour le goût* as the French say.

Come Sunday afternoon, most of the meal was prepared and I would wait until early evening to make the rice since I did not want it overcook and go lumpy. At six o'clock I ran upstairs and told Bruna that I was ready and to please tell Madame to be seated at the table in half an hour when I would bring up the food. She was there when I stepped in and handed the food to Bruna who was waiting for me with Ferruccio at her side. Bruna then told me that Madame was expecting me at the dinner table. I was prepared for the invitation and I had on a shirt, tie and dinner jacket. I knew that Madame Callas liked one to be well-dressed for dinner. As soon as I sat down, I looked up and saw la Callas's eyes on me. They were dark and brilliant and they seem to penetrate my inner self so intense was her gaze on me. I lowered my eyes to raise them up again for fear of making her feel not wanted by me. It was simply a quick gesture of shyness on my part and I knew that she knew it. We had what the French call *une larme d'un petit vin blanc,* just a sip of white wine and then we proceeded to have the hot soup followed by the entrée. We made small conversation during the dinner knowing full well that we would take up our regular conversation after dinner after our coffee. The meal had been relaxed and I was glad that la Callas seemed relaxed herself and not too tense. She asked where we were in our conversation about opera and I told her that we had not quite finished with the conductors. I also thought of advising her that I would like to take up her master classes at Juilliard after the conductors. She agreed with a sly smile on her face.

"Where were we with the conductors, François?"

"Herbert von Karajan."

"Oh yes, Herbert von Karajan the musical perfectionist, that's why I truly liked him. Like myself he did not cut short rehearsals nor was he satisfied with mediocrity. Moreover, he was an elegant man, elegant in his decorum, in his manners and in his dress. He was a true Viennese."

"What operas did he conduct for you?"

"Well there were several. I had some memorable moments with Karajan. I remember **Lucia di Lammermoor** at la Scala that was conducted and staged by him. He wanted everything to be somber, the sets rather bare with stylized outlines and above all dimly lit so that gloom would permeate the stage. That was not to everyone's liking, but the performance was cheered and I remember seeing a rainfall of red carnations coming after the first part of the mad scene. Some called it delirium on the part of the opera goers that night."

"That must have been some night."

"Yes. Then there was the Berlin performance when Karajan surpassed himself and I had a triumphant night with what they called my 'incomparable magic' and there were masses of flowers, cheering and unprecedented applause. It was indeed a memorable evening of opera and Karajan was part of it all."

"That must have been exciting for you."

"Not just exciting but it stirred my heart and soul for noting like that goes without some inner uplifting. And in the recording of **Madama Butterfly** Karajan interpreted the score with penetrating insight and brought all the emotional excitement needed. Yes, I will ever remember Herbert von Karajan with fondness and admiration for his skill and elegance as a conductor."

"He's up there with the other conductors you have known then."

"Yes but Serafin remains at the very top."

"That's how much you admire him."

"I adore him for he was and is the very best in my book."

"May we now talk about your master classes at Juilliard?"

"If you want to. They were my moments of delightful bridging between my stage performances and my stepping away from them. I never abandoned them but they abandoned me in a way. I had to redefine my life and my career and the master classes helped me to do just that."

"Let me tell you about my listening to the recording with nine of your students. If you do not mind I will give you my remarks that I wrote down while listening to every aria."

"No I don't mind at all. Proceed."

"Well, first of all there's Kyo Do Park and Mozart's **Don Giovanni** when you talked about embellishments."

"Yes, I wanted her to be sure of herself and the quality of the embellishments. Embellishments are not to be treated lightly and as a whim. They must be part and parcel of the arias themselves. They must fit like hand in glove. Do you understand?"

"Yes, I do. Then there was Pamela Hebert in Beethoven's **Fidelio** and I enjoyed the comments you gave her."

"Yes, she's a good singer but needs much polishing."

"Next was Luba Tcheresky with Cherubini's **Medea**. You told her that the aria was a very difficult one that she had got to totally open her throat. You told her that repeatedly."

"Yes, I had to in order to impress the importance of opening the throat when one sings such an aria. It's very important."

"What impressed me the most about this part was the fact that when the student said to you 'the way you want it' and you quickly replied, 'No, the way the composer wants it.'"

"It's so very true. It's the composer who composed the opera not me nor anyone else. The composer is the guide and the master of his work. We singers, conductor and orchestra must follow his creative spirit and interpret his opera the way he wanted it. That's why the score and the libretto are so very important."

"Then there was the aria 'Casta Diva' from Bellini's **Norma** with Pamela Hebert."

"Oh, yes."

"You truly went into this aria with agility, strength and dramatic concentration to show this student how to sing it. I realized that diction for you was as important as the singing and the music. You really and forcefully enunciated the words and linked them in a harmonious string vowels and consonants to make them whole and musically complementary."

Yes. If the words are not well pronounced and well integrated within the interpretation of the score then you have mishmash. It won't flow and it will not allow the entire performance to be within the realm of excellence."

"And that's the vision and commitment of the perfectionist."

"But of course. I am a perfectionist and I do not apologize for it. I have committed my entire life to my singing and opera and I will not, NOT, allow mediocrity in any way shape or form including diction."

"I get it. You don't have to convince me."

"Just the budding artists and those who vow themselves to music and singing."

"Then came Rossini's **Il Barbieri di Sivigla** with Syble Young and Rosina's aria. I heard the laughter in the audience when you told the student to come in well- dressed because audiences see more than what one may think they see and to wear longer skirts or slacks if you're a woman on stage. You were quite direct with her."

"Yes, I was. That's because proper dress is a necessity on stage as far as I'm concerned even when it's simply an audition, a rehearsal or a master class. It's all part of decorum, you see, a factor that's way up there in my book. It's very important."

"The perfectionist."

"Yes, the perfectionist. That's who I am and I refuse to recant at any level of any performance."

"You tell the student that the words were clear and that she did not have to overact. Then you told her 'Don't smile,' and always vibrate the sound. By the way that aria was fantastic. I had never heard it before."

"It is a very good one and a challenge to the soprano if she sings it right. I told her to not overdo the drama of the words sung since they are very clear in themselves. Vibrating the sounds are also important in an aria. The sounds must not be static and stuck in the throat."

"Finally, you told her to put more feeling and to forget the hola-balou, I think you said."

La Callas looked at me and smiled with her sly fox smile.

"Precisely. All of the flamboyancy and outlandish features of what I call hola-balou is in itself distracting and should not be allowed for the feeling, the expression of genuine feeling is sufficient to convey the drama and the true quality of the aria, music and words."

"Then came the tenor, Sung Kil Kim and Verdi's **Rigoletto**."

"Yes, the young man with a charming voice but who needs the polishing of words and music in order to express correctly what the composer wanted in his opera. 'Like an animal' I told him, because 'You cry but you hate the idea' I told him. That's how you must view it and especially feel it, I told him. There's a lot of deep masculine feelings in this aria and so the singer must not only feel it but reach deep inside of himself and find the chord that resonated with his feelings of utter frustration and animal gut-wrenching anger."

"I liked the fact that you took time to teach young men as well as young women."

"Male or female, they're all singers that need to learn. I do not have a tenor, baritone or bass register but I know how to put feeling and genuine expression in the words and music the composer wrote. I also told the young man, Kim, in my Farewell words, to never be allowed to close up again on account of auditioning. They seemed to have frightened him, I told the audience. Courage, it takes a lot of courage to sing in front of anybody especially a large audience as I've done."

"I will not forget what you told Sheila Nadler who sang 'Eboli' from Verdi's **Don Carlo**. Elegance you stressed, elegance as the key to the performance of this opera. And at the end, you called for *animato* and the giving of more life to the singing."

"*Animato* is the life from which springs all of the energy of both the singer and the aria she sings. You cannot have anything especially an opera without life and that means soul, the reservoir of spirit and life."

"The next singer was Anita Terzian and Massenet's **Werther**, in the role of Charlotte, the poor suffering girl."

"Yes, she is more than suffering, she's torn by it and she suffers both in her heart and soul."

"Yes, you told the student at the very beginning that Charlotte goes through terrific suffering probably more than any other human being who loves and is painfully separated from her lover. Am I not right?"

"You certainly are. Charlotte is a tragic heroine who undergoes deep sadness and heart-wrenching pain. Werther's letters are both excruciating and horribly hard on her sensibility as a woman who thought she was loved and clings to a vanishing love as she realizes her fate."

"Oh, yes, you tell the student that an 'Ah' doesn't mean you have to breathe. Do you remember?"

"I certainly do. An 'Ah' doesn't mean you have to stop the flow of the singing. A good singer will find the right spot to breathe."

"That must not be always easy."

"No, but we all learn one way or another. Breathing goes with the correct interpretation of the score."

"Towards the end you go into French and I find that more, should I say, authentic."

"You're right. The original is in French and translations are not always the best way to convey words and feelings since any language has its own, should I say, cachet."

"You stress 'Ne m'accuse pas. Pleure-moi' and to act it with your voice, you tell the student. You keep stressing the importance of a commitment to learning and to do the homework."

"It's only through hard work and perseverance that one succeeds in opera. It takes courage and perseverance as I have said but nothing comes out of sluggishness and a lack of agility and vitality. Nothing."

Puccini's **La Bohème** came next with Kyu Do Park in the role of Mimi."

"Yes, I remember her."

"You kept stressing diction as a vital part of her signing."

"Anybody's singing."

"It's that important to you."

"Of course. Why do you think I study languages even those I'm familiar with? Diction is essential in everything, I think, especially opera where words and music meet and form a harmonious whole. If you're an opera-goer you don't want to hear a mishmash of sounds, do you? So, enunciate, pronounce your words so that people can hear what you sing. Besides, you as a singer will feel that much more the resonance of your voice if your diction is correct."

"Perfect most probably."

"La perfection n'est jamais mise de côté dans l'art de l'opéra."[Perfection is never put aside in the art of opera].

"Jamais."

"Jamais."

We both started laughing.

"And finally, there's Akiko Ikuo Hayashi in the role of **Madama Butterfly**. She has a delicate voice and a nice one. The role is delicate and tragically painful to the former geisha and to the audience who listens to her painful cry of anguish and probable despair, don't you think?"

"Yes, François it is despair over her love affair with this coward, Sharpless, who can only utter 'How pitiful.'"

"You try to teach the student how to express the important and fateful word 'Morta.' You keep repeating this over and over again."

"I had to. Those are Butterfly's last words, 'Ah! Morta!' And not the translation 'Oh, let me die!' It's not allowing death but the real presence and dénouement of death as a final realization of the end of her geisha life that she gave up and the promising love affair with the American. It's very tragic and it affects anyone who is young and in love be they Japanese or any other ethnic . Love can certainly fill one with joy but it can also hurt. I know."

"Now, I want to mention your farewell words to the students. You tell them you do not know if you'll be at Juilliard next year and to make the little you have given them profitable in every dimension of opera be it diction, in phrasing and courage because opera is not an easy career. 'Don't ever think that it's an easy career,' you tell them. Then you tell them that the only thanks you want from them if their perseverance and the application of their learning with you. Then you end up with, 'Whether I keep on singing or not doesn't make any difference. (I think it does.) No fireworks, not even applause is worth the effort that students give earnestly and courageously. It's the genuineness of it all that counts in the end, I thought you meant. *N'ai-je pas raison?* Am I not right?"

"Yes, definitely yes."

"Now, what did you mean by saying, 'I am not good at words?' You are good at words and I love your words because they come from the heart. They're at the very core of simplicity and simplicity is the measure of heartfelt words. That's all I have to say to you, la Divina."

"*Merci, mon ami, merci.* Now I think it's time we leave this conversation until next time," and she smiled at me with a smile that I will never forget...sly fox that you are, Madame Callas, more generous and giving than many out there.

26. Eikosieksi

The following day was a day of bright sunshine and very early in the morning, I stepped out to go for a long walk. I was still digesting the many comments on the Juilliard performances by highly qualified students of opera under the command and insightful supervision of Maris Callas. She knew her stuff, I told myself, better than any other singer in the whole wide world. That was very clear to me. Over the years, she had accumulated enough insights and perspicacious understanding of opera to fill anyone's ears and brains. Maria Callas was indeed in my book the supreme Dvina of opera because she had vowed her energies and her passion to her craft, and even more than her craft of singing but her soul and knowledge to her keen understanding of music and how it functions in opera. She understood the composer's craft and genius, not only understood but delved into them with a perspicacious intelligence that seldom an opera singer has. She was truly a brilliant interpreter of opera and she knew so very well how to convey it to her audience and to people who allowed themselves to be touched by her art as a singer. Singing for her was not simply a talent by a gift from God to be nourished and treasured. And she had long ago vowed her gift to the Virgin Mary to whom she had an intense devotion as a mother and a saint. I had come to learn all of these qualities and personal values of hers by watching her and carefully observing her hands and especially her deep dark eyes that demonstrated her inner quality of soul. Such eyes are not common and they let one peer through the inner quality of talent and cherished values as a singer. Not only as a singer, but as a person that Maria Callas was and had been all of her life.

As I was walking on the boulevards and side streets without noticing much of anything that was going on except the morning noises of the busy merchants and the garçons de café, I happen to notice a woman dressed rather shabbily, I thought, wearing a woolen plaid coat with her hair somewhat tousled and hanging on her back. She wore large horn-rimmed glasses and was glancing furtively here and there so as not to be seen or noticed by others. She seemed to be in a hurry and was dashing through the empty sidewalk not exactly knowing where she was going, I supposed. At first sight, I thought it was la Callas hurrying I did not know where, but then I told myself that it could not be her. It just could not be her the impeccable Divina who was always well-dressed and well-made up with her jewelry and her expensive designer clothes. It just could not be. But, I did recognize her walk and her hands that were clutching a small handbag. Was she running away from something or someone, I asked myself. Then I saw this man with a large camera in his right hand who was following her. Then I realized it must be a reporter, *un membre de la paparazzi écarté,* who wanted to take her photo for the papers. Another reporter who was hounding her. She looked askance and seemed petrified. I hurried to intercept the reporter and asked him to please not follow the lady that I knew was la Callas. He started to get angry and throw insults at me like a wild boar. I swore at him not wanting to but the urge was stronger than me so angry was I at this intruder. “Leave her alone,” I shouted. He looked at me and told me to mind my own business. “She is my business,” I said. I struggled with him as hard as I could and I was able to take his camera away from him as he raised his arms to fend me off and retrieve his camera. I struggled desperately with him and by then la Callas had run away and could no longer be seen. “*Allez-vous-en*, I yelled at the reporter and he looked at me with angry eyes. I turned around and started walking away. “*Monsieur,* he said, “*aimeriez-vous faire un peu d'argent? Laissez-moi vous convaincre de venir à mon aide et conduisez-moi chez la Callas afin que je puisse prendre sa photo. Vous devez la connaître assez bien pour l'approcher.*" [Do you want to earn some money? Let me convince you to come to my aid and lead me to Callas so that I can take her photo. You must know her well enough to approach her].I told him absolutely not and that he was a *salaud* for pursuing a woman who wanted to be left alone. I ran away from him as fast as I could. Poor, Madame Callas, I told myself, she must be tired of such hounding and it's no wonder why she wants to remain a recluse, alone in her apartment, her fortress against such people who did not want to leave her to herself. Mad and often vicious paparazzi! Why don't you let people alone? I shouted as I ran as fast as I could.

When I got home to the apartment, I told Olivier about the incident and he told me that several members of the paparazzi had hounded him the past whenever he tried to step outside to take a walk of simply go to the market. After a while, he told the police about the harassment and they stopped hounding him. The paparazzi will not stop hounding you if you allow them to do so. They always smell a story whenever there's an international star in their midst. Any story, any photo or any lead means money for them and their greedy people, he told me with an angry tone in his voice. I had never seen him that way. I did not see Madame Callas for days after the incident nor did I want to see her and face her with it for I knew she would definitely not want to face me either. I would let her live in peace for a while. I certainly did not want to pursue her with my questions about her career. Not now. Not while she was brewing over her disastrous encounter with the paparazzi. I knew that it was not the first time she had had such an encounter but I felt pity for her since she could not step outside early in the morning not even to take a walk. That was a pitiful situation for her and a pitiful sight to see for me who admired her and even revered the woman artist. I told myself that I would wait a while before I approached her again. I would not dare enter her apartment with such a burden on my heart. She carried one much heavier and much more painful.

Bruna did come to talk to me and she told me that Madame

was much appreciative of my conduct that morning and that she was resolved not to let such an incident trouble her to a point of not wanting to anyone especially me who had become her friend and food preparer for she enjoyed what I offered her and enjoyed our evening conversations. She would let me know when the time would be appropriate to resume these conversations again. I thanked Bruna and shed left with a piece of honey and walnut cake that I had just taken out of the oven.

Several weeks went by and I was getting worried that Madame Callas had either forgotten to pursue our conversations about her career or else she was done with them and had refused to see me again. I was hoping that the latter was not the case. I was at a point where I felt rejected and misled by her reclusive self who wanted to be left alone. Was she back to her old feelings of dejection and gruesome self-pity, I asked myself. But, it wasn't Madame Callas' way of taking things for she was a strong and courageous lady that I admired and a came to love as a person. I decided to talk to Bruna.

When Bruna came to our apartment *au sous-sol,* I did not hesitate to ask her how Madame was and how much activity she was doing. Was she walking? Was she listening to her music? Was she sleeping late in the morning? Was she still taking strong doses of sleeping tablets that Madame Devetzi was supplying her? Was she in a good mood? Was she talking at all? Was she….and Bruna stopped me there.

"Madame is feeling much better these days. She is not taking so much medication as she used to and she is eating well, *Dieu merci.*"

"But how is she really?"

"She is fine, I tell you. Please do not worry so much."

"But I do worry since she is not well. I know."

"Her mood changes now and then but she is well, I tell you."

"How are you doing, Bruna?"

"I'm fine."

"Just fine?"

"Yes, just fine."

"But you must feel the tension and the stress of it all."

"Sometimes, but I have to keep the peace and the proper balance in our lives up there. I cannot fail in Madame's service or else everything will fall part."

"You're a good person, Bruna."

"I do my best. *Je fais mon possible, Monsieur François.*"

Bruna left with a smile on her face. Madame was so very fortunate in having her to mitigate the sadness of being a recluse and heighten the joy of everyday living. I know that it isn't easy to struggle through adversity and difficult moments. Oh, the fateful thrusts of suffering and pain and how do they intrude into our lives to caution us that not everything is easy as one would have it. But I told myself that I must not philosophize about life or else I would become a useless philosopher who banters around and talks nonsense. I used to tease my philosophy teacher, Father Marcil, about the description of a philosopher: a philosopher, I told him, is as blind man in a dark room searching for truth that does not exist but he insists on floundering around and "Tater" so that he is assured of some truth although truth as such does not exist. The professor used to laugh and make other jokes about philosophy. I always liked philosophy as a discipline of the mind. It helps to clear the cobwebs of the mind and restore sanity although not complete, but satisfactory.

It was on a Saturday morning in early July that Belle Amie fell ill and complained about stomach cramps. Olivier wanted to give her some medication that he had in the medicine cabinet but I told him not to take chances on an unknown illness and that it would be best to call the doctor. He told me that his doctor, his and Belle Amie's, was dead and they had not consulted one for several years.

"What do you do when you are sick?"

"We simply survive and try to take care of ourselves the best we can."

"You can't keep doing that, Olivier. It's dangerous."

"Why?"

"Because you never know if the illness might be fatal."

"We're old and we know that we're going to die someday."

"You cannot think that way. That's fatalistic and miserable."

"Life is not meant to be endless, I know."

"But, you must accept it as a gift and not as a bad omen, Olivier."

"I know but it greater than me and I cannot cope with life as a bad omen."

"But, it's not an omen at all."

"How do you know?"

"I know, I know that God does not give us life to dispense of it like an old rag or a piece of garbage."

"Here you go philosophizing again, François."

"I'm not philosophizing, I'm rationalizing and counting on my faith in God who will not upset the applecart and dismiss all serious and meaningful thoughts about my being."

"We don't all share your faith, my young friend."

"But you have faith don't you?"

"Yes, but not enough to carry me through the darkness of the soul."

"Don't say that. Please do not say that. You do have enough faith to carry you through. I know that. You are a good person and a faith-filled one."

"Let's get back to Belle Amie and her illness, shall we not?"

I hurried to call a taxi and Olivier and I brought Belle Amie to a local clinic where we consulted with a physician about Belle Amie's condition. They took tests and we waited for hours. The assistant to the physician came to tell us that Belle Amie suffered from a stomach ulcer and that she would have to take special medication to prevent it from turning into a bleeding ulcer that might endanger her life. We left the clinic to go to the pharmacy. I told Olivier that Belle Amie was lucky that the ulcer was taken care of in good time.

"I know that Belle Amie will not live long enough to outlive me. I've always wanted her to live longer than me for I could not stand living without her."

"Now, Olivier, you have to take it as it is and not worry about who goes first and who goes last."

"But you don't have to worry about death, you François, for you're still young."

"Yes, but death is for everyone, young and old. It doesn't matter if you're twenty or eighty."

"Are you afraid of death, François?"

"Not really. I fear the process of dying but not death itself. I fear the illnesses or the disability that precludes death and dying and not death itself because death is a release from suffering and pain and all that is associated with them. I have no fear of death for I know that death will be merciful to me as a transition to blessedness. Do you believe in heaven, Olivier?"

"Well, in some kind of heaven but not the heaven that the priests talk about as in heaven and hell."

"Do you believe in hell then?"

"I do not. I don't believe in devils and certainly not in Satan the great evil one who temps us and leads us down the wrong path. No, I do not believe in devils nor do I believe in hell as place of eternal suffering."

"Then you don't believe in heaven as a recompense and hell as a punishment."

"I know that I'll have to pay for my thwarting from the truth and my uselessness as a human being, but I don't believe in eternal damnation for sins that I have committed as theology teaches us."

"Do you believe in sin then?"

"No, that's for the Jews who first invented it as a revolt against Yahweh, their god and maker as the chosen people."

"But Christ speaks of sin in the gospels."

"I know, but do I have to believe in all that he says, is my question."

"But you are a Christian aren't you?"

"Yes, but not the Christian that priests talk about."

"You seem to resent priests, Olivier."

"I do for most of them are hypocrites as far as I'm concerned, but that's another matter."

"*En tout cas, mon ami, moi j'accepte le pari de Pascal.*"[I accept Pascal's wager].

"*Ah oui, le fameux pari. Il me faudrait y penser plus sérieusement.*"

Belle Amie recuperated very well with the medication we gave her. I made sure that it was administered on time as the physician had prescribed.

Bruna and Ferruccio came down stairs to tell me that Madame was going out for a ride in the limousine. She wanted to visit a close friend of hers on boulevard Saint Michel and Ferruccio was driving her there. Before leaving, Bruna informed me that Madame wanted to see me again and have a light supper the following evening which happened to be on a Friday.

27. Eikosiepta

The following Thursday, I started to prepare a light supper for Madame Callas thinking of what I was going to serve her. I found the right recipe for a delightful soup. Since it was fast approaching summer, I decided to make a vichyssoise. A nice cool cucumber soup would be exactly the right thing, I thought. Then I would serve small sandwiches made of cream cheese, yogurt and chopped walnuts. I was hoping that Madame would not be insulted by my serving sandwiches, but these would offer her a nice opportunity to feel refreshed and not too full. Of course, I would serve a delicious white wine to accompany these sandwiches made with slices of an oven baked bread delicately seasoned so as to offer her something delicate to the palate and delightful to her senses of taste and smell. Then, to top it all off, I would serve some of Berthillon's ice cream that she loved so much like their rich, creamy and unique vanilla flavor. Of course, a few *flutes de champagne* would definitely not be out of order either, not during our after dinner conversation about opera roles.

Everything was decided and come Friday morning I was ready to serve Madame Callas her light supper just as it's done after an opera at the Palais Garnier. Parisians knew how to do things for pleasure and relaxation. It was a beautiful summer day and the flowers were bright and colorful in all of the flower boutiques as well as the flower vendors on the streets. As usual, the flowers were fresh and smelled of a radiant beauty that only fresh flowers can offer. I picked two bouquets, *one* for Belle Amie and one for la Callas. But then I turned around and bought one for myself because I loved flowers too.

I had sliced the fresh cucumbers very thin for the vichyssoise and prepared the potatoes. I had the leeks, the chicken broth and the necessary spices at hand. When I was ready to blend and cook everything, I took a large pan, put it on the stove and poured the wet ingredients to simmer for a while. Then, I put the rest of the ingredients in the pot and stirred and then I let everything stew there slowly and deliberately. When I thought the soup was done, I took it off the stove to cool. I stirred the soup and tasted it for its finished product. It tasted good, just the way I wanted it. I then put it aside for a while and later put it in the refrigerator. In the meantime, I started cutting the bread for the sandwiches. They would be finger sandwiches with the crust edges cut off. I then decided to mix the sandwich ingredients, the yogurt, the mashed fresh fruits, the marinated chicken cut into fine pieces, and the touch of ginger. I mixed it all together and then I made the small sandwiches. They would be just fine for our summer *petit souper* as I called it. I then told myself that you can't have sandwiches without some kind of refreshing condiment or tasty pickles or spicy tomatoes, so I prepared both as a side dish.

I went to Berthillon and got the ice cream for dessert. I was ready. By now the supper was ready to serve and I rested for an hour or two while my two old friends started eating an early meal at about five o'clock. The usually had their dinner around six but today they were both quite hungry and wanted to eat earlier than usual. I obliged them. They ate the vichyssoise, the sandwiches and the side dish ravenously. The both told me that everything was so very good especially the cold soup on a very warm day. Good, I told myself, then la Callas will certainly enjoy this meal.

I brought everything up including the flowers that I had purchased, they were yellow tulips, Van Gogh's favorite color, *le jaune d'accueil*, and told Bruna to alert Madame that's the supper was ready. She told me that Madame had been ready for some time.

I serve the vichyssoise and both Madame Callas and I started eating the soup while Bruna was preparing herself to serve the sandwiches. Bruna then came into the dining room carrying the sandwiches which were all arranged on a large silver tray with radishes cut in the form of a flower, green pepper sticks and small celery stalks which gave the sandwiches an extra lilt of tasty delight. Madame Callas had three of them. She looked me in the eyes and told me how much she enjoyed this supper for she had not eaten much all day long. She hated eating alone, she said. After the cup of coffee, the Berthillon ice cream was served to the great delight of Madame. After the small bits and pieces of conversation, I told her that I had champagne to initiate our evening conversation. Her dark eyes opened up like two big beautiful agates.

"What are we going to talk about?" she asked.

"Well, we are going to begin where we left off. We're going to talk about your roles in opera."

"That's a very interesting topic, François. Let's begin by my telling you that *il y a deux rôles que j'aime beaucoup, La Traviata et Norma. C'est ma nature, tu sais.*"[There are two roles that I like a lot…it's part of my nature].

"I would have suspected that. I knew that the opera **Norma** was one of your favorites if not your very favorite opera with the title role as the preferred vehicle for your voice."

"Yes, indeed. I fell in love with this opera and the role of Norma once I truly got into it. It was my first great role in Florence. I sang with gusto and reverence at the same time. It's such a splendid role, one that can make or break a soprano. It's a real challenge and it takes all that I have to render the role real and musically authentic. The composer Bellini is a true giant and a genius as far as I can tell even to this day."

"What specifically do you like about the role?"

"I love the quality of the music and the vibrancy of the emotions expressed in the lyrics. Of course, the singer has to understand the role and put her everything into it. It's definitely not a passive role. You just cannot play it flat and not put any of the genuine feelings that the composer has put into his art. It is art and art requires a transference of the art of the composer to the art of the interpreter. The performance has to be transparent and clear as far as the virtue of the opera is concerned."

"What do you mean by virtue?"

"It's the genuine quality of the work as determined by the composer. The interpreter or singer cannot deviate from the path the composer has given her and that goes for all the singers in the opera. It's a whole and complete work and demands a whole and complete performance by all the singers."

"You yourself demand complete mastery and total dedication to the opera, I'm sure."

"Yes, of course. Without the mastery the soprano goes off the track so-to-speak. It requires passion and full understanding of the story line and the music and passion requires that one must be totally dedicated to the role that he or she interprets."

"What does that mean?"

"It means countless hours of practice, rehearsals and the endless pursuit of excellence on the part of the singer, the conductor and the entire participants including the *metteur-en-scène*. Visconti and Zeffirelli are true masters of the creation of sets and even costumes."

"Visconti is the one who made Violetta and the entire **La Traviata** such a success at La Scala didn't he?"

"Of course. He's the *grand seigneur*. That's what I call him. He's a creative genius and I trust him in whatever he creates and implements for me. What I want, no, what I demand from a director is truth and justice."

"Truth and justice?"

"Yes, truth in establishing a décor and an ambiance as well as justice in the transfer of what is written to what is visibly true. Can a director make me look real and can he transfer the myth or the story to the reality of art are the two conditions that I look for in a director. The same thing can be said of the conductor."

"You are indeed exacting, Madame Callas."

"Yes, I am and I do not apologize for it. I never did and I never will."

"What is the essence of the opera **Norma**?

"Good question. The essence stems from the fact that the demi-goddess who is Norma is also a woman, a woman of feelings, tendencies and strong passions. She is motivated by all three. As a singer and an actress, I must convey that to the audience and make it look true and valid. That's my task as an opera singer. I've always had a great affinity for the character. She is in many ways like me. I feel for her and with her. Norma may appear to be very strong, even ferocious at times, but in actuality she's a lamb who roars like a lion. She's a woman who is proud to show her feelings and proves in the end that she cannot be unjust in a situation for which she herself is fundamentally to blame. My tears in **Norma** were real."

"That's how much you identified with her?"

"Yes. She's a high-priestess and I'm what they call a Divina; she's a woman through and through and I'm a woman inside and out. She has feeling and I have feelings."

"I read somewhere that the opera **Norma** is a definite challenge to the one who sings and plays the role."

"I must tell you that is very true, but I have met that challenge and have mastered the role and the music, thanks in great part to Tullio Serafin."

"I also read what one critic said about you and your singing in **Norma** at the Covent Garden premiere. He said, 'Callas' fioriture were fabulous. The chromatic glissandi held no terrors for her in the cadenza at the end of 'Casta diva'...nor did the superhuman leap from middle F to a forte high C. One of the most stunning moments came at the end of the stretta to the Act II trio, when she held for twelve beats a stupendous free high D.' I think those were his exact words. I remember them because I have been so struck by these words on your account. He then went on to say that you held your audience in slavery after that. Can you imagine?"

"You're right, François. I did all that because I had practiced for it and had done countless rehearsals. My voice was in very good shape.

Now, I don't know about holding an audience as slaves of my music but I do know that they were ecstatic at the end. Music, good music, well-sung music does that to people."

"I don't know what to say anymore."

"Well, let's change opera and role."

"Let's do Violetta in **La Traviata** the second one you like best."

"Violetta is a true woman of charm and delight. She learned her trade by consorting with the *beau monde* and that's why Visconti placed her in a setting of *la belle époque*. She fits in there so very well and he knew that. Visconti is a great master of fitting in the character, the singer and the conductor into the right ambiance and the right setting. Opera like the theater is a magical happening on stage. It must transfer the audience to place where magic transforms factuality and reality and makes it real as far as the magic of performance is real. Do you understand?"

"Yes."

"Then, Violetta like *la dame aux camellias* is a courtesan who repudiates love and fidelity. That's not in her makeup as a woman of the world. However, she's fragile woman who can easily fall in love with the man who will take her heart and call it his own. So there is a transformation that occurs. From the courtesan that she is Violetta becomes a woman in love ready to sacrifice herself for love which is unusual for her. And, I understand her very well and her dilemma, to love or not to love. However, the choice is not easy when the heart bypasses the brain. Then anguish sets in and desperation too. When Germont, Alfredo's father steps in to reclaim his son, she falters and gives him up in order to save his sister from scandal. Do you follow me, François?"

"Yes, easily."

"Well, Alfredo does not understand the situation and denounces her thinking she has betrayed him. It's then that he throws a handful of money at her saying that's he's repaying her for her favors. She freezes; she says nothing. She just freezes utterly immobile in shock and dismay. That's how I played her and just as Sarah Bernhardt did in her stage performance. She is now poor and must sell her furnishings in order to survive. She is dying of consumption. Alfredo does not understand her plight and tries to make her understand his, stupid lover that he is. She sings in a very low voice the cry, '*Gran Dio! Morir si* giovine' to die so young. I tried so very hard to convey that morose death song at the end. And Violetta dies with that blank stare that shocked even the audience, I am told."

"That's must have been quite a performance."

"Yes, the role of Violetta is one of my favorites because, like Norma, I can identify with the woman beneath the heart and soul of the priestess and the courtesan. They both die of love in some fashion. That's probably how I shall die."

"Don't say that. You'll find your love somehow."

"Yes, I thought I had found it but then I lost it. My only real love is music and my singing and that's fast disappearing. It's vanishing, François, and there's nothing I can do about it. Nothing. As Piaf says so, '*Rien, non de rien. Je ne regrette rien…*' I regret nothing. Nothing. *RIEN*. My only regret is that I'm losing my voice at such a young age…in my fifties when other artists still have theirs."

"Let's change the subject shall we. Things are getting a little gloomy."

"Don't be afraid of my complaints and my deterioration. They're all about my passage from la Divina to the fallen Divina. Now, what's the next role you want me to discuss with you?"

"How about **Aida**?"

"The opera **Aida** is grand opera with a cast of hundreds, animals and all. It was composed by Verdi for a grand celebration but it was never one of my best roles. As a matter of fact, I did not like the opera and I still have strong reservations about it."

"The how about the role of Amina in **La Sonnambula** by Bellini?"

"Of course, it's one of my preferred operas. The role of Amina is one that fitted my singing voice and my love of ballet as well as the illusion of the dream sequence, all fulfilled my desires to play such a role."

"Why?"

"Because Bellini composed an opera that suited me, Maria Callas, the soprano, the actress and performer."

"Can you elaborate on that?"

"Of course. Amina represents for me the ideal woman of dreams, the sleepwalker who crosses the bridge from darkness to light when she finally is reunited with her fiancé. She floats like a ballerina and she is nimble and fragile in her way of being the dream and not just part of it. Visconti had deigned along with Piero Tosi a set filled with colors that reflected the dream world, the pinks, the pearls, the blues and the lusterless whites. I had to inch my way along since you know my eyesight is not very good."

"I didn't know that."

"Yes, that's always been my difficulty. That's probably why Visconti called me a nightbird in **La Sonnambula.** Oh, I loved this opera and the Bellini's music, the *bel canto* music, still resounds in my head each time I think of it. Bellini is a great master of music, but I've told you that before."

"Yes, you did."

"But it's worth repeating."

"How about Tosca?"

"Tosca as a role is a challenging one for those sopranos who do not rely on their dramatic skills. The role is made for drama and strong emotions especially when you have a Tito Gobbi in the role of the Baron Scarpia. He's a magnificent Scarpia that man, simply magnificent. Puccini's opera comes to life with him.

"So you enjoyed playing Tosca with him more than any other Scarpias."

"Definitely yes. Scarpia's role is larger than Tosca's but she makes up for it with the music Puccini, the composer, has given her. I remember the Covent Garden version of 1964 with Franco Zeffirelli as director. I asked for him. It had been a long absence since my last stage performance. He knew how to interpret so well the setting of Rome, the solemn, pompous and grandiose city the Puccini knew so well. His very first beats of music reflect that so very well. It also prefigures the mood as set by Scarpia's presence, a mood of gloom and despair mixed with the bowel sensuality of the Chief of Police, this Scarpia."

"Bowel sensuality?"

"Yes, a sensuality stemming from the bowels of the man, a sensuous, low-down creature who abases the hearts and souls with whom he comes in contact. He has the appearance of a civilized and well-polished man, but deep inside he's a vile and contemptuous being. As for Tosca, she's an exuberant, warm-hearted person rather than a sloppy, casual woman, not a posey-lady and grand diva as Zeffirelli saw her, and I agreed with him. She brings flowers to the Madonna but she soon realizes that jealousy lies at the bottom of her heart when she thinks she has caught her lover cheating on her. We soon realize that she's a fiery, jealous woman, a real Roman woman whose feelings are so quickly fired up at the slightest provocation. I realized that and I knew that and that's the way I played her from the start."

"You really capture a role from the beginning, I see."

"Yes. When we go from the chapel to Scarpia's private chambers, we discover the shadowy and hellish ambiance that linger there just like Zeffirelli wanted it and designed it. Enter Tosca. She has just sung for the Queen of Naples and she looks like a diva, elegantly dressed. Scarpia notices her allurement and precipitates himself at her and then the lustful motions begin. Tosca falls crucified by him as he extends her arms, helpless. I did that because I felt like I was being crucified. I then went into the well-known aria, 'Vissi d'arte.' I tried to not embellish it too much and sing it the way Puccini has composed it. It's a cry of mercy, a cry of suffering since she has devoted her entire life to art and now she sees herself in a position of uselessness and powerlessness."

"Then comes the murder of Scarpia."

"It's rather the killing of the killer of woman's virtue. I see her as religious as she is, plunging the knife into him avenging her own virtue and her lover's innocence. Tito Gobbi as Scarpia does a marvelous death scene, so realistic and so final. There's no catafalque and so Tosca place some candles at his side as a gesture of religious thought. I did it gradually and with serious religious intent. The slow beat of the music accompanied me until I left the body of Scarpia lying there on the floor. Dead."

"That must have been a lugubrious feeling on your part."

"Yes, but remember I was playing a role. Then comes the last scene of the final act when we hear Cavaradossi singing his beautiful song to the stars, 'E lucevan di stelle??' more beautiful than Tosca's 'Vissi d'arte' I believe. Puccini can be truly lyrical when he wants."

"I love 'E lucevan di stelle'. It makes my spine tingle."

"Ah, so you're a romantic."

"I must admit that I am."

"Finally, Tosca runs up the stairs, escapes the guards and jumps like a bird into the vast emptiness to her death. 'God will judge us,' she shouts to Scarpia, and the end comes to all three of them in this tragic story of love and lust. Tosca is not my very favorite role but I enjoy playing it and singing the lyrics to a point where I believe that I am the part and I'm feeling what the diva who feels the joys and the pangs of love when confronted with despair and utter reluctance to cave in as a woman who is being pursued by a hound of a man."

"I'm so glad that we are having this conversation about your roles. I really am."

"Well, I do it for you and with you but I would not do it with others except perhaps with Franco. He is still my very best friend. He understands me and I follow his advice when it comes to opera and his direction. He's precious to me."

"Do you want to do one more?"

"Yes, but the last one for this evening. I'm getting tired, not of the conversation with you but my body is telling me it's tired and I must rest a while before going to bed."

"I understand. How about Lucia?"

"Oh yes, **Lucia di Lammermoor** by Donizetti."

"Yes."

"The role of Lucia that I'm going to talk to you about is the one at La Scala in 1954 with Herbert von Karajan as conductor, one of my favorites. At his insistence, he suggested that Gianni Ratto be the décor master since he wanted a bare, stylized sets with moody, dim lighting and murky rear projections. It was God-awful. I liked making music with him but I detested his visual production. I would have preferred the inimitable style of Franco. He is such a creative genius. But, I followed the directions of the conductor and made music with him in an opera that has one of the most famous Mad Scenes."

"Yes, I know."

"But from the beginning, we see that Lucia is deeply in love with Edgardo and with the fusion of words and music that I managed to control in order to caress broad melodic phrases enabled me to express sensual love. Somehow it was all within me and I could carry it out to the surface and make it subtly transparent. Then, of course, comes the forged letter that upsets everything---ça bouleverse tout---and Lucia suffers in tears: 'Soffriva nel pianto' she sings. All the melancholy, suffering and loneliness is expressed in her heart, in a world of her own. She cannot offer resistance to the madness overtaking her."

"And that's the start of the Mad Scene."

"Only the prefiguration, François. Still on the verge of madness she sings of her misery and added to that are the voices of Enrico, Raimondo, Arturo and Alisa forming a spectacular quintet in my estimation. Their voices combine then separate to reunite once more in a descending sigh with Lucia's desperate voice floating above all the others. Next comes the banqueting hall where we grasp the full dimension of Lucia's madness. She has made a haunting entrance and now her useless wanderings bring her to the moment where she believes that her lover is still with her. Lucia's temporary expression of joy enhances the poignancy of the situation. I could actually feel what she felt then, joy mixed with madness. At least, I forced myself to do so and it came to me. I was playing a role but I was also part of the role. The prolonged trill, the gliding chromatic runs and the unusual stresses in *'Spargi d'amato pianto'* 'Shed a bitter tear' was my way of bridging rapidly with limpid and deeply affecting tones. I love the role of Lucia because it reveals how the mind can go teetering on the brink of sanity while the heart is filled with sentiments of true love. That's the tragedy of **Lucia di Lammermoor .**

"And I'm sure the audience loved it all."

"I can tell you that even after the cadenza of eh Mad Scene, the audience stood up and showered me with red carnations on stage."

"That was a real success and a true conquest of the stage for you and your stupendous voice."

"That was then but now it's so very different."

"It may be to you but you do have those memories and that fame that never left you side."

"Thank you, François, you always seem to know what to say."

"Let's cut it off now, please. I'm tired but joyful at having expressed my thoughts to you about my operatic roles." *Dieu merci* ."

"*Bonne nuit, Madame Callas.*"

"*Bonne nuit, François.*"

I left la Callas's apartment fulfilled and thankful that I had another opportunity to talk to the great diva about her career in opera. I was truly fortunate and especially lucky to be the only one in which she confided her career as an opera star and diva. She may consider herself to be the fallen Divina but, to me she's still up there in the clouds and in the lofty realm of excellence.

28. Eikosioktw

It took a week before I had another chance to talk to Madame Callas about her career and her roles because Bruna informed me that Madame had not been feeling well at all. She was back on sleeping pills that her friend Vasso Devetzi kept mailing her. I told Bruna that those pills will end up by killing her although I did not want to alarm Bruna. She knew it and tried her very best to keep Madame off of those pills. If only I could get Madame Callas to go out more often and probably even travel a bit, I told myself. Being a recluse is a form of malady. It severs you from the outside world and it makes you feel dejected and all alone even though there are people around you. I had to l keep at it and insist to Madame Callas that her health was in danger. Would she listen to me though?

Another week went by and nothing happened. I went to the market for provisions in case that la Callas would want to eat a meal some evening. I always took care of my two good friends who ate well and carried on very well. They went to bed early and got up very early even before the birds, I used to tell them. They were always in a good mood and Olivier liked to tease his wife about living to be over one hundred. She told him that she did not wish to live that long knowing full well that old age beyond one hundred can mean all kinds of hardships and pain. She did not want to end up in a home somewhere. She wanted to stay here with Olivier and François, she said. That was fine with me since I did not have a home and they provided me with one. Northern Maine was far away and long gone for me since both of my parents were dead and buried there. I did miss my mother but I cannot say that I missed my father to be blunt about it. The father/son relationship had never occurred and the ties between the both of us had been severed a very long time ago, probably at my birth. I was no Telemachus and he was no Odysseus.

After several more days, I finally got a message from Madame Callas through Bruna that she was expecting me for dinner on the following Tuesday. It happened to be on July 15, the day after the Bastille. I thought of inviting her to come out with me and celebrate the Bastille outdoor, but then I thought about it and told myself that I might stir up a problem if I did so, especially finding herself among a crowd of people in the middle of Paris. I left that thought behind.

What was I going to serve her was the big question in my mind as I was thinking about that evening meal. I had always served her something delightful and tasty, and even a bit exotic sometimes. How about some *fruits de mer*, seafood, or some fish of some kind? Seafood would be just the thing for her and I would try to find a recipe for it. Why not? I did find one: Seafood and Linguine.

Tuesday morning bright and early I got all of my preparations ready. I had gotten the seafood at a special seafood market not too far from where we lived, on one of the side streets where most people of our neighborhood went to get seafood, fresh seafood delivered in the very early hours of the day by trucks directly from the sea up north and it was always the day's catch by fishermen who knew how to catch seafood. That's exactly what I wanted, clams, shrimps and scallops. Come late afternoon around five o'clock . I boiled my linguine then I set it aside. Then in a large skillet I put olive oil and placed the cut mushrooms until they were ready to greet the seafood. First of all, I placed the clams and the asparagus in a steamer basket and let them cook for a while. Then I placed the shrimps, the scallops and the clams with the asparagus until the clam shells opened. I poured the wine over them and let everything stew not too long but long enough so that the seafood was ready to serve. After, I put the linguine and stirred everything and let the whole recipe absorb the good taste of my seafood dish. Right before serving I would put the grated cheese on top.

For dessert I prepared a special pudding, light and not too sugary with the fresh and pure vanilla taste. I mix the pudding with fresh *crème anglaise* to give it that light and delicious texture that melts in your mouth. I had set it aside in the refrigerator. I thought that this seafood dinner with some white wine followed by rich dark coffee would be just right in anticipation of the pudding. Everything would be light and not too heavy on the stomach exactly what Madame Callas would certainly like.

Come six o'clock I went upstairs and gave the main dish to Bruna and returned with the wine and the dessert. With few instructions I told her to serve when she was ready for I knew that she was well-trained in the art of serving food. I then went to the dining room and found that Madame Callas was not there yet. Bruna came to tell me that Madame would be there in a little while. I sat down and waited thinking that probably I was there too early and that la Callas was getting her face ready. She did not like to appear wan and drawn without her regular makeup. Also, she liked to wear some of her jewelry, that I knew. Finally she came in and smiled while she sat down while I stood up greeting her. After all, that was the polite thing to do with a lady and especially with a diva. We did some small talk while waiting for our food. Bruna came in with the main course since I had not prepared an entrée. The dish looked very good what with the grated cheese spread over it and it smelled so good. La Callas's eyes widened and I could see that she was impressed with the seafood linguine dish that I had concocted just for her that evening. Of course, my two dear friends had already tasted it and found it superb. They loved seafood and did not have it too often. I could only serve seafood now and then since it was expensive and I had limited funds now that my source of income had become if not meager but at least much less than it used to be.

After dinner, we had some more wine followed by a *café noir*. After a while, Bruna served the dessert. She put on top of each cup some fresh raspberries with a spring of mint to make it look much more appetizing. Good old Bruna, I told myself, she always knows how to liven things up. After dessert, la Callas looked at me and said,

"I suppose that you want to continue our conversation about my operatic roles?"

"But of course, Madame. We could probably begin with the opera **Andrea Chénier** although I know that it's not one of your favorites. I just love the soprano's aria, the major one that makes me fell so closely associated with my mother and with the poignancy of the situation when Madeleine sings it and the way you sing it. Ça touche au coeur cette pièce de musique si bien composée par Giordano, n'est-ce pas?"[It goes right to the heart].

"*Oui, c'est une très belle composition opératique.* I did not sing it too often but I Iiked it a lot. The opera is a tenor's vehicle and a good tenor can do justice to the entire opera when he sings his part with inner strength and theatrical conviction. Act III reaches a dramatic high point with the aria '*La mamma morta*', to which you were referring. It begins with a poignant cello solo and I mirrored its tonal color in my voice as I began the first recitative---like the lines of the aria my voice had become lighter in texture, more transparent and somewhat less powerful in volume. That was to transition from the power of the feelings to the control of the voice in order to imitate the pangs of death and mourning."

"That is an emotional moment in the opera, romantic that's I am."

"I don't have much more to say about this opera. However, people do remember precisely Maddalena de Coigny's aria and never seem to forget it."

"Now, how about discussing the next opera, **Anna Bolena** and your interpretation of the queen's role, the tragic and condemned queen."

"I love the role of Anna Bolena because I can identify with it and I am able to sing exactly what the composer, Donizetti, has done so masterfully. First, there's the question of understanding what the singer does and does not do in an opera especially the tiniest part of an opera. The public should know and understand what word, what nervous tension, what fatigue, what love enters each little word or little note apparently without importance not to mention the gestures that are an integral part of each role."

"I understand fully and appreciate your explanation of what you do and what you feel in each and every opera."

"Every gesture means something, every movement and facial expression is aimed toward an emotion or dramatic climax. Everything but everything is aimed at a whole and not just the parts. It becomes a seamless garment where each thread, each color or hue, each part of the texture is a whole and that whole must be achieved in order to claim excellence by the singer, the conductor, the director and, of course, the composer. That's why I demand many practices and rehearsals in order to perfect the whole as it was intended by the composer. Too many people forget the important and vital part played by the composer who is the creator of an opera and its music linked to the lyrics which are an integral part of the whole. You see, one must look at it with a holistic view and not only see parts and useless or worthless gestures and facial expressions. I consider them to be of utmost importance."

"I can see that and that's why your performances are so great and so appreciated by your audiences."

"I earn their applause and their esteem."

"I know."

"Now as for the Queen Anna Bolena, it's her regal position and her dignity in the face of death that I admire and wish to convey to my audience. Henry VIII's second wife, Anne Boleyn, was ever faithful to the king but Henry wanted to discard her like an old rag. He was a thoroughly egotistical man. Since everything transpires in London Visconti, as director and producer, worked to create a décor consistent with the black, white and gray colors of London for sets. It was magnificent as always. The sets were bigger than life and the exuded a grim feature of the tensions happening at court. The King accuses his wife of adultery after having caught her and Percy in a compromising situation. I threw myself on the floor in despair for that's how I saw the scene at that moment. It's at that very moment that I say, 'If this is my trial, judge me, but remember I am your

Queen.' She is ever regal in her composure and dignified in her words and actions."

"Did you really like this role?"

"Yes. I like the woman and the Queen. In the second and last Act, we're in the Tower of London and everything is very dim deep in a subterranean chamber, deep in shadows and grim as a prison is. That's when I sing a prayerful song in the stillness of the enclosure full of pity and coldness. And then the canons and bells are heard in acclamation of Seymour as the new Queen. My voice captures that moment with a soaring of trills and roulades to express both rage and forgiveness for you see Anna Bolena is still a Queen in all of her pride and dignity. Most of all, I admire the grandeur of her forgiveness. She is not a petty person, she's truly a Queen and she behaves like one, unto death. And, that's how I saw her and that's how I interpreted her in my gesturers and in my interpretation of my music. The audiences approved of my playing this role and they applauded over and over again. I felt the excitement and the joy in their response to my playing this role. Yes, I had captured the essence of the opera, its music, its libretto and its deepest feelings as expressed by its composer and I had to go deep inside myself to capture that essence and translate it onto the stage."

"I can only imagine what a performance it was."

"Let's talk about Cio-Cio-San in **Madama Butterfly** by Puccini. It's not a role that I prefer over the others but I had to try singing it in order to grasp Puccini's romantic lyricism and his sense of the oriental mystique. Cio-Cio-San as a personage is an innocent, naïve and gullible young woman who is entirely devoted to the man of her dreams. She does not suspect anything about him and his status as a military man away from home. She expresses her desire to see him again in her lyrical aria, '*Un bel de vedreno*,' not suspecting that he will never return. He had his fling and now he expresses his departure in a letter that his friend Sharpless read to Cio-Cio-San. She is full of dismay and despair. What is to become of her, she asks. I find this opera to be romantic but not truly tragic. For me she's neither a Norma nor a Violetta. She's still a child at heart and mind who lets her sense of disillusionment take a hold of her and breaks her thoughts of love for an unfaithful American. As a matter of fact she has become the embodiment if not the soul of the Japanese geisha who is deluded by an American military man while serving overseas. So many such cases happened during the great wars, be it a Madeleine in France, a Mildred in Britain or Cio-Cio-San in Japan. I can sing the role but I cannot identify with it. She's not me."

"There's one more that I want us to discuss and that's Lady Macbeth."

"Oh, that's a very different role than Madame Butterfly. We go from the child to the woman whose blood boils for power and intrigue. Shakespeare's story is well translated here into opera. A tragedy whose power of seducing the mind and soul of a woman and turning them into lust for power itself. She wants the throne at any cost and she wants it when she wants it. I followed Verdi's instructions as to adopting a full-bodied tone of singing that became appropriately hard and cold reflecting the single-mindedness as an expression of power of a woman seeking power for herself and for her husband. When rubbing her hands she is witnessing her powerlessness and misery singing a mournful pianissimo. With the softest sensual tones rising to a D flat to dip an octave on the final note in *Audiam*, *Macbetto* she is fully in the realm of sleepwalking. I felt those tones and did dipped a full octave on the final note just like the composer would have wanted had he been there directing me. The Sleepwalking Scene is a strong reflection of the guilt and terror haunting the shattered mind. I gave this role its drama depth and the deep feeling that I could muster. Verdi would have wanted it that way, I'm sure."

"I'm sure you did."

"We did not talk about Bizet's Carmen."

"No. ***Carmen*** *ne fait pas partie de mon monde ideal."*[Not part of my ideal world].

"Pourquoi pas?"[Why not?]

"Parce que c'est une personne sans grande moralité. C'est une gitane effleurée qui court pour l'amour et cet amout est un 'oiseau rebelle'. Elle

attrape sa mort parce qu'elle ne sait vraiment pas aimer.L'opéra ***Carmen*** *n'est pas pour moi."*[It's a person without much morality. She's a deflowered gypsy who runs after love and this love is a rebellious bird. She gets her death blow because she doesn't know how to love. The opera is not for me].

"Je comprends. Alors où en sommes-nous? Perhaps the mad scenes you have played? I'd like that."

"Yes, I'm sure you would, you romantic, you."

"But you like those mad scenes in opera, don't you?"

"I suppose."

"You suppose?"

"I must admit that I relish them because they offer me an opportunity to spread my dramatic wings. I can delve into the minds of those poor creatures and reveal the anxiety, stress, ambiguity of senses and feelings as well as the dense and corroded features of motivation not thoroughly understood by everyone. I try to understand them and I try really hard to imitate the tension between sanity and insanity. There's a very fine line between them, you know. On can vacillate between them and in the end fall into the pit of destructive madness. It must be so very terrible and gruesome to do that. The mind makes us who we are as human beings that and the association with the heart and soul. But a clear and logical mind is most important. It's certainly important to a Greek like me."

"Can you imagine a person without a clear mind for reasoning?"

"No. I would never want to lose my mind. Never. Sometimes I feel as if I'm losing it, but not entirely, thank God! I tell myself that I must not lose it and that I need to gain control not only of my mind but of my heart from where come he feelings. But, I suppose the worst danger would be to lose one's soul."

"Do you feel like that sometimes, François?

"Yes, yes, yes."

"Then don't ever take the risk, I beg you."

"Do you take risks like that?

"I am tempted to, but I resist them."

"Do you ever feel that you identify so closely, if not too closely, with a character in an opera during a mad scene that you risk falling mad yourself just for the art of portraying such a person?"

"Sometimes I must admit that the music is so powerful and so enthralling that I feel that I'm being overtaken by it and the lyrics that cause me to project my own feelings and tensions in a role that I have made my own. How can I separate myself entirely from any role to which I have given myself entirely? I just do not know."

"It must be very difficult and hard to shake off once it's over. I mean the role playing with the music and all."

"If a soprano insists on playing a role that requires heart and soul commitment, then she does risk becoming the role itself and falling into the pit of darkness that is insanity, but just for a few moments though, just enough to play that scene. That's the art of it all. Art transcends reality and puts you in a mode of expression that colors and reflects the composer's creation on stage. That's how I see it."

"You have a marvelous way of conceptualizing and analyzing your roles."

"I have worked on it for so many years with much enthusiasm and strength of character. I was shown that by Hildago, the teacher of musicality and brightness of delivery as well as Tullio Serafin, the master conductor and, of course, by the creative geniuses of Visconti and Zeffirelli."

"But you could not have become who you are without being you, Maria Callas. You with your gift of music and interpretation. You and your affinity to languages and drama."

"I know, I know."

"There are one more role that we have not yet discussed and that's Medea."

"Yes, of course, but that's for another day."

With that she got up from the table and left the room. I left quietly and went downstairs to do some reading. I've been reading the biography of Abraham Lincoln. He's a very interesting man, a man of bright intellect and sound mind who desperately wanted to save his country from disunity and prolonged war. I was learning a lot from his thoughtful insights on division and union.

29. Eikosiennea

Belle Amie turned to me as I was preparing the evening meal and said, "*J'ai une fringale pour une bonne soupe chaude.*"

"*Alors je vous confectionnerai une soupe au vermicelle avec des tomates fraîches.*"

"*O, oui.*"

I did not want to disappoint her but I knew that soup with vermicelli and tomatoes was one of her favorites but so easy to do. She could not wait for dinner, so I got started on it right away. When people especially old people have a sudden urge and craving for something good to eat, it has to be right away. Belle Amie was such a refined and delicate lady that I never refused her anything. At least if it was in my power to grant her wishes. After all, she was a mother to me. As for my father, well, he was gone and I did not miss him. I did have Olivier by my side and he was pleasant and accommodating. I fed Belle Amie and gave her *une bouchée de pain* for the French like bread with almost anything especially soup. They like to wipe the rim of the soup plate and get all of what was left as much as possible. You don't waste good soup.

Belle Amie went to bed very early and Olivier and I had our supper. It wasn't much but it was satisfying, potatoes on the grill, a thick slice of cheese and some slices of *charcuterie*. We had some wine and we chatted about the weather and other insignificant things like who had a small white dog who barked all night long and could not be stopped. Olivier remembered that he once had a dog named *P'tite Bouchée* that he adored. He loved that dog and had fun with him. He had brought him up as a pup and named him after what his mother used to say about the dog, "L*ui, il veut toujours une p'tite bouchée. Jamais rassasié. Il avait une faim de loup.*"[He always wanted a little bite. Never satisfied. He was ravenous for food]. So he had named him that, *P'tite Bouchée* . He grew up with the dog and the dog became his best friend. They went everywhere together even at school. The school master did not like having a dog in his classroom but he allowed *P'ite Bouchée* to stay lying down under Olivier's desk. The dog never moved; he never barked. Olivier said that he believed that the school master, Monsieur Valladine, came to like his dog and that's why he tolerated him. With time people called Olivier and his dog, *Saint Roch et son chien* because the saint was known to have his dog wherever he went. That was the legend but the true story behind Saint Roch is that he came from a wealthy family from Montpelier in France and when his parents died he gave away all of his wealth to the poor and needy and went on a long pilgrimage. It happened to be the time of the plague in Europe and eventually Roch caught the disease and he retreated into the forest to die. Miraculously, every day a dog came to see him and brought him some bread and that's how he survived. With time he was healed and that's why one often says about this healing friendship of man and dog, *Saint Roch et son chien.* I had never heard of this legend and this saint but he found it interesting if not amusing. I loved old tales that delighted and inspired. My father never had the time to tell me stories and so I retreated to my room or outside in the nearby woods and read stories, stories about mythic creatures, heroes who rescued people from danger and other stories that made my flesh creep for I also read scary stories about monsters and outer world creatures who came from galaxies far away. I even made up some stories of my own for I was a boy with a wild imagination and could conjure up any tale I wanted to. That's why I loved movies so much because they gave me the fodder necessary to dream up stories based on what I had seen at the cinema.

I'm letting the narrator take over for now. I'm tired.

At one time, François wanted to become an actor but his father discouraged him from such a venture. Then he wanted to become an artist and paint like the old masters like Van Gogh or Rembrandt, but again his father told him, no, for he said, "no son of mine is going to become a sissy artist." Whatever was imaginative, creative or simply fun, Mister Spirounias forbade it. He was an odd fellow, he was. That's what François thought.

Olivier and François went to bed. François kept thinking about his father. He had not thought about him in a very long time and he wondered why all of a sudden he was thinking of him. It must be because I was talking with Olivier and he was telling me tales of old that my own dad never did, he told himself. He fell asleep and dreamt of back home in northern Maine when the weather was nice and warm and he could go swimming in the ocean and jump in the waves and get splashed.

Morning came and Belle Amie did not get up at her usual hour. Olivier was worried since he tried to wake her but she remained motionless in her bed. He hurried to get François. He and François tried desperately to awaken her but she would not stir. She had died during the night. Olivier was alarmed and at the same time worried that he had lost his best friend, Belle Amie. François just sat there and cried. He could not help himself. How could he since she had become like a mother to him and a friend. Death had come to the concierge apartment and mourning was in the air. Olivier and François had to do something about the corpse in the bed, so they called the gendarmes who came right away and got some information about Belle Amie and her unexpected death. Olivier did his best to tell them what he knew, that he had discovered her lifeless body still in bed in the morning and that he did not know that she was ill enough to die. One of the gendarmes told him that only a doctor could tell them the cause of death. So, an ambulance was called and Belle Amie was taken to a nearby hospital where someone was going to go through the procedures of identifying the cause of death and report it to the authorities. Both Olivier and François waited nearly three hours before one of the interns came to tell them that the report would not be ready before another several hours. They waited another three hours. Nothing. They were both nervous, jittery and hungry. They were told to get some food and then return later. After having waited long hours in the waiting room, an official came to ask Olivier where he wanted the body transferred, an undertaker, a crematorium or where else. Olivier told him that he had not thought about that matter and that he would have to think about it. He didn't remember having discussed the issue with Belle Amie. The official insisted that the body had to be transferred and not kept in the hospital overnight. Regulations had to be observed, he said. Olivier looked at François, François shrugged his shoulders and Olivier looked at the ceiling as if he was trying seriously to find an answer there. Then the official started to say, "*Monsieur...*" Olivier blurted out, "*Au crématoire.*" He said that with a raspy glitch in his voice. François took Olivier home.

There was no funeral, no flowers and no ceremony of any kind except that François went to pick up the ashes at the crematorium because Olivier could not bring himself to do so. Once they were in the apartment, Olivier kept them on the mantle for three weeks until one Monday morning he told François that he was going to bring Belle Amie home to a small village in Normandy where she was born. It was called Saint-Roch-sur mer.

The apartment felt a bit empty without Belle Amie for both men, but after two weeks things seem to get better and François did his best to entertain Olivier and he often took him out for a walk in the Luxembourg Gardens to watch young boys sailing their tiny ships on the large water basin.

It was late July when Ferruccio announced to François that he was taking Madame to the chapel on the rue du Bac and that Madame wanted to know if François would like to accompany her. He did not refuse. She told François that she was having one of her spells and feared for her health. She also admitted to him that she had a strange premonition of death and that she wanted, at all costs, to prepare herself for it and was going to plead with the Virgin to give her more time to prepare her soul for the long journey expected by all who suffer the pangs of the fear of death. François tried to reassure her that she was not on the verge of death and that she was not going to die and that she was too young to die. With the unexpected death of Belle Amie and the grief suffered by Olivier that seemed to have affected the entire apartment complex and its residents, Madame was not feeling well about the imminence of death. La Callas and François remained for over an hour at the Miraculous Medal Shrine praying in the front pew before the statue of Our Lady with the rays flowing from her two hands. François just sat there while la Callas was kneeling and praying intently. She wore a plain black dress, a broad brim straw hat with a black ribbon and no jewelry. People did not stare nor did they bother her for François would have shooed them away if anyone had attempted to disturbed Madame Callas, the diva in prayer.

When they got to Avenue Georges Mandel, la Callas asked François if he would like to join him for dinner that evening and that Bruna would serve them baked salmon which was one of her specialties. He was surprised at the invitation but he answered, yes, without hesitating. Olivier was out visiting a friend of his when François climbed the stairs to la Callas's apartment. It was six thirty. Bruna answered the door and told François that the fish was ready to be served and to please have a seat in the dining room. Madame came in looking fresh and joyful. She had a lovely silk summer dress on with a string of pearls at her neck and a gold bracelet with charms around her right wrist. She sat down and Bruna came in to serve the cool *sorbet au citron,* just to open up the palate, she said. Then came the entrée with the baked salmon and egg sauce. She also served them some potato *au gratin* and some white asparagus steamed to perfection. François told Bruna that if he could he would not hesitate hiring her as a cook, so deliciously tempting was her offering. She blushed a bit while Madame told him never in a million years. He smiled and continued to savor the taste of the sorbet still lingering in his mouth. The salmon was moist, just flaky enough to be able to melt in your mouth and the sauce superbly mellow with a hint of onions and a hint of some spice. La Callas and François sat there enjoying their white wine when Bruna asked them if they wanted the dessert during their conversation or after for she knew that Madame wanted to go to bed early tonight. Madame signaled to have the dessert served right away. It was Berthillon ice cream.

"Well François what are we going to discuss this evening?"

"Well, there's the matter of your role as Medea that we did not approach yet."

"Yes, of course, Medea, the great Medea, the sly Medea, the strong-willed Medea, the wretched Medea with the heart of flesh and stone. Medea is the embodiment of wretchedness, supplication, suspense and heart-break. She knows that she has lost he lover, Jason, and will lose her children, so she seeks revenge through death and destruction. She's of the old classical Greek tragedy whereby she's a cursed woman who resorts to sorcery. I love the character even though she horrifies me at times. Cherubini's opera is a fine one and his music allows me to climb to the height of intense drama while sing those lines that horrify and inspire me at the same time."

"But you also did the movie of **Medea**."

Yes, with Pasolini. He was after me to play this role on film. *Ah, Pasolini et son idée fixe. En interpretant **Médée** sans musique, j'ai trahi ma mission*."[By interpreting Medea without music I betrayed my mission].

"*Vraiment?*"

"*Vraiment.* It wasn't the same thing. The film was not the commercial success that Pasolini had envisioned. It was a different kind of experience for me."

"But did you enjoy it?"

"Yes and no. As I said, without music, I could not really get into it and translate my feelings into art as I usually do in opera. It's different and that's all I have to say."

"Pasolini was quite a character wasn't he?

"In his own right, but we remained friends for several years."

"I know I've asked you this before but which role do you like best of all the operas you have sung?"

"There's no other choice for me but Norma. Norma is the epitome of dramatic opera and its composer knew just how to link everything together to create his masterpiece, music, lyrics and built-in directions. You see, good singers, good conductors and good directors/producers discover them and translate them in their expertise while drawing on their own creativity and artistic skills. I know I do. The opera **Norma** allows me to do just that, follow Bellini's instructions cached in his work and evident to those who know opera. It takes time even years to learn and hone to perfection that skill. Of course, there's no perfection in art but there is excellence and I've always attempted to reach that goal."

"Excellence."

"Yes."

"I know you told me that your two favorite roles and Norma and Violetta. Is there another one that you favor?"

"You might say Amina in **La Sonnambula** because it affords me the opportunity to play the role with what I call lyrical ballet stance and gestures. That is, music and the similitude of ballet dance. I try to imitate or simulate the ballet dancer in her gliding and soft steps of evoking lyricism, and I believe the composer Bellini wanted it that way."

"You really know how to interpret an opera, don't you?"

"I try, I try really hard. Most of the times, I succeed."

Tell me again who your favorite people in opera are."

"Well you might say the conductors Toscanini, Tellio Serafin, Georges Prêtre…"

"Leonard Berstein."

"Yes, Berstein for his dynamism and strength of creative baton directions. As for the others well, I would add Visconti, Zeffirelli and Pasolini as great directors/designers. I could name you some of my favorite singers who accompanied me in opera but that would take time and discretion on my part. I don't want to do it now."

"I would add that you Maria Callas are the greatest influence on Maria Callas, the Dvina. You have mastered the true essence of opera and have taken it to new heights."

"Some people say that and that's a great compliment on their part. But, I must be humble and not take all of the credit. Without a voice, I would be nothing. Nothing. That's what bothers me the most in the present time. I am losing it and I know it. People know it and my colleagues know it. *Je suis complètement inutile.* No one wants me nor needs me…*les jeunes et les collègues ne veulent pas de moi.*"[I'm completely useless…the young ones and my colleagues don't want any part of me].

"Please don't say that."

"I mean it. When one loses her most precious gift in life, then very few people cling to her and acknowledge that she was, at one time, one of the most treasured friend there was in their own lives. I truly feel abandoned."

"Probably because you have become a recluse."

"You mean that it's my fault."

"Partly, don't you think?"

"I guess so."

"Well, you have to get over that. You are a diva, a great singer and a great person."

"You flatter me so, François."

"That's because it's true and I fully recognize your talent as an opera star and the quality of the person. This is not flattery but my acknowledgment of the truth as I see it."

"*Je suis qui je suis.*"[I am who I am].

"*Oui.* Did you ever read Jacques Prévert?"

"Non. Who is he?"

"He's a French poet, a poet of the people. I just love his poetry for it transpires everyday life and everyday emotions. Common people really love his poems."

"Like what?"

"Like '*Déjeuner du matin*' *and* '*Je suis qui je suis.*'

"I'd like to heart that one."

"Which one?"

"The last one, '*Je suis comme je suis.*'"

'Je suis comme je suis/Je suis faite comme ça/Quand j'ai envie de rire/Oui je ris aux éclats/J'aime celui qui m'aime/Est-ce ma faute àmoi/Si ce n'est pas le même/Que j'aime que j'aime chaque fois/Je suis comme je suis.... and so forth."

"It sounds like a prostitute song to me."

"Well, I suppose it is."

"It's not to my liking, François."

"Well I guess you're a very moral person, a conservative person."

"I am."

"But, I'm sure you would like the other one. It's about a lack of communication."

"Does it have to do with men and women?"

"Yes."

"Not speaking to one another?"

"Yes."

"Well gave me a few lines."

"***Déjeuner du matin*****-----***Il a mis le café/Dans la tasse/Il a mis le lait/Dans la tasse de café/Il a mis le sucre/Dans le café au lait/Avec la petite cuiller/Il a tourné/Sans me parler.* Do you want me to continue?"

"Why not?"

"I know it all by heart. Here goes, '*Il a allumé/Une cigarette/Il a fait des ronds/Avec la fumée/Il a mis les cendres/Dans le cendrier/Sans me parler/Sans me regarder.*

"Well, continue."

"'*Il s'est levé/Il a mis/Son chapeau sur sa tête/il a mis son manteau de pluie/Parce qu'il pleuvait/Et il est parti/Sous la pluie/Sans une parole/Sans me regarder---Et moi j'ai pris/Ma tête dans ma main/Et j'ai pleuré.* Voilà!"

"That's a pretty good one. It touches me and my ability to respond to real emotions spoken or not spoke. I know how it feels not to have open communication with someone you care about. It hurts. You understand?"

"Yes, I do."

"Sometimes I feel that it's better not to open any communication for when you expect someone to answer you or even talk to you and he doesn't respond and keeps you waiting, then it's utter silence, dull and corrosive silence. But I suppose it's better to have silence than hurtful words."

"I fully agree with you. I experienced that with my father."

"Experience it with my mother."

Once the conversation was over, la Callas retired to her bedroom and François left after talking with Bruna for a while. She told him that she was concerned about Madame's health and that the situation was getting worse. They did not want to prolong the conversation right there and at that moment and so they left it at that.

30. Eikosideka

August came and the humidity that swept across the river could be felt like a wet towel on your skin. The Seine is a very long river that carries with it not only the charm of water flowing but also the many distasteful things like the raw cold in the winter, the intense humidity in the summer and the unenviable darkness of cloudy and somber days. So it was August and François felt uneasy with the temperature as well as the situation of feeling forlorn. He felt that something was wrong with la Callas. He had not heard from her for three weeks. Bruna did not contact him either, nor did Ferruccio. No one. He was getting worried. Situations that one does not understand are a cause of worry.

Now I'm returning the story and conversations back to François.

The reason why some situations are not understood by someone or rather they cannot be understood by anyone since they're impossible to fathom at all, is the fact that human beings are not equipped to manage them properly and so they worry for the lack of understanding or the source of misunderstanding. It sounds all too philosophic but that's the way I see it and rationalize it. Reason is a very important tool but as Pascal says, '*Le coeur a ses raisons que la raison ne connaît pas.* Reason does not necessarily solve anything, it simple explains things.

At least, it does not solve problems of the heart. My problem was my relationship with Maria Callas. It was not a romantic relationship. I did not fall in love with her but I felt as though I had entered her private life and given the privilege of opening up her heart and soul as a recluse. I had opened the doors and windows of her art in the span of her career. I had been allowed to explore the niches and crannies of her art, so-to-speak. They were marvelous niches and crannies. They allowed me to follow Maria Callas in her attempt to justify her art although she did not need to. Her art was the justification of her career. She had more than once displayed her great talent for performance on the stage. Now she was in a dilemma, the dilemma of remaining totally a recluse or trying to get out of her shell. That shell was a heavy one, as hard and heavy as a huge tortoise shell in which the tortoise itself can hardly move much less get out of it. That's its Sisyphean fate. The Greek myth of Sisyphus applies very well to Maria Callas, I believe. Sisyphus had rebelled against the gods so he was condemned to spend the rest of his existence rolling up a huge rock only to see it fall back down once he had strenuously brought it up the hill. He brings it up, it falls back down. He bring it up again and it falls back down. Over and over again. However, Sisyphus is a rebel and he refuses to give up. His fate is his fate. It will never change. He accepts his fate and not only tolerates it but manages to remain happy with it. At least, that's what Albert Camus says in his famous essay on Sisyphus, '*Il faut croire Sisyphe heureux.*' And that's probably Maria Callas's problem with fate. She does not accept it but rather rejects it and fights it, or worse, submits passively to it. She is not the rebel like Sisyphus. She needs to rebel and keep fighting although her situation with her voice is an alarming one. At least to her. But, life continues and the tensions continue and the strains of fighting for one's life in a desert of dryness and loneliness, all lead to the last and important, if not crucial, fight with destiny. Does one give up and die or does one rebel against the forces of destiny. Choose. Maria Callas has submitted to a fate of lost talents when time has already claimed the richness and vibrancy of those talents. But she could transform that loss into a vibrant role of teacher and advocate for music and singing, if she dared to take her despondency and turn it around. Or, has she given up? That's a question I dare not ask her.

The days went by slowly as they do in the month of August. Besides, August was *le temps des grandes vacances*. Paris was emptied of her workers and families who, most of them, went south to seek leisure and repose. That made the streets of Paris practically deserted at times. I went out occasionally but being alone, I walked the streets in total wanderings oftentimes not even thinking what I was doing. It was as if I was like the *Sonnambula* gliding on the sidewalks like a nymph in a daydream. Strange sometimes, we seem to be entranced by these daydreams not thinking clearly about what reality is and where we are going. It's like an aimless child wandering in a daze and talking to himself about little nothings. He has found for himself a world created by his imagination and for the moment lives in that world careless and carefree. I was walking along like that one day when the humidity was high and the few breezes that were in the air from time to time seemed rare and did not refresh me at all. They teased me instead into believing that the Seine would offer me her refreshing breezes that come up now and then. But, no, it was hot and humid. I sought a café where I might take a cold drink with ice cubes. But Parisians do not drink usually cold drinks especially with ice. They haven't been trained that way. They'll have a hot coffee instead even though it's hot outside and inside. I did find an out-of-the-way café that served cold drinks but without ice. Oh well, it was better than nothing. I was wishing that I could be close to Berthillon and get some refreshing ice cream. I took the métro and got to l'Île Saint-Louis and went straight to Berthillon. I ate my delicious and cold vanilla ice cream and decided to take home a pint of strawberry ice cream for la Callas. That should soothe her depression if she was under its spell. There's nothing like Berthillon ice cream to pull you out of the doldrums.

When I got to the apartment, I rushed upstairs and knocked on la Callas's apartment door. The door opened and there stood la Callas's friend Vesso Devetzi. I was stunned and could not say much except to mutter "This is for Madame Callas." She took it without saying anything and closed the door with a slight bang. She seemed a bit insulted that I had dared to intrude on la Callas and herself too. I stood there frigid and *figé* as we say in French. That Madame Devetzi certainly was a doozer, I told myself.

The following day, Bruna came to apologize for the cold reception that I had gotten from Madame Devetzi. I told her that I did not mind because I had not done what I did for her but for Madame Callas. I was sure that she would enjoy ice cream on a hot and humid day like yesterday. She thanked me and quickly told me that Madame was not well at all and that's why Madame Devetzi had been there for several days, coming and going like a busy bee. She had brought with her some more pills and she gave them to Madame Callas enough to put an elephant to sleep, Bruna told me. I was appalled at the revelation. What was she trying to do, kill her?

I realized that Madame Callas was seriously ill and might not make it alive from large doses of those pills her friend was giving her. She was truly at her mercy for she wanted to sleep and escape from the misery of insomnia and despondency. I was hoping that Bruna would call the doctor to look at her mistress and decide if she was a hospital case. But with the friend there, that was not going to happen since she would not want any doctor to discover that she was the source of those forbidden pills. She brought them in or sent them to Madame Callas from overseas since they were not available in France. Dangerous medication especially without professional supervision. Bruna was caught in the middle of things and so was Ferruccio. I was caught in it too since there was nothing I could do about it. I'm sure that la Callas would not listen to me and I was sure that she did not listen to Bruna either. Not on that account. What could I do?

I decided to go and pray at the Miraculous Medal Shrine on rue du Bac. The Virgin Mother would certainly listen to my prayers for the relief of Madame Callas, relief from the tension and pain of her insomnia. I told f Olivier where I was going and why and he told me that my prayers would be useless because they had been useless for him when he had prayed to get Belle Amie back. Nothing, he said in a sad and spiritless voice.

"But, Olivier one doesn't pray to resurrect some loved one. One prays so that the prayers will bring comfort to you and the person you are praying for. You pray so that your grief will be allayed and that you will be able to face the world that seems empty without her. You pray to Belle Amie to give you strength and determination to go on in life. You pray to receive consolation from harm and pain. If you believe in eternity, then Belle Amie is fine and is looking down on you."

"Now you're talking like a priest again."

"Perhaps. There are good priests in the world, you know and they bring consolation to those who ask them for it. They can lead you on the way to strength and courage that you need."

"I don't need that. I already have it."

I left Olivier who looked somewhat dejected but I knew that he would get over it since he was getting ready to step out and go see a couple of friends of his who lived on rue Saint-Jean-de Pauly. I took the métro and went directly to the chapel. There were many people there already, people from all over the world it seems. They wore various dress styles and spoke other languages. I slipped into a pew next to an old lady who was deep in prayer. I looked up and saw our Lady of the Miraculous Medal over the main altar extending her two hands with all the graces she promised to those who prayed to her. I only asked her for one grace, the grace that Maria Callas would shake off those pills and return to her sanity and good health. I whispered, "Please dear Lady, give her the strength to fight this depression and insomnia so that she can continue living as a person and not as a zombie on pills. She's still young, dear Lady, and she needs you desperately for no one else will heal her, I know." '*O Marie conçue sans péché priez pour nous qui avons recours à vous,' as* I read the inscription above her head. "Please, please pray for her, Mother of God. You have to listen to my prayers for her. She's my friend and she needs help. I don't have many friends and I mean to keep her. Please. You know that she has a special devotion to you and wherever she goes she searches you out in whatever place or corner. Please, please help her." The intensity of my prayers were such that the old lady next to me looked at me and asked if I was alright since I was whispering in a deep and moaning tone and she could hear that I was in soul-pain, she said. "Please, *chère Madame*, please pray for a friend of mine who is in dire need of prayers." She nodded, yes, with her head covered with a black scarf. Her eyes were as intent and glowing as the eyes of Madame Callas when she looks at you directly and shows the darkness of her Greek eyes.

I went back to the apartment and told Olivier how consoled I felt after that visit to the shrine. He simply nodded and told me that he was going to bed. In the morning, I felt somewhat relieved that I had not received bad news about la Callas and that meant that she was most probably alright. Her condition had not deteriorated. That's how I interpreted it. Several days went by and no news from la Callas or Bruna. Madame Devetzi had left the apartment. I saw her leave with a suitcase. That meant that things had settled down in the Callas' household and that la Callas was feeling better. I was anxiously waiting for some news when Bruna knocked on our door and told me that Madame was sleeping but that she had a good night. Madame Devetzi was gone and might be returning sometime next week, she said. To me that was some kind of an answer to my prayers to the Virgin Mary at the Shrine. The old lady dressed in black next to me in the chapel, her prayers must have been answered on my account. The Lady of the Miraculous Medal answers prayers in her own time and in whatever way she deems necessary. She's a lady and a mother and she knows best when prayers are said and answered. But, how long before la Callas's troubles surface again? I really didn't know.

The last week of August was simply nice when the temperature is kind to everyone and everyone is kind to everyone else. I did not realize how the temperature affects people in so many different ways. Some are indifferent to it, others live according to its rise and fall while still others are indifferent to it. I much prefer temperatures that hover around 15 degrees Celsius and the sky is bright and Virgin Mary blue. That's what we used to say growing up in Northern Maine where the sky, at times, is bright Virgin Mary blue. I don't know why I keep thinking of the Virgin Mary. It may be because I keep thinking of Maria Callas and her personal devotion to Mary. Lately Maria Callas if ever on my mind. I guess that I worry about her not hearing about her and her situation with her pills and Madame Devetzi. Why does she trust her so much, this lady who intrudes now and then. She must advise Madame Callas on things in her life like her health, her career and her personal matters. I don't know, but it bothers me.

Last night I had a dream or rather a nightmare. I dreamt that I was going through a long dark tunnel and that it didn't seem to end. I had a long thread in my right hand and I was trying to follow it to its final destination. All I wanted was to get out of there but could not. I backtracked and eventually found a huge black bull at the other end. He looked furious and even dangerous. Like the Minotaur, I thought. Where was I? Where was Ariadne? Why was I caught in this situation? Why did my mind ever return to the mythic sources of my life? Why the Greek myths? I turned around and kept following the thread to wherever it would lead me, perhaps outside the tunnel where I could find light and safety. Suddenly, I woke up and felt exhausted. I was disturbed and somewhat dizzy from a lack of sanity that had kept me in my tunnel of darkness and lack of a sense of direction. I hate those dreams that take away your sense of sanity and throw you into a fitful melancholy of dread and insecurity. I got up and had some *café au lait*, warm and soothing. I was glad that I was wide awake now. It was till early in the morning perhaps five o'clock. My mind started to wander and I quickly reached for my book on Lincoln. I started to read a chapter about the Civil War but put it down since I could not concentrate on it. I kept thinking about Maria Callas. How was she doing? How could I help her in some way? Perhaps I should not meddle in her affairs? But I had been given entry into her life, if not her entire life but at least in her career as a singer. That was perhaps the most important part of her life. I had been touched by it and I could not wipe away that part to which I had been introduced graciously and with the elegance of a diva. My life had been changed by it and I just could not feel passive about the lady, the diva or Divina who thought of herself as being fallen. She was not a fallen Divina. No. She had to tell herself that she would rise again like the phoenix if she thought of herself as being fallen. Or she could see herself as Mary Magdalena whom she regarded as being saved from her sinful life. She had told me that she wished that a composer like Bellini or Donizetti would have composed an opera on Mary Magdalena for she would have liked playing that role on stage. No, there is a way out if one thinks that she's fallen and the way out is either by rebelling or by being saved by a savior of some kind. Would that Maria Callas find her savior somehow and somewhere. Nurturing the feeling of being fallen is not beneficial at all. It's a harmful and hurtful feeling. Maria Callas needs to find an outlet to that kind of feeling and I'm going to do my best to find it for her and with her, if she lets me.

It was early September and I had yet to hear from Maria Callas or her maid, Bruna. Now, I was truly worried. What to do? I didn't want to disturb them by calling on the phone nor did I want to intrude in any shape or fashion. I would let them contact me. Bruna must be going through hell, I thought. She was so devoted to her mistress that she had known for a long time. I like Bruna for she was truly a nice person, an affable person and a humble soul. Ferruccio was more suspicious of everything, it seemed to me. He was not a trusting being. I didn't think he trusted me at all while Bruna trusted wholeheartedly and without any reservations whatever. She had the heart of a child and the soul of a saint. Madame Callas was indeed fortunate to have her by her side to watch over her and take good care of her.

Olivier was more and more away from home for long hours at a time either chatting with his friends or walking the boulevards enjoying meeting people and talking to them. He would tell me all about his adventures of the day. I was glad for him since I did not always have time to spend with him. Besides, he was getting on my nerves when he talked about Belle Amie and their past together. I used to tell him to concentrate on the present and look forward to the future, but he always replied that he had no future. He was old and getting older, he said. Old people don't have much of a future, he told me. I used to tell him that everyone young or old all had a future want to or not. He just shut his eyes or looked the other way when I told him that. I think he was afraid of the future. I just let him be and did my things like writing to my friend, Mister Loringdale in New York. I had met him at the opera and we fast became friends and used to discuss operas and their leading sopranos. Tenors too. He loved tenors and their high notes such as Pavarotti and Nicolai Gedda. He never mentioned di Stefano though. We used to correspond occasionally and I enjoyed his news regarding New York City and its Broadway and Lincoln Center. Sandy was his name, Sandy Loringdale. I like Sandy and we always had gotten along well. He too loved Maria Callas but he much preferred Pavarotti. He told me once that it was not that he liked men but he preferred tenors. I told him that it did not matter if he liked men more than women. He then told me that he did not want people calling names like queer and sissy. I told him that names do not really hurt people, they hurt their pride. "Have you ever been called a queer?" he asked me once. I replied, no. "Then you do not know what it feels like," he said with a sheepish grin.

I did not really have many friends. Marcel Lavertu certainly not my friend anymore since he had wanted to exploit me. Strange how a person can change overnight and become a bad guy. Probably I never really got to know him before I started befriending him in Paris. Yet, he was part of my world when he lived in Quebec and I lived in northern Maine. He was a Québécois and I was a Franco-American both of the same ethnic source. Who was I now that I was living in Paris and had not returned to the States since I had landed here in France. I felt that I belonged here and would probably die here. My ashes would be kept in an urn and buried in some garden that I chose or in some distant cemetery somewhere. I didn't care and I didn't worry about it. When you're dead you're dead. I just hoped that the Virgin Mary would take care of me and my dying breath. In that sense I was like Maria Callas, I think.

A week following the departure of Madame Devetzi, she returned and settled in. According to Bruna, she had dropped inconveniently and unannounced. She was like that according to Bruna. Every time she came for as visit she upset the applecart, so said Bruna. She would look into every drawer, every closet, every nook and cranny to see what had happened since her last visit. And especially what la Callas and Bruna had hidden from her. Bruna told me that's she herself was getting tired of being scrutinized and looked over like a guilty slave. She was not a slave; she was a maid who took good care of Madame Callas. Madame Callas kept asking her friend what she was searching for and she never got a response. There was something wrong about her behavior and Bruna knew that too well. She tried to tell her mistress but she would not hear of it. She trusted Madame Devetzi implicitly and without reservation, she told Bruna. Why would she suspect her of anything outlandish? Why would she not believe that her best friend would betray her in any way or by any means? Bruna stopped questioning her mistress and trying to tell her that her friend was not her friend but a devious person who was after something. Bruna was hoping that Madame's sister, Jackie, would come and see what was happening to her sister. Bruna just did not know what to do anymore, so she quit thinking about the matter and she taught herself to concentrate on Madame's immediate needs. As for Ferruccio, he stayed away from the situation and only provided the necessary limousine service wherever la Callas or Madame Devetzi wanted to go. Of course, I avoided Madame Devetzi as much as I could. I did not step out of my apartment if I knew she was coming out of la Callas's apartment. One day, I happened to come face to face with her in the vast foyer without wanting to. She stopped me and told me sternly to forget going to visit Maria Callas anymore that she did not want to see me again. As a matter of fact, she told me, I personally don't want you up there. I asked her why and she told me that I knew why. I really did not know why she was opposed to my going to see Madame Callas. Was she concocting some kind of scheme, I wondered. I felt hurt and afraid of confronting this bitchy witch, as I called her. She was a mean creature. She apparently knew how to play games with la Callas's life and she knew every trick in the book. I even had bad dreams about her. She was the Medea that haunted the deep dark crevasses of anger and revenge and not the Medea that Maria Callas played on stage. That one was a human being although with her failures and passion for love and death. Devetzi's Medea was one of utter wickedness and self-pride. Oh, how I hated that woman. I never hated anyone as much as I hated her. It wasn't in my nature to hate people. Instead I felt truly sad when I felt the coming on of hateful feelings towards anyone. La Devetzi got under my skin like a nasty burrowing insect sucking my blood and devouring my tolerance for anyone or anything. I could not stand her and I wished that she would go away. All that terrible scurrilous manipulation of minds and wills made me feel less than a human being.

It was on a Tuesday afternoon that I decided to prepare a tureen of seafood soup with shrimps, fresh codfish, scallops and mussels simmered in olive oil and splashed with white wine and made with a bouillon that even the Greeks adored, the essence of the glutinous membranes of a young lamb drawn from the best of the shepherd's flock. I was able to get some of that bouillon from an old Greek farmer who tended some lambs and ewes in order to make some money by distilling that bouillon. Wives and mothers ran to his shop in order to obtain some of that rare bouillon. Those who had never tasted it or who had never cooked with it refrained from even going into his shop. Old Madame Troublon used to say that meant there would be more for the rest of us who savored such a delicacy. I knew that Maria Callas would love that seafood soup. As for Madame Devetzi, let her try the soup and it might mellow her to a point where she would allow me to have another conversation with la Callas. I had to try to turn things around in my favor in order to get around the bitchy witch.

I prepared all of the ingredients, washed, scraped and cleaned them, and set them aside. Then, I waited for about two hours before actually cooking the soup so that it would be ready for the dinner hour. When the time came, I put the bouillon in a large pan and let it simmer. I then places all of the seafood in it and stirred gently so as not to bruise the seafood. I let the whole thing simmer some more until all of the ingredients were well cooked but not overdone. When the soup was hot and smelled delicious, I took it off the heat and poured it into a tureen that I found among the DesGrandforts' dishes. I put the lid on the tureen and slowly marched upstairs to deliver the soup to Maria Callas. I wasn't sure if Madame Devetzi would allow me in but I was going to try. It was Bruna who answered the door. She took the tureen and thanked me. I heard a voice shouting, "Who's there?" Bruna responded "It's François with some good seafood soup." There was no answer. I left hoping that Madame Callas would benefit from my soup. She did and so did her friend la Devetzi, I was told by Bruna the following day. However, I did not get the invitation that I so desired.

Apparently, la Callas recovered from her illness or discomfort because la Devetzi left the day after. Bruna came to tell me that Madame wanted to see me for lunch and that she, Bruna, would cook and serve the meal herself as she normally did. I was overjoyed at the invitation. I had not seen Madame Callas in two weeks. We had lunch, sandwiches made of calamari with cheese and we drank some good sparkling wine. Madame Callas did not seem ill at all. Rather, she was joyous and looked content with herself. I was all the more happy for her. Things had fallen into place with la Devetzi gone, I thought.

"Well, François, what will we talk about that we have not touched upon so far?"

"We have pretty much covered everything in your career. However, I would like to hear about your thoughts on it."

"My thoughts?"

"Yes, your thoughts about your career so far for I do not thinks it's over yet, not entirely, not even after your farewell concerts with di Stefano."

"Ah, yes, that fiasco. Pleased don't remind me of it."

"But it was not truly a fiasco. It may have been one in the minds of critics and perhaps in your own mind."

"But, my voice, my dear voice left me. All I could do was come close to the original voice but I deluded myself into thinking I could go back and reclaim the voice that I once had."

"You must not chastise yourself. You still have the voice but a diminished one from what you had."

"But I want the one I had in full dimension and full range of tones. I suppose that will never happen."

"I do not think so and you know better."

"I should. You see I'm an idealist and a perfectionist and I can only live with excellence not mediocrity. I want my voice back, François, I want it back the way it used to be."

"I know but it's not possible. You have to take yourself as you are now, now in 1977 and not in 1957."

"Why do we get old and lose some of our powers and talents? Tell me why."

"I cannot."

"Then I will spend the rest of my life listening to my tapes and stand in awe of that beautiful voice I once had. And he range of sounds I was able to acquire."

"You do that but don't give up on yourself."

"If only I could sleep and have a good night's sleep not just spurts of troubled sleep."

"Why not trey fresh air walking in the morning or traveling to Greece or other parts of the world?"

"I tried that but I'm hounded by the paparazzi or people who want my photo or autograph. I'm hounded on every side and I don't like that. Can't they leave me in peace?"

"That's the price you pay for fame, Madame la Divina."

"Now the fallen Divina."

"Maybe fallen in your mind but not in mine."

After lunch and a cup of coffee, la Callas went to her room and closed the door. I thanked Bruna for her fine meal and we parted with my saying to her, "Please let me know how Madame feels in the morning." Bruna nodded her head in compliance. I went downstairs and started listening to one of Maria Callas' recordings specifically the aria from "Andrea Chenier," *La momma morta.*" I felt goose bumps just listening to it. Oh, those initial cello notes followed by Maria's singing, pleading, grieving and deeply dramatic tones of hers. How could I not react to this singing with so powerful an emotion of loss and sadness. Sometimes we listen to music simply because it soothes and relaxes while imitating the plaints of the soul in response to the tension within us. Why could I not give Maria Callas the strength of heart that was needed to buoy her up and lift her soul so that she would not feel dejected and lost. I knew what I would do. I would urge her to come with me to the rue du Bac chapel and place her sorrow and loss of talent in front of Mary's altar. Not talent, really, because she still had the talent to sing, but her voice had grown fainter or rather she could not reach the high notes as she used to, and all of this had disappointed her when she truly wanted to sing in her full-bodied voice of the soprano she once had been, the diva, now the Divina, fallen or not. "The splendor in the grass" was gone, the splendor of excellence and the grandeur of perfection was gone. Lusterless and tarnished by time and overuse.

31. Eikosidekaeva

The narrator will now take over since François is, as he says, indisposed.

François got up late this morning of September 15. He thought that he had missed his appointment with the dentist. He had been having problems with his lower right wisdom tooth and it had bothered him for days, sometimes in severe pain. He had suffered long enough and Olivier told him to consult his dentist, *Monsieur le Docteur Germain Faré* over on boulevard . François had made an appointment some time ago and was anxious to get it over with. He dreaded the dentist but he could not stand the pain. He had gone to the pharmacy to get some analgesic and he pharmacist had given him some medication that was better than an analgesic, he told him. It worked for a while but the pain throbbed all the more during the night. He was at a point where he did not eat nor drink since all he wanted to do was try to sleep. He was taking several sleeping pills and that seemed to help him sleep, but he felt drowsy most of the day. Now, he realized how Maria Callas felt after taking so many Mandrax. That was the name of the medication that she got from Madame Devetzi as well as from some other friends or even acquaintances. That's what Bruna said.

He went to the dentist and suffered through the painful procedure of tooth extraction and then went home relieved that it was all over.

His lower gum hurt but it wasn't the tooth pain that he had withstood for so many days. He went to bed right away not even telling Olivier about his encounter with the dentist. Olivier let him sleep most of the day. Bruna came to see François but Olivier told her that he was sleeping and that he was not going to wake him. She agreed. By the time darkness had set in, François asked Olivier for something to eat. He gave him so soft food, some cottage cheese with fruit that was in the refrigerator. François went back to bed. Olivier tried to tell him that Bruna had come to see him, but François was not in the mood to see anyone.

The following morning François felt no more pain. All that was left was a sensitive lower gum. He had his usual *café au lait* with pieces of a croissant dunked in his coffee. He got dressed and went outside to see what the weather was like. Cool but nice and sunny. A perfect September day. He went back inside and checked the calendar, September 15.Olivier was getting ready to step out and visit his friend, Jacques Dudevoir on rue de la Dentelle. François thought that it was too early to go and pay someone a visit. Olivier told him that his friend did not mind since he lived alone and loved to have company. François had realized that his old friend was lonely and searched out for companionship especially of his own age. François himself felt lonely at times especially when he did not have any meaningful conversation with someone he cared for, like Maria Callas. She was continuously on his mind nowadays. He knew that he should gout more and meet people his own age, but he did not have the taste for it. He thought of going to the opera but found nothing to his liking at the Palais Garnier. He was ever hoping to meet another Mister Kapalodous but chances of meeting someone like that and striking a conversation about opera were slim indeed. So, he stayed home either listening to music or reading some good book. He loved reading the classics like "Madame Bovary" by Flaubert or "Un Coeur Simple" by the same author. He read Albert Camus's "La Peste" and Simone de Beauvoir's,"Mémoire d'une jeune fille rangée." He truly liked this one. She was a good writer. He sometimes read magazines where the latest men's fashions were on display but he knew that he could not afford the prices. Paris offered many a fine selection of men's clothes and François loved to stroll on the avenues where the expensive shops were only to do *lèche-vitrine*, window shopping but that was all. He usually went back to the apartment somewhat disappointed but content of having only wiped the windows with his tongue and not his pocketbook. He liked playing with words and their translations.

The day went by without too much commotion and very little activities in the vast apartment complex and Number 36, Avenue Georges Mandel. The night was calm and the moon shoe bright and silvery. By the time François went to bed, it was past midnight and he could not fall asleep. Something was bothering him and he did not know what or what for. He tossed and turned until he finally fell asleep. He woke up suddenly and he felt as if he had a premonition of some kind. But he did not know what. He fell back to sleep and woke up early in the morning around five thirty. Olivier told him that while he was out doing window shopping, Bruna had come and had asked to see him. François told himself that he definitely had to go up and see Bruna for she might be in some distress. After his *café au lait* and his usual croissant, François started getting dressed and he put on his best shirt and tie. He did not know why the shirt and tie, but he felt like it. Some days were like that, he told himself. Perhaps he would meet la Callas and they could have a short conversation of some kind. He waited until it was later in the morning for he did not want to disturb Madame if she was sleeping late. One never knew with la diva and her pills, he told himself. Not that he wanted to imply guilt or shame for taking a lot of those pills, but he did worry about the situation. She took those pills because she was suffering in her mind and in her body if not in her soul. Poor diva at the mercy of pills. Who would have thought that such a Divina with all of her glamor, riches, and international renown would one day be so miserable as a recluse, *renfermée dans sa coquille de plomb et de perles*?[All closed in with her shell of lead and pearls].

François did go upstairs around eleven o'clock. He knocked on la Callas' apartment door. Bruna answered but she told him in a whisper that Madame was sleeping and that she had had a very bad night.

"S'il vous plaît revenez plus tard" and she closed the door abruptly. François did not know what to make of this kind of brush off, but he insisted on pardoning Bruna for her loyal and insistent service to her mistress. He told himself that Bruna was most probably under great stress and that she was being protective of Madame Callas as well as herself. He did not know. He went quietly downstairs and entered his apartment very quietly with a glum face.

François had a quiet lunch of bread and cheese with some raspberry jam and a cup of hot herbal tea. He then started listening to opera music, the aria "*Visse d'arte*" by la Callas. He loved that aria devoted to the art of performance and singing. Tosca pleading with Scarpia to release her from his clutches. Suddenly there was a loud knocking, repeated knocking at the door. He got up and rushed to go and open it. It was Ferruccio winded and strangely pale. He told François to hurry and come upstairs because there was something very wrong with Madame. They both scurried upstairs and went into the bedroom where Maria Callas was lying motionless and deathly drawn. Bruna was crying. Her eyes were red with tears. She tried to speak and tell him what had happened but she could not hold even her breath not alone speak to be heard much less understood. Ferruccio started to talk and he told François that Madame was dead and that she had died around one o'clock.

"She took too many pills, some to sleep and some to revive herself. It was too much for her heart. Her blood pressure was very low, you know. That's what her doctor had told her. She told Bruna about it. We tried to tell Madame Devetzi about the pills, and she replied to let her have them if she wanted. What could we do, Monsieur François? What could we do?"

Bruna took a hold on herself and started telling François what had really happened.

"Madame got up on Friday morning as usual. She went to the bathroom and washed herself. I was in her room fixing the bed when she came back into the bedroom and she suddenly knelt down on the floor. I was terrible, truly terrible. I didn't know what had happened or why. She said she needed help and I got her on the bed and she asked for the coffee I had brought. She took one sip and then she died. She's dead, Monsieur François, she's dead. I called Ferruccio and when he realized what was happening, he phoned Monsieur Roire who called the doctor, but it was too late."

"The doctor left with Monsieur Roire and they told the both of us not to touch anything and that they would be back sometime. I, Ferruccio, who was always at Madame's command and now she's dead."

"What are we to do, Monsieur François?" asked Bruna in tears."

"Nothing but wait. I'm sure someone will come and settle things."

"But who? I'm sure that Madame Devetzi is bound to come and take control of everything. She's like that." Madame has a mother and a sister. We did not know she had a family because she never mentioned them to us."

"Well, you see someone will come and manage things for you. I must go since I don't belong here and I do not want to be found here where I don't belong. It could cause some friction and make trouble for both of you."

"We understand," said Bruna with a dejected glance.

"Please keep me informed."

"Yes, we will."

François then leaned over the body of Maria Callas and placed a soft kiss on her forehead. He looked around the room and found it to be cold and dimly lit like a morgue. He left sad and filled with grief for a friend he had known for a short time but who filled his heart and soul with the joy and excellence of music.

I'm now turning the story over to François who needs active rapprochement.

I didn't know what to do now that Maria Callas was dead and I would have no more long conversations with her about her career. I would not get the chance to prepare a good meal for her and I certainly would not be able to talk to her about her greatest moments of her career that I wanted to talk about but had no chance to do it.

Strange how we postpone things a never get the chance to make is happen. It's gone. Gone like a restless wind that sweeps away our plans and our dreams. Gone.

The following morning, I realized that people started coming to the Callas apartment that I had never seen before. I sat in the foyer and looked at some of them either taking the lift or walking up the stairs. The newspapers were already splattered with news items and photos dealing with the diva's death. People came flocking to Avenue Georges Mandel to gaze at our large complex and pinpoint the apartment where Maria Callas had lived and where, at some intervals, she could be seen in the large window pushing the curtains to look outside. Notwithstanding all of the publicity hounds, the many fans who came to pay their respects, and those who had nothing better to do than seek the latest news item, the surroundings were calm and not too boisterous since people maintained a sense of dignified mourning for a great lady of opera. We were all waiting for the person who would take charge of the situation and give it some impetus. The sister Jackie arrived the very next day and then Madame Devetzi arrived and took charge. After all, she had the Moral Right, the Power of Attorney to execute all wishes and plans. She made things move. Bruna told me all about what this woman thought and what she did. She could overhear her from her kitchen.

The first thing that happened was the placing Madame Callas in a coffin then sealing it in preparation for the funeral service at the Orthodox Cathedral on rue Georges Bizet. After the religious service Madame Devetzi insisted that the remains be cremated even though cremation was opposed by the church and Maria's family, her sister,Jackie, and her mother, Evangelia, were totally in the dark about Maria's last wishes. However, the Archbishop of the Orthodox Cathedral, St-Étienne, Archbishop Meletinos, agreed to the cremation and that was that.

I went to the Cathedral on rue Bizet and tried to get into the church but couldn't, so I stayed outside. The funeral was being held at four thirty in the afternoon of Saturday, September 20th. There were several dignitaries there including Princess Grace of Monaco.

I could hear the beautiful Greek psalms being chanted inside the cathedral and they transported me back to the monastery of the Transfiguration where I had stayed years ago. After the funeral service, people started coming out. There was a mob outside where I was and people shouted, Callas, Callas, Callas, Brava, Brava. They were throwing roses on her casket as it was being carried out of the cathedral and into the street. I stood there frozen and unable to move so intense were my feelings of grief and sorrow. The Maria Callas that I had known was no more. She would live on in my memory as an elegant, charming, reflective and passionate lady, passionate about her art and her hunger for excellence and perfection. The world had lost a great singer and a great person and I was witnessing her descent from the top of her strength and her ability to perform with passion and dramatic creativity. The word passion kept popping in my mind. I knew that it meant intense, extreme and compelling emotions that drive one to an overpowering desire to think and especially to act. That, to me, identified Maria Callas for she surely had the drive of passion within her. Now it had been extinguished. Only the memory remained. People would recognize Maria Callas to be the eagle soaring high above the mountaintop of opera. She was an innovator and a champion of excellence in opera. Everyone recognized that and they saluted her for it. There were many many roses to show the people's love and admiration for her. I only wished at that very moment that I had an armful of red carnations to throw at her coffin in tribute to her and as a farewell gesture on my part. I waited silently until the crowd dispersed and found myself alone on the steps of the cathedral waiting for I do not know what. A little boy went by, stopped in front of me and asked me why I was still standing there. I answered that I was waiting. "Waiting for what, Monsieur?" he asked. "I'm waiting for the curtain call," I said. The Divina had just gotten her grand ovation, but I was still waiting for her curtain call.

I slowly walked back to the apartment. Olivier asked me how things had gone, and I replied that they had been solemn and brief. "Were there many people there?" he asked. "Thousands maybe, yes, thousands cheering and chanting the name of Maria Callas," I said. "That's nice," he replied.

That Sunday afternoon, I went to the Miraculous Chapel on rue du Bac and deposited an armful of red carnations that I had just bought on the steps of the main altar of Mary with the graces flowing from her two hands. I placed a note with the flowers, "À la douce mémoire de Maria Callas---In memory of Maria Callas. One of the sisters came to pick them up and carried them to the back of the altar. I detected a smile on her face as she read the note. I did it out of my tender moment and I was not afraid to show my romantic side since Maria Callas would not have rejected my gesture. She understood me and I understood her. I went to sit in a pew facing Catherine Labouré and just sat there without moving a limb. I said nothing for nothing came out of me. When nothing comes out of your lips, it's better to remain silent. So, I sat there for about an hour. Not that I could not feel for Maria Callas but I felt nothing as if my insides were empty. I'm sure that she felt like that sometimes when she was depressed and terribly blue. Nothing. Empty. Then I got up, stepped out of the pew, genuflected and turned around to go out of the chapel. As I was nearing the exit, I turned my head to gaze at the Miraculous Medal Virgin Mary and I realized that my heart felt empty and my soul filled with silent pleas. That was my mourning, my grief being expressed the way Maria Callas would have understood. Silence is a prayer.

I took the métro to go home. As I walking inside looking at all the people who were going and coming in a hurry, I happened to see a young woman standing in front of a large poster board writing something in large bold letters that read, *"Homage à Maria Callas, la divina aux ailes de cire qui a voulu s'envoler trop près du soleil et qui a chuté vers le néant."*[Homage to Maria Callas the divina with the waxen wings who wanted to fly too close to the sun and fell towards nothingness]. I watched her finish her huge poster and smiled at her. She smiled back. I said to her, *"Non, vers l'infini."* and I put a large coin in her cup and walked away.

Maria Callas had no written memoirs. She once told me, "My

memoirs are in my music that I interpret---the only language I really know." That's how I will remember her as well as millions of people who recognize her powerful influence in music and opera.

The Friday after the funeral, Bruna came to see me to talk. She looked relaxed and relieved that the whole thing was over.

"Monsieur François I want to tell you that I will be leaving soon and return to my family in Italy. So will Ferruccio. Although Madame Devetzi told us not to tell anyone, she and Madame Callas's sister gave us both a good sum of money. Signor Meneghini did not want to but Madame Devetzi prevailed. I thank her for her good will towards me. You see, Madame Callas never gave Ferruccio and I a salary. She took care of us, fed us and lodged us, but to money. I could not afford to buy new clothes and that's why I always wore the same old dress. I loved Madame Callas but I found her tight with her money. She must have gotten that from her husband. He was very tight with money and he's the one who handled all of the money. I thank Madame Callas for her friendship and will keep her in my thoughts and in my prayers. So now, I tell you goodbye, Monsieur François. I must tell you before I leave that Madame truly enjoyed your conversations with her and also the meals you prepared for her. She enjoyed that very much."

"I know."

"I want to thank you too for your special friendship for myself and for Madame. You were so kind to her. I told Ferruccio that I admired you for that."

"Madame Callas was a very special person to me and I was happy to be with her when she refused to talk to other people since she had become a recluse."

"Yes, it was a sad situation, I know. I tried to talk her out of it and so did some of her close friends, but she refused to listen. Now, she's gone."

"Farewell my dear friend and I will not forget you either since I know the faithful service you rendered Madame for such a long time and admire you for that. You're a good person, Bruna. Where are you going now?"

"I'm going back home to my village in Italy."

"Ferruccio?"

"He's going to work for Christina Onassis."

She had tears coming to her eyes and I hugged her as she turned around to leave. I did not want to embarrass her so I let her go. The door closed and I was left standing there stunned by the moment. I did not cry for I did not want to show my romantic side, but I did feel like crying. Such a tender moment in my life.

The following day, I happened to be in the foyer when I met Madame Devetzi. She stopped and came towards me.

"Monsieur Spirounias, I want to talk to you."

"Yes, Madame Devetzi."

"I want to ask you something. I know you had several long conversations with Madame Callas about her career. She told me herself and she appreciated the meals you prepared for her. Now, these conversations are part of the estate and you cannot profit from them."

"I never intend to."

"If you ever have them published the estate owns a good part of them and I want you to realize that."

"But I own them. I'm the one who initiated them and they belong to me."

"No. They belong to the estate. If you ever dare to publish them or even go on a speaking tour with them, I'll have you know that when it goes public these conversations are part of the estate and since I have the Power of Attorney, I'm obliged to safeguard the estate. These conversations are with an international star, a diva who's very well known in the opera world and they're worth money."

"Don't worry, Madame, I will keep them private, in my heart and soul as a precious memory of a woman I have come to love and greatly admire."

"Just don't you forget that I'll be watching you wherever you are. Goodbye."

I had wanted to tell her how much I admired her gesture towards the maid and the butler/driver, but I was glad that I had not done so, for now I did not admire her anymore. She was still the bitchy-witch that I had gotten to know and will never change. *Elle ne changera jamais de peau, celle-là*, I told myself—she will never change skin that one.

It was late Sunday afternoon following my encounter with la Devetzi when a man in his thirties knocked on my door. He was a newspaper man, he said, and he wanted to interview me about Maria Callas. I asked him if he was part of the paparazzi. He smiled and told me, "Yes, I'm earning a living. Is that wrong?" I told him, no, but that I did not want to be exploited nor did Maria Callas want to either, Besides she's dead, I told him, and I shut the door in his face. The following morning he was there at my door again. I told him to go away and get lost. He raised his camera and took a photo of me. I lunged towards him, took his camera away from him and threw it in the busy street. Some people saw me do it and started applauding. I was so angry. Then and here I decided to get away from the Avenue Georges Mandel and even from Paris until my blood cooled and the paparazzi had gone away from my life. I decided to go back to northern Maine. I wanted peace and quiet for I decided to write my own memoirs. Just those with Maria Callas in Paris on the Avenue Georges Mandel Apartment #36. My pilgrimage was over and now was the time to move on and reap the harvest of my experiences from Maine to Boston to New York and then Paris. I had come full circle, the circle of trying to understand myself and comprehend the world around me as it moves towards more and more challenges for me and for others. I still have a long way to go but I'm ready for it now that I have music anchored in my soul, the music of Maria Callas. The only thing that came to my mind like a haunting refrain was Baudelaire's pantoum poem, *Harmonie du Soir*, that kept spinning and spinning and throwing facets of light in every direction of my brain. It was like a mystical moment for me and I was enthralled by its clarity and emission of light. Was I dreaming? Was I romanticizing all of this? Maria Callas was right, I was a romantic. But, I wasn't a sad or crazy romantic. I had done it. I had climbed the mountain to where the recluse Maria Callas had insulated and hidden herself from all the world out there. But, I had penetrated that asylum and that prison of hers. I had done it. No one else was able to accomplish that. I did, from the far distant region of northern Maine to the capital of the world of glamor and lights, Paris. Maria Callas "*ton souvenir en moi luit comme un ostensoir.*" [Your memory within me shines like a monstrance].

Vissi d'arte, vissi d'amore/non feci mai nale ad anima viva!/Con man furtiva/quante miserie conobbi auitai/ Sempre con fé sincera/la mia preghiera,/ai santi tabernacol sali./Sempre con fé sincera/diedi fiori agli altar. TOSCA

I lived for art, I lived for love:/Never did I harm a living creature!/ Whatever misfortunes I encountered/I sought with secret hand to succor/ Ever in pure faith,/my prayers rose/in the holy chapels./Ever in pure faith,/I brought flowers to the altars.

Milton Keynes UK
Ingram Content Group UK Ltd.
UKHW011322101123
432329UK00001B/224